THE PATRIARCH

THE
PATRIARCH

CHAIM BERMANT

St. Martin's Press · *New York*

Library of Congress Cataloging in Publication Data

Bermant, Chaim, 1929-
The patriarch.

I. Title.
PR6052.E63P3   823'.914   81-510
ISBN 0-312-59804-1   AACR2

Design by Paul Chevannes

10   9   8   7   6   5   4   3   2   1
First Edition

TO TMcC

without whose encouragement this book would
never have been started, and without whose guidance
it would never have been finished.

CONTENTS

CHAPTER I
THE WICKED UNCLE

EVERY FAMILY HAS RELATIVES THEY DON'T TALK ABOUT AND OTHERS about whom they rarely stop talking. Uncle Hector somehow entered into both categories, for he was at once a source of embarrassment and controversy and, as a result, a source of fascination. To my generation he was known, not without a touch of admiration, as the Wicked Uncle (or, rather, as *the* wicked uncle, for we had several).

Mother would not suffer his name to be mentioned at table. He had been married to her sister Arabella (or Ara, as she was generally known), and she firmly believed that he had killed her. When I first heard her use the expression, I imagined that he had taken an axe to her—which, from what one heard of Aunt Ara, had seemed a perfectly reasonable thing to do—but, as I grew older, it became clear that the process was rather more subtle, and there were even those who argued that Ara had "killed" Uncle Hector, which was their way of suggesting that she had robbed him of his manhood, though as a matter of plain fact Uncle Hector is alive and Aunt Ara is not.

I, for some reason which I still fail to understand, was Hector's favourite nephew, but when my family moved from Glasgow to London in the early fifties (I suspect that one of the reasons we moved is that Mother feared his influence upon me), we almost lost contact. I wrote to him sporadically and he answered even more sporadically, usually on my birthday or Christmas to enclose a small cheque (which annoyed Mother deeply, first because she did not like the idea of his communicating with me at all, and second because she felt that a Jew had no business sending other Jews Christmas presents. "It's an impertinence to intrude upon other people's festivals," she said).

Years passed. I went to University and then into the army to do my National Service, and I was stationed in Malaya, and he either stopped writing, or Mother intercepted any letters that he did write. In any case, I lost all contact.

Then in the late sixties I obtained a lectureship at Glasgow University, and I found myself in rooms only two streets away from him. I didn't warn him of my arrival, but as soon as I settled in I went round to pay him a call. He lived in what in my boyhood had been regarded as an expensive block of flats with a tiled close, a wrought-iron stairway and richly ornamented front doors with stained-glass panels. It had not only looked opulent, with the rich glow of polished brass and expensive timbers, but had smelt opulent. Now the glow was gone, and instead of opulence there was the smell of decay— decaying fabric, decaying food, decaying lives—which become more pronounced the higher one moved. Hector lived on the top floor, and the stained-glass in his front door had been replaced by smoked glass, like the door of a public-house. He had a pull-bell and a push-bell, neither of which worked, and I rapped on the letter-box and the glass window for about five minutes before a vague figure loomed out of the darkened hallway and came towards the door. Two fingers pulled a thin lace curtain aside, and a nose pressed against the glass.

"Who is it?"

"It's me, Sammy."

"Sammy who?"

"Sammy Krochmal."

"Who?"

"Krochmal."

And then came a sliding of bolts and a rattling of chains and a clanking of keys, as if he were guarding the Crown Jewels, and the door was open.

At first I thought I had come to the wrong door. It was nearly ten years since I had last seen him, and I remembered a tall, erect picture of a man, even if a somewhat washed-out one, while here stood a bent, shrivelled figure, leaning heavily on a walking-stick. When he switched on the hall light, I recognised him at once. The slightly battered balding head was the same; so was the long nose, now looking slightly longer and redder, and so were the melancholy, washed-out blue eyes with their red surrounds, as if he were suffering from chronic hay-fever. His face did not brighten at the sight of me, either with delight or, it would seem, recognition.

"I'm Sammy," I repeated, "Caroline's son."

"I can see. Deaf I may be and crippled I am, and my memory's going, but blind I'm not. You haven't changed. I thought in the years I haven't seen you, you might have grown up a bit, but you're like your late father, a dwarf." He led the way into the kitchen as he spoke. There were the remains of a meal on the table and the remains of a previous meal in the sink. "Pardon the mess, I wasn't expecting company."

"Did I interrupt your meal?"

"No, I was just thinking of clearing up. I'm glad of the excuse not to. I suppose you all think I'm dead."

"Why should we think you're dead?"

"Because nobody writes, nobody phones, and in any case at my age I'm entitled to be dead—I often wish I was. I fell down the stairs last week, and one thought stayed uppermost in my mind as I rolled over and over. I don't mind being killed, but for Christ's sake I hope I'm not injured. I was two days at the bottom before they picked me up, which is not unusual in this part of town. They thought I'd been celebrating and left me to sober up. That's one thing in Glasgow, they respect your privacy. As a matter of fact, I'm just out of hospital."

"Why didn't you let anyone know?"

"I had no reason to believe anyone cared."

"Why didn't you write to me?"

"Why didn't I do what?"

"Write."

"Who to?"

"Me."

"To you?"

"You used to write."

"When I had a cheque to send, but I can't afford cheques, I can't even afford a cheque-book."

"I didn't expect you to send cheques."

"I know you didn't, but when an uncle can't even send a miserly cheque, what is there left to his uncleship? Lay there for two days at the bottom of the stairs. Didn't break a thing, but I did catch pneumonia, and I thought, ah, this is it. We'll clear it up in a jiffy, said the doctors. Over my dead body, I said, but they did, they cleared it up. There's no stopping these buggers."

I invited him to my rooms from time to time, but he felt too unwell to come out during what he called "the cold weather." The cold weather lasted for a long time that year, well into the spring, and I developed the habit of dropping in on him for tea once or twice a week, bringing him a packet of Paterson's, his favourite short-cake biscuits, or a Fuller's walnut cake.

We always met in the kitchen, presumably because it was the only warm room in the house. It was spacious, and he had it fitted up as a living room with a sofa, which doubled as a bed, in the alcove, and two leather armchairs by a gas fire. His cooker and pantry were in a small, stone-floored scullery by the side. I was never admitted to any of the other rooms, except the bathroom, which was large and ornate with black tiles and frosted glass and a huge geyser, whose sobbing and snuffling must have had a paralytic effect on the gastro-urinary system of anyone who used it. There were, if I remembered rightly, two other bedrooms, a dining room and a drawing room, but all the doors were kept firmly shut, even locked, as if he were afraid of what might be found behind them.

I asked him why he didn't move to a smaller flat, which would be cheaper to heat and easier to maintain.

"It's on a long lease," he said. "It would cost me more to rent a garage than I pay for this flat. In any case, what would I do with all my things?"

I remembered his "things" from boyhood. They had all seemed enormous, possibly because I was so small. The rooms themselves were cavernous, with lofty ceilings and tall windows. There were huge, heavily upholstered armchairs with velvet buttons; a long brocaded couch; vases large enough to accommodate a small boy (and which had, on more than one occasion, accommodated me); heavy velvet drapes; delicate porcelain in indelicate show-cases; worthless paintings in expensive frames; embossed, fleur-de-lys wallpaper; a lace-covered baby-grand supporting a copper jug with pampas grass and a host of photos; and, over the black marble fire-place, an oil painting of Ara in the role of Desdemona, her face a deathly white.

In the dining room, with its long heavy table and large heavy chairs and richly carved dresser, there was a portrait of his father, Nahum, whom I had once described as looking like a Victorian worthy. "Yes," said Hector, "when he was younger, for he used to model himself on the English gentleman, as known in Scotland, but as he became older he shrunk a little, and he became more and more like the small Russian Jew he was." He spoke frequently of his father and brothers, rather less frequently of his mother and sisters, and hardly ever mentioned his wife.

He had a family photo which he kept in the kitchen, which had been taken some time during the first World War and which clearly represented, if not his golden age, then a nodal point in his existence. Nahum was in front with his wife and three young children, Jacob, Victoria and Benjamin, between them, while at the back stood the three older children, Sophie, Alex and Hector. Alex and Hector were both in officer's uniform.

"It was a real war, that one," said Hector. "The last do was fun and games in comparison."

Sophie, a large woman with a dark complexion, was also in a uniform of some sort, which I could not identify.

"She was in the voluntary something-or-other. There wasn't a good cause going which she didn't try to make better. She had pips, if you can see. She was a sort of lay mother-superior. Had we been Catholics, Father would have bought her a convent, or perhaps she'd have started her own order. A saintly, high-principled woman. She might have been canonised."

"She's still alive, you know."

"That, as far as I know, is the only thing which could count against her."

The photograph made her look severe; I remembered her as a handsome, Italianate woman, who looked rather like an over-blown Madonna.

"People found it difficult to believe I was her brother," he said. "We were a varied bunch, in appearance as much as anything else. Look at the faces, no two features in common. Alex, the Ram-rod, we used to call him—ram-rod thin, not ram-rod straight—priggish, donnish, old-maidish. If Soph was the soul of the family, he was the brain."

"Isn't Vicky very brainy?"

"Isn't who what?"

"Vicky, brainy."

"Oh, she has brains all right, but she's never had occasion to use them. Then there's Jacob, good-hearted fellow, but an enigma. I always thought him a bit dim, but in some ways he's done better than the rest of us. As for Benny, I thought he was backward, and look what's happened to him." A loud sigh escaped him. "But what's the use of talking? They're all gone, and it's all over."

"They're not *all* gone."

"The ones that count are. That's usually the case with people that count. When you get to my age and you're still around, you begin to feel you've been overlooked."

He usually continued in much the same vein about relatives past, with disparaging asides about relatives present, while I sat quietly beside him, till the daylight faded and the dusk thickened into darkness. What, I wondered, did old men do who had no dead relatives to take pride in and living relatives to complain about?

"We were an odd family," he said.

"Most families are."

"What's that?"

"Most families are."

"Most families are what?"

"Odd."

"But our family was odder than most."

"I suppose, given its size, it had a right to be."

"You see, we became rich too soon and English too quickly."

"But you lost your money."

"That was the trouble. We bought our way into English life, then didn't have the funds to keep ourselves there. The least an upstart can do is to be rich."

One cold, blustery evening, I was in my rooms working on some papers when there was a knock on the door. I had a shaggy little student from Skye, who importuned me at every opportunity with arcane problems. I thought this was he again, and I rose impatiently to give him a mouth when the door opened and Hector appeared, wearing a battered homburg and a heavy black overcoat with a moth-eaten astrakhan collar.

"You look startled," he said.

"Surprised, rather. I didn't expect you to be out on a night like this."

"I feel better. I thought I'd take an airing."

He still carried his stick, but, possibly because of his homburg and ornate collar, he seemed taller and more erect. He took off his hat and sat down in an armchair, and we had the usual exchanges about the weather and his health and his conviction that everyone thought he was dead, or wished he was, or was treating him as if he was. I had the feeling that he had not come out on a night like this—the windows rattled and the wind howled—for a mere chat, and I waited a trifle impatiently for him to get to the point, but he continued much as he had always done, and I was wondering how I could terminate his visit when, à propos of nothing, he asked: "What would you do if you suddenly came into a fortune?"

"Do everything I've always wanted to do."

He shook his head. "At my age you'd be too old to do them, or even to want to do them."

It had not at that time occurred to me that the question was not academic, but a few weeks later he was in every paper, and one in particular had banner headlines reading: GLASGOW WAR HERO INHERITS AMERICAN FORTUNE.

"That's the second time in my life I've been in the headlines," he said, "and it's almost as unpleasant as the first."

According to the papers, he had been left two million dollars.

"I wish it was," he said. "What they do is to think of a number and double it. Where there's a will there's a lawyer—British lawyers, American lawyers, accountants, clerks, excise men—and after they've all had their bite, I shan't have more than a few bob." But his protestations notwithstanding, the sum was clearly substantial, and anyone who thinks money cannot buy youth is mistaken. He was rejuvenated. His step was lighter, his air more buoyant. His conversation became more animated both in content and tone. He ceased to be hard of hearing. His memory improved. He was no longer a peevish old man, or at least his peevishness assumed a livelier form.

"No man knows how many relatives he has till he becomes rich," he said. "Until I came into money, everybody thought I was dead, and I could pass whole weeks without hearing a human voice or seeing a human face. I was thinking of having my telephone disconnected; it was beginning to look like an ornament. Now it hasn't stopped ringing, and I'm assailed with invitations by every post—bar mitzvahs, engagements, weddings, silver weddings. A month ago I knew nobody; now suddenly everybody knows me. Do you think I'd go to their bloody weddings?" —He gave a two-finger sign—"Their funerals, maybe."

Later that year he invited me to join him on a Christmas cruise. I was startled by the offer, for if everything else about him had changed, his parsimony remained the same. My first instinct was to accept with alacrity, but I was afraid he might have booked steerage accommodations on some rusty, broken-down old hulk, and I said I would need time to think about it. Besides, I had arranged to spend the holiday with my mother, and I was unhappy about letting her down, but then one evening he arrived at my door with glossy travel brochures and pictures of a vast floating resort, and my hesitation all but vanished.

"Isn't it all going to be rather expensive?" I asked.

"A fortune, but what are you worried about? I'm paying for it."

We travelled first-class. The average age of the passengers was about ninety and not a few looked as if they might have been a good bit older, and they travelled with nurses and whole teams of medical auxiliaries. It was not an exhilarating experience and the weather was dreadful, and I cheered myself as best I could with the food and drink, which were splendid.

Even mealtimes, however, were not without their drawbacks. Passengers would arrive with whole basketsful of medicines and arrange them on the table like chess enthusiasts marshalling their men, and every now and again there would be a rush of stewards as this ancient or that gave up the ghost and slumped forward into his soup or sank quietly under the table. Such dramatic intimation of mortality tended to have a dampening effect on one's appetite. Also, one or two ancients, who could hardly move their feet, vanished mysteriously overboard, and there was the suspicion that their nurses might have helped them over the rail, so that the atmosphere was not particularly congenial, and I could not wait for the voyage to end.

I had the feeling that Hector had some ulterior motive in asking me to accompany him, and the speculation as to what it could be made it rather difficult for me to relax, but gradually I came round to the view that he wanted nothing more than my company. Then, the night before the ship docked and passengers were hobbling around in false noses and funny hats, he said to me: "You're an historian, aren't you?" His tone of voice made it sound like a vaguely improper occupation, which perhaps it is.

"An economic historian," I said.

"Which means what?"

"I'm something of an authority on the history of coal in South Ayrshire during the latter part of the nineteenth century."

"Doesn't sound very exciting to me."

"I'm afraid it isn't very exciting to anyone, but I try to liven it up. I bring in personalities as often as I can and tell something about their lives."

"And is that your whole life, digging into coal?"

"It's becoming that."

"I'll tell you something more exciting. Why don't you dig into the history of the Jewish family Raeburn?"

"Because it isn't the sort of specialty which would get one a university job or a doctorate. Nor is it the sort of subject which anyone would care to publish, if only because not all that many people would want to read it. The Raeburns, nés Rabinovitzes, might want to, but there aren't all that many of them around, and of those who are, not all can read, not all wish to read, and of those who wish to read, not all would be prepared to put their hands in their pockets for something as outlandish as a book."

"Yes, but think of the Raeburns who are gone. We've got—or at least we had—everything in the family, saints, wealth, scholarship, eccentricity, madness, scandal and—as your mother would have us believe—even murder. What more do you want? Cannibalism? Incest? It would be a best-seller."

"I doubt if I could convince my publisher of that."

"Never mind your publisher. *I'm* convinced, and, what is more to the point, I'm prepared to finance it. Haven't you ever been tempted to write a *real* book?"

"Tempted? I dream of the chance. But where would I begin? Are there archives, papers, diaries?"

"I've got all my father's business papers, and Sophie's a jackdaw, she's kept all the letters from everyone, and I think Alex kept a diary. There's loads of material."

"I'm afraid it might be as dull as my books on coal. When I said that I yearn to write a *real* book, I meant a book with dialogue and real people using real language."

"Use your imagination, put dialogue in."

"That wouldn't bother you?"

"Not at all."

"You mean I can write a novel?"

"Call it what you like, as long as all the characters and situations are drawn from life."

"And I would be free to describe everything I discovered?"

"Everything."

"Even how you came by your two million?"

"It wasn't two million, it wasn't even one million, but whatever it was, it's come in useful."

"But who left it to you?"

"I have my suspicions, but I don't really know."

"How is that possible?"

"That's for you to find out."

CHAPTER II
GENESIS

THERE ARE STORIES LINKING THE RABINOVITZES TO SAUL BEN YE-
huda Wahl, a sixteenth-century Jewish merchant who, according
to legend, was king of Poland for a day. The first is as devoid of
foundation as the second, or as the numerous other legends linking the
Rabinovitzes to every Jew of distinction who ever lived or died or set
foot in Lithuania or Poland. It is only when one comes to the nineteenth century that some of the stories circulating in the family for
generations begin to acquire the buoyancy of fact. A jotting in a family
Bible here, a scrap of paper there, touch on actual names, none of
which, however, establishes any serious claim to fame. What one does
find is a consistent amalgam of Torah and trade, the former generally
deriving from the male side and the latter from the distaff side, with
the daughters of merchants tending to marry the sons of rabbis. (It is
not clear what happened to the daughters of rabbis, for they tend to
fade from the narratives. Were they drowned at birth, or were they
carried off by cossacks?)

The family was large and scattered, with branches in Poznan, Bara-
novich, Vitebsk and Volkovysk. Only the last was to survive, and its
survival may be traced to a letter dated Sivan 5652—which would
correspond to about May 1892—from Yechiel Ben Meir Rabinovitz,
merchant of Volkovysk, to Moshe Ben Yechiel Moss, merchant of
Glasgow. It is written in a fine Yiddish hand and reads:

Please forgive the long gap since my last letter, but bad news travels of
its own accord and of good news there is little. We have so far been
spared the horrors which have overtaken the southern provinces,
thank God, but one rises with anxiety and goes to bed in despair. Men
turn in all directions wondering where to go. Some are on the move to
Austria, some to Germany, others to America, Argentina, Africa,
anywhere, but out of this vale of tears. Only business is at a standstill.
I too would move but am a prisoner of my possessions. Who will buy
into the flax trade when no one is buying flax? I am not even like a
farmer who can eat his own corn or a baker who can eat his own bread.
My store-house is full and my counting-house is empty and my anxieties

are endless, and my only hope is that my children, with the help of God, can start upon a new life. My son, Nahum, now sixteen (may he live to be a hundred and twenty), is a young man of great promise who, in happier times, I would have sent to Yeshiva, for he seemed destined to walk in the ways of our exalted ancestor, the saintly Reb Nahum Phaebush of Kalisch, but, as it is written, where there is no flour there is no Torah. He is my only son, and if he is not to be the provider, who will? His sister, Esther, is a year younger, pretty as an olive sapling and intelligent, with golden hands, well able to cook, clean, embroider and everything she sets her mind to. But when sons are on the move, what hopes are there for daughters? I should like her to accompany Nahum in the hope that with time they will both be blessed and the hopes that I and their mother have for them will be duly fulfilled. Nahum, though young, is responsible and well able to look after both himself and her, but could they encroach upon your hospitality for the first few weeks of their stay? Your father, of blessed memory, was known as the kindest man in Volkovysk. It is said that he never turned anyone away from his doors, no matter how persistent the caller or outrageous his demands. My children, thank God, will not be arriving penniless. I know you to be the son of your father, but I hope you will not be offended if they should insist on making some small payment towards the costs of their stay. . . .

One does not know the nature of the reply. Perhaps Moss wrote that he could only accommodate one person, perhaps Yechiel felt that he could not, after all, let his daughter leave the family hearth. If so, it was, in the light of later developments, a singularly unfortunate decision, but whatever happened, Nahum, after travelling via Riga and Newcastle, arrived in Glasgow on his own. There is a picture of him taken about the time of arrival, looking lean and hungry and a good bit older than his sixteen years.

Moshe Moss—or Moss Moss, as he was known locally—"merchant of Glasgow," was, in fact, a chicken dealer, who bought chickens, sold chickens, talked chickens, smelt of chickens and, towards the end of his life when he became small and shrivelled, began to look like a chicken. His wife, a shrill scold of a woman who felt a little hard done by the world—as indeed she was—berated everyone within sight, her husband, her daughter, her guests and, failing everything else, her chickens. Any chicken too old, too scraggy or too tough to be sold found its way into the pot, and the family rarely ate anything else. It was, said Nahum in later years, like living on boiled rope, and the experience turned him off chickens for life.

Nahum at first found it difficult to get employment, and Moss Moss offered him a share in his chicken business.

"You can't fail with chickens," he said; "the world lives on chickens."

"That's true," said Nahum, "but I was hoping to try something different."

"Why not open a bank?" suggested Moss acidly. He was a trifle offended at the rejection of what was in many ways a generous offer, though in fact Nahum took up his suggestion, albeit on a minute scale.

He had arrived in Glasgow with a few rubles and, more than that, a few gold sovereigns—family lore puts the figure at five—which he lent out on a weekly basis—one doesn't know at what rate—and after a few months he had doubled his assets. Then, having profited from lending short, he turned to lending long and gave out money on a monthly basis. And even here, as he used to put it, the Lord was with him, and by the end of the year he had profited sufficiently to open an office and there suffered his first major setback. He had lent out something like half his capital to a small trader called Goodkind on the security of his home. Three months passed, six months, a year, and still Goodkind couldn't pay. Or, rather, he took out new loans at a higher rate to repay the old, so that by the end of the year, he owed more money than he could ever hope to earn—let alone repay—and Nahum finally sent him a formal letter demanding immediate repayment of at least part of the loan and threatening foreclosure. When a week passed and there was no reply, he descended on Goodkind, who lived a few streets away, in person. He knocked; there was no answer. He tried the handle, and the door opened. It was midwinter, and the house was as cold as the grave. There was no fire in the kitchen grate, and the kitchen itself was largely bare of furniture or cooking utensils and, but for some crumbs on a windowsill, did not look as if it had ever contained food.

"Henry, is that you?" cried an angry voice from another room.

"No, it's me, a visitor."

"What the hell do you want?"

He opened a door, and there on a large bed under a dirty pile of rags lay an ashen-faced slattern, clutching a small misshapen infant. He had never, not even in Volkovysk, seen such poverty.

"Who are you? What do you want?"

"I'm looking for Mr Goodkind."

"Everybody's looking for him. I don't know where he is, the devil should take him. And I've got no money, if that's what you're after. I haven't eaten for two days."

Nahum fled from the scene. Then, on an afterthought, he went into a corner shop, bought some bread, milk, butter and eggs, left them in the kitchen and fled again.

A few days later, he ran into Goodkind and upbraided him for neglecting his family.

"My family?" he said. "Where did you see my family?"

"Then who was that woman in your house?"

"My tenants, that's my whole trouble. I can't get them to pay rent, and I can't put them out on the street, either. I was going to clear them out last summer, but then she had a baby. I suppose by the time it gets to next summer she'll be having another."

"So when will you start repaying the loans?"

"Today, if I had the money. You're not the only person I owe money to, but you'd be the first I'd repay, and you will be as soon as I get hold of a penny, though frankly I'm surprised you're still in business. Do you lend out money to everyone the way you lent it to me? You didn't even look at my books."

As a matter of fact, the sort of businessmen Nahum lent money to didn't keep books, but he saw what Goodkind meant.

It was a long time before Goodkind was in a position to repay the loans, but by way of compensation he offered what he called his expertise. He spoke English, could write it, was a British citizen and looked fairly respectable (if a trifle untidy), which, in Nahum's circle, were uncommon qualifications.

Glasgow, said Goodkind, was filling up with Russian and Polish Jews, anxious to get to America. There were ships sailing from Glasgow every day, but they weren't always sure which ships went where and which lines gave the best terms. He, Goodkind, had some dealing with ships and shipping and knew everything, but couldn't speak Yiddish and didn't have money, while Nahum had money and spoke Yiddish. Together, he believed, they could make an invincible partnership. And they did.

They, of course, had their small differences, the most frequent of which arose out of Nahum's readiness to give credit. There were many prospective travellers who found themselves a few shillings short of a price of a ticket. Goodkind, who was not a harsh man, was prepared in certain cases to accept goods in lieu of cash and acquired a mass of bric-a-brac, with which he was later to open an emporium. Nahum, on the other hand, was frequently ready to extend credit on the strength of an IOU, even though, as Goodkind pointed out, some of the creditors did not even know how to write their names to an IOU, let alone repay it, but even so their partnership prospered.

Now, Moss had a daughter called Miri, a lively child with large eyes and a delicate appearance. There is a photograph of her taken together with her parents, and she seems so refined compared to the pair on either side that it is difficult to believe they were her natural parents. Nahum was alive to her attractions, and frequently, when she knocked on the door of his room to give him a message or to bring him a glass of tea, he felt tempted to ask her to stay but never amassed the courage to do so, for he was afraid that she would almost certainly refuse, which suggests that he had little insight into the character of either Miri or her father.

It is clear that once Nahum showed himself to be a young man likely to go places, Moss hoped to have him as a son-in-law, but no sooner did he begin going places than he went, at least from the Moss menage (or "the chicken house," as he called it), and got himself rooms, or at least a room and a kitchen, on the south side of the river in the Gorbals, and it was also then that he wrote home suggesting that his sister might wish to join him. His father replied:

I am happy that God has blessed your efforts so far that you are already in your own home and you are able to send for your sister. Is it not written "for unto the pious shall be given and that they who seek the paths of righteousness shall have their reward"? I do not—for fear of the evil eye—wish to anticipate good news, but your sister may shortly be betrothed to a young man of great promise, a grandson of your godfather, the saintly Reb Yechetzkel Meir of Klotsk (of blessed memory). He is Yerucham Mikhols, a scholar renowned throughout the province, who has lately become a Rabbi. You should remember him for he spent many days in our house and it was always my hope that he would—God willing—become my son-in-law. Had we lived in happier times I would have been content to support him and his wife and any family with which they might be blessed, for can there be any greater honour for a man of means than to support a student of the Torah? Unhappily, business is so slack as to be almost at a standstill and although I am, thank God, still in a position to give Esther a start in life and to provide her with a house and furniture and linen, I cannot see myself supporting another generation and I therefore feel that Yerucham would be well-advised to find a post before he marries, and to this end he has travelled the length and breadth of the land without finding a position in keeping with his rightful expectations. He is, as I have said, and as you must have heard, a great scholar and a good teacher, of fine appearance, and all the world speaks well of him. Would there perhaps be something in Glasgow?

And it happened that there was indeed a vacancy for a rabbi in

Glasgow, a position which offered a house, a modest but regular salary and some social standing, but Nahum doubted if Yerucham was the right man for the job.

There were, in those days in eastern Europe, a great many *Yeshivoth,* not all of whom were in a position to feed their *bochur,* as their students were called, and it was customary for them to eat different days in different households, and Yerucham used to eat Mondays with the Rabinovitzes. Nahum recalled him as a solemn young man, some three or four years his senior, tall, cadaverous and dark of garb, beard, complexion and mood. He was fine-featured and might have been considered handsome had he been able to smile, but Nahum could not remember him smiling or even talking, for he rarely raised his eyes from his plate and, when not eating, would sway back and forth as if lost in holy thought. He would also sway through the Grace after Meals, which he would intone in a hissing voice, his eyes screwed up tight as if he had a violent headache. And the minute it was over, he fled, and if he thanked his Maker profusely, he never, as far as Nahum could remember, thanked his hosts. Nahum's mother remarked upon it, but his father said: "Why thank me, when all I have is the Lord's?"

Nahum was not too happy with his father's letter. He did not know his sister well (for he had spent much of his own youth in *Yeshiva*), but the little he did know had not prepared him for the possibility that her affections would alight on such a figure. She was a worldly, well-read, high-spirited young woman, who had perhaps been a trifle over-indulged by her parents, and he could not imagine her as a rabbi's wife. Moreover, although fairly devout himself, he tended to recoil from excessive holiness, and he felt that having someone like Yerucham in the family was a little like installing a high altar in one's living room. He found it easier to admire Yerucham than to like him, and he was not even quite sure that he admired him. On the other hand, if both his sister and father had set their hearts on him—as they clearly had—he saw no point in making his feelings known, but he discussed the matter with Moss, who was a person of some influence in the community.

"They'll want a man with a good English and maybe a University degree," said Moss, "but the sort of man they want will not want them, and they'll have to settle for what they can get. Is he a decent-looking man?"

"Very," said Nahum and brought out a photograph.

"It's a nice picture," said Moss, "but is it the man we're talking about?"

"Of course. I know him, I know his family."

"And when was it taken, ten years ago, twenty years ago?"

"It's recent, he's only twenty-two."

"He's got a birth certificate? Because you don't know what frauds we've had to put up with."

"He's got everything."

"And will he trim his beard, or at least his moustache? If his moustache is not trimmed, he'll have soup stains all over his lapels, and if nothing else, they'll want a man with clean lapels."

Nahum did not say much about the young man's piety, for what he knew of Glasgow suggested it was no recommendation.

Moss was able to persuade his colleagues on the synagogue board of management to invite Yerucham to address them, but they were not prepared to pay his fares. There were enough candidates on the spot eager to come without cost, and Nahum sent him the money. He arrived a month later, and Nahum, accompanied by Moss and a small delegation from the synagogue, went to meet him at Queen Street Station, and they were immensely impressed by his appearance and bearing; Nahum almost failed to recognise him. He had filled out somewhat, and, if not erect, he had lost his *Yeshiva bochur*'s stoop. He was also respectably, even elegantly, dressed, and he had trimmed both his beard and moustache, and he smiled incessantly, showing a fine line of healthy, regular teeth. A short speech of greeting was read out on the platform by Moss on behalf of the delegation, and he replied in kind. When he spoke in synagogue two days later, the place was packed to the rafters, and the women in the gallery craned so far forward to catch his words that they threatened to topple over onto their menfolk below.

"Marvelous!" "Wonderful!" "Out of this world!" were the opinions uttered on every side. The only drawback was that he could not speak English. Neither could they, but they sought a rabbi who would not only be their spiritual leader, but who would be their ambassador to the *goyim*, and *goyim* didn't speak Yiddish. Both Moss (who seemed to have taken up Yerucham's cause as his own) and Nahum assured them—as did Yerucham himself—that he would lose little time in learning English. He began taking lessons on the very next day, and before the week was out, he was already greeting people with "good morning" (unfortunately, even at night) and "nice day" and "how do you do?" and there was a move to engage him there and then. They had, however, already arranged to hear another candidate, who could speak English, and they could not reach a final decision until he had been heard.

"I know him," said Moss. "He turns up here, there and everywhere like a bad penny. He may speak a good English, but he's got a bad everything else, and he and his wife quarrel with everybody so that he can never keep a job for more than a year and sometimes doesn't even keep it for as much as a month. He's no good. You can tell Yerucham the job's his."

Nahum lost no time in sending the good news home, and his father wrote back urging him to expedite matters. "The poor child is pining for her loved one, and she will not be herself until they are married."

The English-speaking rabbi arrived, a short, thin man with a tall, thin wife, both of them beautifully spoken, and he an M.A. He got the job. The decision split the community, and Moss and several others broke away to form their own congregation in a small shop-front synagogue and appointed Yerucham as their rabbi. They could not offer the salary paid by the previous congregation, or a house, but Moss assured Yerucham that he would receive both in due course.

Nahum was not sure how to present the news to his father and alighted on every crumb of comfort he could offer.

"The main thing," he wrote, "is that Yerucham will now have a foothold. He will receive a small salary, but it is only a small congregation, which will make the smallest demands on his time. In the meanwhile, he will be able to learn English (he has already picked up quite a few expressions) and perhaps even enter University and get a degree, and if he does, every road will be open to him."

He also felt reassured by the fact (though he did not mention this to his father) that Yerucham had matured a good deal, even in the few weeks he had been in Glasgow, and was not quite as black and holy as he had feared. He swayed with less fervour during prayers and raised his eyes from his plate during meals. He could engage in light, casual conversation without dragging in God's name on every breath. He could even be gallant and charmed the ladies everywhere. Nahum had no doubt he would do well, even if his immediate prospects were slight, and he urged his father not to delay the marriage plans any further, to which his father replied tartly: "It's not for me to delay or advance anything."

A few weeks later he wrote again: "I don't know if he wants to wait till he becomes Chief Rabbi of the British Empire, but Esther doesn't, and I wouldn't want her to wait even if she did. I think he should come back here to get married right away, and they can then both return to Glasgow as man and wife. Can you lay out the money for the fares? If not I'll send you the money by the next post. I don't read Esther's letters, but I know that he doesn't write as often as he should, and when the letters do come they don't bring her as much joy as they did, at least that's the feeling I have. She never says anything to me. She says a little more to her mother, but her mother tells me nothing. That's how it is. I pay for everything, I worry about everything, and everybody tells me nothing. Sometimes I feel like a stranger in my own house. Could you have a word with Yerucham and find out what's happening?"

Yerucham was in lodgings with Moss (which took the edge somewhat off his elegant appearance and air, for he was beginning to smell of chickens, but he liked Mrs Moss's cooking and, indeed, was growing large on it). Moss, moreover, was his patron and mentor, as well as his English tutor (an imperfect one, as it happened, for Moss's English was coloured by rustic expressions which he picked up from the Lanarkshire farmers who supplied him), and Nahum felt that the best he could do was to take Moss aside and ask him to speak to Yerucham.

"Certainly," said Moss. "I'll speak to him like a father, and I'll tell you what he says."

Nahum was then living in what was called a but-and-ben, consisting of a kitchen and bedroom. The kitchen was spacious with an alcove at the side with a bed and made up his living quarters; he sub-let the bedroom to a Russian Jew who spoke no Yiddish, who, indeed, hardly spoke at all, who came and went silently, but who paid his rent regularly, sometimes even—when he was away for days at a time—in advance.

One evening Nahum was alone in the kitchen, drinking tea and doing his accounts which, from all accounts, was his favourite evening activity, when he heard a coughing and spluttering on the stairs; a little later there came a knock on the door. It was Moss who stood for a moment by the open doorway, trying to recover his breath before sinking into a chair.

"The stairs will be the death of me," he panted. "I don't know how Glasgow people live so long with the stairs—the stairs and the fog. I think I must have breathed a ton of soot on the way here, and I couldn't see further than my nose—which you may say is no short distance—but I had to tap, tap my way in front of me with my umbrella like a blind man. Remember the wide open skies of *der heim,* eh? The clear air? The clean streams? The fields, the trees, the lakes, the meadows? And we gave it all up for this our *golderneh medineh.* I sometimes think we need our heads examined."

Nahum did not pursue the matter. He knew that Moss was not a man for social calls. He made him a glass of tea and waited apprehensively for what he might have to say. Moss took his time over it, crunching the loaf-sugar between his teeth, slurping loudly, warming his mittened hands on the sides of the glass. The room was bitterly cold.

"You don't believe in over-heating your place, I see."

"I'm out of the house first thing, and by the time I come home I'm almost ready for bed, so what's the point of lighting fires?"

"And besides, the winters here aren't winters," said Moss, "not compared to Russia. In fact, if you dress warmly enough you can manage without lighting a fire from one end of the year to the other. The important thing is the underwear. If you've got warm *gatkess,* the weather can't touch you."

He slurped in silence for a while, then he said: "Yerucham and your sister, what relationship have they got?"

"I thought you knew."

"I also thought I knew, that's why I'm asking."

"They're waiting to get married."

"*They're* waiting?"

"She's waiting."

"Ah."

"Why the 'ah'?"

"Because I did as you asked me. I took him aside and said, you know, this poor girl is pining for you, you should write more often, she wants to know what's happening. It wasn't an easy thing to do, as you can imagine. After all, he's only my lodger, I haven't bought his heart and soul, but even if I say so myself, I'm a diplomat, and I put it very diplomatically. The poor girl has a right to know what's happening, I said, and——" He broke off.

"And?"

"He said there's nothing formal between your sister and him, and nothing informal, either. She's a lovely girl, a beautiful girl, an intelligent girl from a good family, a girl whom any man would be proud to marry, but——" he paused to take a long slurp of tea as if to fortify himself——"but he's fallen in love with my Miri and wants to marry her."

"Miri?"

"Miri."

"She's only fourteen."

"Excuse me, she's fifteen. Next year, please God, she'll be sixteen. My mother married at fourteen. And, in any case, she's a mature girl, my

Miri, whatever age she is. Anyway, he's fallen in love with her, she's fallen in love with him, so what can I do? I mean, what would you do in my place?"

"I would throw him out of the house."

Nahum made himself a glass of tea and sat down in the chair vacated by Moss, wondering what to do next, what to say to his father and how to say it. He took out a pen and a sheet of paper, but his fingers were too numb, and he felt too desolate to write. He would sleep on it. But he could not sleep and lay awake, staring up at the ceiling and seeing the tormented faces of his father and sister. He tried to comfort himself with the thought that it was perhaps a blessing in disguise, for he had been having doubts about Yerucham which he had kept subdued but which now began to crowd his mind as the night progressed. He had changed from holy man to man of the world to, indeed, something of a man about town a little too suddenly. His side-curls, which he had kept tucked behind his ears, had vanished after a week, and his longish beard had atrophied by the day, till it was hardly more than a small outcrop on the tip of his chin. The very fact that he was content to remain in lodgings with Mrs Moss raised further doubts. Nahum had noticed that Mrs Moss (through what at first he took to be forgetfulness) washed her meat and milk dishes in the same sink, and he suspected that Moss himself, instead of taking his chickens to the *shochet* for kosher slaughter, sometimes saved himself a few pence by wringing their necks. Yet Yerucham, rabbi though he was, seemed content with the situation. And, finally, there was the Miri affair. His sister had clearly been saved from a charlatan, and with this thought he eventually fell asleep.

The next evening he grappled with the letter and decided to break the news by degrees.

Was it definite, he asked his father, that Yerucham and Esther were formally engaged, because the more he saw of Yerucham, the less he was convinced that he was the right man for her; he also had serious doubts about Yerucham's prospects, he said, for there was a glut of rabbis in Glasgow, and he was no longer sure that he would ever get a decent job. His letter crossed with an anguished letter from his father that rumours too dreadful to contemplate had reached him about Yerucham, which he regarded as a slander "on the pious and saintly young man"—such news travelled fast even then—and he begged Nahum to reassure him that none of them were true. Nahum had to reply that the rumours were indeed true, and that Esther had been saved from a catastrophe; he only hoped that she would see it that way.

His father took time to absorb this and eventually came back with a prayer thanking God "for visiting upon us those small calamities which save us from large ones. As for Esther," he added, "she is so cheerful and has been taking it all so well that your mother and I fear for her." There was a postscript: "Now that we have, for the time being, been disappointed with Esther, perhaps—God willing—we may soon hear good news from you."

The news of Yerucham and Miri had, in fact, come as a double shock to Nahum, for he had often comforted himself on cold nights in the Moss menage with warm thoughts about the daughter, and he took great pleasure in looking at her, especially on the Sabbath and festivals, when she was washed and scrubbed and almost free of the all-pervading odour of chickens. He was particularly fond of her smile, which he thought had a slightly derisive edge, as if she were laughing at him, his shyness, his awkwardness. He did not mind being laughed at, at least not by her, for it showed that she was aware of him. Had she been older, and had he been more established, he would have thought seriously about marrying her. She was exquisitely pro-portioned, except for her bosom, which seemed excessive for her age, and, indeed, for her size, and made her look top-heavy. She had a fine neck and large, dark, mischievous eyes, and once, when she and Nahum were alone at table, she confided that she hoped to be an actress, but in the meantime she seemed to spend much of her time helping her large and slatternly mother pluck chickens, gut chickens and keep house.

Even after he had moved to his own rooms, Nahum frequently ate with the Moss family at weekends and regarded the mother's cooking as a small price to pay for the daughter's smile, and although he had given no hint of his intentions, he had been under the impression that he was regarded by her parents as a long-term, prospective suitor. Yerucham had clearly been more direct and definite in his approach.

They married on Miri's sixteenth birthday. It was a large wedding, with everyone receiving their fill of chopped chicken liver, chicken soup and various parts of the animal served in various guises, and it is said that those who stayed through all six courses came away clucking.

The happy couple left for a week's honeymoon. When they returned, Yerucham returned with his chin bare (though with his moustache intact). He also let it be known that in future he was to be called James. A month later he left the rabbinate to become a partner in his father-in-law's enterprise.

Nahum was still troubled about his sister and in some way felt personally responsible for her misfortune, and he wrote home suggesting that she might like to come over and join him. Glasgow, he explained, was full of eligible young men, and he had no doubt that she would find a suitable partner. In the meantime he was planning to move into a larger abode where she could keep house for him. His father was noncommittal. He seemed to blame Glasgow for the way things had developed with Yerucham. "From what I hear, it doesn't seem a fit place for a true daughter of Israel." A few weeks later there came a terse note: "Your sister has gone out of our lives. We have sat *shiva* for her. You should do the same. I hoped too much for her, aimed too high. Pride comes before the fall."

Nahum walked around in a daze, not knowing what to make of it. He presumed it meant she had converted to Christianity, but he found that difficult to believe, for his sister had never given him the impression that she had ever thought deeply upon such things. His father could not be drawn to add anything, and it was with something like desperation that he wrote to his mother in the hope that she might be more forthcoming, but all she would say on the matter was: "It hurts too much to go into detail, but if what happened surprised your father, it did *not* surprise me." It was only some weeks later that a newcomer from Volkovysk told him the full story. His sister had eloped with a *sheigatz,* "a red-haired ruffian, a soldier, a deserter, a double deserter, who had run away not only from the army but from his wife and children."

"That," said Moss Moss, "is what I call *tzores.*"

CHAPTER III
THE DEATH OF RABINOVITZ

THERE WAS IN VOLKOVYSK A MUCH-QUOTED SAYING: "OPEN THE door to the devil and he brings in his relatives," which Nahum recalled with frequency. Almost everything that could go wrong had gone wrong. He could not only imagine his father's anguish, he felt it, not only in what his father wrote but in what he didn't write and in the long silences, which seemed to be becoming longer, between his letters. He found it more difficult to sense how his sister felt, for, although she was his only sibling, he had never really known her. On the other hand, he could never have imagined her doing what she had done, or how a woman who could have loved a man like Yerucham could have eloped with a Russian soldier, yet he had always had vague feelings that the womenfolk in his family had never quite shared the same outlook and loyalties as his father and himself, and that they showed irritation with some of the more awkward ceremonies and traditions of their faith.

Every year there was a large family reunion on Passover, and his father would sit enthroned at the head of the table like a king, with Nahum by his side like a crown prince, and various relatives from far and near—uncles, cousins, aunts. The menfolk clustered towards one end of the table, the womenfolk around the other. The latter, and especially his mother, his sister and his Aunt Katya, tended to be a slightly disruptive influence, for, while the menfolk read through the *Haggadah,* and discussed the Exodus and other events commemorated on Passover at one end of the table, there was chatter and giggles at the other, and Yechiel had to stop from time to time and bang the table till the wine quivered in the wine cups.

"This is Passover," he would shout, "not a fish-market," and for a moment there was silence, but only for a moment.

Nahum suspected that his mother fasted only half a day on the black fast of *Tisha B'Av* and that his sister did not fast at all, but he had thought that, whatever her feelings about Judaism and Jewish tradition, she had shared his respect and affection for their father.

How, he kept asking himself, could she have done this to him, and what had happened to her now that she had done it?

He would bump into Miri and Yerucham from time to time, and although he tried to avoid conversation, Yerucham was either insensitive to his contempt or chose to overlook it, and he once said to him: "You're worried about your sister, aren't you? She'll be all right. There can be wars, revolutions, the world can come apart, but whatever happens, your sister will be fine."

Nahum was not disposed to draw comfort from such a source, and he was anxious to go to Volkovysk to find out exactly what had happened and to see how his father was, but the one spark amid the surrounding gloom was his success in business, and he did not want to jeopardise it by the long absence which a journey to Volkovysk would have entailed. He was not in a hurry to get rich, but he felt that, as things were declining in Russia, the burden of supporting his whole family might eventually rest on him.

For the first year or so of their partnership, Nahum and Goodkind ran their business out of their waist-coat pockets, but they soon grew to the point where they had to acquire premises, and premises meant a name on the door; they had to decide what they would call themselves and to place their partnership on a formal basis.

They consulted Tobias, a lawyer, a lean man with a deep voice, thick glasses and a crumpled face with warts like nipples.

"Rabinovitz is a bit of a mouthful to carry through life. There're a thousand ways to spell it, and you'll be asked to spell it every time you say it."

"But it happens to be my name," said Nahum.

"You were born with a foreskin," said Tobias, "which doesn't mean to say you're required to hold onto it. Do you realise how many times you write your name, say your name, spell your name in the course of a lifetime? But what is more to the point, you hope to grow, don't you? You hope to establish international contacts? Well, foreigners like to feel they are dealing with an olde English firm, and there's nothing English or olde and certainly not olde English about a name like Rabinovitz."

Goodkind agreed.

"But it seems dishonest," said Nahum.

"Mr Rabinovitz, let that be the most dishonest thing you will ever have to do in your life."

"And the name stands for something. We're a well-known family."

"In Volkovysk, maybe, but you're in Glasgow now. A new world, it calls for a new name."

"Such as what? Rabin?"

"No, if you have to change, change it properly. Why not Raeburn?"

"Raeburn, is that English?"

"It's Scottish, which is better still. The best English names are Scotch."

"So we call ourselves Raeburn and Goodkind?"

"Why not drop the 'and' and call yourself simply 'Goodkind-Raeburn'? It sounds good, you can almost sing it—like the opening lines of a Christmas carol:

Good-kind Raeburn last looked out,
On the Feast of Stephen . . .

"See what I mean?"

And Goodkind-Raeburn it was, though Nahum was never entirely happy about carrying a name which was not his father's and was not his; it was a little like sailing under false colours.

There is a photograph of the partners standing outside their office, a converted shop, on what appears to be a blazing hot day, both in black and bowler hats, both moustached, Raeburn dapper, Goodkind large, with a third figure standing a little behind, the tall, thin figure of their clerk, the admirable Colquhoun.

Initially they called themselves shipping agents but soon found themselves dabbling in insurance and transport. At first they were content to hire horses, carters and vans, but they soon discovered that whenever there was a rush of traffic, there were no horses or vans available, and so they established what Goodkind called their own "fleet" and which consisted of two vans, one horse called George and one carter called O'Leary.

Nahum continued to live in his small Gorbals but-and-ben, though when his tenant moved he did not seek another, and Mrs O'Leary called for an hour or so each day to wash, cook, clean and light fires. He permitted himself few luxuries, for his costs seemed to grow faster than his income. Goodkind complained that he was far too hesitant about putting his hands in the till.

"I'm supposed to be a partner in this business," he complained. "I'd be better off as a clerk."

Which was indeed the case. Colquhoun once invited them home to a meal; he lived in a comfortable, well-furnished terrace house. He had an attractive wife called Jessie, who prepared them a meal of a quality they had never tasted in their lives, including large helpings of poached salmon which they washed down with generous quantities of whisky.

"You and I don't live like that," said Goodkind huskily as they staggered homewards through the night.

"He's free to spend everything he earns," said Nahum, "we're not."

"When can *we* start spending?"

"When we're established, properly established."

"When will that be, when we own the White Star Line?"

In spite of the growth of his business, Nahum felt curiously unsettled and dissatisfied, especially on summer evenings. The winters seemed conducive to hard work and application, and he liked to come home to a cheerful fire with the kettle on the hob and dinner in the oven, all prepared by Mrs O'Leary, and after the meal he would sometimes fall asleep in a chair by the fire. In the summer, when the skies glowed with the setting sun and the stone tenements exhaled the accumulated heat of day, he was reluctant to go home, and he was filled with vague longings and undefined stirrings. When Miri was still single, he used to drop in on the Moss household on such evenings, and he had felt refreshed by the sight of the girl, even with a dead fowl between her legs, but the Moss household had lost what attractions it had had, once the daughter was gone, and Nahum never found it easy to make new friends. In all his boyhood years in Volkovysk he had made but one friend, a boy called Shyke, who, though highly intelligent, was as boisterous and wild as he, Nahum, was placid, but until he had moved to Glasgow, or at least until Miri married, he had never found the absence of friends a serious deficiency. For the first time in his life he felt lonely. Once, after walking round and round the streets, he knocked on Goodkind's door. At first there was silence, and a few minutes later Goodkind appeared, looking a trifle flushed.

"Is there anything you want?" he asked in a less than welcoming tone.

"No, no, I was just wondering how you were."

"How I was? You saw me just an hour or two ago."

"Yes, yes, so I did, so you're all right?"

"Yes, I am. Are you all right?"

"Fine. Well, I'd better get on, then."

Nahum saw more of Goodkind than any other living soul and had immense faith in him, yet knew nothing about his private life beyond the fact that he had a wife and children living with his mother in Liverpool. He often wondered why, now that he had a regular income, he didn't bring them to Glasgow. Goodkind never touched on the matter and perhaps the answer lay behind that door, but Nahum did not feel encouraged to call on him again. The rebuff added to his feeling of desolation. He half wondered whether he should drop in on Colquhoun or O'Leary.

Mrs O'Leary, who often offered unsolicited advice, said to him once: "Marriage is no paradise, but sure man needs a woman waiting for him when he gets home after a long day."

Nahum still attended synagogue on the Sabbath with fair regularity, and, especially after word got around that he was not doing too badly in business, he was frequently invited out to meals and as frequently found himself seated next to an eligible daughter. There was also an elderly rabbi who acted as a part-time match-maker—or, rather, an elderly match-maker who acted as a part-time rabbi—who importuned him almost daily with his collection of somewhat shop-soiled wares, and there were times when Nahum had the feeling that Glasgow Jewish life consisted largely of a conspiracy to get him married.

He was also aware of his parents' constant yearning for "good news," and, although he tried to cheer them with accounts of his growing prosperity, which was good news in its way, it was not quite *the* good news his father, in particular, was waiting for; his letters were filled with admonitions from the sages that "a good wife was better than rubies" and that "no man knows happiness who has no children and grandchildren," but Nahum felt that to rush into marriage merely to please one's parents was carrying filial piety a little too far.

As time passed, the letters from home became more frequent and less desolate, but on the matter on which he was most anxious to hear —his sister—both his father and mother remained silent, and while they remained silent he did not feel able to ask questions. Instead, he wrote to Shyke but got no reply and later learned from a newcomer from a small town near Volkovysk that Shyke had emigrated.

"He didn't get on with his father," he said, "but then, who does? I think he's gone to America."

One evening Nahum was invited to the table of Black, a local businessman with whom he had had some dealings, and as usual he expected to find himself next to a daughter. What he did not expect was to find himself next to three, none of them unattractive and all of them substantial.

"They came in quick succession," said the father after the meal, "one more beautiful than the other—*kein-ein-horeh*."

"They're healthy-looking," said Nahum.

"They are, *kein-ein-horeh*, and is there anything more important in life than good health? And they're intelligent girls, cultured. None of them was born here, but they all speak a beautiful English, it's a pleasure to listen to them. You also speak a good English."

"I try to."

"With a bit of an accent, though. You listen to my daughters, no accent at all, you'd think they was born here. You a British subject yet?"

"Not yet."

"I am—I was nationalised three years ago. I voted in the last elections, you know. Conservative. If the Liberals have their way, it won't be worth anybody's while to become a British subject. They're destroying the country, tearing it apart. They play the piano, all three of them. Want to hear?"

Nahum didn't want to hear, but he listened all the same as each took her turn to give a brief recital.

"Now, that's something you didn't get in Volkovysk, eh? Jewish girls playing the piano like that. In fact, you didn't get pianos at all. And, thank God, I'm in a position to see that none of them get their hands dirty."

All three were a trifle like overblown roses, with good teeth and good complexions, pink cheeks, light brown hair and dark eyes. Any one of them would not have been too displeasing an eyeful; a phalanx of all three, however, amounted almost to an assault on the senses.

One afternoon he bumped into one of the three walking with her mother, next to whom she seemed almost slight, and he stopped to talk to the mother, though he felt aware that the daughter was regarding him with warm approval. Suddenly there was a downpour, and they sought the shelter of a shop doorway. The mother noticed something in the shop she wanted, and Nahum, to his embarrassment, found himself alone with the daughter. For a time they looked at each other in silence.

Then he said: "You're the middle one, aren't you?"

"No, I'm the youngest, Elsa. I'm seventeen."

"Are you?"

"Yes."

Silence.

Nahum searched his mind in desperation for a likely topic.

"Where does your father come from?"

"Oh, Russia, somewhere, he doesn't like to talk about it."

"Why not?"

"I've never asked."

Silence.

"Are you still at school?"

"My goodness, no, do I look like a schoolgirl?"

He agreed that she didn't. The mother seemed to be taking an unconscionably long time buying whatever she wanted to buy.

"Do you like Alice?"

"Who's Alice?"

"My oldest sister—Father was hoping you might want to marry her."

"Marry her? I only met her that once."

"But she's nice, isn't she?"

"You're all nice."

"Do you think so?"

"Yes, you in particular."

"I'm fat, and I'll be like Mother before I'm much older. They're all very fat in her family. You should see my Aunt Sarah. She could be in a circus."

As a matter of fact, he had seen her Aunt Sarah, and she was not exaggerating.

"Where do you live?" she asked.

"In Portugal Street."

"That's not far from here. Do you look after yourself?"

"There's a woman who comes in to do the cooking and cleaning."

"And does she look after everything you need?"

"No, not *everything* I need." He felt an almost overwhelming urge to touch her, and, unless he was seriously deluding himself, she looked as if she yearned to be touched. Her bosom was heaving up and down and almost brushing his lapels. Her mother appeared at that moment, and he greeted her with a stifled cry of relief.

That evening he was alone in the house when there was a knock at the door. It was Elsa. He stood gaping at her, open-mouthed.

"Quick," she said, "I can't stay long. My mother thinks I'm with Aunt Sarah." Then, as he led the way into the kitchen, she stopped and gazed around her with dismay.

"Is this where you live?"

"Yes, of course." What did she think he was doing there if he didn't?

"Father said you were a big businessman."

"A what?"

"A big businessman."

"I'm a businessman, but not a big businessman. Why do you ask?"

"It's only a but-and-ben, this."

"So what, it's all I need."

"It's not all *I* need." And she picked up her shawl which had fallen on the floor and fled.

Nahum stood there for a moment, feeling slightly dazed. The ways of his mother and sister had often mystified him, and he had never quite understood how a woman's mind worked. What had brought her to the door so unexpectedly and had raised his hopes so dramatically?

He had never imagined that disappointment could be so painful. After that chance encounter in the street and their conversation in the shop doorway, he had imagined himself to be in love. He had gone back to the office without being able to do any work, and when he had gotten home he had kept looking into the plate of smoked haddock Mrs O'Leary had prepared for him and seeing Elsa, and when she had suddenly appeared in person, it was as if a vision had been made flesh. And then, when she had disappeared as suddenly, he felt it must have been a vision after all. But it had all felt to real, and certainly there was nothing imaginary about the desires which the thought, and then the sight of her, had provoked. For a moment he felt it must have been a vision after all. But it had all felt too real, and into the street. It was raining, which calmed him a little, but he could not stand the thought of going back to his rooms. He did not know where to go, and after wandering around the streets for about an hour, he went into a pub.

It was his first such visit, and his sudden appearance, with the rain dripping from his clothes, halted all conversation. He approached the bar hesitantly, aware of the dozen or so pairs of eyes watching him with curiosity and bemusement.

"A whisky, please," he said.

"A hauf?"

"A what?"

"A hauf?"

"Yes, a half bottle should be fine."

The barman looked nonplussed but produced a half bottle of whisky and a glass, and Nahum retreated to a corner table where a small, elderly figure, like a battered dormouse, was sitting half asleep by an empty glass. He came to life at the sight of the bottle.

"Would you like a drop?" asked Nahum.

The man looked at him open-mouthed as if he couldn't believe his ears. "Eh?"

"Would you like a drop of whisky?"

"Aye, just a wee drop, if you can spare it."

Nahum, who was as yet unfamiliar with British understatement, gave him what he asked for.

"Well, perhaps a drop more than that."

Nahum gave him a drop more, which he gulped down as if afraid it might be taken away from him. "To your guid health," he said when the glass was empty.

By this time others had noticed what was happening in the corner, and Nahum found himself surrounded by five or six people who were ready and eager to drink his health. The half bottle was soon empty, and he ordered another, and a third.

When Mrs O'Leary came in to clear up the following morning, she found him laid out, fully clothed, on top of his bed, as if for a funeral.

"Holy Mary, Mother of God!" she screamed, at which Nahum stirred to life and sat up, holding the sides of his head in both his hands as if afraid it might come apart.

"You poor man," she said, "you look as if you've risen from the dead."

"It's how I feel," he said.

There was a public bath a few streets away to which he normally resorted on a Friday afternoon (there was none in his own place), and he soaked himself in hot water for about an hour. The hot water helped to clear his head, and as he emerged he sat down on the edge of the bath with his towel to his mouth in what his father used to call a *din v'cheshbon*—a self-appraisal. He had been in Glasgow for nearly five years. What had he done with himself? He had built up a fairly thriving business, but he was friendless, alone. He could not help reflecting that, if he had been sufficiently quick off the mark, he might have married Miri and wondered if the feelings he had once had for her could stop him from developing a proper relationship with anyone else. That encounter with Elsa had been a mere spasm, yet he could see as he looked down that even the thought of her affected him physically, if not emotionally. Colquhoun's wife Jessie, a cheerful, bright-eyed, pink-cheeked, full-lipped woman, had a similar effect on him, and he was half-afraid to be in the same room with her in case he should lose control of his hands. Once, when she had pressed against him to wipe some cream from his lapel, he had had to remain seated at the table long after the others had risen, and they had thought he had had too much to drink. Drink may have had something to do with it, but he believed that it was mainly loneliness which made him so prone to arousal, so vulnerable to temptation. That was why the Talmud counselled marriage at eighteen. He was nearly twenty-two, and without a sign of anyone he might possibly want to marry. He felt rather less assured in managing his life than his business. And there was no one he could talk to on any personal matter, not Goodkind, not Colquhoun, though he sometimes thought that Jessie would be a ready listener. The nearest thing he had to a confidant was Miri. He had kept his distance from her and her husband in the first months of their marriage, but she had been gravely ill after her first child, a daughter, was born. He visited her a number of times in hospital and when she was convalescing, but the frequency of his calls dwindled after that. Her second pregnancy had been almost as difficult as the first, and she was again in hospital when he went to visit her and she said: "Do I have to have a baby every time I want to see you?" He would have liked to call more often but found Yerucham —who, in fact, went out of his way to be friendly to him—a deterrent. Had he felt mere hatred for the man he would, he was sure, have gotten over it by now, but the feeling was more one of revulsion. Yerucham had a curious habit of touching people as he spoke to them, putting a hand on their shoulder, or holding them by the arm, as if they might try to get away, and he shuddered at his touch.

"You should see my wife more often," Yerucham said, "you're the best medicine." A few months later they moved to a large house in one of the suburbs, and Nahum hardly saw anything of them at all. Strange how he found it easier to talk with women than with men, and then only with women who were beyond his reach. He wondered if perhaps he had left home too soon, before he had had time to mature. And then suddenly he felt a pang of longing for Volkovysk, for his parents, for home, so intense that he almost writhed. Perhaps it was due to the feeling of contrition which comes after a debauch, or the dread of the long, hot summer ahead, but there and then he decided to visit his family. He was no longer nervous of leaving things in Goodkind's charge, for he had grown more restrained, and in any case there was always the steadying hand of Colquhoun.

Three weeks later he was on the train. He travelled first-class. He felt he owed it to himself. But it was not only that. He had, without trying to mislead anyone, built up a picture of himself in his parents' eyes as a highly successful businessman, initially in an attempt to console them for their disappointment with Esther, and also because the sort of turnover he had—when translated into Russian terms— seemed large, and now that he was about to materialise in person, he felt obliged to live up to the image. He always believed in being reasonably well dressed so that he already had a good wardrobe. He now bought expensive leather luggage and expensive presents for his parents, for his Aunt Katya, for his cousin Lazar, his Uncle Sender and his children, and others.

This was the first time Nahum had set foot in a first-class carriage, and the moment he settled in his seat and the train pulled out, he felt he was embarking on a new experience. Previously he had merely moved from one place to another; now he was a *traveller*. The first thing that struck him was not so much that the seats were more comfortable, the carriages more spacious and better appointed and the company more elegant, but that there was almost no smell. All his previous experience of travel had involved smells, not only the acrid smoke from the locomotive, which passed almost unnoticed, but the smells of humanity. People, when brought together, smelt of herring, onion, garlic, fish, cabbage and other less definable smells, and, of course, sweat. First-class passengers, he discovered, were almost odourless, as if they came from a different environment, or, if from the same environment, they had left it behind. Also, on entering the first-class carriage, he felt he had set foot in his own natural milieu. It seemed to him that there were people who, whatever their circumstances, were natural first-class passengers, and he felt he was among them. He would not, he promised himself, travel third-class again. It would mean that he would be putting back less into the business and that he would expand more slowly, but the best time to enjoy luxury was when it was still something of an extravagance.

He was sorry he had not planned his holiday some six months earlier, for he could have added the pleasures of anticipation to the pleasures of the journey. The thought of the expense—he had never spent so much on himself in so short a time—nagged a little at his peace, but he enjoyed the journey as he had enjoyed no other. He travelled from Glasgow to Newcastle, and Newcastle to Hamburg, and Hamburg to Berlin. From Berlin he took the Great East European Express as far as Bialystock and from there changed to a local train, where he was instantly overwhelmed by a wave of nostalgia wafting over him like the warm wind through the open window. It was the smells that finally brought home to him the fact that he was again in *der heim,* back home—the smells of dust and dried pine needles and resins which immediately evoked Russia in high summer. He could not quite understand the thought processes that made him so happy to be back in a country from which so many of his fellows had fled for their lives. It was not only the thought of being back with his family that thrilled him; he was overjoyed to be back in Russia itself. He had no complaints about Britain, and certainly not Glasgow. They had given him a freedom and opportunities which he could never have hoped for in Russia, but he had never felt at home, and after five years of exile, he was beginning to doubt whether he ever would. He presumed the hold which Russia had on him arose simply out of the fact that he had been born there: one loved one's mother country as naturally as one loved one's mother, even where—as happened in this case—the love was unrequited.

He had fond memories of Volkovysk and would have been content to remain there had his father not urged him to move. He remembered clear, fast-flowing rivers, great open skies, cobbled streets, wooden houses with brightly painted shutters, spacious forests, lakes, echoes across the water on quiet summer evenings.

Train arrivals were infrequent events in Volkovysk, and the station and its surroundings were filled with teeming crowds—small boys, old men, peasants with sheep and goats, barking dogs, clucking hens, quacking ducks, waggoners with whips and restless horses and porters clamouring to carry the baggage of the few passengers who alighted. The appearance of Nahum caused a stir. One did not see many well-cut suits in Volkovysk, especially in hot weather, or immaculate leather luggage, and he was immediately surrounded by a curious crowd; the driver who took his luggage almost had to whip his way out of the railway yard, and he was followed much of the way home by a crowd of barefoot boys.

Nahum had sent a letter to say he was coming but without giving precise times or dates, partly because he was not too sure of them himself—the time-table beyond Bialystock was sometimes erratic— and also because he presumed that at that time of the year, the end of July, the family would be at their dacha, and he didn't want to make them feel obliged to come to the station. Besides, he had always hated to be greeted or seen off at railway stations.

As he guessed, the house stood empty and shuttered, and he asked to be driven to the *dacha*, about fifteen miles from the town, a squat timber house surrounded by a wide verandah, set amid pine trees on the edge of a lake. It was nearly dark when he arrived.

He had happy memories of the dacha. They used to go there every summer, his parents, Esther, aunts, uncles, cousins, servants; it was loud with chatter and laughter, and when they assembled on the verandah in the cool of the evening as the sun was beginning to set, the noise rang out across the water, and distant sounds, snatches of music and laughter, the cries of children, the barking of dogs came wafting in on the evening breeze. But now the verandah was empty, and the lake was like a mirror with only an occasional insect disturbing its surface. There wasn't a sound. He found the silence ominous.

CHAPTER IV
VOLKOVYSK

As HE WENT TOWARDS THE HOUSE, A CLOTH-CAPPED FIGURE emerged and stopped short by the open door. Nahum recognised the long nose and small, bright eyes of his cousin Lazar. He had become a head taller since Nahum had last seen him but was as thin as ever and had acquired a stoop.

"*Nu*, Lazar," said Nahum with a show of joviality, "don't you recognise me?"

The young man approached him, eager, envious, disbelieving. "You look so rich," he said. "If I wasn't told you were coming, I wouldn't have known it was you. Did you know about your father?"

Nahum felt a stab of alarm. "Father?"

"He's been very ill, poor man, but he's pulling through. He was upset that you didn't say you were coming; he would have liked to meet you at the station. He always likes an excuse to see a train."

Lazar led the way into the house, and there, at a long table under a green lamp-shade, sat two silent figures drinking tea, both in dressing gowns, his father in a large, square skull-cap, his mother with what looked like a towel around her hair.

"I've brought you a visitor," said Lazar.

The mother turned but at first could not make out the figure in the darkened hall; then suddenly she jumped to her feet and put her hands to her face.

"It's Nahum, Yechiel, it's Nahum."

The father also attempted to rise but fell back in his chair. Nahum rushed towards him, and they embraced in a show of emotion which they all felt to be slightly excessive. Lazar looked away with embarrassment. The mother bit her lip.

"You'll have to excuse me," said the father. "I haven't been too well."

"Too well?" said the mother. "He's lucky to be alive."

"Why didn't anyone let me know?" asked Nahum.

"What could you have done? I've had a slight stroke, but I've still

35

got one good arm and"—he laid a hand on Nahum's shoulder—"one good son."

Nahum was shocked by his appearance. His father had been what they called in Yiddish a *Yid mit beinner,* a Jew with bones, as if such Jews were uncommon in Eastern Europe, which perhaps told one something of the image which Russian Jews had of themselves, for it was an expression used only by Jews among Jews. He was a stalwart figure, straight-backed with a magnificent head of hair and a long, dense beard of Assyrian proportions. His hair was now snow-white, though he was only in his fifties, his beard had become thin and wispy, and his mouth was twisted. He was blind in his left eye, and his left arm dangled limply at his side. He tried to treat his condition lightly.

"I'm not the man I was," he said, "but what does it matter as long as I've got my health?"

He wanted to stay up to talk to Nahum, but his wife ordered him to bed.

"You see what it is to have a wife? You can't even talk to your own children." But he did as he was told and was soon asleep.

"He's taking it heroically," said Nahum.

"More heroically than I could have believed. Remember how peevish he used to be? He's more of a *mensch* now, and his mind's as good as ever."

"Why didn't you let me know?"

"He didn't want me to, and, in any case, how could I have put it? 'Your father's had a slight stroke'? What would that have sounded like two thousand miles away? How slight can a stroke be? At first I thought he wouldn't live and was preparing to send you a telegram, and then, when he pulled through, I was hoping he might make a complete recovery. I'm still hoping, though, in fact, it's a miracle he's not worse. There is perhaps one thing which could possibly make him better. He said to me, *nebbich,* 'I look and feel like a grandfather, which wouldn't be so bad if only I had grandchildren.' I suspect he had Esther in mind."

"Still?"

"Still? She's never been out of his mind, but he never talks about her directly—not in his waking hours. If you married, it would lighten his heart a little, but you know, ever since the Yerucham affair, he's had the most terrible apprehension about Glasgow girls. When he acquires an image about a person, he never changes it. Yerucham, as far as he knew him, was a saint, so a saint he remains, and the fault must have been the girl's."

36

"What I can't understand is how Esty could have fallen for a man like that—not the sort of man he turned out to be, but the sort of man Father thought he was. What did she have to do with saints?"

"He was very good-looking—but she was doing her little best to desanctify him, to shorten his beard, improve his manners. I suspect she realised he was a fraud but regarded it as his saving grace. It gave her the hope that she might civilise him. She thought he was hers to make, and it was a shock when she found he wasn't. What's his wife like?"

"Small, pretty, but she's put on years since she married and—if it's any consolation to anyone—I don't think she's very happy. Do you hear anything of Esty?"

"Not a thing. Her name isn't mentioned in this house, except by your father in his sleep."

"Where is she?"

"No one knows. I'm not trying to hide anything, I just don't know. But what about you? What's been happening to you?"

"Nothing."

"Isn't it about time something did? As your father put it, 'I wish he was a husband and father first, and a millionaire later.' Isn't it time to settle down?"

"Perhaps I might find it easier to settle down if I thought things here were a bit more settled. Why can't you and Father move to Glasgow? What is there to keep you here?"

"The business, for a start."

"He never stops grumbling about it."

"What businessman doesn't grumble about his business?"

"Look, if it's a going concern, you can find a buyer, and if it isn't, then cut your losses and pull out."

"Are things that straightforward in Glasgow? They're not in Volkovysk. Your father has no idea whether he's making a profit or a loss. What he does know is that thirty families depend on him for a livelihood, and that he somehow manages to pay wages and earn enough to keep me and your Aunt Katya and Lazar and Uncle Sender and the rest. And, in any case, supposing he did sell out, what would he do with himself at his age?"

"At his age? How old is he? Fifty-five? That's nothing."

"In England, maybe; in Russia that's old—especially with all he's been through. Here, at least, with all his grumbles and headaches and heartaches, he's among familiar people in a familiar setting. What's he going to do in England? He'll never be able to learn the language."

"I know millionaires who don't speak a word of English."

"But they didn't start out when they were fifty-five, and after a stroke. No, Nahum, we'll come to your wedding; otherwise we can stop here."

"You talk as if your future is assured. Russia is not a stable country."

"No, and it never has been, but with all its instability, it's lasted a thousand years, so it should last another couple of hundred—enough, in any case, to see us through."

The next day was hot and heavy. Nahum had vivid memories of the cold winters, but he had forgotten exactly how hot the summers could be. He spent much of the morning talking to his father on the verandah; then, as the heat became impossible, he changed and went into the lake for a swim. Lazar paddled among the reeds on the edge of the water.

"Can't you swim?" asked Nahum.

"I daren't. Father died in a swimming accident, and Mother won't let me near the water. She would have a fit if she even saw me paddling." He was sixteen or seventeen but sounded like a five-year-old.

A few minutes later the mother appeared but ignored her son altogether and stood looking admiringly at Nahum. "Aren't you coming to kiss your aunt?" she asked.

"I'm all wet."

"I don't mind getting wet, especially on a day like this."

He came out and kissed her, a trifle hesitantly, on the cheek.

"That's no way to kiss your aunt," she said, and pulling him to her she kissed him on the lips. He retreated breathlessly, not quite sure what had happened. It took him some time to regain his composure.

"You're looking well," she said.

"And you."

"I feel hot and dusty. I wouldn't mind jumping into the water fully clothed." Then, as if in answer to a challenge, she sat down, unlaced her boots, took off her stockings and jumped into the water. Her son looked on as if she'd gone mad and scrambled out of the reeds in alarm.

"It's not so long since you used to bathe naked in here. You've grown up quickly. Have you got a mistress?"

"A what?"

"A mistress."

"You've read too many bad Russian romances, Aunt Katya."

"Don't call me aunt, it makes me feel ancient. You're very successful, aren't you? And don't successful men have mistresses in England?"

"First of all, I'm not that successful, and, second of all, I'm from

Glasgow, which is in Scotland, and in Scotland they're a good deal more strict about such things than they are in Russia."

"So you've no mistress?"

"No mistress."

"What a waste."

Katya was his mother's younger sister, a plump, excitable woman, with what someone once called *shikseish*—good looks—which is to say she was pink and blond, with lively blue eyes and dimpled cheeks. She was always known as the "naughty" sister and tended to revel in the title and take pleasure in asking scandalous questions and making scandalous remarks.

"Let's swim round to the other side of the lake," she said.

"Aren't you bothered by the weight of your clothes?"

"I am, but I'm going to take them off as soon as we're out of sight."

Nahum hesitated in mid-course, not knowing whether to believe her or not. He had never been certain when to take his aunt seriously. But then, as if by way of reproof, the weather broke. There was thunder and lightning. Shrill gusts of wind ruffled the surface of the lake and whistled through the reeds, and it began to pour and the lake was suddenly covered with a million small eruptions. Nahum loved it and stood upright in the water and let the rain wash over him. Katya was, or claimed to be, a little afraid and huddled against his chest till the storm subsided.

They ate supper on the verandah, one of those delicious summer meals he remembered from his boyhood—diced cucumbers, radishes and spring onions mixed with caraway seed and garlic and served in sour cream; smoked buckling, and, finally, wild strawberries in lemon juice.

"I suppose in England you had half a cow for supper," said Katya. "I hear that in England they do nothing but eat cattle."

"I've never tasted anything as delicious as this," said Nahum, "not in the five years I've been away."

"Who looks after you?" asked Katya.

"A woman comes in to do some cooking and cleaning for me."

"And then she goes again?"

"Yes."

"We know what you're getting at, Katya, but keep off it," said the mother; "the poor boy's already had enough from me."

The two sisters sat on one side of the table, Lazar and Nahum on the other, and the father, who seemed oblivious to the conversation around him, at the head. With his white hair, limp arm and twisted face, he looked like some poor cripple who had been brought in for a meal. No one could have imagined that Eva was his wife. She had reddish hair which was beginning to turn grey and green eyes, but otherwise, with her snub nose and generous build, she was very much like her younger sister. Their necks could have been a trifle longer and more slender, but they were an attractive pair, their ample size well contained both by corsetry and their buoyant personalities. They looked as if they'd stemmed from well-to-do peasant stock and lacked the soulful, dark-eyed appearance Nahum associated with Jewish women. There were vague stories that their mother had been raped by a cossack, but from what he remembered of his maternal grand-mother, it would have taken a brigade of cossacks—fully armed—to perform the task. Both his mother and aunt took what had struck him as an unseemly pride in the fact that they did not look Jewish, and neither was particularly Jewish by temperament. His father's family had apparently objected to the marriage partly because it was thought that he was marrying beneath him—the Rabinovitzes being a well-known and well-to-do clan—and partly because there were serious doubts about her religiousness. She came from Odessa, which was the largest Jewish centre in Russia and which, though proud of its enlightenment and its rich cultural traditions, was thought of among Orthodox Jews as a latter-day Sodom. His mother had agreed she would keep a kosher home and observe the Sabbath but made it clear that she would, in no circumstances, wear a wig (as was custom-ary among devout Jewish matrons in Yechiel's family) or even keep her hair covered with a kerchief, though, in fact, she did keep it cov-ered on those occasions when Yechiel entertained a rabbi or some visiting Jewish sage in the house, and it had been as happy a marriage as any in the town and happier than most.

Nahum had never enjoyed the close relationship with his mother that he had with his father, but he was proud of her good looks. He kept her photograph in his room; it was the subject of frequent com-ment and admiration, and Miri had said to him that if he hoped to find a wife like that he would never marry. He himself had inherited the fine features, dark eyes and erect bearing of his father, but he liked to think that he had something of the self-assurance of his mother.

"How long are you here for?" asked Katya.

"Two weeks."

"Are you going to stay here all the time, or are you going to travel?"

"I've no plans at all—though I hope to see Shyke's family."

The two sisters exchanged glances, and he thought Katya changed colour, but he might have imagined it.

"He's gone to America, hasn't he?"

Katya leaned forward till her forelock touched his. "He did an Esty," she whispered.

"You should visit his father, *nebbich*," said Yechiel.

"I don't think I'd call Grossnass a *nebbich*," said Eva.

"He's big now," said Katya.

"I don't remember him ever being small," said Nahum.

"She means in business," said Eva. "He has tanneries, distilleries, tobacco, everything."

"But it doesn't add up to anything," said Yechiel. "He's a *nebbich*, you should go and see him."

They remained at the *dacha* for another three days, but the weather turned cool and overcast, and they returned to Volkovysk.

Nahum's presence caused a stir in the town. It had a population, including the outlying areas, of only ten thousand, of which about half was Jewish, and visitors from beyond the Russian border were few and far between. Anyone who emigrated to the West—especially as far west as Britain or America (and the former figured in the local imagination as an offshore island of the latter)—was presumed to prosper. Anyone who prospered sufficiently to afford a return visit, however (and only a visit; to return and stay was a public confession of failure), was taken to be a minor Rothschild, and Nahum's parents' house was filled with an endless succession of visitors, relatives, friends, acquaintances, contemporaries at school and *Yeshiva,* pilgrims who wished to feast their eyes on this protegé of fortune and shake his hand, possibly in the hope that something of it might rub off. His father's stock in the community, which had declined with Esther's elopement, was restored to its old heights.

Nahum himself was depressed by it all, as perhaps any return to scenes of childhood is depressing. His memories of Volkovysk were of nippy, glittering, wintry mornings; of gleaming snows in the setting sun; of summery days and cool, tranquil evenings; of bright hues; of openness—clear skies, clear waters, clear vistas. It was rather less attractive amidst the grey skies and mists of early autumn. Grey, indeed, was the predominant colour—grey streets, grey homes, grey faces, grey lives, decay without mellowness. There was hardly a building in good repair in the entire town. Bridges, public buildings as well as private, everything seemed to be falling apart as if everyone was content to let things slide into oblivion. And the streams where he used to go fishing, which he remembered as transparent and swift, were murky and sluggish. Eaves sagged, domes sagged, windows sagged, faces sagged, but at the end of it all he had to ask himself whether what he saw reflected his own mood or the actual scene.

Uncle Sender came to visit them, which further depressed him. He recalled his uncle, who had always been referred to by his father as "the brains of the family" as a large, jovial man, but now he looked shabby and ambling and was painfully pedantic. He was widely read in the Talmud and Russian and German literature, but his conversation was full of quotations, some of which sounded phoney even to Nahum's untrained ear, and where Nahum had previously admired his relaxed, easy-going manner, he now found Sender feckless. He had an ailing wife and six children, and they were all supported by his brother; it struck Nahum that Sender might have had more to be jovial about if he read less and worked more. It was all right to have a relaxed, leisurely attitude to life if it was not dependent on another man's earnings.

"Have you a nice home?" he asked Nahum.

"It's a small home, but for the time being I don't need anything big."

"But have you room for books? Was it not your Shakespeare who said that you can judge a man by his books? Have you seen my library? When Wachsman was in Volkovysk—you know who I mean, *the* Wachsman—he said what you have there is worth more than I'll ever have in my bank, and that was ten years ago. My library grows by the day, *vechein yirbu*. My house has become too small for it; even the children have books. You may remember the saying of Rab Assai: 'Give your children spiritual nourishment, the rest they will find themselves.' "

The children did not, indeed, look undernourished, but they were bedraggled and unwashed, and Katya, who was an obsessively tidy woman, went from one to the other, blowing noses and wiping mouths.

"As a matter of fact, I'm thinking of making my home in England," said Sender. "It's a cultured country, England, no?"

"I wouldn't know. I live in Scotland."

"Scotland, England, they're the same."

"You might as well say Poland and Russia are the same."

"Well, they are the same, except Poland's a bit different. Do you think I would like Scotland?"

"No," said Nahum firmly.

Nahum regretted his impatience with his uncle, but, apart from feeling depressed, he was deeply worried about his father. His mother had insisted that his father's mind was as active as ever, but it was so only intermittently. Whenever he sat down to relax, he tended to fall asleep and seemed half asleep even at mealtimes, and yet, with all his infirmities, he still attempted to put in a full working day. Nahum asked him if he had ever thought of selling out.

"Everybody thinks of selling out if he gets the right price, but the only offers I get are from people who want to buy me with my own money. They'll give me a kopek in cash and pay off the balance out of profits for the next two thousand years. They think because my arm has withered, my mind has also dried up."

He showed Nahum his books. They were kept partly in Yiddish and partly in Russian and both in a highly idiosyncratic manner, and Nahum couldn't make head or tail of them.

"Neither can I," his father confessed.

The following day he obtained a rough evaluation when he visited Shyke's father, Grossnass, a large, round man with a short, square beard. He received Nahum with open arms and engulfed him in a cloud of garlic.

"An English gentleman," he said. "I wouldn't have recognised you. They tell me you're another Wachsman, or soon will be. *Nu*, so what's it like being rich?"

To which Nahum nearly retorted, "You should know," but answered instead: "Much nicer than being poor."

"You haven't come to see me, have you? You want to know about Shyke; everybody wants to know about Shyke, as if they didn't know already, and all I want to do is forget. Your father's got his little pile of *tzores*, and I've got mine. You've heard he isn't here?"

"I've heard various things, some of them contradictory."

"He's forsaken his God, his religion, his family, his people. He doesn't keep *Shabbos* or *Yom Tov*, he doesn't eat kosher. He's not a Jew. He's not my son."

"Where is he?"

"Don't ask. I don't know, I don't want to know—you're opening wounds." He put a pudgy hand on Nahum's knee. "Let's turn to more cheerful things. Tell me about yourself. You've become a good-looking man, you know, like your father when he was a young man, *nebbich*. The calamities the poor man's been through. Well, at least he's got some joy from his son, which is more than I have. I must tell you it's a pleasure to look at you, you dress nicely."

Nahum rose.

"No, no, don't go, there's a lot I've got to ask you. You married?"

"No."

"Got somebody in mind?"

"I really haven't come here to discuss that."

"No, but you're here, so we might as well discuss it. I suppose you know I've got the prettiest daughter in Volkovysk, and her father, thank God, isn't a poor man, either; an unfortunate man, maybe, but poor, no." He rose from his chair and shouted down the hall: "Sorke!"

And instantly there appeared a slender young girl with dark eyes, red cheeks and long hair.

"Go on now, feast your eyes on her and tell me if I'm wrong."

"Mr. Grossnass, I can't claim to be an authority on such things."

"Who better than you, a man of the world, a man who has travelled, an English gentleman?" Grossnass felt the lapel of Nahum's jacket. "What a beautiful suit. An English tailor?"

"A Jewish tailor."

"But English material, what quality." He felt the lapel again. "They don't make stuff like that around here. Our tailors have golden hands, but the material's rubbish."

The young girl spoke up. "Can I go now, Father? I was in the middle of something."

He waved her away with his hand. "Well, do I exaggerate? And not like your sister, bless her. She was brought up to honour and obey, the same with all my daughters. I'm not, heaven forbid, criticising your father, but he let Esther do what she wanted. The books she was reading, the company she was keeping, it was bound to happen. My daughters don't read Russian, they don't read German, I'm not sure I should have taught them to read Hebrew, though they write and read a very good Hebrew. A compensation, my daughters, for the misfortunes I've suffered with my son." He put his hand on Nahum's knee again. "She's only seventeen, you know, and golden hands, cooks as only her mother —may she rest in peace—used to cook, sews, cleans. Look at my house. Thank God I've got servants, but you need somebody who can handle servants. She does—and only seventeen. You can't realise what a loss she'll be to me, but she can go tomorrow as long as she goes to the right man. You're in shipping, aren't you?"

"I'm a shipping agent."

"Right, I'll buy you a ship."

"It's a generous offer, Mr. Grossnass, but the fact is, I've got other things on my mind."

"You mean your father? Your marriage would be his cure. He'd be a new man. He'd come and live with you; I don't mean on top of you, but he'd move to Glasgow. What is there to keep him here, his crazy sister-in-law?"

"He's reluctant to leave his business."

"Leave his business? His business is leaving him."

"Is it? I have the impression it's picking up."

"He has a decent turnover, but on what terms? He gives credit as if he's scattering manna. I nearly bought him out a year or two ago when I found myself short of flax and he came to me with a ledger of debts which he asked me to regard as assets. 'Assets?' I said. 'Assets,' he said. 'I'm owed the money, that's assets.' They're liabilities, I told him; the more people owe you, the more you're in their debt. If your father could recover even half his debts, he'd be a rich man. I'm not saying, heaven forbid, that he's a poor man, but he thinks his business is a gold mine, when, in fact, it's a hole in the ground."

"But in round terms, how much do you think it's worth?"

"Depends to whom. I personally wouldn't take his business as a gift."

Nahum had been in business long enough to recognize an opening gambit when he saw one, and he was confident that if his father would be prepared to dispose of his company, Grossnass would be in the market. He made further inquiries and found other prospective bidders, but he could not get his father to apply his mind seriously to the possibility of selling out, and he began to doubt that his father still had the mental capacity to take a balanced view of his situation.

"There's nothing wrong with his mind now that there wasn't before," said his mother, "but you'll get nowhere with him. When things are going well and there are buyers around, he feels no inducement to leave, and when things are going badly and he can't sell, then he can't leave. Nothing short of a major calamity would force him to move."

CHAPTER V
POGROM

IF THERE WAS ONE THING WHICH NAHUM MISSED IN GLASGOW, IT was the advent of the Sabbath—the advent perhaps more than the Sabbath itself—the minutes before sundown on Friday afternoons, when the frantic last-minute preparations ceased, shops shut, transport stopped, candles began to glow in front parlours and fathers and sons emerged in their Sabbath best—their faces scrubbed, their nails clipped, their boots polished—on the way to synagogue. The confluence of minor tributaries from the minor roads thickened to a broad stream in the major ones. The synagogues were packed. There was an air of serenity to those minutes which was not to be experienced in Glasgow, where, if anything, the town grew more boisterous and profane as darkness approached, and one had to make one's way to and from synagogue through streets thronged with drunks. The menace surrounding Jewish life in Russia was of a far more serious kind, yet it was somehow forgotten for the duration of the Sabbath, and the harassments of the workday week seemed to dissolve in that one day of bliss .

One Friday, Nahum had been wending his way slowly to synagogue with Lazar, his father between them, leaning heavily on their arms. The hot days had made an unexpected return and the sky was scarlet with the setting sun, when Lazar pointed out that there was a glow coming not only from the west, but from the east, as if there were two setting suns. Others stopped to gaze at the phenomenon, and distant, excited voices came wafting in on the evening breeze, but no one seemed unduly alarmed. The summer had been very long and very hot, and rain had ben sparse. The forests and, indeed, the towns were like tinder, and fires, some of which raged for days on end, were not infrequent. Nahum felt a trifle uneasy, but his father merely shrugged his shoulders, and they continued on their way. But then, towards the end of the service, some latecomers entered, and somebody whispered the word "pogrom." The cantor immediately quickened his pace to a gallop and completed the service in a rushed jumble of words, and some of the timorous, or less devout, hurried home before the close.

Usually, after the service, everybody turned to everyone else to wish each other *Good Shabbos*, to ask after their families, to exchange gossip, while Yankelson, the *Shammos*, waited impatiently for the building to clear so that he could get home for his supper. This time, the building emptied within minutes. Yechiel could not be hurried and hobbled home slowly on Nahum's arm, while people darted in all directions. (Lazar, too had run ahead.) The glow of candles vanished as shutters were closed, and worried voices echoed through the darkened streets. Nahum was becoming alarmed himself, but his father seemed untroubled—and his weight on Nahum's arm had a steadying effect. By the time they got home, all the windows and nearly all the doors had been barricaded, and Katya was screaming, "We'll be raped, we'll be raped." Nahum wondered if it were hysteria or wishful thinking.

No one had much appetite for food, except Yechiel. They hurried through the meal without the usual accompaniment of *zemiroth* (table hymns), and the women bit their nails impatiently while Yechiel insisted on droning through the grace after meals as if nothing were happening.

"I really do think he's senile," Katya whispered to her sister. "I really do." Nahum wondered if it was that, or whether he drew more reassurance from his faith than the others. Their old Russian servant, Anna, tried to calm them, without much effect.

"It's all right for *her*," said Katya.

When the meal was over, they asked Anna to put out the lights. Yechiel went to bed. The rest sat huddled together in the darkness, talking in subdued voices. Lazar began to cry.

The most painful part of the situation to Nahum was the feeling of utter helplessness. In towns like Volkovysk, the Jews outnumbered the gentiles. They were better educated, more intelligent, more prosperous. He felt that they should have been able to organize some sort of self-defence effort but instead sat there, quaking in the dark. The more spirited, the livelier elements in the town, the Shykes, who might have been the natural leaders (even the semi-Shykes, like himself), had all left, and the young men who remained seemed dispirited, feeble and old; he was not sure whether they had become that way through remaining where they were, or they had remained where they were because they were so inclined. He listened to Lazar's sobs and wondered if he had been as timorous the last time the town had been threatened with a pogrom. He could not remember.

It was a long night, or seemed like one, and they sat upright with ears strained for every sound. Dogs barked, but there was little movement outside. Occasionally the gallop of horses could be heard, and

Katya clutched at him and did not ease her grip till long after the sound had faded into the distance.

"Perhaps it's a false alarm?" said Nahum.

"There was nothing false about that glow in the sky," said his mother; "it was a real fire and a large one."

"But there's no sound, nothing."

"That's what worries me. That's how it began last time. Silence, and then . . ."

Katya began to whimper.

"Why don't we all go to bed?" said Nahum.

"Who can sleep?" asked his mother.

"Father seems to be sleeping."

"Your father's stopped caring what could happen to him or anyone else since Esty left."

"I'm leaving Russia, I've had enough," said Katya. "If we get out of this alive, the first thing I shall do is to get tickets for Lazar and myself. We'll go back to Glasgow with you." She sounded in earnest, and Nahum found the thought more discomforting than the prospect of a pogrom.

He wanted to go outside to see what, if anything, was happening, but they all screamed their alarm in one voice, and eventually he fell asleep. When he awoke, the first light of day was glowing through cracks in the shutters. Lazar said a prayer for being saved from calamity.

"Don't pray too soon," said Katya. "Who knows what the day will bring?"

But somehow they felt more relaxed with daylight, and Nahum stood up to open one of the shutters.

"Not yet," screamed Katya, "it's not safe."

"For God's sake, control yourself," said her sister.

"Do you remember in Odessa, they hurled torches through the open windows?"

"This isn't Odessa."

"It's all right," said Nahum, "see for yourself." There was nothing to be seen, save for chickens pecking unconcernedly amid the cobbles and the occasional stray cat. He went outside. At first he was alone, and his footsteps echoed strangely in his ears. Later, others ventured out in ones and twos, looking around apprehensively for signs of destruction. There were none, at least not in Volkovysk. There had, however, been a disturbance in a nearby town. A worker in Grossnass's distillery had been dismissed for stealing. He had returned later in the evening and set fire to the distillery and an adjacent warehouse. The fires had quickly gone out of control and spread to nearby shops and homes. The local synagogue had been burned down and there had been incidents of looting and, it was said, rape, though such reports were difficult to substantiate, for in those days victims of rape did not readily confess to their misfortune. The culprit had been apprehended and there were no deaths, but nevertheless, the events of the night had an unsettling effect on a sufficiently unsettled community, and at supper that evening, Eva declared that they would have to sell out and go: "I will not live through another night like that."

Migration always went in waves, and nothing more induced a Jew to move than the sight of other Jews moving. Nahum noticed that the local ticket agent was besieged by clients, and he wondered if it were not perhaps the agent (or a close friend) who had whispered the word "pogrom."

Katya, he was glad to hear, had had second thoughts about Glasgow. A relative of her late husband's in Chicago had written on several occasions, urging them to join him, and she thought that Chicago held out better prospects for Lazar than Glasgow.

"It's not important where you go," said her sister, "as long as you get out of here. We're all leaving. Whatever happens, I shall not go through another night like that."

When Yechiel pointed out that nothing had, in fact, happened, both sisters turned upon him.

"Do you want us to wait here till we're massacred?" asked Katya.

"But it was only a drunk settling a private account." He turned to Nahum. "Don't you have drunks in Glasgow?"

"We hardly have anything else, but that's beside the point. You can live with drunks if your nerves aren't on edge. We're afraid of our own shadows here. You only need to whisper the word 'pogrom' to send the whole town quivering."

"Weren't you afraid yourself?" asked Katya.

"A bit, but fear is infectious."

He had been less alarmed than humiliated by the events of the night, and he wondered if he would have felt as humiliated if there had been an actual pogrom, and he agreed with his mother that they should make immediate arrangements to emigrate.

"It's a bad time to sell," said Yechiel.

"Give it away," retorted his wife.

"That shouldn't be necessary," said Nahum. "You've got a responsible foreman. Sell the company to him, and he can pay you so much out of the profits every year."

"He's responsible while I'm around, but if he would have to pay me out of profits, he would see to it that there were no profits."

"If your business is that important to you," said Eva, "you can stay, but I'm going."

Nahum had arranged to leave that week but felt unable to do so while things at home were so unsettled, and he telegraphed Goodkind that he was delaying his departure by a week.

"You must have a reliable partner if you can stay on just like that," said his father.

"I've got a very reliable partner."

The next day he received a telegram:

AM HAMBURG-BOUND URGENT YOU JOIN ME IMMEDI-ATELY IN EMPEROR HOTEL CHANCE OF A LIFETIME GOODKIND

Nahum's hands were shaking as he read and reread it.

"Bad news?" asked his father.

"Incomprehensible news," said Nahum.

"Has he done the usual?"

"I don't know what he's done or what he's trying to do; all I know is I've got to stop him."

There was a train leaving in under an hour. He packed at once.

"Are you leaving just like that?" said his father. "Your mother isn't here, or Katya; they'll be upset."

"You'll have to give them my apologies."

As he stepped towards the waiting *isvoschick*, he looked back and saw his father by the garden gate, one shoulder lower than the other, one arm limp by his side, one eye lifeless, the other in tears. He hesitated for a moment, wondering whether he should stay on after all, but on an impulse climbed into the coach and was hurried out amid squawking chickens through the dusty streets.

CHAPTER VI
SIGN NOTHING

NAHUM HAD A TROUBLED JOURNEY. HE WAS TROUBLED AT LEAVING before he had settled his father's affairs, troubled at leaving his father at all, for he seemed so old and broken that Nahum doubted he would see him again. And he was troubled about Goodkind's telegram.

He valued Goodkind as a colleague, for, if messy and somewhat gross in appearance (and, Nahum suspected, in private behaviour), he was beautifully spoken and had infallible judgment in small things, but he suffered from what he called "spasms of ambition," which made him rather dangerous in large affairs, and every now and again, usually towards the end of the month (which made Nahum suspect that it might have had something to do with phases of the moon), he came out with a scheme so hare-brained and wild that Nahum had serious doubts about his sanity. He had a particular weakness for enterprises on the point of collapse. He sniffed them out like a vulture sniffs out carrion.

"They're desperate for a penny," he would argue. "You can buy your way in for next to nothing and put them on their feet." To which Nahum retorted, "With your own money by all means, but not with ours," and, as Nahum was the larger shareholder in partnership, he always had the last word.

Before leaving Glasgow, he had demanded and obtained a solemn promise not to enter into any commitment involving the expenditure of more than a hundred pounds.

"But supposing the chance of a life-time crops up?"

"I'll only be away for a fortnight."

"It could still crop up."

"Then it'll have to crop down again. I have a terrible fear that the moment my back is turned, you'll go out and buy a liner."

At which Goodkind's great pan of a face lit up.

"What a brilliant idea! It's the ship-owners who make the real money, you know. We're just their servants, and we're making it for them on a paltry commission. We're at their mercy. If there's a cut-price war, traffic may shift from one line to another, but we lose out wherever it goes. And they've got social standing. Think of the big names in the shipping world, knights and barons to a man, while the shipping agent can never be anything but a nobody, a hanger-on."

Nahum recalled these words and the wild look in Goodkind's eyes as the train rolled through the night, and he feared that the aim of the Hamburg mission was neither more nor less than to buy a boat. He told himself that they did not have enough money to buy a barge, let alone a craft large enough to ply the oceans, but there was no telling what credit he might be able to obtain, for, if he was unimpressive in appearance, he was impressive in speech and had a certain awkward grace that appealed to some people. When he changed trains at Bialystock, Nahum rushed to the telegraph office and wired: AM ON MY WAY SIGN NOTHING REPEAT NOTHING. This eased his mind a little, and he was soon asleep.

When he reached Hamburg and entered the foyer of the Emperor Hotel, his anxieties returned. He had never set foot in so magnificent a building. It was a palace with marbled halls and mirrored walls, glittering chandeliers, vaulted ceilings, brocaded furniture, with guests every bit as elegant as the setting. Wherever one turned, one saw silks and satins and gold braid, and Nahum, who was still a trifle dusty and crumpled from his journey, felt somewhat like a menial who had strayed from the servants' quarters. He had to wait about twenty minutes before Goodkind appeared, and then he almost failed to recognise him, for Goodkind was descending upon him in evening dress with a silk scarf around his neck and a top hat in his hand.

"Mr Rabinovitz, I presume. What have you done to yourself? Two weeks in Russia, and you again look as if you're just off the boat. You've lost the air of the English gentleman, and your suit looks as if it's been slept in."

"It has been slept in. We can't all afford to stay in marble halls."

"To make money you've got to spend it, dear boy. We have a major transaction in the offing, and we cannot afford to look or live like *schnorrers*. I've booked you a room. Why don't you have a bath and change, and we'll have a bite together."

"A room here?"

"Where else?"

"How much will it cost?"

"What's happened? I had hoped that when you set out for Russia in a first-class carriage that you had finally woken up to the fact that you're a man of means. Now we're back where we started. What's brought on the lapse?"

"The fact that I've spent one fortune is no reason why I should go on to spend another, and, besides, I paid it out of my own money."

"All right, I'll pay."

"What do you mean, you'll pay?"

"I'll pay for your room out of my income, if you insist."

"I don't insist, but I don't see why we've got to stay in the most expensive hotel in Europe."

"Actually, it's the second most expensive. The most expensive one was full. But look, there's no point in talking to you while you're in this mood. Go and have a bath and then we can chat, though, if it eases your mind, I can tell you that I received your telegram and have signed nothing. I only hope the delay will not jeopardise the deal."

The bath—huge, deep and ornate, with elaborate bronze taps—was about the size of a dock, and every time he settled back in its soothing waters, he had visions of a huge liner steaming in with a receiving order nailed to its mast.

Goodkind came into his room as he was dressing. "Feeling better?"

"A bit."

"Good. You must be starving, so I thought—"

"Before you do anything else, I want to know what this is all about. What are you doing here? What am I doing here? Do you want to buy a boat?"

"Did I tell you?"

"I was joking, but are you serious?"

"Perfectly. Unfortunately, we're not in a position to do so on our own, but I think I've found a partner. Would you mind putting on one of your better suits, one has to impress these people."

"What people?"

"You'll know in a minute, but first, would you mind if I clipped your moustache and hair a bit, you look somewhat bedraggled."

Nahum calmed himself and sat down before the bathroom mirror, while Goodkind tended to his hair and moustache with a dexterity which suggested that he might once have been a barber.

What had brought him to Hamburg, he explained, was the fact that the small shipping company which had plied between Hamburg and Newcastle, and for whom they had acted as agents, had gone bankrupt. Its fleet was in the hands of the receiver and, unless otherwise disposed of, would soon be up for auction. The so-called fleet consisted of four vessels, only one of which was sea-worthy, and even *it* was less than A-One at Lloyds, but Goodkind had had it surveyed and had been told that it could be put into first-class condition for seven or eight hundred pounds.

"You use the words seven or eight hundred as if there was no difference between them," said Nahum.

"Right, let us say eight hundred."

"If it costs eight hundred to repair, I can imagine what it must cost to buy."

"Frankly, I don't think you can, because you're not used to thinking in such figures."

"Well, what is it?"

Goodkind hesitated.

"I'm waiting."

"Twenty thousand pounds."

"You must be out of your mind, which I knew, but you must think that I'm out of *my* mind."

"It's a chance of a life-time."

"Of a life-time? We can go bankrupt at any time, though this is probably the quickest way of doing it. But, in any case, where do you think we could possibly find twenty thousand pounds? Have you suddenly come into an inheritance?"

"We would only have to find ten. I've found a partner, I told you, and we wouldn't even need the ten. The banks would lend us five. I could raise two from my own resources, and you should be able to raise three without much difficulty."

"As a matter of fact, I can't. I've just arranged for my family to come over from Russia."

"But they're not penniless, are they?"

"They may have some money when Father disposes of his business, but it'll take time; in the meantime, I'd have to find them a house and other things. It's out of the question, I haven't the money."

"Is your family ready to move now?"

"Not immediately, no."

"You'll have the money by then."

"Go on, tell me the ship will pay for itself."

"But it will."

"Goodkind, you and I have been lucky so far, let's not push our luck."

"Don't you see that once we've got the ship in hand, we'll have all the reserves we need, a solid, tangible, negotiable asset worth tens of thousands of pounds? Think of the money we could borrow."

"Think of the money we would have to repay."

"Nahum, you'll never make a millionaire."

"I've never had any ambition to be a millionaire. All I want is to be solvent, which I am, and to stay solvent, which I won't be if I should listen to your hare-brained schemes."

"Let's not argue, wait till you meet Eizenberg."

Herr Eizenberg was a tall, severe-looking man who spoke English with a harsh German accent and enunciated each word as if he were engaging in an elocution exercise. He was a shipper who had been badly put out by the collapse of the line, and if Goodkind-Raeburn was prepared to refit at least one ship and return it to the Hamburg-Newcastle route, he was prepared to guarantee a long-term contract, which, in turn, could be used to secure a long-term loan. Nahum listened impassively to his proposals, then said he and his partner would need a day or two to think them over.

Eizenberg protested: "Mr Goodkind has already had a week to think them over. How long must the thinking go on?"

"I shall let you have a definite reply by tomorrow," said Goodkind, throwing a grim look in the direction of his partner.

"You know," said Goodkind later, "we can't keep a man like that hanging on forever. We're not the only people in the market."

"But we're probably the only ones who would listen to his proposals without throwing him out of the door."

"Then you couldn't have understood him—though I'll admit there were times when I found him a bit hard to follow myself. Don't you see that by giving us a long-term contract, he's not only underwriting our loan, he's providing us with ready money to cover a large part of our operating costs?"

"In which way is he underwriting our loan? If we collapse, it will be our assets they'll seize, not his."

"But it's his standing with the bank which will make the loan possible in the first place. I got nowhere till I met him, but with the Eizenberg contract, and especially with Eizenberg by my side, every door suddenly opened. He's obviously a man of substance."

"Then why doesn't he buy the wretched hulk himself? I'll tell you why he's interested in the contract. Shipping rates are low—which is probably why the line collapsed in the first place—and are unlikely to go lower, and he hopes that with a long-term contract he can assure himself low rates forever."

"Do you think I haven't thought of that? He's agreed to pay the average rate over the past three years."

"They've been declining over the past three years. Would he accept the average over the past ten years?"

"We could discuss that."

"We can, but I don't think we should, because, frankly, I'm not really interested in the Hamburg-Newcastle line. If we buy a ship at all, we should ply between Riga or Danzig and Leith, because given the present state of the market we couldn't compete with the other lines. But we can compete with the railways, especially in transporting passengers *and* baggage, because in my experience those East European Jewish families who have household goods worth transporting are frightened to be parted from them, and if we can go from Riga or Danzig, we can cut out a large part of the railway journey and grab a good slice of the market."

"But where is the money to come from? I've spent a week rushing from bank to bank—and not only in Hamburg. I've been to Hanover, Frankfurt, Cologne, tried everyone from the Rothschilds downwards."

"Have you tried Wachsman?"

"Who?"

"Wachsman."

"Never heard of him. He's probably some jumped-up money-lender."

Wachsman was one of the legends of Volkovysk. Everyone claimed to remember him as a ragged urchin running barefoot through the streets—even people who were born long after he had left the town. His home was, in fact, no poorer than most Volkovysk homes, and if he went barefoot it was in the summer, when children from even comparatively prosperous homes preferred to discard their footwear. He was also spoken of as a child prodigy and while at *Yeshiva* was said to have known whole tracts of the Talmud by heart by the age of ten, and by the time he was *bar mitzvah*, he was advanced enough to dispense with the guidance of his teacher and studied on his own. It was said that Nahum's grandfather had given him his first job. Others made the same claim, and it would seem that he had worked for half the town, but he could not have worked for any of them for very long, for his family moved to Germany when he was fourteen or fifteen, and when he returned ten years later to endow an orphanage in memory of his father, he was already a millionaire (or was spoken of as such, which was not always quite the same thing).

Nahum was nine at the time of the visit and he recalled it in every detail, for the whole town had turned out to greet him, including the fire-brigade band in full uniform. The more prominent families vied for the privilege of entertaining him, and the honour finally fell upon Yechiel, who brought in extra servants and even imported English crockery, as if his household were about to be graced by a royal visit. Nahum still remembered the sense of anticlimax when a great coach pulled up and a small figure with a pointed beard, carrying a white cane, emerged. He patted Nahum's head as he entered the house and pinched his cheek, and when Nahum returned to Volkovysk as a sort of minor Wachsman, people reminded him of the occasion and wondered if some of Wachsman's good fortune had not rubbed off on him.

Wachsman was a banker and had his head office in Berlin, but he had branch offices in several German towns, and Nahum and Goodkind called at the Hamburg branch with the intention of arranging an appointment to see the great man in person.

The Hamburg office was disappointingly small and shabby, and Nahum was received by the manager, a short man with a thick neck who said Wachsman was very busy and rarely received callers.

"Tell him I'm the son of Yechiel Rabinovitz," said Nahum.

"Everyone who wants to see him appears to be the son of somebody," said the manager. "The best I can do is to send a telegram and see what happens." Some hours later, there came a reply to say that Wachsman was at Menton on the Riviera and would be there till the end of October.

"And that I suppose is that?" said Goodkind.

"No, no," said Nahum, "it's now or never. There's no time to be lost."

Nahum marvelled at his own enthusiasm. Only the previous day he had given passing thoughts to ending the partnership because he felt Goodkind had a tendency to drag him into dangerous waters; now he was racing ahead, with a breathless Goodkind following reluctantly in his wake. What, he kept asking himself, had brought the change— the taste of good living from his night in the hotel? The splendour of the surroundings? The conviction that he was about to become a Wachsman in his own right? It could hardly be Goodkind's enthusiasm, for he was less than eager now and seemed a little apprehensive about what he had started. Was it that in transmitting his enthusiasm to Nahum, Goodkind had been cured of it himself? He was aghast when Nahum ordered first-class tickets for the train journey to Menton.

"Didn't you say yourself that we've got to spend money to make money?" asked Nahum.

"Yes, on a hotel, but that's to impress people. There's no one to impress on a train."

They travelled via Hanover and Cologne, and thence down the Rhine valley to Frankfurt. Nahum felt like a child on his first outing and was as enchanted as much by the train and his fellow passengers as by the scenery—the winding river, the vineyards climbing up the hillsides, the castles. The journey across the great European plain to

Volkovysk had been comfortable, but once he had become used to the novelty of his surroundings, it had turned dull, and his fellow passengers had been mostly plump businessmen, with bulging briefcases and lusterless eyes: it was a means of getting between two places in the shortest possible time. His journey to the south took on the aura almost of a mystical experience, his road to Damascus. He had felt a presentiment when he set foot in the first-class carriage in Glasgow that he had at last entered upon his natural domain, but it had faded after his sojourn in Volkovysk. Now the feeling returned in force that he was at last among people of a class for which nature had intended him. His father had always looked to him like an aristocrat fallen upon hard times, and perhaps he was destined to restore the family to better times; the plush surroundings of the train, the carpeted corridors, the rich veneers, the elegant company made him feel that he had already done so.

While in Hamburg, Nahum had insisted on eating in a kosher restaurant, where, according to Goodkind, "the food was poisonous, the service dreadful, and the prices outrageous," and Goodkind waited with interest to see what he would do about food on the train. Would he rush out to buy a roll and butter at the station buffet every time the train stopped, or would he be prepared to make use of the dining car? Goodkind was agnostic himself and was not quite sure about the exact degree of Nahum's religious observance. In the event, he sat down to a fish meal which came with a rich sauce which Goodkind was certain contained shrimps and other forbidden matter. Nahum seemed to be enjoying it, and Goodkind remained silent lest he should interfere with Nahum's pleasure.

They also had wine with their meal. Nahum had, of course, tasted wine before, the heavy, rich, sweet, spicy wines used on the Sabbath and festivals in most Jewish homes. He had also tasted spirits in their different forms, including vodka, gin, whisky, cognac, schnapps and something known as *ninetziker* (or "nineties," which, as its name implied, was almost pure alcohol), but a dry, chilly, tingling table wine was a novel and exhilarating experience.

"The *goyim* know how to live," he said and ordered another bottle. When he rose a trifle unsteadily to return to his carriage, he found himself following a tall, exquisitely groomed woman with a slender figure, blondish hair, a regal, upright bearing and a perfume which seemed to fill the dining car. He yearned for a glimpse of her features, but as he tried to squeeze alongside her, the train roared into a tunnel; he saw her face briefly reflected in the carriage window—a fine neck, small chin, a rather large mouth and high cheek-bones. But then, as he was summoning courage to accost her, he heard his name being called, and a waiter tapped him on the shoulder.

"Excuse me, sir, a gentleman wants you."

It was Goodkind. "You're behaving like a millionaire already," he complained. "I've hardly any money, and you've not paid the bill."

Nahum wondered whether he had actually seen the woman, or whether she was a product of his imagination, but he searched from one end of the train to the other without catching sight of her. The train had not stopped in the meantime, so she could not have alighted. Could she have been conjured up by the wine? He had a further bottle at dinner, but it only gave him a headache, and he went to bed feeling somewhat like a small boy who had been given too much pocket money and had over-indulged himself.

When he came into breakfast the next morning, Goodkind was at table, counting his change with a rueful expression on his face.

"A coffee and roll on this train costs more than a three-course meal in Glasgow," he said. "This is the ruin express. I couldn't sleep last night; the clatter of the wheels kept saying the same thing, louder and louder as they went faster and faster—crash, crash, crash, collapse, collapse, collapse, what'll-we-do, what'll-we-do, what'll we do, r-u-u-u-u-in, r-u-u-u-u-in."

"You needn't put on a theatrical performance at this hour of the morning, you know."

"Don't you think this is ruinous?"

"You're hardly one to talk. Who started this idea?"

"I did, but it looks as if you'll finish it."

By the time they reached Menton and booked into their hotel, they were hardly on speaking terms.

Menton in those days was greatly favoured by the Jewish upper-middle class of Eastern Europe—bankers, merchants, industrialists. It was not a sizable class, and its members came mainly from the larger cities of the Russian empire, cities from which Jews, as a whole, were generally excluded. They spoke Russian or Polish or German or French, and sometimes all four, but the sound of Yiddish was never to be heard among them. They had transcended their poverty, had lapsed from their faith (without formally abjuring it), and what was left of their Jewishness consisted mainly of their tendency to come together on the Riviera. Here they found husbands for their daughters and wives for their sons and the assurance that Jews could still make their way in this world.

Nahum had an aunt—his mother's oldest sister—who had been in Menton, and his mother kept evoking the fact whenever she complained that she had never set foot outside Russia. He had never met his aunt and she was never mentioned in any other context, but a look bordering on alarm came into Yechiel's eyes whenever her name was raised, and Nahum presumed that she had moved beyond Menton and out of Jewish life altogether. To his mother Menton represented the symbol of worldly success, and to his father a warning of what worldly success could entail, and Nahum wondered if the main reason he had gone trailing after Wachsman was to behold this city of legend with his own eyes; by finding Wachsman in Menton, he would be alighting on two legends in one move.

"We've come on a wild-goose chase," said Goodkind. "You don't even know if he'll see you."

"If he knows I'm here, he'll see me. He stayed in our house."

"So you keep telling me."

They went up to their rooms to rest and change, arranging to meet downstairs later in the evening. Nahum came down first and was passing the dining room when he noticed a familiar figure, a small man with a large, bald head and a small, pointed Louis-Napoleon beard, with his glasses by his side on the table, and head so low over his plate as to be almost in it. It was Wachsman exactly as he remembered him, and he went over to greet him.

The small figure looked up from his plate with screwed-up eyes.

"I'm Nahum Raeburn—Rabinovitz—Yechiel's son from Volkovysk."

At which the man jumped to his feet, threw up his arms and began shouting: "Out, out, throw him out, impostor, out!"

Diners looked up, waiters and attendants darted from all directions.

"Throw him out!" His voice became frantic. "Out, out! Impostor! Out!" Nahum quickly withdrew to Goodkind, who had descended in time to witness the scene from the hallway.

"Am I correct in believing," he asked, "that your presence was unwelcome?"

"The old chap must be senile, or perhaps he's mistaken me for someone, but that's a strange way to behave."

"Look, I made a mistake in dragging you to Hamburg, you made a mistake in dragging me here, so let's call it quits. I'm going on the night train. If you insist on staying on, I suggest you pay the expenses out of your own pocket." He went back upstairs to pack and left an hour later without a word. Who said fat men are good tempered? thought Nahum.

They had had their differences before, but Nahum felt that this was more serious. Goodkind underwent a change in appearance and even personality when he was displeased. His face grew redder, his underchin larger and more taut, his eyes more protuberant, his voice high pitched. Above all, he lost his self-assured Englishness and became peevish and petulant. Nahum began to wonder whether their partnership would survive this particular excursion, though when he paused to look at his own actions, he had to admit they were not always rational. He had travelled a thousand miles across Europe to see a man without assurance that he would be received in the first place. He felt almost as if he had been dragged along, in spite of himself, by his own destiny. He had always been the cautious, prudent member of the partnership. "You act like a natural Scotsman," Colquhoun had said to him once, and he had taken it as a compliment, for that was, indeed, how he liked to see himself, but he had acted on an impulse in travelling to Russia, and it almost seemed that one impulse begets another, and there were moments when he was no longer in control of his own actions.

He went out to snatch a breath of sea air, his thoughts darkening with the day, when he felt a tap on his elbow and turned to find the short figure with thick glasses and a pointed beard.

"Excuse me," he said, "but don't I know you?"

Nahum felt like answering, "Yes, you had me thrown out of a restaurant tonight," but presumably the man had forgotten the incident.

"My name's Raeburn—Rabinovitz. I'm—"

"Raeburn-Rabinovitz?"

"No, it used to be Rabinovitz—I'm from Volkovysk."

"From Volkovysk? You know, I thought so. Then you must be . . . but you can't be . . . you're too young. I'm from Volkovysk myself" He turned and looked about him, then lowered his voice: "My name's Wachsman."

"*The* Wachsman," said Nahum, as if he didn't know.

"Yes, but not so loud, please. There are *schnorrers* everywhere, claiming to be *lantsleit* from Volkovysk. Even here in Menton, I was sitting in a restaurant having a quiet meal, when a young impostor comes up to me with the usual story—he's from Volkovysk. Suddenly, everyone I talk to is from Volkovysk—as if it entitles them to a pension. So you're from Volkovysk, eh? A lovely place."

"It seems lovely when you're out of it."

"Nice people, a bit simple, but nice. What did you say your name was?"

"Rabinovitz."

"Rabinovitz? Then you must be . . . no, you can't be. You're not Nahum's son, are you?"

"I'm his grandson."

"A saintly man, a good businessman and a fine scholar, taught me everything I know, or used to know, but knowledge is like your private parts—stop using it and everything dries up. You know me as a banker, a philanthropist, a public figure, but did you know I was once a scholar, an *ilui*, a child prodigy? I could have been a *godol bador,* one of the great men of my generation. Not that I'm a small man now, but my father died and there was the family to support, and I had to go into business. I wouldn't say I did badly in business, but a *godol* in banking isn't the same as a *godol* in learning. I always promised myself, when I've made my fortune I'll go back to my books, but once you're caught up in one sort of books, it's hard to get back to the other. And what do you do, young man?"

"I'm in shipping."

"That's a very good—shipping, did you say?"

"Yes."

He stopped and put a cautionary hand on Nahum's arm. "Get out of it if you can, young man. Start with ships and you finish at the bottom of the sea. The number of ships and shippers I've had to fish out of the deep water, or thrown back in because they were too far gone to save. I've got whole fleets laid up in settlement of bad debts, and they're worse than bad debts. It costs more to keep one sizable ship idle than to keep a hundred men at work. What are you in, cargo, passengers, what?"

"Passengers, with a bit of cargo."

"You'd be better off in cargo with a bit of passengers. Passengers are a pain in the neck. With cargoes, you establish a rhythm; some goods go here, others there, and you can hope for a full load, coming or going. Passengers go in spasms, in waves, thousands upon thousands, all wanting to go at the same time. You pull ships out of one route and push them into another, and before they're on steam, the whole thing's over. And what's worse, it's all in one direction—everybody wants to go to America—so that even if you go out full, you come back empty. And they're such trouble. One death on board from I-don't-know-what, and the word goes around you're carrying the plague—as if people never die on land. And then there's the competition. North German Lloyd are offering passage from Bremen to America for two pounds a head—imagine it, two pounds a head—and that includes food. Hamburg-America will do the same, you can't undercut Ballin. Where is there room for competition with those sorts of prices?"

"But I'm not in the Atlantic. I would run a local line. People still have to get from Russia to Bremen and Hamburg. They go by train now, which is expensive. I'd take them by ship from Riga or Danzig, and, in fact, I know from my experience that there's a constant traffic between the Baltic and the east coast of England. Perhaps people don't know about the cut prices, or they want to stop off in England to draw breath before they go on, but whatever the reason, I can tell you we've been busy."

"You operate from England?"

"Yes."

"You know Kagan?"

"Kagan?"

"My London agent, everyone knows Kagan. You talk to him about ships, and see what he says."

"We've done all right so far."

"You mean you're actually making money?"

"Yes."

"A lot?"

"Enough."

"I don't know how you do it. I suppose you carry passengers to England. But what do you carry from England?"

"Coal, machinery, textiles."

"You mean you use cargo vessels for passengers? A dangerous thing, especially in the North Sea. It's very rough, the North Sea. You batten down the hatches, and before you know what you've done, you've asphyxiated half your passengers—it gives a ship a bad name. But look, you see Kagan, tell him I sent you—better still, I'll send him a telegram. See what he says."

Wachsman was as good as his word. When Nahum got back to London, he went straight to Kagan's bank and was immediately ushered into a large, panelled office smelling of leather and cigars, where a large, bearded figure came towards him, offering a hairy hand in greeting. Kagan, but for his bare head, looked like an over-fed, over-cossetted rabbi.

"If you've just been with Wachsman, you've just come back from Menton, no doubt," he said. "One only has to look at the calendar to know where he is at any particular time. Very regular in his habits. A bit irregular in his judgments, but still a genius, a genius. I suppose you're from his part of the world. My own people came from that part of the world—centuries ago, of course. Are things as bad there as they seem to be from here? Because I must tell you, they're not as good here as they seem to be from there. People come here thinking London's paved with gold. They lose their faith almost as soon as they set foot in this unholy place but rarely get rich in the process. What profits it a man if he lose the mortal soul and does not even gain a livelihood? I can't claim to speak from my own experience, but if one does have to be poor, I should imagine one is much better off in Russia or Poland than in the East End of London."

"Except that they have no fear of pogroms in the East End."

"Not yet, but if Jews continue to pour into London at the present rate, there is no knowing what could happen. There is tremendous opposition to immigration—tremendous—only verbal for the time being, but it could erupt into violence any day, any day. People hate the sight of poverty—they have enough of their own to contend with—though, frankly, I can't see Jews being welcomed here in any number even if they arrived in top hats and frock coats. However, let's change the subject. Presumably you haven't come here to talk about Jews."

"In a way I have," said Nahum and explained the scheme he had in mind.

"Did Wachsman try to sell you a boat?"

"On the contrary, he told me to have nothing to do with ships or shipping."

"It's his opening gambit. That man's a genius, a genius. If he tried to sell gin, he'd appear in the guise of a teetotaler. He's the greatest salesman in the world. Not only can he sell almost anything he wants, he gives you the impression that you've bought it against his advice, so that if, in fact, you do come a cropper, he can turn around and say—I told you so. So he's sold you a ship?"

"No, but I'd like to buy one."

"I thought as much. You've come to the wrong address, I'm afraid. I'd do anything for Wachsman short of cutting my own throat, but if I was a party to increasing the flow of Jews to London, I would be cutting my own throat."

"But they're moving in, in any case."

"That's as may be, but it is not up to me and, if I may say so, not up to you to help them move, at least to this country. We're a small and crowded island. Jobs are scarce, poverty is rife and anti-Jewish feeling is high. There are already far too many Jews in the East End for their own good or anybody else's."

"But I have nothing to do with the East End. All the ships I deal with dock in Newcastle or Leith or some other port on the northeast, and most of the passengers go on to America."

"That's always their intention, but if they haven't the price of a ticket they stop here to see if they can earn it. If they succeed, they feel no inducement to go on, and if they fail—as they so often do—they haven't the money and have to be supported by the Jewish Board of Guardians. I'm a trustee of the board, and I can tell you it's almost bankrupt, bankrupt; yet you're asking me, Amadeus Kagan, to add to their number. Never, not a penny." His voice rose as he spoke. His eyes bulged, his beard bristled, his face reddened. Nahum waited till he calmed down before repeating that about eighty percent of his passengers went on to America.

"How do you know?"

"Because I arrange the transshipment."

"And the rest, I suppose, filter down to London."

"Probably not. From what I can see, most of them settle in Glasgow or the northeast, and it would seem to me that if you could build up sizable communities in the provinces—"

"One would have a counter-magnet to London?"

"Exactly."

"I've heard the argument. I'm not convinced, but I am prepared to study your figures."

Nahum went back to his hotel and cabled Colquhoun to compile the necessary figures and get down to London on the first available train. He had been irked by Goodkind during their few days together, and he felt that he could work more satisfactorily with Colquhoun.

The papers he asked for arrived the next morning, carried by a sandy-haired, pink-cheeked young clerk called Cameron whom Colquhoun had described as "'a boy of extraordinary promise." He could not have been more than fifteen or sixteen, and Nahum was surprised that Colquhoun, of all people, should have entrusted so important a mission to a mere schoolboy.

"Mr Colquhoun couldn't come," said the clerk; "he asked me to give you this letter."

It was brief and cryptic. "Goodkind has had to leave for Liverpool (domestic troubles), which makes it impossible for me to leave Glasgow. Young Cameron has all the papers you asked for. When can we expect you back?"

"Can you add anything to this?"

"Not a thing. Mr Goodkind, as you know, never says much about himself."

He studied the papers over breakfast and sent them around to Kagan with a covering note, asking if it was possible to have a further meeting that day as he was anxious to catch the night train to Glasgow.

He didn't expect to have a reply before lunch, and he took a walk down to Whitechapel, which was no great distance from his hotel. It was his first visit, and as soon as he got beyond Aldgate he stopped in amazement. He was on the brink of a different world. The poverty and squalor reminded him of Glasgow, but it was Jewish poverty and Jewish squalor, and the faces were the faces one might have seen in Russia. There was Hebrew lettering and the sound of Yiddish everywhere. He could have been in Volkovysk, but it was a hurried, jerky Volkovysk, and a noisy one, with trams and dray-carts clattering over the cobbles and steam locomotives thundering over viaducts which criss-crossed the area and left whole streets in darkness, but even where there were no viaducts, the neighbourhood seemed trapped in an eternal twilight, and soot particles descended like black sleet.

He went into a small restaurant which seemed to be a club room, rather than a dining place. There were several groups of people chattering around different tables, but very few of them seemed to be eating. The chatter stopped as he entered, and twenty pairs of eyes followed him to his place.

"Moishe," shouted a voice, "you got a customer."

The proprietor, a stout man with a black skull-cap on his head, emerged, took one look at Nahum and came back with a newly pressed soup-stained tablecloth, which he placed over the old one which was both soup-stained and crumpled.

"Where does a Jew come from?" he asked in Yiddish.

"Glasgow."

"And before that?"

"Volkovysk."

"Ah, a lovely town."

"Do you know it?"

"No, but my brother-in-law's son-in-law comes from there."

"What's his name?"

"His name? Look, I'm not on speaking terms with my brother-in-law, so I should know the name of his son-in law? You here on business? I don't know why I ask. Can you imagine anyone coming here for pleasure?"

"What have you got to eat?"

"Anything you want."

"Where's the menu?"

"Who needs menus? You name it, we'll cook it, but my wife's specialty is *tzolent*."

"In the middle of the week?"

"Listen, *tzolent* is like wine, the longer you keep it, the better it tastes. She makes it on Friday, by the following Wednesday it's in its prime."

"But this is Thursday."

"Then it's in its prime plus."

"Have you got duck?"

"Yes, we've also got chicken."

"I don't eat chicken."

"You don't eat chicken?"

"I don't eat chicken."

"You got a disease?"

"No, I haven't got a disease."

"I've never heard of nobody not eating chicken, but if you want to have duck, my wife can cook a chicken so it tastes like duck."

Nahum rose.

"What's the matter? You lost your appetite?"

"I've lost my patience."

He went to another restaurant where he was promptly served with what he asked for and it was deliciously cooked, but he was importuned by a constant succession of vendors—one man selling bootlaces, another matches, a third skull-caps and candles and another who wasn't selling anything but had, or said he had, a daughter to marry off and wanted ten shillings.

As he was finishing his meal, he was joined by an elderly figure with a walking stick and glasses, who wasn't selling anything and didn't ask for anything but sat there opposite him, as if he had never seen someone having a meal before, though his glasses were so thick that Nahum wasn't sure if he was staring at him or into space.

Finally he said: "You in a nice way of business?"

"Why do you ask?"

"Nice suit, nice tie, clean shirt. Look around you, go into the street. You won't see another suit like that this side of Aldgate. On *Shabbos* and *Yom Tov* maybe, not on weekdays. You got a shop?"

"No, I haven't got a shop."

"You don't mind my asking, do you?"

"As a matter of fact, I do."

"You're beginning to sound like an Englishman. How long have you been here?"

"Five years."

"Five years, and you already expect people to mind their own business? I mean, you look as if you was doing well, and I wanted to know how you do it. For myself, I've tried everything and succeeded in nothing. I'll tell you something, it was easier in Russia."

"Do you think so?"

"I think so. In Russia, no matter how bad things were, you could always hope that when you moved they would be better. And so I moved to Germany, I moved to France, and finally I moved to England, but they only got worse. Of course, in Russia I was single and here I'm married, so maybe it only seems worse. *Tzores* shared is *tzores* doubled."

"Why do you stop in the East End, why don't you move to the provinces?"

"The provinces? Here, at least, I've got my religion. In the provinces, they're all *goyim*."

"I'm from the provinces."

"I can see that, you're eating without a hat."

By the time he got back to his hotel it was nearly three, but there was still no message from Kagan. He spent a couple of hours reading papers and writing letters, and when he still hadn't heard, he walked around to the bank and was directed from one clerk to another, until he found himself before a very officious-looking personage with flopping jowls who said Kagan was too busy to see anyone.

"I think he'll see me," said Nahum; "my name's Raeburn."

"You're the gentleman who was here yesterday and sent around some papers this morning?"

"Yes."

"I'm afraid he can't see anyone. Not today. I'm sure if you called tomorrow—"

"I've a train to catch tonight."

At that moment Kagan emerged from his room and, on noticing Nahum, seemed half-minded to go back into it.

"Ah, there you are," said Nahum; "could I see you just for a minute?"

"I'm a very busy man, Mr Raeburn.'

"I'm hardly idle myself. It won't take a minute."

"Oh, very well." He led the way into his office and stood behind his desk. Nahum sat down, at which Kagan did the same.

"Have you seen the papers I sent you?" asked Nahum.

Kagan sighed. "I have, which is what makes me think that we may be wasting each other's time. You see—"

"May I interrupt?"

"If you must."

"I have just been to the East End and could see what you're afraid of. You've got another Russia on your doorstep."

"It's not what I have on my doorstep. It's what their neighbours have. They're Englishmen and want to stay in England. They're beginning to find themselves in a foreign town, a foreign country, and they won't stand it for much longer."

"Which is why I think I deserve your support. I would build up new centres of Jewish life in Edinburgh, Dundee, Newcastle, Sunderland—"

"So you told me yesterday, but I've been examining your books in some detail, and, frankly, you're not equipped to do any such thing."

"Not at the moment, but once we've expanded—"

"Have you any idea what sort of sums you would need?"

"I do."

"Mr Raeburn, one's borrowing must have some relation to one's assets. I am not suggesting that you purposely misled me, but I did get the impression—especially as you came with an introduction from no less a person than Wachsman—that you represented a substantial concern, especially when you began to talk about acquiring an actual boat, but, frankly, you are hardly more than a petty trader. You talk about boats, yet still have sums outstanding on a horse and cart."

"There's nothing wrong with owing money if you're paying it off. We have a consistent record of profits and a consistent record of growth."

"Be that as it may, the sums you would need are quite beyond your range, quite beyond it. We must learn to walk, Mr Raeburn, before we can run. Ambition is one thing, but this is fantasy, Mr Raeburn, fantasy. Nobody in his right mind or, indeed, out of it would, given the sort of assets you are able to display, lend you the sort of money you hope to raise. You may have a tidy little business which makes a tidy little profit, but that's as far as it goes. You are not what one would call a class-A risk."

To which Nahum could not help retorting: "Which is why I've come to a class-B bank."

Kagan drew in his breath and stood there, large-eyed and open-mouthed, struggling to find his voice. Then he said abruptly: "You'll have to excuse me, I have another appointment."

CHAPTER VII
MAN OF PROPERTY

NAHUM BOARDED THE TRAIN EMPTY-HANDED AND SAGGING WITH exhaustion, yet feeling oddly triumphant. He had felt smaller and smaller as Kagan continued his tirade, but got angrier and angrier, and then, finally, something snapped, and he answered back. It was not something he had done before. He had moved mainly among amenable people who did not browbeat, or heckle, or lecture, and he could thus be amenable himself. He had discovered a new faculty which reassured him. It suggested he was still developing, still growing. He had regarded himself as a replica of his father, who hated getting angry and was prepared to forego a deal if it meant losing his temper. It now seemed that he, Nahum, was, on the contrary, prepared to lose his temper even if it meant foregoing a deal, and he fell asleep in a euphoric haze.

When he reached Glasgow he went straight to the office and, although it was still early in the morning, he was surprised to find the lights on and Colquhoun at his desk.

"My goodness," said Nahum, "you look as if you've been here all night."

"I feel as if I've been here all week. I've been doing all Goodkind's work."

"What's happened to him?"

"I wish I could tell you. The day he got back I walked into his office, and I saw him with a telegram in his hand and tears streaming down his face. Goodkind crying, can you imagine it? Streaming down in torrents. I asked if there was anything I could do. He shook his head, and all I could do was leave him. He collected himself, washed his face, apologised and said he'd have to be away for a few days. He's been gone nearly a week now."

"He didn't say where?"

"Not a word."

"What was in the telegram?"

"I tried to have a squint but couldn't make it out. I think it was in Yiddish."

"Yiddish? Goodkind doesn't speak Yiddish."

"Then maybe German, but I couldn't make it out."

"When he gets back, I'll have to ask what's been happening to him. I think we have a right to know, don't you?"

"No, we don't."

"What do you mean, we don't? We're supposed to be his best friends."

"Aye, but friends should know when to mind their own business."

Nahum spent much of his day going through the mail and dictating replies, too busy to notice how weary he was, but when he got back home, he felt like a man returning to sobriety after a prolonged debauch. His whole excursion—Volkovysk, Hamburg, Menton, London, the first-class carriages, the grand hotels, the sumptuous meals, the exchanges with Kagan—all seemed vague and unreal, like something experienced in an alcoholic haze, and when he looked around the cramped rooms, the drab interior, the bleak view, he couldn't face it; he felt as he imagined a man might feel on returning to his homely little wife after a night with a beautiful woman. His previous self seemed dead.

He lit a fire, unpacked, put on the kettle and made himself something to eat, but he wasn't hungry.

He stood up and looked out on the desolate little green and the surrounding tenement at the back. It was getting dark, and the pale green glow of the gas-lights shone from every window. He could see women at the kitchen sinks coping with the detritus of the day, and from here and there came the harsh sound of altercation and the crying of small children. He began preparing for bed. It wasn't late, but he didn't feel there was anything else he could do with himself.

He began to undress but, on an afterthought, dressed again and took a walk through the noisy, crowded streets. Houses were small and cramped, and, weather permitting, people spent what little free time they had in the street; although it had been dark for some time, urchins obstructed the pavements with their games, and the night echoed with their clamour. It was uncommonly warm for the time of the year.

He walked down through the Gorbals without any intention of going anywhere in particular and after half an hour found himself amid the spacious homes and clipped gardens of Pollokshields, where the more prosperous gentry of Glasgow lived and where Miri and Yerucham (or, rather, James) had lately acquired a house. He looked at his watch. It was ten o'clock, not he hoped, too late for a man to call on a friend.

A small, large-eyed girl whom he recognised as Miri's daughter, Sophie, came to the door and announced in one breath: "Daddy's not in. Mummy's in bed. Mummy's sick. Mummy's sick a long time."

Miri was sitting up in bed reading, with a cardigan over her shoulders, her face swollen and blotchy.

"I didn't want you to see me like this, but it's so long since I've seen anyone. James is always away. Can't blame him staying away if I look like this."

"You don't look so bad."

"You don't look so good."

"I've had problems."

"Who hasn't? The maid walked out this morning and left me like this. Look at the mess—no, don't look at the mess—left me all on my own, helpless in bed, with my three ragamuffins."

"Does your mother know?"

"No, and don't you dare tell her. That's all I need on top of everything else, my mother. Last time the maid walked out, Mother moved in—for a week only"—she drew in her breath and cast her eyes up to the ceiling—"the longest week of my life. She has hardly anything to do with herself, poor thing. You know Father's sold out?"

"I didn't, who to?"

"James."

"But they were in partnership."

"They were, but James started dealing in pork, and Father wouldn't have it—silly, really, it's not as if he'd be *eating* the stuff, though it wouldn't surprise me if James did. But he wouldn't have it, and James bought him out. That's one of the reasons I hardly see him. Remember all the travelling Father did? James does it now, only he goes much further—Holland, Denmark, Germany. In the meantime, the children run wild. They're supposed to be in bed, listen to them. If I have to get out of bed again, I'll kill them. The nanny's walked out as well, by the way, everybody's walking out. I would myself, if I could get to my feet."

"Is there anything I can get you?"

"Get me? I've got everything I need. Look." She pointed to her dresser, which was cluttered with perfume bottles, all of them gathering dust. "There's enough there to float a liner. And jewellry, and odd little bits of bric-a-brac too tasteless to expose to public view. Every time he shows his face, he comes back with a little something as a sin offering. To think that he was once a rabbi—no, a saint—wasn't that the word you used, a saint? Saint Yerucham."

"That's what my father called him."

"I suppose having been a saint for the first twenty years of his life, he feels he can make up for it for the next eighty. He's a rotter. You don't know what a favour I did your sister by marrying him. Sometimes, when I'm lying awake at night and he's snoring next to me, I feel like leaning over and cutting his throat, but then, of course, I think of the children. That keeps echoing through my head every time I want to do anything—think of the children, the children, think of the children."

"I didn't know things were that bad."

"How should you know, you haven't been to see me in months."

"I've been away."

"You're beginning to sound like my husband. And I can see you don't even want to stay. You're bored."

"I'm not bored."

"You look bored."

"I'm just tired."

"Tired of me."

"I've been travelling all day. All I need is a good night's sleep."

"Oh, if only I could sleep, if only I could sleep, I could forgive everybody everything. The doctor's given me something, but it doesn't work, not in the doses he's prescribed, and James keeps hiding the stuff in case I should take an overdose. Wishful thinking. I told him, I'm determined to stay alive if it's the last thing I do—if only to make his life a misery." She broke down and drew a handkerchief from under her pillow. "I don't know what's happening to me. I wasn't like this when I was younger, was I?"

Nahum sat down on the bed and put an arm over her shoulders. "Of course, you weren't, you're unwell. You'll get better."

"Will I? How can I, if no one knows what's wrong with me in the first place? If only I could sleep."

Sophie opened the door, then quickly closed it.

"That child's spying on me," said Miri. "I'll kill her, I'll kill them all." But she grew less excited and gradually subsided into sleep. Nahum tucked in her sheets and blankets and went on tip-toe out of the room. As he was crossing the landing, a door opened and Sophie appeared.

"Aren't you going to kiss me goodnight?"

"Shouldn't you be in bed?"

"No, I can't, not until Mummy's asleep. I've got to keep my eye on things, but the boys are asleep."

"Are they? I could hear them jumping up and down."

"They're quiet now. I banged their heads together—hard."

He kissed her on the forehead.

"Good night."

"Good night."

He sympathised with Miri. He had anticipated her predicament and could not imagine anyone being happy with Yerucham as a husband, but at that particular moment he felt rather more sorry for himself. He ascribed his feeling to travel weariness more than anything else, though, to be sure, he had plenty to worry about.

There was, first of all, the situation in Volkovysk. His mother had agreed that they would leave the town without delay, and once her mind was made up, he could not see his father changing it, but he had rushed off to Hamburg without settling any of the details. When would they come? How? Where would they live? Knowing his mother's tastes, he was sure they would want a house and garden, rather like Miri's, though, of course, smaller, but they had not discussed how much they wanted to spend, or, indeed, how much they were in a position to spend.

He was worried about his business. He was beginning to feel the effects of the collapse of the Hamburg-Newcastle company. He would have to negotiate a new long-term agreement, and on reflection he felt he might have been too quick to dismiss Goodkind's Eizenberg plan. He was worried about Goodkind, whom he regarded as his closest associate, but worried how close their association could be if he did not allow himself to be helped in distress. No one had any idea where he had gone, when he would come back, or, indeed, if he would come back at all. Nahum did not—or had not hitherto—put great store by his business judgment, but he was a good sounding board, an able negotiator and excellent at handling people, so that a business meeting with him took on the nature of a convivial social call. But, above all, Nahum regarded him as a sort of talisman, who had brought him good fortune in business. Goodkind had only been away about a week, and they were already feeling the effect.

When he got to the office the next morning, Goodkind was there in his usual place. He might have embraced him but for the fact that he almost failed to recognise him. Much of the colour had gone out of his face, there were rings around his eyes and he seemed deflated, like a thin man in a fat man's clothing. And when he began to speak, his voice was without its rich resonance.

"Are you all right?" asked Nahum.

Goodkind turned a wan face to him. "Why shouldn't I be?"

"You don't look yourself."

"Well, that's an improvement, to start with."

"You've lost a lot of weight."

"I had a lot to lose."

"Seriously, though, you don't look too good."

"I've felt better."

That was as far as Nahum got. Colquhoun seemed to find such reticence natural and healthy. Nahum found it unnatural and unhealthy

and even vaguely offensive. He felt rebuffed and thought that Goodkind's attitude was impairing their business relationship.

They spent much of the morning in conference. Nahum opened by
outlining the results of his meetings with Wachsman and Kagan. When
he mentioned his retort to Kagan, Colquhoun laughed, but Goodkind
was not amused.

"So the whole thing was a waste of time," he said.

"I wouldn't say that."

"What would you say?"

"I've established contact with Wachsman which could be useful on
a later occasion."

"But as Kagan's his London agent, how useful can it be? If you had
done as I suggested, you'd have had everything tied up with Eizenberg
by now. As it is, we've been caught at the top of the market, and we'll
be paying out more than we've taken in."

"Eizenberg couldn't have helped us in the present situation."

"Yes, but what makes you think the present situation can't continue?"

They had had differences before, but Nahum resented his inquisitorial
tone, and he felt that Goodkind was asking questions less to elicit information than to put him in his place. It was as if he had shed his
bonhomie with his bulk.

Nahum had other troubles. He had been searching for a suitable
house for his parents, but as he knew little about such things he had
engaged Miri's help, and eventually they found a comfortable terrace
house with a sizable garden at the back in the West End of Glasgow.
The property was in sound condition and the price was very reasonable,
though Miri thought it was a bit too near the centre of town.

"Why not buy something near us in Pollokshields, it's like living
in a garden."

"There's no synagogue in Pollokshields."

"There's isn't now, but with your father there, and James, they could
start a synagogue themselves."

Nahum was surprised at her suggestion. Was she forgetful, insensitive
or stupid? He had been worried about the possibilities of his father
and Yerucham meeting, and one of the advantages of a West End
house was that it was a safe distance from Pollokshields. He was satisfied
that he had found the right place and sent the details to Volkovysk to
make sure that this was the sort of house they had in mind. His mother
replied that it had possibilities. His father was aghast.

"Is that what people really pay for a house in Glasgow? Here in
Russia, I could buy the Winter Palace for that. Who do you think I am,
Wachsman?"

Nahum wrote back to say that if he was short of capital, they could rent a property rather than buy one, but that in the long run it was better to buy. Some weeks passed before he got a reply, and when Miri asked him what was happening, he said his father had bridled at the price.

"It's a bargain."

"But even for a bargain, you need to have money. Father has always been convinced that he's on the edge of bankruptcy."

"Couldn't you buy it?"

"No, not at the moment."

"But I thought you were rich."

"Who says I'm rich?"

"Father says you're rich."

"Father thinks everybody's rich."

"James could probably help you."

"That's all I need."

"What have you got against him?"

"What have *I* got against him? Wasn't it you who told me you'd like to cut his throat?"

"I'm his wife and am entitled to cut his throat and I've every cause to, but he's all right outside the house. He's helpful and considerate—generous."

"I'd rather do without his generosity, thank you."

A few days later Yerucham came to see him. Nahum was not at all surprised at the visit; in fact, he had expected him earlier.

He was a good-looking man, thought Nahum, but his jowls were too heavy and too blue, and his lips were too full and red, like a woman's. He couldn't stick the sight of him, and he asked himself why he didn't take him by the scruff of the neck and throw him down the stairs, but he was polite, in spite of himself.

"I know what you're here for," he said, "and the answer is, no, thank you."

"If that's your answer, then you don't know what I'm here for. It's about your father. Like everybody who's ever known him, I adore him, he's the saint of his generation." He used a famous biblical phrase to explain himself, and Nahum felt that Hebrew, the holy tongue, sounded obscene in his mouth. "I hear he's been ill and has had difficulties and that he would like to come here. I want to buy him a house."

Nahum took some time to find his voice. *"You* want to buy him a house?"

"A comfortable place near a *shul,* with a garden—"

"Do you still understand Russian?"

"Of course."

"*Gay kibeni matri.*" Which, roughly translated, meant, "Go right back up your mother."

"I didn't know you used such language," said Yerucham, rising and picking up his hat and gloves. "Where did you get it from? Not from your father, I'm sure."

As he left a clerk entered with a telegram. Nahum's father was dead.

He left for London on the night train and was in Berlin thirty-six hours later, but beyond that, progress was slow. There was flooding on some parts of the route and heavy snows on the other, and it took him a further four days to reach Volkovysk. When he got there, the *shiva,* the week's mourning period, was over. He was not sorry, for if anyone in Volkovysk died, the bereaved were visited by the whole town, and Nahum was not sure if he would feel able to face an endless succession of comforters.

"He died as he always wanted to die," said his mother, "of overwork. He returned from work one evening, and as he reached up to hang up his heavy sheepskin pelts, he gave a slight gasp and dropped. It was all over before we knew what had happened. No pain, no agony, at least not for him. If I'll go the same way, it'll be a blessing."

The next morning he found his mother at work in the counting house.

"I've been helping out for months," she said; "it's a busy season, and life must go on."

Nahum was not surprised by his mother's composure in the face of her bereavement, for she had never been an emotional woman; what surprised him was his own, as if he had already discounted his father after he had suffered his stroke. No one in the world had meant more to him, and what remained of his belief in religion derived mainly from a belief in his father, whom he had always thought of as the embodiment of goodness; the fact that he was also successful had reassured him— until his stroke, at least—that here was one small corner of the universe where God had not muffed things. He was no longer so sure. Yechiel had been only fifty-six and had not enjoyed the one blessing which every Jewish parent looks for in his children, grandchildren, yet Nahum did not feel deficient as a son. If he had any regrets at all, it was his failure to insist that his father sell out his business there and then, while Nahum was still in Volkovysk. He had been under the impression that his parents had been taking active steps to dispose of the business but found to his dismay that they had done no such thing. His father had made out a traditional Jewish will and, in keeping with biblical injunctions, had left his entire estate to him and had appointed him sole executor, and he proposed to put both the business and the house on the market without delay.

"I can't stop you selling the business," said his mother, "but I can stop you selling the house, and I will. I'm not ready to move out this week or next. I want to have time to put my thoughts together."

"How much time?"

"I can't say, but I shall *not* be rushed."

"I can't stay here indefinitely, you know."

"Who's keeping you?"

"But what are you going to do here all by yourself?"

"I've got friends, I'll travel, and, of course, there's Katya."

"Katya will have to come as well."

"Oh, she will, will she? Have you spoken to her about it?"

"She spoke about leaving last time I was here. She can come with you."

"And Lazar?"

"And Lazar."

"You'll need a big house."

"I'll get a big house."

He was approached by prospective bidders even before he had put the business on the market, but few were in a position to offer cash; these few did not come within sight of his reserve price, and he considered the possibility of selling it off in small lots.

"Don't," Grossnass advised him, "and I'm speaking to you as a friend of the family. You may get more in cash for small lots, but it'll take ages to get it. Besides, a business is a living thing. Your father was proud of it, and he had something to be proud of. If you keep it as a going concern, you've got a living memorial. If you break it up into pieces, you break up your father's good name—may he rest in peace."

Nahum didn't know how to take such advice, especially as Grossnass himself was a bidder for the whole, and his price was by no means the highest. On the other hand, he was prepared to pay cash, and Nahum's mother urged him to accept.

"This can go on for months. You're impatient to get back to Glasgow, I'm tired of the haggling; let's get it over and done with."

He, however, felt that to give Grossnass the business at the price he offered would be too much of a gift, and the haggling continued for a further fortnight before the transaction was complete and Nahum felt able to make arrangements for his return journey.

Shortly before he left, he was visited by Yankelson, the synagogue beadle, a tall, lean man with a long, grey beard, sad eyes and large teeth, which even the undergrowth around his lips couldn't obscure and which gave him an eternal smile at odds with the rest of his face.

"I know you're a busy man," he said, "and I didn't want to bother you, but your saintly father—may he enjoy the glowing lights of paradise—spoke to me before he died—not immediately before, because he thought he had recovered by then, but when he was first taken ill and he was preparing himself for the end—and he said to me he wanted to be buried in holy soil, and I said to him, Reb Yechiel, any place in which you're laid to rest will be holy, Jewish bones make soil holy, and he said, no, he meant Palestine. . . . His father of blessed memory, Reb Nahum Yosef, whose name you bear, was buried on the Mount of Olives, and he wanted to be buried next to him, well, if not next to him, at least on the same mountain. Then he recovered, and we didn't do anything about it. I thought of mentioning it to your mother, but I didn't think she would be interested, so the best I could do was to put a little bag of holy soil, brought by my own saintly father from the Holy Land, under his head. I thought you would like to know."

Nahum took out his wallet, but Yankelson raised his hands in protest.

"No, no, for a *mitzva* like that I should be paid? It was a privilege, and, besides, your mother paid me."

"My mother, bless her, is not a generous payer."

"Generous, no, but when you had a man as generous as your father, it was useful to have a woman as level-headed as your mother."

Nahum sometimes doubted if his mother was quite as level-headed as she was thought to be. He had been in Volkovysk for over a month and hoped to have her affairs in order by the time he left, but she seemed oddly secretive and was reluctant to discuss her affairs at all. She had promised to fix a date when he could expect her in Glasgow, but finally she said she didn't like to plan too far ahead. "Who knows if I'll be alive in six months or a year?"

Before he left, he spoke to Grossnass and asked him, as a friend of the family, to make sure that his mother and aunt settled their affairs without delay. Grossnass assured him that he would see to it personally that his mother received a good price for the house, that he would help her with all the necessary papers and documents, and make sure that she would not remain in Volkovysk a moment longer than necessary.

"They're still attractive women, your mother and your aunt," he said, "especially your mother, and she's not too old to start a new life. *Meshane hamokom meshane hamazel*, a change of place is a change of fortune. I envy you, I envy her. I'd leave myself if I could, this place is a graveyard."

Katya saw him off to the station, and he said to her: "I expect to see you and Mother in Glasgow within six months, and if I don't, I shall come back here and fetch you both by the scruff of the neck."

"We'll be there," she promised. "I may even send Lazar out a little earlier. He wants to learn English and can't wait to leave. He wants to go to University. Imagine, a son of mine, a University student."

"Everything's possible in Glasgow."

"Will you have a large house with servants?"

"Why the servants?"

"You can't have a large house without servants."

"I'll have you and Mother, two women in the prime of life, to look after things, why should I need servants?"

"You're rich, that's why. There's no point in being rich without servants."

"I've never been poor."

"But now you're *très riche*. I had no idea your father was that well off."

"He used his money carefully."

"You mean he didn't spend it, but what's money for if not to spend? We lived far better than he did when poor Brasha was alive, and we couldn't have been worth half as much. Eva, of course, is also careful with kopeks—they made a likely pair in that respect, if in no other. She always kept complaining how difficult business was and I was almost sorry for her, but they were sitting on a gold mine. You'd think they'd have travelled, to a spa somewhere, or the Riviera, even. My older sister almost lived on the Riviera."

"And look what happened to her."

"It wouldn't have happened to Eva, not while she was married to Yechiel. Anyway, I hope she'll begin to live a little now and spend something on clothes."

"Clothes? Mother was always the best-dressed woman in Volkovysk."

"That's saying a lot. I think that your dear old mother will be giving you a few surprises in the years to come. Being married to a saint was a terrible strain to a woman like her. It must have been worse than being married to a rabbi. With a rabbi you can always tell yourself that he has to be good because it's part of his job; with Yechiel it was the real thing. But it may not be too late for her to flap her wings a little. And if it comes to that, it's about time you flapped yours."

"What do you mean?"

"If you don't know what I mean, then there's the danger you may never flap them. But be careful, dear boy, you're very innocent. Some little hussy could grab you for your money." She reached up on tip-toe and kissed him on his mouth.

"If you were a bit older, or I a bit younger, I'd grab you for myself, money or not."

CHAPTER VIII
HOPE

NAHUM REGARDED HIS SUDDEN INFUSION OF WEALTH WITH MIXED feelings. He had taken pleasure in the process of accumulation and in the thought that, but for the few rubles his father had given him, he was a self-made man. Now, suddenly, through no effort of his own, he had acquired five times as much as he had been able to accumulate in six years. He had had presentiments at various times of a sudden onrush of wealth and had not been particularly happy about them. Now that the presentiments had been fulfilled, he was not exactly distressed, but neither was he excited or elated or delighted. He resigned himself to the thought that he would be a rich—possibly a very rich—man. With his mother and Katya on his hands, he would have to be.

He was surprised at the amount his father had left, especially after his protest over the price of the Glasgow house, and he could only presume that, given the eccentric way he had kept his books, Yechiel had had no clear idea of the extent or value of his assets, or the amount he was worth.

Nahum's new situation opened several options to him. He still intended to buy Goodkind out. The very thought of the man was gnawing at his rest. The only reservation he had on the point was that Goodkind-Raeburn sounded better on the ear than Raeburn on its own.

As soon as he was ready to leave Volkovysk, he telegraphed Wachsman to say what had happened and to ask for a meeting, and when his train pulled into the Silesischer Banhoff in Berlin, there was a coach waiting to collect him, and he was driven to a nondescript building in a narrow street. Neither the building nor the street quite went with his vision of the House of Wachsman, but once inside he felt reassured, for the interior was palatial, and Wachsman, behind a vast desk in a large office, was waiting to receive him with open arms.

"My dear, dear boy," he said, clasping Nahum's hand between both of his, "I've just heard about your dear father. Such a young man, such a tragedy."

Nahum presumed, from the warmth of the greeting, that Wachsman had also heard about the inheritance.

"And your dear, sweet mother, how is she? Such a beautiful woman. Such a wonderful family. Such a misfortune. It could happen to any of us. We struggle, we climb, we reach the peak, but where does it get us? We're all back where we started before we know where we've been." He let out a deep sigh. "It was a terrible shock. I was just about to write you a letter of condolence when I got your telegram. As a matter of fact, I began it—here it is. Uncanny coincidence. Still, a man like your father has nothing to fear from his Maker. It's sinners like us who have to worry. I only hope that the good I have done for my fellow men will count against the sins I have committed before God."

He continued in that vein for about half an hour before Nahum could bring him back to earth with a very mundane question.

"What would you do if you suddenly came into a fortune?"

"Spend my days in study. Unhappily, I had to make my fortune as I went along, so that there was no time for that. And now that I have a fortune, it's too late. That's life."

Nahum wondered if the old man were not senile, for it was becoming impossible to conduct a normal conversation with him, but, as if sensing Nahum's impatience, he cleared his throat and changed his tone from that of philosopher to that of banker.

"The first thing I would do is to move to London. The provinces are no place for a young man with a large fortune. Rothschild began in Manchester, but he had to come to London before he got anywhere, and Glasgow isn't Manchester. He also didn't marry before he got to London, that's the important thing. A young man like you needs a wife with a bit of polish, culture, grace, and you'll not find it in the provinces. As a matter of fact, I'm not all that sure you'll find it in London. Perhaps you should settle here in Berlin."

"I wouldn't call that business advice."

"Believe me, it is. I only deal with larger issues. If you want to talk about shillings and pence, I'll put you onto Kagan."

"Kagan? I wouldn't talk to Kagan."

"Why, what's wrong wiht Kagan?"

"He's pompous, patronising—"

"Yes, but only to people without money. Now that you've got a fortune, he'll treat you like a king. The trouble with Kagan is that he's got a good eye for the prospects of a company, but not the prospects of people. As soon as I set my eyes on you, I could see that you were a young man with prospects, that you'd make a fortune, or marry it, or inherit it, perhaps all three, and, as a matter of fact, if you've got the one, the others come of their own accord. He told me off for sending him Russian paupers with grand illusions, and I told him that illusions are a start and that one day he'd eat his words. You'll do me a personal favour if you go back to him. He's got a pretty daughter, by the way. I think he's waiting for the Prince of Wales to leave his wife and propose to her instead. You see, when I—"

"Mr Wachsman, if I may interrupt. Last time I spoke to you, I discussed the possibility of buying a ship."

"And I told you to forget it."

"That wasn't the advice Kagan gave."

"Kagan? What's he got to do with ships? He doesn't know a dreadnaught from a dredger. Look here, young man, you may be a whale in Volkovysk, but you go into shipping and you're a minnow. All the money you've got, which your father accumulated in a life-time, could vanish in a day."

"How do you know how much I've got?"

"There's very little that I don't know. All the money you've got, and more, would be just about enough to buy one ocean-going craft. But supposing you're caught up in a crisis, and there isn't a day without a crisis. You're in Salonika, and there's a Balkan war. You're in Shanghai, and there's an uprising, what happens to your fortune? I'll tell you what happens; it's sunk. I'm speaking to you as a friend; go and have a word with Kagan, and if he invites you to his home, look out for his daughter. She's a princess, not perhaps the princess he thinks she is, but a princess, none the less. I don't know how such parents—his wife is as homely as her father was rich—could have such a daughter. Matilda's her name. Give her my love, and tell her my offer of marriage still stands."

Nahum, against his better judgment, finally felt persuaded to call on Kagan, and he was not only received more cordially than on the previous occasion but was invited to lunch in the partner's dining room.

The room was large and panelled, with a long, polished table and portraits of heavily built, unsmiling, hirsute figures lining the walls. There was a waiter in attendance who, but for the napkin over his arm, might have stepped straight out of one of the frames.

"Long telegram from Wachsman," said Kagan. "He appears to think I owe you an apology. I rather feel you owe me one, because, frankly, if you came to me with the same balance sheet that you brought last time, I would give you precisely the same advice, precisely the same."

"You gave me more than advice, Mr Kagan, you gave me a lecture."

"Anything wrong with offering a young man at the beginning of his career the benefit of my experience? I have completed forty years in banking, Mr. Raeburn, forty years, and even a dullard, which I like to think I'm not, would pick up something worth imparting within that time. The food's kosher, by the way."

The meal consisted of a cold soup, which seemed too cold to be merely hot soup which had been left off the boil: it was tasteless. He watched his host carefully, half wondering if possibly it was a finger-bowl, but Kagan slurped it with gusto, and he followed suit. The next course was duck and orange, which again was a novel experience, for although he had eaten duck before and orange before, he had never had the two combined, and the result was a little over-rich and sticky for his taste; finally, there were strawberries in brandy, which he enjoyed without reservation. One delicious wine accompanied the soup; another even more delicious, the duck; and a brandy accompanied the strawberries in brandy. The waiter refilled his glass every time he emptied it, and by the end of the meal it developed into something of a race.

Kagan did most of the talking, and by the time they reached the third course, the wine had begun to have its effects, and Nahum had only the vaguest idea of what he was talking about or to what, if anything, they had agreed.

He was at breakfast in his hotel the next morning when one of Kagan's clerks called on him.

"I have prepared the scheme of arrangements you asked for, sir, which you may wish to study at your leisure, and I have also made an appointment with Messrs Crude, Carter and Reynolds—"

"Crude, Carter—"

"The shipping people, sir."

"Ah, yes, the shipping people." Then an alarming thought seized him. "I—I haven't bought a ship, have I?"

"Oh, no, not yet, sir."

"But you mean I'm buying one?"

"We thought this was a subject on which Messrs Crude, Carter and Reynolds could be the best people to advise you."

It was an odd experience, spending an afternoon examining the possible craft "within your price range, sir," as if he were choosing a suit length, and he kept asking himself—every time a proposal for this or that vessel was put to him, each involving the expenditure of thousands of pounds—whether he was not out of his mind. He drew some assurance from the fact that he was not only putting his own money into the project, but that Kagan was prepared to advance him a considerable sum, but Kagan would at least have the vesstl as security if it failed. What would he have? *Kadoches,* as his father would have put it, a fit.

But—and this was something he had experienced on previous occasions —he felt almost as if his own destiny was pulling him on.

The mass of papers he was given filled up his briefcase, and he reckoned that it would take the better part of a fortnight to study them in detail. He began work on them in the train but found it difficult to get into them, for he was troubled by the thought of Goodkind, who was, indeed, becoming something of an obsession. He recalled one of his father's favourite sayings: "If you've something nasty to do, get it over and done with, for the thought can be as nasty as the execution," and when he got into Glasgow, instead of going home, he took a cab to the house of Tobias, his lawyer. Tobias was entertaining friends to dinner and invited Nahum to join them, but Nahum was in no mood for company, and Tobias took him to an upstairs room.

"How does one go about getting a divorce?" asked Nahum.

"Well, as a start you get married," said Tobias, "or have you got married already?"

"I'm talking about Goodkind."

Tobias's eyes grew so large that they filled his glasses. "You're not splitting with Goodkind?"

"It was always an unequal partnership—"

"I know it was, but it worked and worked well. You had complementary talents. You may have a decent command of English, but you will never feel at home among Englishmen, or Scotchmen, for that matter."

"There's Colquhoun."

"Yes, but he hasn't got Goodkind's geniality."

"*Geniality?* Have you seen anything of Goodkind in the past few months? He's not the same man."

"Why, what's happened to him?"

"I wish I knew, but that's part of the trouble, you can't talk to him. He had some sort of breakdown last year."

"What caused it?"

"I don't know."

"Some partnership."

"That's the very point I'm trying to make. And it's not only that. As you know, my father left me a bit of money."

"I heard it was more than a bit."

"Who told you?"

"Moss Moss."

"He would."

"But look, even if you've come into a fortune, it's no handicap. It means you may have to reorganise the company, it doesn't mean to say you have to wind up your partnership."

"In ordinary circumstances, I wouldn't want to wind it—"

"Only you feel you're no longer working with the same man."

"Exactly."

"Leave it to me."

"Leave what to you?"

"Leave the whole Goodkind business to me. I'll look into it; in the meantime, don't you do anything."

"In the meantime, I've got to work with the man. Time's of no consequence with you lawyers."

"Give me a fortnight."

"A *fortnight!*"

"A week."

Tobias was as good as his word. A week later he asked Nahum to call on him and gave him a paper with all the details.

"I don't see why you couldn't have found out for yourself. You knew he had family in Liverpool."

"I had a vague idea, but nothing more."

Goodkind was married, with two children in Liverpool. He had separated from his wife about ten years previously, but he was attached to his children, who in turn were attached to him and extremely attached to his mother, who still lived in Liverpool. They would stay with her frequently, and he would travel down to see them at weekends. His wife, who appeared to have been a woman of dubious character, had been living with different men. Lately, however, she seemed to have formed a more stable relationship with an American, and one morning she, the American and the children vanished without trace. This had happened while Goodkind was abroad. His mother had gone to the police, had seen one of the local rabbis, tried in every way to find out what could have happened to the children. She was a woman in her seventies, and the exertions and distress proved too much for her. She died before she could let Goodkind know what had happened, and he only found out when he went down for the funeral.

Nahum was in tears long before Tobias had finished his account, and he left with streaming eyes, though he managed to pull himself together by the time he got to his office. He felt he couldn't face Goodkind at that particular moment and sent him a note, asking him to dinner. Goodkind sent it back, with a scribble: "I'm not hungry." Nahum then waited by the window all afternoon till he saw Goodkind in the street and quickly ran down the stairs after him.

"I've got to talk to you," he said breathlessly.

"You are talking to me," said Goodkind.

Nahum couldn't take that and lost his temper. "For God's sake," he shouted. "Why don't you let me speak to you? Why can't I help you? Why are you bottling everything up inside yourself? What have you got to hide?"

Goodkind turned to him with a mixture of wonder and alarm, studied his face for a moment in the pale light of a gas-lamp, and broke down and cried, at which Nahum also broke down; as they stood there weeping on each other's shoulders, a small crowd collected.

Nahum had intended to take him to a restaurant, but they took a cab home and Goodkind sat by the kitchen table and talked while Nahum prepared supper.

"You've never met my wife, have you?"

"How could I?"

"Beautiful woman. I've always wondered what she saw in me and why she married me. I suppose it was because I was well spoken. My people were never well off, but I was an only child, and they went to immense sacrifices to send me to a posh school. I didn't receive a particularly good education, mainly, I suppose, because I was not particularly educable, but, as Father used to say, it's not what you know in life that counts, but who you know, which was the main reason why he sent me to that school, though the efforts to keep me there broke him, and he died nearly penniless. In fact, my education, what there was of it, was a handicap, for I acquired tastes and expectations which did not go with my ability. I could not keep a job. Then I met Rachel. She was a Polish immigrant en route, she said, for America. I don't know how her parents could have sent her out on her own—she was only seventeen; perhaps she had run away from home. I tried to help her get a passage but couldn't, though by way of compensation she got me. We were together for about six years and lived with my mother. She got a job in a sweatshop owned by a chap called Kriger, but I found it almost impossible to get work. She kept bringing things home which made me suspect that her relationship with Kriger was something more than the normal relationship between employer and employee, but, to be honest, I was too relieved to see the children decently clothed and fed to complain. In the meantime, I travelled further and further afield in search of a livelihood and eventually found my feet, but by then it was too late. She had moved out of my mother's house and had moved in with Kriger, but again I was not too distressed, for I had presumed that exactly that would happen, and, in fact, as long as she put no obstacles between me and the children, I was happy. They came to see my mother almost every day, and I saw them nearly every week-end and spent my holidays with them. And they had a beautiful home, a governess, all the things I could not have hoped to provide."

"You could now."

"Yes, but that was nearly eight years ago, and I didn't know how long my good fortune would last. I had had false starts before. I had also gotten to know Kriger, a dear chap, much older than my wife, a good bit older than me, in fact, quite elderly, a widower, with a sad face and mutton-chop whiskers, who was devoted to her and the children and had certainly done a lot more for them than I had. I wouldn't have dreamt of taking them away. In fact, I had established something of a friendship with Kriger myself, and he always sent flowers and baskets of fruit to my mother, for, although he was an immigrant with hardly a word of English, he was quite a gentleman. And everything continued happily until last September, when suddenly my whole world and, I dare say, his came apart. My wife was being unfaithful to me, but under licence. What I didn't know was that she was also being unfaithful to Kriger, and one day she took the children with her and vanished. She had finally made the passage to America. Mother knew nothing about it; she was expecting the children for tea the following afternoon, and when they didn't turn up, she went round to Kriger. Together they made inquiries with every shipper and every shipping agency. She died three or four days later. The first I knew of it was when I went down to her funeral."

"Have you tried to trace them since?"

"Tried? I've spent almost everything I have on lawyers and private detectives."

"But you couldn't trace them."

"Unfortunately, I could. They weren't in America, but Holland. I immediately began proceedings to claim custody of the children, and my wife replied that they were not, in fact, mine. I thought this was a mere gambit and went to see Kriger about it, and he said that that was a distinct possibility—though they weren't his, either." At which he broke down again.

In later years, when Nahum felt desolate and thought that fate was being harsh to him, he had only to think of Goodkind and immediately remembered his blessings.

Goodkind was never again the Goodkind he had known, but their exchange had cleared the air, and if their relationship was not as happy as it had been, he was no longer impossible to work with, which was perhaps just as well, for the next few months were amongst the busiest in Nahum's life.

He was reorganising his company, arranging to acquire, refit and reequip an ocean-going vessel, appointing agents at the various points of call between Riga and Leith, and looking for a house large enough to meet the different requirements of his mother, his aunt, his cousin and himself. The last he left to Colquhoun, who, in turn, left it to his wife Jessie, who found Nahum a substantial, two-storied, red-sandstone terrace house with a sizable garden in Carmichael Place, in the new suburb of Langside. It had four bedrooms, a maid's room, two reception rooms. Jessie also selected the furniture and furnishings. "All you need now," she said as she showed him around, "is a wife."

"You're beginning to sound Jewish," said Nahum.

He left his small but-and-ben with a slight feeling of guilt, as if he were abandoning a lowly companion who had seen him through hard times.

The reorganisation of the company posed some problems, which were solved finally by liquidating the partnership and creating a limited liability company. Goodkind was allocated a considerable share of the equity in lieu of his shares in the partnership, and Colquhoun was also given a share and made a director; Nahum, who held seventy percent of the equity, became chairman.

He left Tobias to work out the details and concentrated his attention on his ship, which he proposed to call *The Tikvah,* which was Hebrew for hope. When he first set eyes on her his heart sank, for she was a rusty hulk, barely water-tight, with hardly a part in working order, but his surveyor thought that she was basically sound, with immense possibilities and a good fifteen to twenty years of working life. She was being refitted and reequipped in a Newcastle dockyard, and there was a period when Nahum spent more time in Newcastle than in Glasgow, for her special features were to include a synagogue and kosher kitchens, which were outside the experience of the builders, and he remained on hand for consultations.

He took pleasure in observing the gradual resurrection. The ship had not only been rusty in herself, but she was surrounded on every side by rust—rusty scaffolding, rusty cranes, rusty chains, rusty plates, junk amid junk. Gradually she rose from her surrounds like a phoenix. Her hull was painted black, with a bright blue band around the top. Her superstructure was painted white, with two funnels in orange with a blue band. He felt the exultation which he imagined a mother must feel in the later stages of her pregnancy, plus something of the labour pains, for there were technical problems on every side which involved him in hurried meetings with architects, engineers and surveyors, and financial problems, for the estimates bore little relation to the final costs, and he had to make anxious journeys to London to explain the situation to Kagan, who seemed incapable of parting with a penny without some homily. He would sometimes lie awake at night marvelling at his own effrontery, though he came to realise that the more Kagan lent him, the more difficult it was for him to refuse further loans. The amounts made him feel light-headed.

Jessie Colquhoun was furnishing his house while he was away, and she wrote to ask how much she could spend on this or that item, but the sums involved, even when taken together, were so piffling compared to his debts that he wrote back to tell her to use her own judgment. "I don't want the place lined with gold," he added, "but I want everything to be of good quality and in good taste."

Problems arose with some of his prospective agents, and he had to make several journeys to Eastern Europe. Once, while in Riga, he managed to get down for a hurried visit to Volkovysk and found, to his dismay, that his mother and aunt had not finalised their arrangements to move and that his mother had not even disposed of the house. He had not pressed them earlier, because he did not want them on top of him in Glasgow while he was busy with other things and before the house was ready to receive them, but he was irritated by their lackadaisical manner, and for the first time in his life he found himself raising his voice to his mother.

"Look, are you coming to Glasgow or not?"

"Of course we're coming, but you can't bring together the accumulations of a lifetime overnight."

"Overnight? This has been going on for over a year. Look, I've booked you a cabin for the maiden voyage. The ship sails in six weeks, and I want you to be on it whether you've sold the house or not."

His mother was a trifle taken aback by his tone. "If he's like that with one boat," she said to her sister, "what will he be like when he's got a fleet?"

His exertions often left him too exhausted to eat, or sometimes even to undress, and he would fall asleep fully clothed on his bed. He became so worried by his lack of stamina that he went to see a specialist who told him: "It's not stamina you lack, young man, it's sense. You're racing to an early grave."

But he couldn't rest, for there was always some small crisis somewhere, and he alone felt equipped to handle it. He had supper with Colquhoun about three weeks before the sailing, and Jessie was startled at the sight of him.

"You can't go on like this," she said.

"I'll rest when she sails."

"You'll be resting in a wooden box if you're not careful."

Some trouble had erupted with one of the Polish agents who was fairly central to his organisation, and he had planned to leave for Danzig that night, but she wouldn't let him.

"You're stopping right here for a good night's rest," she said.

"I'd go instead of you," said Colquhoun, "if I could trust you two alone together."

"I'll have a good rest on the night train," Nahum protested.

"You'll do nothing of the sort. You're staying right here." He had, in fact, developed a heavy cold and remained in bed, nursed carefully by Jessie, for the better part of a week, and Goodkind went to Danzig instead.

His great day finally came. If Jessie had had her way, the ship would have sailed without him, for he was still rather shaky, but once in Riga, he felt braced by the sense of occasion.

He had taken rooms in the Imperial Hotel to supervise the final preparations, and there was a whirl of messengers coming and going with papers to read and to sign and bills to pay. The ship's rabbi, who had given himself the title of Holy Captain, came to complain that some of he crew had brought whole sides of bacon on board.

"For their own needs, I presume," said Nahum.

"But how do I know it won't get into the kitchen?"

"It's your job to see that it doesn't."

"I've only got one pair of eyes."

"If you keep them open, they should be enough to get on with."

The ship's doctor complained that the operating room was too cramped.

"Too cramped? What do you think I'm running, a ship or a hospital?"

"Women have babies."

"Not on my ship, they won't. I've told the agents, no passengers in the final stages of pregnancy. And no sick passengers, either."

"Are you going to have medical inspection at the quayside?"

"Our conditions are printed in three languages at the back of the tickets. We've got four stops between here and Leith, and anyone taken seriously ill is to be landed. You're only there to cope with emergencies and as a form of reassurance."

"If anybody dies, it won't be my responsibility."

"People also die on land, and nobody blames the doctors for it."

The ship's captain came to complain that the first engineer was drunk and incapable, and demanded a replacement, and the second engineer came to demand that he be appointed first engineer.

Amidst all the commotion, Nahum almost overlooked the fact that his family, whom he had expected at the hotel the day before the voyage, had failed to arrive. The next morning he was already on board when Katya and Lazar appeared on the gangway, perspiring and breathless. There was no sign of his mother.

He descended upon Katya as soon as she was on board.

"Where is she?" he demanded.

She blinked at him. "Are you all right?"

"What's happened to Mother?"

"I'm not your mother's keeper, so don't shout at me. This is not the only ship on the ocean. If you can't talk to me without shouting, I'm getting off."

"I'm sorry."

"I should say so."

"But what's happened to her?"

"It's a long story, and I haven't slept for the past two nights. I must lie down."

"But is she all right?"

"Yes, she's all right."

He was speechless with rage. Here he was in a frock coat, striped trousers and with a large carnation in his buttonhole, the proprietor of an ocean-going liner, which, if not quite a Cunarder, could transport several hundred passengers in reasonable comfort and safety from one continent to another. He had a captain working for him, a *doctor,* a rabbi, nurses, engineers, cooks, stewards, sailors by the score. There was a band on the quay and various dignitaries, including the British consul, to see them off, but his own mother wasn't there. He had made all the necessary arrangements, had reserved a suite for her in his hotel and a state cabin—*the* state cabin—on the ship. Had he been able to snatch a minute of privacy, he would have cried. As it was, he was being tugged from all directions. Passengers who had booked cabins complained that the cabins were too small, others who had booked dormitory class wanted to travel cabin-class. One old gentleman wanted to know what sort of rabbi the ship's rabbi could be because he shaved under his beard, and another wanted to know where the ship's doctor had qualified and whether there was a ship's dentist; finally, as the ship raised anchor and blew its horns, he pulled himself free and sought refuge on the bridge. His great day was ruined.

He had saved Katya a place at the captain's table, but she did not come down for the evening meal, and when he went to her cabin he found her and Lazar fast asleep. He was still fuming with suppressed resentment when he saw her the next morning.

"You've got a very comfortable ship," she said brightly; "you should be proud of it."

"What's happened to Mother?"

"Nothing's *happened* to her."

"Then why isn't she here?"

"Did she never hint that she might stay behind?"

"Never."

"She is an odd girl, my sister. I know she's secretive by habit, but you have a right to know, and even if you didn't, you'd find out. It's bound to come out—only she did swear me to secrecy."

"What are you talking about?"

"She's getting married."

"Mother?"

"Yes."

"Getting married?"

"Don't sound so incredulous. People do, you know, even at her age. Only she's still hesitating, which is why, I suppose, she swore me to secrecy."

"Who is he?"

"Who is what?"

"The man she's going to marry."

"I wish you wouldn't get so agitated, it doesn't become you. Your eyes begin to bulge as if you've got the goitre. It's not as if she's a young girl who's just gotten herself into trouble. You can rely on your mother to do the sensible thing."

"Never mind what she's done," he shouted, "who's she doing it with?"

"I never answer people who shout."

"I'm sorry."

"Didn't she throw out any hints at all, name any names, tell you who she's been seeing?"

"No, nothing."

"No friends of the family?"

"She didn't tell me a thing."

"Did she never mention the name of—Grossnass?"

"Grossnass?"

"Fatty. He's as ugly as sin but *very* manly and powerfully built, with thighs like cedars, and he's as rich as he's ugly."

"Mother doesn't need the money."

"She may need the company, and, in any case, no matter how much you have, it's always nice to have that bit more. He's been after me for years, and I suppose your mother's the nearest alternative."

The voyage turned out to be a nightmare. The ship was virtually one class—*chazar* class, as one critic called it—and had been fitted up like a troop ship with row upon row of bunks, though there were also a few cabins for the occasional moneyed passenger. The cabins were all taken, but the bunks were not. The synagogue and kosher kitchens had added marginally to the cost of the ticket, but he hoped that prospective customers would regard the ship as a sort of floating Jerusalem, and he had described it as such in the Jewish press. He had taken many pages of advertisements and had the voyage heralded even in announcements from synagogue pulpits; the ship's rabbi had travelled throughout Eastern Europe extolling *The Tikvah* as a temple, stressing that one would be able to travel from Russia to Britain without ever having to miss a synagogue service or be exposed to non-kosher food. There would, he said, even be a Talmud study circle aboard. But there was no rush for tickets at Riga. Nahum hoped that he might pick up some passengers who had left arrangements to the last minute at Danzig, Stettin and other ports of call, but they were few. Whenever he stepped on deck, he was pulled at in all directions by passengers with complaints—that the bunks were too hard or too narrow, that the ship was too unsteady, that the food wasn't kosher enough or too expensive, that the crew was anti-Semitic. Many of the passengers had brought their own provisions. The expensive kitchen facilities were hardly used, the restaurants were half empty and the kitchen staff stood around idle. The synagogue was well used, but there were complaints that it was too small, cramped and ill-ventilated (Nahum could not recall a synagogue which was anything else and might have presumed that ventilation went ill with prayer), and all the prayer books he provided vanished on the first day. The dispensary was overwhelmed, and passengers queued for attention almost from the moment they embarked. The sea was rough. People kept toppling from their bunks, sustaining various minor injuries and not a few fractures, and an emaciated little figure who claimed to be a lawyer did a roaring trade advising passengers how, and for how much, they might sue the company. On the second night out, a drunken Polish kitchen hand grabbed a meat cleaver and went berserk, shouting "Death to the Jews," and, before he could be restrained, jumped overboard. By the third night out, Nahum felt like doing the same.

Katya was a good sailor and managed to promenade on deck while most of the passengers were retching below, and she was a great favourite with the captain and crew, to say nothing of the ship's doctor, a little man with a huge head and large glasses. Nahum wondered if his journey would ever end. Goodkind and Colquhoun were waiting at Leith for what was to have been a triumphant homecoming, but as he disembarked, he felt as he thought Napoleon must have felt on the retreat from Moscow, and not even a hug and kiss from Jessie Colquhoun could ease his spirits.

In an odd way he blamed his mother for it all, as if she had been a missing component which had made everything come apart, and he could not stop himself from brooding over the news Katya had brought. There was no reason why his mother should not remarry. She was a handsome, well-preserved woman in her early fifties, who had spent the last ten years of her life helping to sustain an ailing man broken in body and spirit, and she was entitled to a new life, but did she have to choose a rancid heap of quivering flesh like Grossnass? He was rich, to be sure, but she wasn't poor. He was said to be pious (though Nahum found it hard to reconcile piety with bulk), but that, if anything, might have been a defect in her eyes, for she had complained of Yechiel's piety often enough. The religiousness in the family had emanated largely from his father, a refined-looking, handsome man with the bearing of an aristocrat and he could not understand how the widow of such a man could marry someone like Grossnass.

"She hasn't married *yet*," Katya kept telling him, "she's only thinking about it." But he couldn't see how she could even think about it, yet, as it happened, the first thing which greeted his eyes when he returned home was a letter from his mother apologising for her absence from the voyage, wishing him good luck, urging him to keep "a very careful" eye on Katya and Lazar, and informing him that she was now Mrs Grossnass.

CHAPTER IX
KATYA

NAHUM HAD NEVER QUITE HAD TIME TO GET USED TO HIS NEW home, for he was away so often that on the rare occasions he got home, he felt almost as if he were staying in a private hotel. Katya imposed her own personality on the house almost as soon as she arrived, with little boxes here and figurines there, vases, a glowing bronze samovar, paintings and photographs. Nahum did not much care for the photographs—they were mostly of Lazar in various stages of growth and he found him as unattractive as a child as he was as a man—but otherwise he approved of the changes.

With Katya installed as chatelaine, or possibly because of the wealth of bric-a-brac she had deposited about the place, the house did not seem as large as he thought it was. Katya, though not small, had an expansive personality which made her seem even bigger than she was, and she wore a rich perfume which warned one that she was coming and reminded one that she had been. Her son, on the other hand— lean and sullen—was like a shadow. He ate silently, moved silently, and his mother complained that he had turned into a ghost, for he made so little impression on his bed that it looked as if it had hardly been slept in. Nahum employed him as a clerk, and he applied himself to his work with intense deliberation. As the day wore on, he seemed to glow with a white sweat and spent all his free time, including his lunch breaks, learning English, which he picked up quickly. He already knew Russian, Polish and a smattering of German and was useful in dealing with the many-tongued letters which poured into the office. "Another few years," said his mother, "and he'll be able to take over the firm."

Nahum's father used to say that all Jews were *shadchonim*—marriage brokers—a belief which was certainly confirmed by his own experience, and he sometimes felt that every married Jew resented the sight of anyone over twenty who was still single. He often joked about this trait, but Katya had not been a year in Glasgow when he found himself, a little to his surprise, engaged in the very same effort, and one evening he invited Goodkind to dinner.

He told himself that he wasn't really arranging a *shidduch,* because, apart from anything else, he was not quite sure whether Goodkind had ever formally divorced his wife and was free to marry, but he hoped that an association with Katya might raise his spirits a little.

Goodkind had never really recovered from his domestic tragedy, and sometimes in the middle of a meeting Nahum would look at his face and notice that he was lost in thought. He was still an able administrator and a useful member of the team, but no longer so full of ideas, even wild ones, and no longer the able negotiator he had been. Where he had shown flair, he now showed only application and worked late into the night, and although there was certainly enough to keep him busy, it suggested that he had no life outside the office.

The evening was not a success, for Katya found pretexts to be in the kitchen most of the evening, and the three men found themselves talking mainly about *The Tikvah* and her prospects, which were topics Nahum preferred not to discuss with his meals.

When Goodkind had left, Katya accused him of trying to palm her off onto a tramp.

"A tramp? He's one of my oldest and closest friends."

"In which case, you should tell him how to dress properly. His clothes look as if they've been slept in, he was covered in cigar ash and all he can talk about is ships and insurance."

"You didn't give him a chance to talk about anything else. You were hardly in the room."

"I didn't like the way his little piggy eyes stared at me."

Nahum would have liked to see his aunt married, for he was troubled by her presence, especially towards the end of the evening when Lazar was in bed. He often brought papers home and worked late into the night in a corner of the lounge. His aunt would occasionally try to engage him in conversation, and he would point out politely but firmly that he was working, and she would sit in silence for a while, or write letters, or try to read a book, but always restlessly, which had an unsettling effect on him.

About ten she would make tea and bring it in on a tray and would engage him in conversation, whether he liked it or not. She called it "Talk Time."

"You'll make a dreadful husband," she said. "You're far too fond of your own company. I know you work very hard, but you don't seem to have all that much to say when you're not working—at table, for instance, or do you think I'm too stupid for words?"

"The Talmud says that God created ten measures of speech. Nine were given to women. I'm just keeping to my tenth."

"When you begin spouting the Talmud, you begin to sound like your father. It suited him, it doesn't suit you; it makes you sound old."

"I'm not all that young."

"I know, and in another few years you'll be past your prime. Jewish men don't wear all that well, you know."

"It's because they're generally married to Jewish women."

"But really, Nahum, what are you waiting for? It isn't as if you've still to establish yourself or get somewhere. You're good-looking, you're of good family, you're rich, and I'll be surprised if you'll get much richer—"

"As things go, there's every chance that I'll be getting much poorer."

"Exactly, so what *are* you waiting for?"

"Haven't we been over all this before?"

"Maybe, but you're still single."

"But why are you worrying about me? You've still got a son to marry."

"He's five years younger than you and has got nowhere yet. He'll get places, and when he does, that'll be the time to marry. But you've already got there. People talk of you in hushed voices, point you out in the street and say, 'You know who that is—that's Raeburn, the shipping magnate.' And look"—she put a hand through his hair—"it's beginning to go. Your father, who had such a lovely head of hair when he married, was almost bald at forty, and you're beginning to put on weight, which he never did."

"That's your cooking."

"I'll have to starve you." She passed her hand down the back of his neck and caressed his cheek. "Don't you feel the *need* to get married?" She pressed his head against her bosom and remained silent for a moment. "It's unfair, don't you think, that uncles can marry nieces but aunts can't marry nephews. The old rabbis knew how to arrange things for themselves, didn't they?" She grasped his hand and kissed it and laid it to her cheek, and then, breathing heavily, she quickly loosened her bodice and pressed it against her naked breast. "Do you think I'm an old woman? I don't *feel* like an old woman, do I? But I sometimes wonder if you're not perhaps an old man. We've been alone like this so often, have you never wanted to touch me?"

"All the time."

"Then why didn't you?"

"You're my mother's sister."

"What's that got to do with it? I'm not your mother."

He gazed at her in silence, with a distant look in his eyes as if he was dreaming it all, but with his hand still on her breast, caressing softly.

"You don't really think this is wrong, do you? You don't keep kosher any more. You eat shrimps. This isn't worse than shrimps."

"It's much, much better," he said in a choked voice.

She jumped to her feet and, without buttoning her bodice, led him by the hand to her room.

If ever a ship was misnamed, it was *The Tikvah*. She was proving an expensive disaster, and Nahum kept recalling the sage words of Wachsman: "Start with ships, and you finish at the bottom of the sea." The traffic was light, the expenses heavy and the complications endless, and the only person who seemed to be doing well out of it was his solicitor, Tobias. Wachsman had sent him his best wishes when he heard that Nahum had, after all, acquired a vessel but added the warning: "Remember, when you're carrying Jews, you've not only got passengers, you've got litigants," and hardly a day passed without a writ for lost luggage, or broken bones, or missed connections, or all three. He had incurred a slight loss in his first year, which he expected, and more than a slight loss in the second. The third year threatened to be even worse, and the prospect of bankruptcy stared him in the face. He would come home in the evenings, weary and bent, as if his world were falling about his ears, but after a night with Katya, he was content to let it fall.

Shyke, whom he had regarded as an authority on everything and who claimed to have had his first taste of sex on his *bar mitzvah* (and thus gave new meaning to the traditional declaration: "Today I am a man"), had said that there was no experience on earth and, he would guess, in heaven to compare to it. Nahum had had to wait till he was double *bar mitzvah*—twenty-six—to discover this for himself, and it began to affect his work. He found himself looking up from his papers in the course of the morning to ponder over the events of the night before and would almost see Katya in all her fullness, naked before him, and if someone entered his office, he would start with embarrassment, as if he had been caught in flagrante delicto. He stopped working late at night and not infrequently would make hurried visits to his home at lunch. Katya prepared him a small snack, which he put aside for what she called the *entrée*. Lazar went to synagogue religiously every Saturday morning, and, as religiously, they would dive into bed the moment his back was turned, and, not infrequently, even before. On one occasion, Lazar returned home unexpectedly and nearly found them together on the kitchen floor, another in the kitchen pantry, a third on the dining-room table, as if the thought of one carnal pleasure provoked them to another, though there was not a corner of the building, from attic to cellar, which had not at one time or another felt the flare of their passion.

Occasionally, when drawing breath, Nahum would pull himself up with a start and ask himself if he knew what he was doing. The fact that in consorting with his aunt he was in breach of Jewish law— "Thou shalt not uncover the nakedness of thy mother's sister, for she is thy mother's near kinswoman"—worried him not at all, for it seemed to be without reason or justice, except that, given the normal run of aunts, it was a law which he imagined was rather more widely observed than others. What did worry him was that he, a man in his late twenties, the head of a sizable enterprise with scores of employees, was behaving like an infatuated schoolboy.

Colquhoun, who had more than a suspicion of what was going on, would sometimes pull him aside and point out that important papers, which had been awaiting his attention for weeks, had not been signed, or worse, papers which had been signed had not been properly scrutinised. At such times, Nahum would turn hermit and would lock himself in his office, not emerging even for food or drink. Or he would travel over to Leith and work in the office there for one, two or even three weeks at a time. In the first week he felt her absence keenly; the second was rather less painful. By the third, he was tempted to remain there for good if only to avoid the tears and reproaches on his return, which grew more bitter the longer he stayed away. Then there came a day when he had to go to Hamburg, and she asked to come with him.

"To Hamburg?"

"Why not? I've never been anywhere since I've come to your metropolis."

"I'm going by train, you know, not by boat—think of the expense. Besides, what would people say?"

"Who do you know in Hamburg that it matters what they say? You're ashamed of me."

"Ashamed of you? Why should I be ashamed of you?"

"I don't know why you should be ashamed of me. I dress as well as anyone in Glasgow—which, heaven knows, doesn't say much—but I can't afford to dress any better and I look reasonably well, but you're ashamed of me. You're transporting whole towns halfway round the world, and you're quibbling about the price of a train ticket. I don't mind travelling third-class, at least, I do, but I'd rather travel third than be left here on my own. I might as well have stayed in Volkovysk.

You're hardly in town, Lazar works all day and all night. I'm all on my own."

"I'm sorry, Katya, but if I go on a business trip, I like to treat it as a business trip."

"And you won't take me?"

"No."

"Not even third-class?"

"Not even third-class."

"How long will you be away?"

"Three weeks."

"Then don't expect to find me here when you get back."

He was half hoping that she would be as good as her word, but when he got back, she greeted him with smiles and open arms, and although he welcomed her embrace, he was beginning to feel imprisoned.

A few weeks later it was his twenty-seventh birthday, a fact which he had been careful to keep to himself, but Katya remembered the date—she had, as she reminded him, been at his circumcision—and had arranged to make a party for him—"a very private party," she added, "just you and me and a bottle of champagne, so that, whatever happens, keep the evening free," which he did. On the morning of his birthday, however, he received a telegram from Kagan, asking him, indeed, almost ordering him, to come to London without delay. He sent a message to Katya to say what had happened and arranged to leave for London on the afternoon train. When he got to Central Station, he found Katya by the ticket barrier with a small suitcase in her hand.

"I've bought my own ticket," she said.

They travelled in silence for their compartment was full, but Nahum had little to say in any case and busied himself with papers he carried in his case.

"You're angry with me, aren't you?" she said when they reached Euston.

"Don't you think I have a right to be?"

"No, you haven't. It's nine o'clock now, are you going to see Kagan this minute? Couldn't you have gone on the overnight train?"

"I sleep badly on the overnight trains, and I wanted to have a good night's sleep in a good hotel and a clear head when I see him in the morning. It's a crucial meeting."

"You're tired of me, aren't you?"

"Yes, yes, I am." The words emerged without thought and in a loud shout, and passengers turned to look at the source of the commotion.

"That's all I wanted to know," she said, and, grabbing her case from his hand, she strode rapidly back along the platform. He ran after her.

"Where are you going?"

She looked him in the eyes. "Does it matter to you?"

All the generosity and warmth had gone out of her face. There were lines under her eyes and tiny folds around her mouth. She had suddenly turned into an elderly woman. All she needed was a black shawl over her head to look like a Russian *babushka*.

"You're not going back, are you?"

"To Glasgow? I'd rather jump under the train."

He took her by the hand and led her to the station hotel where they booked a room as man and wife. It was a twin-bedded room, and each occupied a separate bed, but neither of them slept. She cried all night— a tinkling sound oddly reminiscent of her laughter—and he was kept awake by her crying.

He saw her onto the morning train back to Glasgow, a slow-moving, downcast, elderly figure—even her clothes seemed to have aged with her—and he turned with something like relief to his meeting with Kagan.

It was not a pleasant occasion. Kagan's bank had arranged standby credits to see Goodkind-Raeburn through its early difficult years and which, it was assumed, would be gradually drawn on over a period of six years. Instead, the sum had been all but exhausted in under three.

"It's not only the rate of exhaustion which troubles us," said Kagan, "but the trend. One expects major withdrawals in the first year and less and less in the second and third, whereas you have reversed the process. The longer you go on, the heavier the withdrawals, and at this rate you won't have a penny by the end of the year, not a penny."

"Traffic has been light."

"Indeed, but not more so than in the earlier years, which brings me to what is perhaps the most painful point. We do not feel that there is the same careful hand in control of affairs that there was before. Suggestions remain ignored, urgent queries, letters, even telegrams unanswered, and when the answers do come, they sometimes bear no relation to the questions asked. There is, of course, a limit to the amount any man can get through in a day, and we wonder if you haven't perhaps taken on too much too soon." He broke off for Nahum was staring into space. "I shall repeat that, Mr Raeburn, since you do not appear to be with me. We feel you may have taken on too much too soon. Frankly, I was horrified by your accounts—horrified."

"Are you asking me to resign?"

"It's your company, Mr Raeburn, and we are not in a position to do so, even if we had any such thought in mind, but we are aware that you invested the greater part of your fortune—"

"All my fortune."

"Worse, all your fortune in the company and that you may not have done so without our help and encouragement, so that we would feel partly to blame for any debacle, which, I'm afraid, is all too likely if present trends continue, all too likely."

"Are the other lines doing much better?"

"They have larger reserves, and, as a matter of fact, business has been picking up somewhat. Let me get to the point. Is there any way in which you can cut down your borrowing?"

"Not this year, and not without withdrawing the ship from service."

"What are advance bookings like?"

"Light, but then they always are. It's one of the disadvantages of handling Jewish traffic—there are others. They tend to make their arrangements at the last minute and sometimes even try to board the ship as it's moving, as if they were boarding an omnibus. We've solved most of our teething troubles and reduced our overhead."

"Can't you cut down on extras, like the synagogue?"

"It's a small corner, and in any case there's no point in closing it while the traffic is light. We're at the mercy of the market. Our prices are competitive, our service is reliable, but if there's little traffic—"

"There's little Jewish traffic. Traffic elsewhere is picking up. Now, I know immigrant traffic is your specialty, but it seems to me that you're too specialised, and if you're nervous of dabbling in general traffic, then it might be an idea to sell the boat. You wouldn't lose on it; prices have picked up."

"But do you know how much I've put into it?"

"A wise man knows when to cut his losses, Mr Raeburn."

"But if the market is rising, is there anything to be lost by holding onto the ship?"

"Yes, if it's losing money, especially as it is by no means certain for how long the market will continue to rise. It's been very erratic, very erratic."

"I take it the credits are still there for me to use."

"Indeed, while they're still there, but when they've gone, they've gone."

"And what you're trying to tell me is, I shan't get more."

"My dear Raeburn, we're not here to tell anyone anything. We're here only to advise. On the other hand, I could not upon my conscience do anything which might land you in deep water—"

"And another loan might—"

"There is that danger, is there not?"

They were to have had a further meeting after lunch, but while he was at his hotel, a clerk from the bank called to tell him that Kagan had been summoned to an urgent meeting and would not be free till the following morning.

"Tell Mr Kagan that I am not free tomorrow," said Nahum; "perhaps he will be good enough to write to me."

He returned to Glasgow on the overnight train, and as he went for a cab, a headline in a morning paper caught his eye and made him rush to the bookstall. There had been a pogrom in Kishinev in southern Russia, but on a scale and virulence unknown before. Dozens of Jews had been slaughtered, hundreds maimed. Jewish property had been pillaged and set ablaze. Thousands were homeless.

CHAPTER X
THE MAGNATE

K ISHINEV WAS IN SOUTHERN RUSSIA, BUT NEWS OF THE MASSACRE
sent a tremor throughout the Pale of Settlement, and whole Jewish communities, many hundreds of miles from the scene of the tragedy,
pulled up their roots and headed toward the West, by ship, by train, by
wagon, even on foot.

Nahum anticipated that exactly that would happen as soon as he
read the news, and, even before ascertaining that he would have the
necessary funds, he chartered two more boats, each as large as *The
Tikvah*. Kagan thought he was mad and refused to advance a penny,
and Nahum appealed over his head to Wachsman, who proved rather
more amenable. He then travelled eastward to see how his agents were
coping with the new situation. He found that the facilities at Riga were
no longer adequate, and he acquired a new depot at Danzig and persuaded a remote relative called Schwartzman, who had been planning
to emigrate to America, to stay on to look after it. He also abandoned
the intermediate stops between the Baltic and the Forth and put on
extra men at the docks, working day and night so that ships could be
turned around without delay.

"Kishinev made me a magnate," Nahum was to say in later years,
"and instead of one ship, which limped along half-empty, I had three,
crammed to the gunwhales." He soon amassed a fortune, which, as he
himself said, was based on Jewish misfortune. "I grew rich with a heavy
heart. How much nicer it would have been if I could have made my
money taking gold prospectors to the Cape." But he comforted himself
with the thought that he was providing an essential service at a low
price and to that extent was helping to ease the burden of Jewish suffering.

As soon as the news of the outbreak reached the West, emergency
committees of leading Jews were established in London and the other
major Jewish centres to help the victims, and, a little to his surprise,
Nahum found himself on the executive of the Glasgow committee. He
had not thought of himself as a leading Jew and had not been active in
Jewish life since the death of his father, but he had given a large dona-

tion to the emergency fund so that he had become a leading Jew almost in spite of himself.

There was a time when he went to synagogue, if not religiously, then with fair regularity, but he found the small building with its unwashed windows suffocating, though he felt less affected by the physical atmosphere than the psychological one. It was Volkovysk on the Clyde, with the same tunes sung in the same tired voices, much the same garb, the same sort of gossip, and the same troubled faces, and it seemed to him that they came together less to celebrate their faith than to recapture the world they had left. He could not quite understand their nostalgia, for he had come from a comparatively prosperous home and was quite glad to forget it, whereas they had come doubled up with poverty and, to all appearances, had not quite straightened themselves out yet. Whenever he appeared in synagogue, one man would rush to him with a prayer book, another with a prayer shawl, a third would guide him— sometimes even pull him—*eiben on,* to a place of honour near the ark, and at the close everyone would crush around him to shake his hand. He did not regard humility as one of his virtues, but he hated to be fussed over. His father had been fussed over in the same way in Volkovysk, but then his father had been a scholar, a man of genuine worth, while he had only money to commend him, and not so much money at that; gradually he ceased to attend synagogue, and his contact with organised Jewish life became more and more attenuated, until it virtually lapsed altogether.

And then came Kishinev. He recalled a remark of Wachsman's: "We try to sidle out quietly when we think nobody's looking, silently, inch by inch. We look around, we look up, we're in the clear, we think we've made it, but then, one crack of the whip, and we're back with our fathers."

He found himself back in synagogues, not because he had recovered his belief (which he had never either defined or formally abandoned), but because the synagogues were the main centres of concern and the principal venues for the meetings, and, as the meetings frequently began and ended with prayers, he felt compelled to join in. There was, moreover, the pressure of expectation. As a leader of Glasgow Jewry, he was expected to be seen in synagogue, at least on the major festivals, and gradually, and without even giving thought to the matter, he resumed synagogue attendance. Cynics, including Katya, saw a link between the apparent recovery of his faith and the upturn in his fortune.

Nahum's involvement in Jewish affairs brought him not only extra burdens in the form of frequent and sometimes acrimonious meetings, but new anxieties, for, as he watched events in Russia, he asked himself if something similar could not happen in Britain. In Russia, all gentiles were thought to be anti-Semites, unless they showed definite proof to the contrary. In Britain, they were taken to be philo-Semites, unless they could show themselves to be Jew haters. Nahum thought both positions were perhaps exaggerated, but clearly one of the attractions —perhaps the main attraction—of Britain was that Jews could live and work in an atmosphere free of the hatred and anxieties which had surrounded them in Russia. In Volkovysk, the last act of the night was a tour of the house to make sure that everything was securely fastened, that the shutters were drawn tight and all the doors locked and bolted, with a heavy bar thrown across the front door: in Glasgow, one turned the front-door key, and that was that. When he travelled abroad and he was asked how things were with the Jews in Britain, he could say unhesitatingly that they could hardly be better, for he had to search his memory for an utterance or incident which could be construed as anti-Semitic. But everything seemed to change with Kishinev, and the very papers which had shed crocodile tears over the plight of Russian Jews belaboured them as "alien scum" the moment they set foot in Britain. The Scottish papers were less hostile, but he received cuttings from the London press which made his blood run cold.

One day a reporter from a London paper called on him to enquire about the growth of his company. Nahum had been interviewed before, and he found he had been reported fairly and accurately, and the publicity helpful, and from time to time short pieces had appeared about him, describing how he had arrived in Glasgow as a penniless refugee and was now the head of a shipping line, which were rather less accurate, but the tone was always favourable and the intention, he believed, benign. This reporter seemed rather more intelligent and better informed than the others, and his questions were more searching, though not hostile. Nahum took pride in the growth of his business and was relaxed and expansive, and, he hoped, perfectly frank, so that when he was asked if his vessels did not sometimes tend to be overcrowded, he said that, while, of course, he kept within the limits laid down by law, he could not turn away people who were in fear of their lives, and that the crowds were sometimes too large for comfort.

The result of the interview appeared a few days later, and Nahum felt as if he had undergone a private and personal pogrom.

The reporter had travelled on *The Tikvah* from Riga and described it as "a floating black hole of Calcutta, stifling, dangerous and perhaps not even sea-worthy, every corner crammed with reeking humanity" and Nahum himself as a penniless refugee now growing rich on the misfortunes of the Jewish poor.

"It's all lies," said Colquhoun, "every word of it, lies, but they've left themselves wide open. Smells are a matter of opinion, but not sea-worthiness. The ship was inspected only last month and passed A-One. I'd see Tobias right away."

Tobias, Nahum's lawyer, had already seen the article.

"In normal times, this would be an open-and-shut case," he said, "but these aren't normal times."

"What do you mean?"

"The case would have to go before a jury, and I very much doubt if any jury in a case like this would deliver a verdict in favour of a Jew, especially a Jewish alien—"

"I beg your pardon, I've been a British subject now for several years."

"Sorry, an ex-alien, who derives his income largely from bringing in other aliens. You wouldn't get damages, and, if you did, they would be nominal, and you mightn't get costs."

"We might as well be back in Russia."

"We might, indeed. You've got to understand this country; it goes through ugly spasms. There is strong anti-alien feeling—alien being the polite word for Jew—and while it lasts, don't start scattering writs. You wouldn't do yourself any good, you wouldn't do the Jews much good— indeed, the whole case could be used as anti-alien demonstration. My advice is, batten the hatches and lie low till it's over."

Nahum felt as he imagined a lover must feel when a woman he had adored for most of his adult life had suddenly turned ugly. Britain had figured in his imagination almost in idyllic terms as open, free, fair, compassionate, honest, just. His father had often been spoken of as a successful trader and an honest man, as if the two were incompatible, which, in Russia, they often were, and even his father had had to prac-tice subtle evasions to stay in business. In Britain, Nahum had found that one could survive and even prosper without them. One could trust people unless they showed themselves untrustworthy, whereas in Rus-sia, one began by distrusting them and generally continued to distrust them.

He had once said all this to Wachsman who replied, "It's true, it's true, which is why when you're stabbed in the back by an Englishman, it's all the more painful."

He had been stabbed in the back by a young man to whom he had taken a liking and whom he had trusted and in whom he had confided, but what was infinitely worse was the suggestion that he could not be assured of justice in an English court of law.

For some weeks after the article appeared, Nahum was nervous of showing his face in public, especially the Jewish public. Colquhoun told him he was being unduly sensitive. "Nobody who knows you, knows of you, or who has ever done business with you would ever believe a word of the article," but he felt otherwise. It was his experience that people with little money tended to draw comfort from the belief that people with a great deal of money generally came by it in unseemly and underhand ways.

One day while at lunch with Colquhoun, he told him he was thinking of emigrating.

"Ah," said Colquhoun, "you're turning native."

"What do you mean?"

"It's a thought which strikes every Scot sooner or later; it doesn't mean they always emigrate, but they like to play with the idea."

"I'm playing with the idea because the Jew will never get the chance to turn native."

"You're still fuming about that bloody article."

"Not only that one, there have been others like it, and I've been reading the speeches in Parliament."

"Aye, aye, and you think the country is ready for its first pogrom."

"Don't you think it could happen?"

"Are you talking about London?"

"Would it be any different here?"

"Of course, it would be different here. You're talking about Scotland, man, it's a different country. All you bloody foreigners make the same mistake. There's never been any anti-Semitism to speak of here, because there haven't been any Jews to speak of, which doesn't mean that those who are here have been loved. They're shrewd, they're fast, they're sharp, they drive a hard bargain, they're ambitious, they're restless, but then, so are the Scots, and I can't see many Jews coming here for that reason—the competition's too keen. In England, it's a different matter. They're a lot of lazy bastards in England, especially in the south, and a bit slow, and they're no match for the Jew—they're not even a match for the Irish. The English aren't really interested in being rich, but they don't like being overtaken by those who are."

"I thought this was meant to be a land of opportunity."

"It is, if you don't grab at them too keenly."

"And you think the Jews grab at them too keenly?"

"They grab at everything going and a few things which aren't."

"That's why I want to emigrate. If even you talk like that, can you imagine how the others feel?"

"But how do you expect them to feel? And what makes you think they'll feel different anywhere else? Take Germany—" He paused in mid-sentence. "You're not saying, are you, that I'm a Jew hater?"

"I wouldn't call you a Jew lover."

"For God's sake, I'm a nobody lover, I take people as they come. I've nothing against Jews, but you know and I know that you've got to be on your toes when they're around, and when they start crowding in among people who don't like being on their toes, you can expect trouble; that's why there's this commotion about the immigrants."

"And that's why I'm thinking of emigrating."

"You'll get over it."

And he did—for a time.

As a result of the new Jewish influx in the aftermath of Kishinev, there was a growing clamour in Parliament and the press for an end to immigration, which, in turn, quickened the influx, which, in turn, increased the clamour. Kagan urged Nahum to curtail his business before it was curtailed by law and not to renew the charters of the extra vessels he had taken on.

Nahum had, in fact, decided for himself not to renew his charters, because it was perfectly obvious that the bill to close British doors to further immigration would soon become law, and he doubted if there would be enough immigrant traffic to keep even *The Tikvah* in business. As a result, he made strenuous efforts to use the experience his company had gained to establish a more varied clientele and become a more general carrier. Goodkind, Nahum was delighted to see, was particularly adept in establishing new contacts—as if the very scale and pace of their enterprise had given him new life—which, in turn, added to his self-confidence, and when they arranged to enlarge their office in Hamburg, Goodkind volunteered to look after it. Nahum reminded him that he didn't speak German.

"I have a smattering and I could pick up more, and, in any case, anyone with any intelligence in Germany can speak English—or at least they jolly well should."

Nahum didn't know if he could spare him, and he tried to persuade Tobias to leave his law practice and join his company.

"You couldn't afford me, dear boy," said Tobias. "Besides, there will always be a need for lawyers; I'm not sure if I can say the same about ships," but he did agree to serve as a part-time director, and Goodkind was able to move to Hamburg.

The accession of Tobias to his board revolutionised Nahum's domestic situation. One evening he brought him home for dinner, and after he had left Katya said: "He is not a thing of beauty, and you could hang a hat on his warts, but he dresses well, and he has beautiful manners."

Tobias had lost his wife a year or two before and had been left with two children to look after, but Nahum had never regarded him as a possible husband for Katya and had certainly not brought him home with any such thought in mind, but Katya had obviously thought that this was a further attempt at a *shidduch*, and on the whole she approved. Tobias, for his part, did not disapprove. She asked him to call again, and he called again. Six months later, they were married.

It was a small wedding. Lazar, who was now a law student at Glasgow University, was the best man and wore a frock coat and top hat several sizes too large for him. Tobias's two children, Arabella and Caroline, exquisite little girls aged ten and eight respectively, were bridesmaids. Colquhoun was there with Jessie, and, a little to Nahum's surprise, so were Miri and Yerucham. Miri had been unwell for some time from a nervous disorder which affected her skin, and she had put on weight at the same time, but she appeared to have made a complete recovery and seemed to have shed both years and bulk. Nahum could not take his eyes off her, and Katya, in a hurried aside, chided him for it.

"You're a bit obvious, my dear. She has a husband, you know, whom she loves on and off, and, by the look of things, this is one of the on days."

Nahum did not know what loneliness was until he returned to his home that evening. He thought he had been lonely in the Gorbals, but he had lived in a tiny flat, and there wasn't the space to echo his solitude. Now he felt it on every side—it almost whistled in his ears— and as he moved from room to room he would have been glad to get even a sight of Lazar (who had moved into Tobias's house that day to look after his young step-sisters while his mother was on her honeymoon). Katya had been substantial not only in size but in presence, sound and impact. He thought he might miss her, but it never occurred to him she would leave such a void.

Colquhoun and Jessie had frequently urged him to come down to their country cottage and meet a friend called Verity. They did not say who or what sort of friend she was, and Nahum usually found some excuse for not doing so. He presumed she would not be Jewish and, though he had drifted far from his origins, he could not yet contemplate the thought of marrying a gentile, if only out of deference to his father's memory. On the other hand, he yearned for company, and he was particularly anxious not to be on his own that weekend, and a warm, vivacious Scottish woman—an unattached Jessie was what he hoped for—could, he imagined, make exciting company.

Still, when he accompanied Colquhoun to St Enoch station to catch the Gourock train, he felt somewhat like a small boy about to embark on his first major sin, and he moved furtively, as if afraid someone might see him. Why, he asked himself, did he quiver at the thought of consorting—probably innocently—with a *shiksa,* when he had already consorted—anything but innocently—with his own aunt? Two reasons suggested themselves. The first was that sins within the family were generally discreetly handled and were allowed to go no further, whereas if one went beyond the family, there was every chance of discovery. The other was that the *shiksa*—to any observant, or ex-observant Jew—epitomised forbidden fruit in its most fruity and forbidden form. He could not wait to meet Verity and the forty-minute journey to the coast seemed endless. When he reached Gourock, however, and was introduced to her, he almost turned back. Verity was a boat.

"Well," said Colquhoun proudly, "what do you think?"

"What should I think?" (What he actually thought was that if Colquhoun and his boat had at that moment sunk to the bottom of the sea, it would not have been a bad thing.)

Colquhoun gave him a life-jacket and unfurled the sail, and, as they were carried along briskly by the wind, Nahum's spirits picked up a little; half an hour later they reached the island of Great Cumbrae where Colquhoun had his cottage. Jessie was waiting for them on the shore. She put her arm through his.

"You look downcast," she said.

"I'm a bad sailor."

The following morning all three went out on the boat. There was a slight breeze blowing, and they skimmed swiftly through the glittering waters. Nahum had never experienced anything so exhilarating in his life. He was taken completely outside himself, away from all his concerns, worries, loneliness, arguments with himself and others.

"You should see yourself," said Jessie, "your brow is unfurling like a sail."

"I've fallen in love with *Verity*."

"Why don't you get yourself a boat?" said Colquhoun. "I mean a real boat, where you can lean over and touch the water."

"Or break your head on the boom," said Jessie.

"How long have you been doing this?" asked Nahum.

"Och, I was born on the water. My father was a sailor. I wanted to be one myself, but Mother wouldn't hear of it, and I got myself a job in a shipping office, but it failed. Then Mother came home one day and said: 'There's two Jews starting up a shipping office, and they need an experienced clerk, and I told them you're their man. You canny go far wrong wi' Jews,' she said, and she wasn't far wrong."

Nahum felt almost intoxicated by the blue sky, fresh breeze and glittering waters.

"As soon as I feel more calm and settled," he said, "I am going to get myself a boat."

"If you wait that long," said Colquhoun, "you're never going to get yourself a boat. I got myself a boat as a way of feeling calm and settled. You've got to get out on the water to flush your head; there's no other way of doing it."

They found a visitor waiting for them when they got back to shore. It was Cameron, who had come in his own boat. He had been passing and wanted to show off his craft. He was an extremely attractive young man—lean, tanned, muscular, with a cleft chin—but his twinkling grey eyes always seemed to carry a slightly derisive look. Jessie asked him to stay for lunch.

"Sorry, my love, I'm already expected to lunch."

"By someone with a pretty daughter, I hope."

"Leave the lad alone," said Colquhoun.

"I thought only Jews were like that," said Nahum.

"It's something she's picked up from you," said Colquhoun.

When Cameron was gone, Nahum said: "We must be paying him pretty well if he can afford his own boat."

"Och, you can afford anything if you're single," said Jessie.

"We are paying him well, but he's got a responsible job," said Colquhoun, "and he's put the thing together with his own hands, you know. He's one of the most capable youngsters I've ever come across."

"Your blue-eyed boy," said Jessie.

They lunched on smoked fish, brown bread, baked potatoes, green salad and whisky.

"I'll bet it's a bit different from your usual Sabbath lunch," said Jessie, "but it's all kosher."

"And all delicious," said Nahum.

"Then I wish you'd eat with greater gusto. You're nibbling at your food as if you're afraid I've put poison in it. What's bothering you?"

"No, nothing's bothering me, but when I'm enjoying something, I prefer to sip it rather than gulp it."

But something was bothering him, for he thought he was falling in love with Jessie. He wondered if it was induced by his loneliness, for there were times when he thought he had fallen, or rather refallen, in love with Miri, and when he saw her at the wedding, he was convinced that he would never meet another woman whom he would find as pretty, as pert, as vivacious, or who would instill him with the same sensations, though not the least of her attraction was the sense of assurance she gave him, that his feelings were not unrequited. Now, hardly a month later, he had almost exactly the same feelings about Jessie. Miri reminded him of one of the three little girls at school in *The Mikado*; there was always a slightly mischievous glint to her eyes, as there was with Jessie, but there the resemblance ended. In build, Jessie was more like Katya, and she had Katya's buoyancy, plus a warmth which Katya lacked, and he felt an ease in her company which he found nowhere else. But she was a married woman, as Miri was a married woman. He and Jessie often held hands and met and parted with a kiss on the cheek, and he wondered how she would have reacted if—as he had been often tempted—he had kissed her on the mouth. He never tried. There was forbidden fruit and forbidden fruit, and his aunt had been the limit of his transgression. It would seem that only married women could arouse his affection, and he wondered if he would ever marry.

Two months later he had an encounter which set the matter at rest.

CHAPTER XI
LOTIE

FROM TIME TO TIME NAHUM RECEIVED LETTERS FROM WACHSMAN, drawing his attention to trends in the shipping world, but Wachsman, too, liked to play the *shadchan*, and with each letter he asked Nahum if he had met Kagan's daughter Matilda.

"She's a princess," he kept repeating, "even without her money. I know you're not very fond of her father, but you wouldn't be marrying him. I want you to meet her and tell me if you don't think I'm right."

Nahum was not in the least averse to meeting the young lady, but he could not see how he could do so without an invitation to Kagan's house which he never received. Wachsman wrote back to say: "I shall see to it. Wachsman can arrange everything."

And lo, a week or so later, an invitation did arrive, but it was to a wedding, Matilda's wedding.

It was held at Stanwell, Kagan's country home in Suffolk. The ceremony was performed by the Chief Rabbi. The cream of Anglo-Jewry was there—the Rothschilds and Montefiores, Goldsmids and d'Avigdor Goldsmids, Montagues and Samuels, Waleys and Waley-Cohens, to say nothing of famous names from the continent like Bleichroeder and Warburg and Bischoffsheim and Fuld and also, to judge from the accents, a fair sprinkling of Americans.

There must have been about five hundred guests, and Nahum moved among them, glass in hand, without a soul to talk to, until he was stopped by a beaming, white-haired figure.

"You don't remember me, do you?"

"I'm afraid I've got a bad memory for faces."

"People who make money always have bad memories. Before you became a magnate, you'd have known who I was. Polack, remember me?"

"Yes, yes, of course," though Nahum still could not place him.

"You used to like my daughter Elsa, remember?"

"Yes, lovely girl."

"Well, she's married a Dacosta, what do you think of that? A Dacosta."

"*Mazeltov*, I'm very happy for her."

"Would you like to meet them?"

"Later, perhaps. I'm looking for somebody."

What Nahum was looking for was a way out. His train had been delayed, and he had missed the actual wedding ceremony. He had hoped that Wachsman would be there. When he established that he wasn't, he saw no point in hanging around, especially as he had a train to catch for the continent early the next morning. He was look-ig for Kagan and his wife to make his farewell when he came across the bridal party lined up for a photograph, and he stopped in his tracks. The bride, a tall, slender young woman with large, dark eyes set in a small, pretty face, was every bit as beautiful as Wachsman had said, but his attention was caught by the bridegroom, a heavily built young man with a large, square jaw and a face wreathed in smiles. He felt he had seen him before but couldn't place him. Then, as his eye travelled down the line of relatives, he caught sight of a young woman who seemed to be staring at him; when their eyes met, she smiled. He smiled back and raised his glass, and she nodded appreciation. He had not seen her face before, but again there was something familiar about her, and he had the odd feeling that he might have been at Stanwell in a previous existence. Kagan gave him a hostile glare, and he retreated out of sight, but as soon as the photographer was finished, he rushed over towards the young woman.

"Hullo. I'm Nahum."

"Na—what?"

"Nahum."

"How do you pronounce that?"

"Na—"

"Na."

"Whom."

"Nahum. I'm Lotie, or rather Charlotte, though nobody calls me Charlotte. I'm Edgar's sister. Edgar's the bridegroom." She spoke with an American accent.

She, in fact, looked rather like the bride, tall—or looked tall, for she had her hair piled high on her head—with a long neck, large, lustrous brown eyes set well apart in a broad forehead, upturned nose, high cheek-bones, small chin and teeth rather too large for her mouth.

"Have we met before somewhere?" asked Nahum.

"No, unfortunately not. I'd have remembered if we had."

"I have the feeling I've seen you, and I've almost certainly seen your brother."

"That's quite possible, he's been everywhere. Where are you from?"

"Scotland."

"Your accent isn't very Scottish." As they were talking, they were joined by a short, squat woman with silvery hair and blue eyes.

"Oh, Mother, I'd like you to meet Nahum."

"Nahum Raeburn," he added.

"Raeburn?" she said. "I've heard that name before. Where are you from?"

"Scotland."

"You don't sound Scottish."

"I wasn't born in Scotland."

"Somehow I didn't think you were. Lotie, come."

Lotie went, but she was back a few minutes later.

"I'm sorry about Mother, she's like that. She doesn't like me talking to people she doesn't know."

"That's very limiting."

"Not really, she thinks she knows everybody who's worth knowing. Are you related to Matilda?"

"I'm related to nobody, and, in fact, I know nobody. I'm not quite sure why I was invited."

"Oh, dear, Mother's giving me looks. I don't think we'll get much chance to talk here."

"Where are you staying?"

"We'll be here overnight, but we'll be in London tomorrow, at the Cecil, in the Strand."

"I have to leave early tomorrow, but I suppose I could postpone things for a day."

She clasped her hands hopefully.

"So can we meet in the Cecil?"

"What time?"

"We're going to the opera at seven. Could you be there about six? Don't ask for me. Just wait in the lobby. I'll be down."

He was at the Cecil the next day on the dot of six, pulled out a paper and waited. From time to time he lowered his paper to see if there was any sign of Lotie, but there wasn't. Finally, when half an hour had passed and still she had not turned up, he went over to the desk, gave his name and asked if there was any message for him. There was none. He then asked if the Althouse family had been staying in the hotel.

They had, but they had booked out earlier in the afternoon.

Where were they now?

He couldn't say.

Nahum presumed that whatever had happened was due to the machinations of the mother, and he wondered why she had taken such an immediate and intense dislike to him. He presumed Kagan would know where they were, but, if so, he was unlikely to tell him, and in any case he did not feel inclined to ask.

Feeling tired and dispirited and angry at the loss of a day, he returned to his own hotel, the Great Eastern, and, as he entered the foyer, he found Lotie by the desk. She was almost speechless.

"How did you know I was here?"

"How did I know? I didn't, I'm staying here."

"It's a miracle," she said. "It's fate. Mummy suspected that we might have arranged to meet in the Cecil, that's why we moved here. You're actually staying here? I can't believe it."

"What's your mother got against me?"

"I don't know, I'm sure. I think you're wonderful. I wonder what Kagan could have told her. I suppose she thinks you're an adventurer. She thinks nearly everybody I talk to is an adventurer."

"But why an adventurer?"

"Don't you know who I am?"

"You're what-do-you-call-him's sister."

"But don't you know who my father is?"

"I take it he's American and probably very rich."

"Don't you know my name?"

"Yes, Althouse."

"So you do know who I am."

"Well, of course, the name was on the wedding invitation."

"But it means nothing to you, otherwise?"

"No."

"Have you never been to America?"

"No."

"That explains it. We're Althouse stores."

"How do you do? I'm Raeburn ships."

"Seriously, though, we're one of the biggest stores in America, and by far the biggest in Philadelphia. Mummy thinks I'm silly and hare-brained and that I talk too much—which I do. Look at me, we've only just met and I'm telling you my whole life story, and my mother's afraid that somebody will marry me for my money. Oh, and she also thinks I'm plain."

"How can anyone, especially a mother, think you're plain?"

"The gaps in my teeth are too wide, and I show too much gum when I smile, which I do—look. Mummy always gives me a look or a nudge when I smile. I never smile when Mummy's around, not that I feel much like smiling when she's around, though I love her dearly. And it's not the end of the world, really, is it, when people marry you for your money—after all, it's something you inherit, like intelligence or good looks. People say Daddy married Mummy for her money. Her family is very rich, or was, and Daddy is very good-looking, or was—he's run to seed a bit now, poor man. Mummy hasn't got looks, but she's got pedigree, and she's very intelligent, very. Father never makes a move without her—very good business brain. But again, like some very intelligent people, she can be very stupid about some things, which is a comfort, don't you think, for it does mean, doesn't it, that very stupid people can sometimes be very intelligent. She's been very ill, poor dear, which is why I nearly always give in to her. I nearly made a scene about moving from the Cecil, but I was afraid she might have another breakdown if I upset her."

It was a balmy night, and Nahum asked her if she wanted to go out.

"Now? Together? Alone?"

"People do, you know."

"In London, perhaps, not in Philadelphia—not in my family. Oh, but I'd love to. But why not? Mummy'll be in bed and asleep by midnight. Can we meet here?"

"Why not?"

She looked at him with fond, smiling eyes for a moment and then turned and ran up the stairs as fast as her hobble skirt would permit. She was back a minute later.

"Silly of me, but if you don't mind my asking—you're not married, are you?"

"No, and never have been."

"You somehow don't look married."

He held her hand. She disengaged herself reluctantly, and, blushing from ear to ear, she bolted up the stairs, turning every now and again to see if he was watching her, which he was. It was seven o'clock. The five hours which followed were about the longest he could recall. He went to his room to study some papers he had in his case but couldn't apply his mind to them. He ordered some food but couldn't eat and spent an hour or so watching darkness gathering over the City. When she appeared shortly after midnight, he pounced upon her and engulfed her in an embrace which almost broke her bones.

"For goodness sake," she squealed delightedly, "what will people say?"

He wanted to take her out for a meal, but she said she didn't feel hungry, and, "in any case," she added, "I always think it's a pity to waste time eating when you're enjoying good company. People don't look their best when they're eating. I know I don't." They took a ride in a cab, instead. It was a soft, velvety night, warm for the time of the year, with a huge copper-coloured moon like an illustration from a child's storybook.

"I daren't think what Mummy would say if she saw me now."

"Can't you forget your mummy for a minute?"

"I'll shut my eyes and try, shall I?"

And as she did, he leant over and kissed her on the ear.

"That's nice, do it again.."

Which he did, again and again. "You know," he said, "I still feel I've seen you before."

"Perhaps you met my sister-in-law Matilda; people say I'm her doppelgänger. I wish I was; she's much prettier."

"She isn't."

"She is, too, and much more intelligent. She speaks five languages fluently and plays the piano beautifully. I think Edgar's very lucky, though not half as lucky as she is. He's the most marvelous man, kind, generous, gifted. I don't know how I shall face Philadelphia without him; we were very close." She was almost in tears. "What's going to happen after this?"

"What do you mean?"

"We're leaving for Europe tomorrow."

"So am I."

She brightened. "Are you? Don't tell me you're going to Mulhouse."

"Why Mulhouse?"

"That's where we're going. I've an aunt in Mulhouse."

Then suddenly he remembered. "Mulhouse, that's it, Mulhouse," he shouted in a voice so loud that he startled both her and the cab driver. "I knew I'd seen you before, you and Edgar. It was on the train in the dining car. You must have got off at Mulhouse. How long ago was it, nine years ago, ten years?"

"Nine years ago, but I don't remember seeing you."

"You didn't. I saw Edgar, and I saw your back. I fell in love with your back—"

"You mean you prefer it to my front?"

"No, I don't mean that. I'm talking about that train journey. I was engrossed in conversation with my partner and then looked up and saw this magnificent figure of a woman moving along the carriage. It was almost like a vision, for I had the feeling that your feet didn't touch the ground, you seemed to be floating."

"You were drinking."

"I was drinking."

"That explains it. If only you had called me back. We were on the grand tour, Edgar and I. It was my first trip to Europe. Oh, if only you *had* called me back. Nine years, can you imagine it? I resent all the times we could have been together and weren't. How old are you? Can I guess? Are you sensitive about age? I am. I'm ancient, you know, all my friends married years ago. I was nearly married myself two years ago. Everyone thought it was about time I married, and so did I. That's how he met Matilda."

"Who did?"

"Edgar. I nearly married Richard Kagan, Matilda's brother. You'd like Richard. No, perhaps you wouldn't. He's a bit stiff but with beautiful manners. He's quite charmed Mother, but there were little things—perhaps not so little—about him which irked me. He's got a rather loud voice and seemed to address me as if I was an audience. He stayed with us in Philadelphia, and we stayed with them in Stanwell, and we had lawyers to draw up a settlement, and we nearly married."

"What stopped you?"

"I kept asking myself the same question, because there were so many things I liked about him, and I did so desperately want to get married, but I couldn't. Mummy, of course, thought I was mad and wanted me to see a doctor, and by the time she had finished with me, I did have to see a doctor. She made me ill, but not half as ill as I made her. She nearly died. Poor Mummy, I seem to be causing her upsets all the time. I think she'd disown me if she saw me now, sitting with you like this." She kissed him under the ear. "How old are you?"

"You asked me before."

"But you didn't tell me."

"Thirty-one."

"Thirty-one!"

"Don't I look it?"

"I'm only surprised that someone so attractive and eligible should have remained single for so long." She sat up and searched beseechingly into his face. "You're not a fortune hunter, are you? Silly question, you wouldn't admit it in the first place if you were."

"And if I said I was, would that be proof that I wasn't?"

"Mummy will think you're a fortune hunter, whatever you say—she thinks almost everybody is."

"Even Kagan?"

"He's heir to a fortune himself."

"So it's all right to be a fortune hunter if you've got a fortune already?"

"As a matter of fact, I don't even care if you are a fortune hunter. You know, it's only just occurred to me that I don't even know what you do."

"Didn't I tell you?"

"I don't think so."

"That's because I own a fortune myself, and I was afraid you might be after *my* money."

"But seriously, what do you do?"

"I'm a ship owner."

"Are you? That sounds exciting, but you don't look like a ship owner."

"What are ship owners meant to look like?"

"Oh, I don't know. I imagine someone salty and weather-beaten, like an old sea captain, and smelling of the sea. You look like a lawyer or a banker, except that there's something still a little bit unpolished about you which I like. But tell me, why aren't you married? Were you ever married before—or—or anything like that?"

"Anything like what?"

"Well, you know what men are."

"Do I?"

"Of course you do, at your age, you must."

"I come from a provincial town in Russia and live in a provincial town in Scotland. You can't be more innocent than that."

"And you mean, you never—"

"I don't know what you mean."

"I'd be upset if I thought that you ever, ever—well, you know."

"Shall we change the subject?"

"Which means you have." She sat upright and pulled a handkerchief from her bag.

"Lotie, my darling, look at me." She turned her face slowly, and he wiped a tear from her eyes. "We've only just met, and we're already quarreling about something which may or may not have happened before I knew you. Aren't we mad?"

She nodded. "I'm sorry."

They kissed. There was something moist, tender and delicate about her lips, like a touching of souls. He could not help comparing it with the experience of kissing Katya, who always approached him with a gasping, wide-open mouth which made him feel he was about to be swallowed.

"I'm going to ask Mummy to invite you to Philadelphia."

"Isn't it a bit soon?"

"Do you think it is? I feel as if I've known you all my life. In any case, we're leaving in the morning, and I want to see you again, and where can I see you if not Philadelphia? Oh, I shall be so miserable tomorrow, it makes me miserable to think about it—unless you could come with us."

"It already is tomorrow, and I've got a busy day ahead."

"I'm sorry, I'm being presumptuous. Perhaps you don't even want to come. Perhaps you don't even want to see me again. All you have to do is to say so, and I'll jump under an omnibus."

He kissed her again. "I'll come to Philadelphia in the morning."

"What do you mean, in the morning?"

"It's the words of a song."

"Now you're making fun of me."

"I'll come, only I'm worried about your mother."

"I'll look after Mummy," she said in a determined tone, which did not quite go with the impression he had of her otherwise.

CHAPTER XII
TO PHILADELPHIA
IN THE EVENING

EVER SINCE HE HAD BECOME A SUBSTANTIAL CARRIER, NAHUM HAD contemplated extending his interests to America. As it was, most of the passengers he landed at Leith continued across Scotland to one of the Clyde ports and then onwards across the Atlantic, and Goodkind-Raeburn was hardly more than a feeder line for the Atlantic. They earned considerable sums in commission, but it was his ambition to have a ship of his own plying between Glasgow and the American East Coast.

Both Tobias and Colquhoun thought that such an idea was so far beyond his means that he could only be day-dreaming.

"Even if you can find the money," said Colquhoun, "what makes you think you'll always have the traffic? How many Jews can there be in Russia?"

"Four million."

"And will they all want to leave?"

"Not the rich, and not the very poor, but as for the rest, pogroms or no pogroms, once they've got relatives overseas, it's only a matter of time before they move themselves. Over a million Jews have already moved to America. You can expect another million to follow, which'll be enough to keep us busy for a while yet." Colquhoun remained skeptical. Kagan was even more so.

"You want to launch out into the Atlantic? To what end? You have the same anti-Jewish clamour in America that you have in England, only with less justification. Britain is a small and crowded island, America is a vast continent with great, empty spaces crying out for people, crying out for people, but they're afraid of being overrun by Jews. Immigration is stopping in this country, and by the time you have your venture in hand, it will have stopped in America. In any case, have you any idea what competition is like on the Atlantic run?"

"The traffic is heavy, but the ocean is large and the seaboard is long."

"To all intents and purposes—as far as your traffic is concerned—

the seaboard consists of New York. That's where everybody wants to go to, everybody, and that's part of the trouble. If only they scattered a bit and moved to the South or the West, they would arouse less opposition, but they all want to be in New York, all of them, all of them, much as the Jews in this country all want to be in London, and the East End of London, at that. That's always been our trouble, everybody wants to be where everybody else is."

"I managed to divert them."

"Temporarily, temporarily. Your passengers weren't interested in getting to Leith or Glasgow—they hadn't heard of the places. If they hadn't seen New York as their journey's end, you'd never have sold a ticket, not a ticket. Well, that's all going to stop, and if I was you, I'd get out of immigrant traffic altogether. Doors are closing everywhere—especially for Jews."

"All the more reason for making every effort to get them out of Russia now."

Nahum took pride in the fact that, in spite of the discouragement offered by Wachsman and Kagan, he had been able to make his fortune outside the usual run of Jewish businesses and gloried in the role of shipping magnate, a status which he regarded as second only to that of landed gentleman, and, indeed, there were times—in calm weather, at least—when he strode along *The Tikvah*'s deck and examined its various departments, he felt as he thought a landowner must feel in looking over his estates, especially when sailors—even officers—jumped to touch their forelocks when he appeared. But, as he soon discovered, there were shipping magnates and shipping magnates, and their standing depended almost as much on the length of their voyages as the number and size of their ships. When he moved among others in the trade, the talk was of distant oceans and faraway places, whereas he, with his Riga-to-Leith run, was hardly more than in the coastal trade, and the thought of the Atlantic pressed upon him with such force that he would sometimes wake in the morning with the sound of the waves in his ears.

He had, however, allowed the idea of a westward operation to lie dormant, not only because it would stretch his resources but also his personnel. He had hitherto thought of cash and credit as the only limitations on expansion, but in the past year or two he had discovered that it was even more difficult to get the right people to do the right jobs, people like Goodkind and Colquhoun whom he could entrust with a given function and be certain that it would be carried out. He thought he had found such a man in Schwartzman, a second cousin, who looked after his interests in Danzig, and considered bringing him over to London, only he could not find an adequate replacement. There was also young Cameron, who, though only twenty-two, seemed capable of the highest responsibilities, but he was now in charge of the Leith office and could not be spared. Lazar had qualified as a lawyer, and although Nahum did not care for him as a person, he had a high respect for his abilities and offered him what he thought of as a generous (and what Colquhoun described as an extravagant) salary to join the firm, but Lazar preferred the law and joined his step-father's practice. As a result of these difficulties, Nahum had allowed the thought of the Atlantic to drop from his agenda.

Then he met Lotie and rarely thought of anything else; he told her that he would be visiting America "at the earliest possible moment." Three or four months passed before the moment arose, and in the meantime he received recriminatory letters from Lotie suggesting that he had forgotten about her and didn't really want to see her; other-wise, he would have been in America by now.

He assured her that he would be coming well before the end of the year but could not give her a firm date in case, as not infrequently happened, something intervened to delay him.

When his ship docked, she was waiting for him at the quay and fell upon him with such force that she half-stifled him and at the same time drenched him with tears.

"I thought I would never see you again," she sobbed.

"But I said I was coming."

"I know you did, but you were so slow about it, and your letters were so dry and impersonal—almost business letters—but, never mind, you're here."

At her suggestion, he had booked rooms at the Murray Hill Hotel which she said was around the corner from an aunt with whom she often stayed—"a dear, understanding woman who is as sane as my mother is crazy. She thinks I'm with my aunt now, that's how I was able to get away."

She couldn't stay long because she had to get back to Philadelphia that evening, but she was expecting him to join her tomorrow.

"No," he said firmly, "not tomorrow. I've arranged a few business meetings which I must get out of the way."

"How long will that take?"

"A week."

"A *week!*"

"We've waited this long, we can wait a week longer."

"But a week is forever, as far as I'm concerned."

"It'll pass quickly, I promise you."

They kissed, and for a moment he was disposed to forget all about his business meetings and go with her to Philadelphia there and then.

Later that day he was called downstairs and found a reporter from a Yiddish paper waiting to interview him. Nahum looked at him with surprise.

"How did you know where I was staying?"

"I didn't, but this is where all the big people stay, and here you are. I recognised you from the papers." And he held out a clipping from an English paper—*the* clipping—in which his ship had been described as a floating dungeon. The reporter asked him if there was any truth in the story.

"Do you think there is?" asked Nahum.

"I don't know. It's hard to make a living these days. My boss exploits me, I exploit my lodgers, everybody exploits everybody else. Why shouldn't you exploit your passengers? English papers have a high reputation here."

"So you think it's true?"

"What I'm saying is that, even if it is true, it's nothing to be ashamed of—a man's got to make a living."

"Look, I crossed the Atlantic on a Cunarder, but I went down to see conditions in steerage, and, believe me, my passengers are better off. They're less cramped, they've got a synagogue, kosher food, a dispensary. They feel at home the moment they're on board and the crew doesn't treat them as if they've done them a favour to let them on in the first place. I'm not the only carrier on the route. If things were half as bad as described, I wouldn't have sold a ticket."

"But everybody knows how you came penniless from Volkovysk only five years ago and that now you're a ship-owner and a millionaire."

"I didn't come penniless, I've been in Britain nearly fifteen years, not five, and I'm not a millionaire."

"But you give away fortunes."

"These things are comparative."

"You married?"

"No."

"Not married?"

"Not married."

"You must be about thirty."

"I'm over thirty."

"And not married?"

"You asked me before."

"It's just that I'm surprised. You don't find men with money, single at thirty—not in New York. You get many who wish they were single,

or pretending to be single, but honest-to-God single, with money—
you're the first. You won't be single long—not in New York."

Two days later, there was a long article on him in one of the Yiddish
papers so flattering and obsequious that he wasn't sure if he did not
prefer the slanderous piece in the English paper. The following morning, the advertising manager of the paper came around to ask if he
would like to place an advertisement.

Though Kagan had advised him against venturing into the Atlantic,
he had given him letters of introduction to various associates in New
York, and one evening Nahum was invited to the home of a Mr Kurtzhammer, a short, bald-headed man with a thick neck and a large
moustache, who lived in a large and elegant apartment on the south
side of Central Park with a large and silent wife and two glum daughters.

"So, you're a precipitate young man," began Kurtzhammer.

"Precipitate?"

"That's how Kagan describes you—'an able but precipitate young
man.' He doesn't want you to go into more ships."

"He doesn't want me to go into more anything. I think he's warned
me off every venture I have ever mentioned. I suppose that's his way
of reserving the right to saying I told you so if anything goes wrong."

"But everything has been going right—yes?"

"So far."

"And you want to go into the Atlantic?"

"If possible."

"That's what he means by precipitate. If I may say so, New York
isn't Leith. Everybody wants a berth in New York, and the difficulties—"

"Actually, I was thinking in terms of Halifax, Nova Scotia. It would
save at least one full day at sea, which is a lot for Jewish travellers,
they're bad sailors. Jewish passenger traffic, moreover, is erratic and
may thin out in a year or two, whereas there's a fairly constant flow of
traffic between Glasgow and Halifax. My idea is to use the Atlantic as
an extension of the North Sea run. I'd disembark passengers at Leith,
put them on special trains to Glasgow or Greenock and then straight
on to Halifax."

"Have you ever been to Halifax? It's Siberia."

"But no worse, I take it. Don't forget that nearly all my passengers
are from northern Russia. Canada is still a wide-open country—like, I
suppose, America was fifty years ago."

"Except that it's much colder."

"But they're used to the cold. Most letters from America that I ever see complain about the heat. There's a future for Jews in Canada. Doors are closing in Britain—"

"They'll be closing in America."

"But Canada is still wide open."

"It won't be, once you start bringing in Jews by the boat-load."

"Strange how discouraging bankers are."

"It's the job of a banker to discourage."

"And the job of the entrepreneur to ignore discouragement."

And Kurtzhammer turned and put a hairy hand on his knee.

"Which is exactly what I want to hear, young man. Before you leave New York, I shall find you everything you want. Now, enough for business, it is time for pleasure. Have you heard my wife and daughters perform on the piano? They are out of this world."

It was past midnight before Nahum got back to his hotel, and, as he picked up his key, an embarrassed clerk took him aside and whispered that "a lady" was waiting for him, in a tone which suggested that the lady was anything but. "She's been here all evening," he added.

Nahum looked into the lounge and found a tall, rather hard-faced woman advancing towards him.

"You've put on weight," she said in Yiddish, "and look prosperous, but otherwise you haven't changed at all. I don't suppose you recognise me."

He scanned her face for a familiar feature.

"I'm sorry—" he began.

"I'm Esther," she said, "your sister," and broke down.

He hurried her to his room and ordered some food which she ate ravenously, while he watched her with disbelief. She obviously was his sister. There were her slanted, grey-blue eyes, her freckled complexion, but she had verged on the plump, while here was a tall, gaunt, middle-aged woman, and all the warmth and tenderness had gone out of her face.

"I picked up the paper by chance and read all about you," she said between mouthfuls, "only I couldn't believe it was you. You were such a duffer, and shy and awkward and slow. I didn't know how Father could send you off on your own, and when he did, I was sure you'd be back within a year, robbed of the few rubles he gave you, but here you are, a ship-owner, a millionaire, a magnate."

"I've been lucky."

"Which is more than I have, but perhaps luck comes to those who deserve it. I can't complain. I deserved everything I got, and more. Father's dead, isn't he? I can even tell you when he died. It was on a

Friday afternoon. I was visiting Simyon—my first husband—in hospital, and we were chatting cheerfully when suddenly, for no reason that I could think of, I was overwhelmed with grief. I suppose you think I killed him?"

"This isn't the time to discuss it."

"I think I killed him, and by way of punishment, poor Simyon, who was as innocent as a child—who was a child—had a sudden relapse and died." She broke down again. "Why Simyon and not me? I don't know if there is a God, but if there is, He's got an odd way of going about His business."

"Where did all this happen?"

"Odessa. I was alone and pregnant."

"Is the child all right?"

"A little girl. You'll meet her."

"Why didn't you write?"

"What was there to write about? Who'd have answered?"

"I'd have answered."

"I remembered you as a callow *Yeshiva bochur* without sensitivity or imagination; I didn't think you'd be interested, or that you'd understand. I can't quite believe you're Nahum, even now."

"How did you manage?"

"I found friends—women with small children always do. My difficulties began in earnest after I married again, and instead of having two mouths to feed, I had three. I sometimes wonder if I married Arnstein in a fit of penitence, to punish myself for all the suffering I've brought upon others, except that I wonder what he's done to deserve the suffering I've brought upon him."

"What does he do?"

"Nothing, though he's tried everything. He is—or at least regards himself as—an *intelligent,* a thinker. He's an ex-*Yeshiva bochur* like yourself. Almost everybody I meet seems to be an ex-*Yeshiva bochur*— perhaps I married poor Simyon because he was an exception. He reads a lot and writes for two or three Yiddish papers, none of which pay him—in fact, he's half expected to pay *them*. He did a bit of peddling and set out with books under his arm and a pack on his back, and not infrequently lost both pack and books. Small boys and dogs used to chase him, farmers set their bulls on him—or he said they did, though I'm not sure he knows the difference between a cow and a bull. He got a job in a sweatshop but lasted only a day—he said he was too delicate for it, he had to have air."

"So how do you live?"

"I work, he looks after the child, does a bit of *cheder* teaching on the side, prepares the occasional boy for his *bar mitzvah*—and him a sworn atheist, though he claims he never teaches anything in conflict with his beliefs, or, rather, the lack of them. He says that *cheder* teaching is one way of doing away with religion, and that it's a vaccine which immunises the child against the onset of the real thing."

"What do you do?"

"Anything, everything. It's the high season now, so I work in a sweatshop, but I've worked as a waitress, I've scrubbed floors—how is that for your dainty, delicate little Esty, with her lace handkerchief and her leather-bound books, who was not even allowed to make her own bed?" She held out her hands. "Look." He remembered her hands, fine, long-fingered, silken. They were now large, calloused and a coarse brown.

"I've also worked in a laundry, and some of the dye seems to have stuck. Still, it could be worse. Once a beautifully spoken young man— also an ex-*Yeshiva bochur*—wanted to put me on the streets."

"On the streets!"

"Don't sound so incredulous. I wouldn't have been the first Jewish daughter who's ended up that way, or the last. Come down our way and you'll have to fight them off with umbrellas—so much for your *golderneh medineh*."

He went down her way the following evening, and what she said was substantially true. He was oddly intrigued by the sight of Jewish prostitutes. He had discovered, both from his reading of the Talmud and the behaviour and language of some of his contemporaries, that Jewish men were not always the souls of virtue, but he had been inculcated with the belief that Jewish women were chaste and pure. The behaviour of his own sister had raised the suspicion in his mind that the case was perhaps overstated, but nothing had prepared him for the phalanx of whores who lined the streets like a guard of honour and who chatted in loud, grating Yiddish voices; as he was looking around for his sister's apartment, he was pulled aside by a harridan who invited him to come upstairs, *lekoved Shabbos*—in honour of the Sabbath.

It was Friday night. Nahum had arrived in a cab clutching a bottle of wine and a bottle of vodka in a large paper bag, but he had alighted at the wrong door, and it took him some time to find the right one. His sister lived on the fourth floor of a crumbling building, and he had to hold his breath as he made his way up through an effluvia of urine, cat's droppings, stale cabbage, fried fish and the general odour of decay. Esther and her husband waited for him on the darkened landing and led him into a room illuminated by a single gas-lamp with a faulty mantel sending up a greenish glare which made everyone look like corpses. There was a small girl, who looked a good deal less than her five years, asleep in a cot in a corner of the room with rags thrown over her as blankets. The husband, dressed in a grimy white suit, was a slight figure—a little like Wachsman—with a pointed beard, abundant black hair and a pair of spectacles attached to a long black ribbon.

He stood for a moment with his hands behind his back, contemplating Nahum over the top of his glasses.

"So this is the famous brother, eh?"

"He's not famous," said Esther, "he's only rich."

"In this country, riches is the only kind of fame that counts."

Nahum was surprised to find no sign of preparation for the Sabbath— no candlesticks, no candlelight, no white tablecloth, no white bread, nothing to suggest that this night was different from any other. He presumed that Esther had abandoned her faith as had many other Jews of his acquaintance, but those Jews still somehow clung to the Sabbath— or at least the Friday night part of it—or the Sabbath clung to them, at least to the extent of candlelight and a festive meal.

There was nothing festive about the scene which greeted him now. The room which he entered served as a bedroom, living room, kitchen and, to judge from the number of books stacked in the corners and under the beds, study. There was a grubby cloth stretched over a small rickety table and two rickety chairs. Nahum sat at one end of the table and Arnstein at the other. Esther, propped up by a couple of pillows, sat on the bed. The sole source of ventilation was a steamed-up window which looked out upon a darkened courtyard, and which remained firmly closed because, as Esther explained, "You wouldn't believe the smells which come in"—and in any case it was stuck fast. Moisture climbed up the walls and dripped from the ceiling, forming dark stains on the tablecloth.

"A bit different from Volkovysk, isn't it?" said Esther.

"A bit."

"Father at one end of the table, Mother at the other, a regal pair."

"The damask tablecloth, the silver candlesticks, the candlelight."

"The *Zemiroth*."

"Which you always sang out of key. The chicken soup, the dumplings. Father would unbutton his waistcoat and drop off to sleep before the meal was over."

Her eyes filled up.

Their meal consisted of black bread, herrings, onions and potatoes. Nahum enjoyed it, especially the herring—something which Katya had refused to have in the house on the grounds that it "smelled of poverty"

—but the setting tended to take the edge off his appetite till he suddenly remembered the two bottles he had brought in his bag.

Arnstein regarded the vodka with approval, but the wine—which was sweet, heavy, kosher wine—with distaste.

"Are you expecting me to make *kiddush?*" he asked.

"It's *Shabbos,*" said Nahum.

"The *Shabbos* is something we left behind in Russia along with the pogroms—the one brought on the other. We don't have anything to do with religion in this house, and it's the same with our neighbours, our friends and most people we know. In New York, religion is a thing of the past—thank God."

The vodka went particularly well with the herring and onions. They took it in copious quantities, and Nahum soon discovered that the mellowness which he associated with the Sabbath could be had straight from the bottle without the benefit of religion, except that the devout Jew could have both his Sabbath and the vodka, and not infrequently did.

"You still religious?" asked Arnstein. "I suppose you are. Religion goes with money, money with religion."

"You think so? I find most people—when they've made a pound or two—feel they can manage without religion. Most religious people I know are poor, and most poor people I know are religious."

"It's religion that keeps them poor," said Arnstein.

"If you'll forgive me for saying so, you don't strike me as particularly rich."

"I'm another matter. I'm an intellectual, and we intellectuals have never cared about material things. As long as I've got my books and I can afford to keep the fire going under the kettle, I'm satisfied."

"You can't afford even that," his wife interjected.

"Coming to America has had one important effect," he continued. "In *der heim,* people could still dream. America, they all thought, would solve their problems, that their daughters would be in silk and their wives in velvet, that they would dwell in stone houses and dine on leviathan, that they would come in peace and go in peace and sleep in peace. Nothing of the sort. They have the same *tzores* here as they had there, even the anti-Semitism, except that here the police are sometimes on the side of the victims, so that pogromchicks can get their heads broken as well as Jews. And, of course, nobody's going to send you to Siberia for political opinions, but how many people in *der heim* had political opinions? They had *tzores,* all sorts of *tzores,* and the cure for them all was America, or so they thought, but now that they're here and discovered that even America is no paradise, their minds are at last beginning to open to the possibility that it isn't only Russia which is one dark prison, but that the whole world isn't as ordered as it should be, and they're turning to socialism."

"Were there no Jewish socialists in Russia?"

"Of course—there was hardly any other sort—but they were a handful, but here in America we've got—or are about to get—the masses. Jesus knew what he was talking about when he said that the poor will inherit the earth, except that they're not going to wait to inherit. They're going to take it here and now, and the place where it'll all begin won't be Russia, because in Russia they can still dream about America, but here in America itself, where the dreaming must stop." He paused to refill his glass: "So, brother Nahum, forget about your ships and your trains and your passengers and your through-tickets. It'll all come to nothing." He raised his glass: "To the revolution."

"I've got to put up with this every night," said Esther. "I'm going to get myself a night job."

"Weren't you something of a socialist yourself?" asked Nahum.

"Sure, I was, until I tasted poverty at first hand, since when I've become a capitalist *manquée*. In my case, listening to him would cure anybody of socialism."

She walked him down the stairs and into the street.

"You seem to be fairly cheerful in spite of everything," he said.

She laughed. "You've caught us in one of our prosperous weeks. I've got a job, and he picks up a few cents from tuition, but there have been times when there wasn't a piece of bread in the house. Nobody really knows what poverty is until they've got a child to feed and no food to feed it."

"Why don't you come to Glasgow?"

"I don't know if I like the idea of moving yet again, and I don't know how Arnstein would fit in. He's a sort of somebody here. He may not be able to make a living, but that is something which he has in common with a great many people around here, and he enjoys some standing among them. What would he do in Glasgow?"

"I'd find him work of some sort."

"Doing what? He's useless, not merely unwilling to hold down a job but temperamentally incapable of it. Everything he touches wilts. The best assurance you can have that the revolution won't come is that he's working energetically—insofar as he does anything energetically—for it. He's not only a failure himself, he inspires failure in others. Throw him in together with three or four good, hard-working men, and they seem to lose their sense of direction or purpose."

"Forgive my asking, but why did you marry him?"

"He was my ticket to America. I was a single woman with a child—Simyon and I were never properly married, in fact, we were never married at all—and I would never have gotten in without a husband, and a single woman without money and with a child in no *metziyeh*. There weren't many men who'd have leapt at the chance of marrying me, though quite a few tried to leap at the next best thing, which was another reason why I needed a husband. Arnstein used to frequent a café where I worked as a waitress. He was there every day and looked reasonably well dressed and fed, and, as he didn't seem to do anything for a living, I thought he had private means, perhaps even very private means. On the other hand, he thought he was saving me from 'a life of degradation,' as he put it. When he asked me to marry him, I told him I had a child, and he said, 'Well, that's all the better, I like children,' and he does. He's very good to my little girl and will do anything for her, short of finding a job. Still, I've thought of leaving him a hundred times, if only for the sake of the child, but I couldn't do it to him. He's my atonement, my private *Yom Kippur,* but there's no reason why he should have to become your *Yom Kippur* as well."

Nahum saw her the following evening, and again on Sunday morning. The day was moist, heavy and unseasonably warm.

The night obscured or softened some of the harshest features of the immigrant's New York. He found it at its worst in broad daylight, or what passed for broad daylight. People spoke of Russia as a prison, but there were always the skies, whereas in New York the very skies seemed hemmed in. There were rivers not far away, but again they were not like the rivers of Russia, where one could go down to the waters and paddle and swim and catch fish. Here the waters were grimy and threatening and did not look as if they would suffer any living thing to be in them or near them. In Russia there were fields, meadows, grasses, flowers. Here there was only asphalt and stone, and the very rivers seemed to be composed of a sort of fluid concrete. He did not know how Esther could live in such surroundings, and when, after further discussion, she definitely decided that she did not want to move to Glasgow, he arranged for her to move into a large, four-room flat in a better neighborhood with, as he insisted, "windows which will admit both light and air." He paid the first year's rent in advance and for the furniture and furnishings, but when, shortly before he left America, he called to see how they were thriving in their new surroundings, he found that they were still living in one room. The other three had been let to three other families, and Arnstein had had his beard trimmed and was wearing a new suit.

Kurtzhammer acted as Nahum's guide throughout his stay in New York and had drawn up a long list of people he thought he should see—

bankers, lawyers, shipping brokers—but Nahum had had to ask him to postpone some of the meetings while he coped with his sister's affairs. It was not until his sister was settled that he felt able to turn his mind to business.

"You're a good brother," said Kurtzhammer, "but a bad businessman. If family is all that important to you, perhaps you shouldn't start playing about in the Atlantic. It's a big place, the Atlantic, and it will need all the attention you can give it."

The one thing Nahum discovered in America was that it was a good deal easier to raise capital in New York than in London, and even where bankers were hesitant with their money, they did not accompany their hesitancy with a sermon. He liked the brisk, vigorous, go-ahead atmosphere of the place and even envisaged the possibility of leaving the Glasgow operation in the hands of Tobias and Colquhoun and starting afresh on his own in New York. They would probably have to curtail some of their European operations and recall Goodkind from Hamburg, which might occasion some difficulty, for he seemed to be happy there and was almost his old self again. The main problem, however, would be the formation of a new team in New York, and possibly the best way of going about it was to buy out an existing concern. The very fact that he could even consider such a possibility made him wonder if he were already banking on Lotie's fortune, though, given her mother's attitude to him, it was very likely that if they did marry Lotie would probably be disinherited, and he ascribed his visions to the exhilarating influence of New York. There were clearly many New Yorks. His sister had introduced him to one; Kurtzhammer had introduced him to quite another.

The day before he left for Philadelphia, Kurtzhammer introduced him to the head of a small shipping line whose interests, he said, were almost complementary to his own and who was as anxious to extend his line eastwards as Nahum was to gain a foothold in America.

"You'll make the ideal couple," said Kurtzhammer, rubbing his hands, "and it will be the ideal marriage. You should live happily ever after."

Nahum was not quite as sanguine, but he agreed that the idea had immense possibilities, but he didn't want to rush into too many marriages at once, and he told Kurtzhammer that he would have to discuss the proposals with his colleagues in London.

"But this is too good an opportunity to miss," protested Kurtzhammer; "cable your colleagues to come here."

"No," said Nahum firmly, "I want to consider this on my home ground."

He left for Philadelphia the following afternoon, and Lotie, distraught, white-faced and red-eyed, met him at the station. She was clutching a small case which she dropped with a clatter when she saw him, and she threw her arms around him and broke down.

"Lotie darling, what's happened?"

"Everything."

"But what?"

"The New York train's leaving in a minute, let's catch it, quick."

He took her firmly by the hand and led her to the railway waiting room, wiped her eyes, blew her nose and put an arm around her shoulders.

"Now tell me what happened."

"I told Mother I wanted you to come and stay here, and she was speechless for a minute. Then she said, 'But you've hardly spoken to him,' and I said we had spent hours together and that I knew everything about you that counts. She wouldn't say anything more till Father came home, and he said, 'Who is he, what is he, what does he do, who are his friends?' and I mentioned Kagan, which raised you instantly in his eyes—though I suppose it may have opened some wounds in Mother, and she said she had spoken to Kagan, and he'd told her that you were small and took chances and that you were too ambitious. That's the word which frightened Mother—'ambitious.' She thinks all ambitious men are adventurers."

"Would she rather I was unambitious and a failure?"

"I don't care what she would rather. I wouldn't want you to be anything other than you are."

"But you're close to your parents, aren't you?"

"I was."

"And you wouldn't want to hurt them?"

"I don't know, they don't seem to mind hurting me."

"Wouldn't it be best to go back and talk this out with them?"

"I've talked it out with them, shouted it out with them, screamed it out with them, and it didn't help."

"Screaming rarely does, and they do have a point. I am small, and I am ambitious, perhaps too ambitious for my own good, and we have only known each other for a day—if that."

"Are you trying to take their side?"

"Of course not, but I would hate to come between you and your parents."

"I don't want to have anything more to do with them."

"You're tired and distraught, you'll feel better after a good night's sleep."

Her eyes filled with a sort of tearful fury. "Nahum, I'm catching that New York train. If you're not coming with me, I'm going alone."

She slept on his shoulder all the way to New York with her face closely nuzzled against his neck. The carriage was full, but he did not feel in the least embarrassed, rather as if he was comforting a tired child.

When they reached their hotel, she insisted on sharing his room, and when he suggested that she might be sorry in the morning, she became almost hysterical. They finally compromised by taking a suite of adjoining rooms, and when he put her to bed she drifted into sleep, though only after many kisses and good-nights, and he half expected her to ask for a bedtime story.

Early the next morning he was awakened by someone nibbling on his ear and the presence of something soft and warm pressing against him. He turned to find Lotie beside him, and he rolled over on top of her.

"Not now, darling," she pleaded, "please, not now, I want to save it for our wedding night."

"Women who want to stay virgins shouldn't climb into bed with strange men."

When they came downstairs, arm in arm, they found a large, plump, bald-headed man waiting for them. Lotie tried to pull Nahum away, but when they sat down to breakfast, the man joined them.

"Lotie, my dear, won't you introduce me to your friend?"

She remained silent.

"My name is Althouse," he said. "I presume you are Mr Raeburn." Lotie kept her face averted but could not maintain her distance for long. He obviously knew how to handle his daughter.

"It's a pity we have to meet like this on strange territory," he said. "Wouldn't you like Mr Raeburn to spend a few days with us?"

"And what would Mother say?"

"Didn't you know? Mother's gone."

"Gone?"

"Aunt Frederika's been taken ill, and she's gone to stay with her."

"Aunt Frederika is always ill."

"But she's very ill now, poor thing, and we're standing by for the worst. Terrible strain."

Nahum travelled back in the train with Lotie on one side of him and her father on the other. He didn't know why, but he felt oddly like an escaped prisoner being taken back under escort.

When he got to their house, he began to understand why her parents had thought of him as an adventurer. It was like a pocket Windsor, including one wing which looked vaguely like the round tower, and he half expected to find a moat and drawbridge and even sentries in bearskins and scarlet tunics, but there was a small army of servants, all in livery—some white, some black—and he couldn't turn his head without finding one or two of them in attendance. Through the arched windows of his room he could see acres and acres of ground rolling away into the distance as far as the eye could see, all forming part of the estate. He had been thought of—and had even begun to think of himself—as a rich man, but this gave him an inkling of what real riches meant. What would Lotie and her parents think of his modest, red-sandstone terrace house in Glasgow and its tiny garden. He felt out of his class.

Lotie must have sensed his unease, for she came over to him and grasped his hands.

"Big, isn't it? Too big. Nobody is happy here. Edgar was nearly always away, but you'll like the gardens." The gardens overawed him even more than the house, for there were fountains and waterfalls and a lake and ornate flower beds laid out in successive terraces.

"Have you a garden?" she asked.

"Yes, but it's a tiny bit less formal than this."

"You're making fun of me, aren't you?"

"I never knew people lived like this."

"Kagan lives like this, and his grounds are bigger, much bigger, though less ornate, and his house is genuine Stuart—ours is only mock Plantagenet. It's Mother's taste. There's a whole history of wandering in her family, and they were expelled from here, there and everywhere. They had huge estates in Bohemia until they were thrown out by Maria Theresa, and also in Bavaria until they were dispossessed, and I suppose this is her way of getting her feet firmly back on earth."

"She must have big feet."

"Oh, stop making fun of me. You just think we're upstart Americans."

"Could you see yourself living in Glasgow?"

"I can see myself living anywhere, as long as you're there."

"In a small house?"

"I'd prefer it to a large one."

"In a *very* small house?"

"In a tent—as long as it has a garden. I must have a garden. I can't live without gardens."

"I have a garden, but I'd better tell you here and now that it has neither fountains nor a lake."

"A pity about the lake. I love waterfowl, and watching the water in the rain when it spouts up like tiny fountains, but Scotland's full of lakes, isn't it?"

"Yes, but none of them are in my back garden."

"I'll make one. Our lake's artificial, you know. Oh, and I can cook, I learned that in finishing school in England. Do you like French cuisine?"

"Is that what they teach American girls in English finishing schools, French cuisine?"

"And Italian, but I prefer French."

"I think I prefer Jewish cuisine."

"Mother would die if she heard you."

"Pity she can't hear me."

They both laughed.

"Why is she anti-Semitic?"

"She's not anti-Semitic, but she hates everything Jewish except religion. She's very religious or, rather, thinks religion is a very good thing. She's given away fortunes to temples and seminaries."

"But she doesn't like Jews?"

"Not the sort who like Jewish cuisine, but I'll cook Jewish cuisine if you want me to—I'll even eat it. And I'm good at household management, though Mother thinks I spoil the servants, which, she says, is always the sign of the upstart. You can't imagine how I look forward to being in your house and cooking and cleaning and making breakfast."

"And lighting the fire?"

"Lighting the fire?"

"I suppose you have the fire going on all the winter here, like in Russia. In Scotland you let the fire out each night and light it each morning. It's my daily chore on wintry mornings because my aunt, who used to look after me, found it difficult to bend down or straighten out. You wake in darkness in a house which is as cold as the morgue and put your feet down on a linoleum floor like ice. You then grope your way down the darkened staircase into the kitchen, which, at that hour of the morning, is the coldest room in the house, take out some old newspapers, put them down by the stove, remove the ashes from the night before and clean out the grate. You then crumple some papers up, put firewood on top, and coal on top of the firewood. You light the paper and blow with all your lungs so that the wood should ignite, and if the wood ignites, the coal eventually does, but sometimes the paper burns out before the wood catches fire, or the wood burns out before the coal catches fire, and you clear out the grate and start all over again. I've got it all down to a fine art, and as a rule the whole operation doesn't take me more than an hour or two, though if things go wrong it can take me all morning, by which time I'm in a mood to set fire to the house."

She listened with fascination and disbelief, her hands clasped under her chin, as if he were describing never-never land.

"I'd love that, I love rising early, only nearly everybody I know sleeps late so that there's nobody to talk to till lunchtime, and there's little to do with the mornings except stay in bed. I haven't done much with my life, really, I suppose because there's only about half a day to my day."

Nahum was aware from the minute he set foot in the house that Althouse was waiting for an opportunity to talk to him on his own, and he seemed to lurk in dark corners—of which there were a great many in the house—to pounce on him, but whenever he came near, his daughter's rapid footsteps or fluting voice forced a retreat, and they were not able to get together until the following morning over breakfast, for Lotie, whether she liked rising early or not, was still asleep.

"I need to leave shortly, so I had better get straight to the point. My wife's absence—as you probably surmised—has nothing to do with her sister's illness. She felt that if we had you under our roof, it might in a sense compromise our daughter, but it seems to me that, unless I'm very much mistaken, our daughter has already been compromised and that we are dealing with a *fait accompli*. My wife, if I may be direct, thinks you're an adventurer, and once she gets an idea into her head, nothing short of a pistol will get it out. Kagan told her that you took chances. Nothing wrong with that, chances are there to be taken, and I, for one, am not prepared to stand in your way. I don't know what obstacles her mother might put in the way, like cutting her throat, but supposing you should decide to marry, as I take it you will, would you plan to live in Scotland?"

"We haven't discussed it, but, as you know, my business is in Scotland."

"Beautiful country."

"Very."

"I was rather hoping you might be interested to join the organisation."

"Organisation?"

"My organisation. You see, Edgar, my son, prefers to be a farmer, but I was hoping my son-in-law might be interested to join me. It's a large concern—public—and I've good staff, but I'm always on the lookout for able young men."

"I'm not all that young, and I'm not sure if I'm all that able, but I've built up a sizable business in Glasgow, and I wouldn't like to give it up."

"Perhaps I should explain my position. I'm a reasonably comfortable man—some might say unreasonably comfortable—but all my money is tied up in the company or in trust, and I can't pull out a sizable chunk without endangering the whole stack. Now, if you were here in America, as part of the company, it would be quite another matter."

"But, if I may interrupt, why are you telling me all this?"

"Because Charlotte—sweet, adorable child though she is—is perfectly incapable of running a home without an army of servants."

"She's looking forward to running the small house I have."

He laughed. "Mr Raeburn—"

"My name's Nahum."

"Nahum, you obviously don't know my daughter. She's a child, and she thinks she'll be playing with some sort of enlarged doll's house. She'll need a substantial place with a carriage and servants. Such things shouldn't be too expensive in Scotland, and, of course, I'll provide them, but that's not the point. What worries me is your business. I understand you've been trying to buy a trans-Atlantic liner."

"A trans—! A *share* in a trans-Atlantic liner, a small share at that, in a small liner, or a share in a company involved in the Atlantic trade."

"But involving tens of thousands, possibly even millions of dollars."

"Involving a lot of money."

"Precisely, and there I may be unable to help you."

Nahum struggled to find his voice. "Forgive me, but did I ever suggest that I might need your help?"

"You misunderstand me. It's not what you expect, it's what people expect of me. What would people say if they knew that Althouse—who only has one daughter—had a son-in-law running some ten-dollar outfit somewhere in the wilds?"

"Mr Althouse, I had the impression that you were too big to have to worry about such things."

"The bigger you get, the greater the range of your worries. We're a quoted corporation, a public company. You don't know how sensitive the market is to every breath of gossip. There could be a run of confidence. I put this house on the market two years ago, and the shares began tumbling, and it looks as if I'll be condemned to live here for the rest of my life. Your life isn't your own once you go public."

At this point they were joined by Lotie, who kissed her father on his forehead and Nahum on the lips.

"What's he been telling you? That I'm a child who can't be trusted to boil an egg? Actually, one of the reasons I want to get married is to show them I'm not quite as useless as they think. But listen, I've been thinking. I want to have a party, an engagement party, to show off Nahum to my friends."

"But, my dear, I haven't actually proposed."

"You haven't?"

"No."

"Then isn't it about time you did? Don't you think so, Daddy?"

"You must keep me out of this, my dear, but I do feel that no one should feel compelled to propose marriage on an empty stomach. Can't you let Nahum finish his breakfast first?"

She returned to the idea of a party over lunch. "It's years since we've had anything like that in this house—and we can announce our engagement then. I look forward to seeing their faces, they all think I'm on the shelf, you know."

"Don't you think we should wait till Mother comes back before we do anything like that?" asked her father.

"But will Mother ever come back?"

And at that moment an outraged voice cried out: "Mother is back," and they all turned. Her formidable figure was quivering with fury. "So it's all settled, is it?"

"Oh, please, Mummy, please don't make a scene, it upsets me so."

"And do you think I'm not upset? If you marry that young man, I'm leaving the house."

Her husband put an arm round her. "My dear, this isn't the time or place to argue about such things."

She shrugged herself free. "When is the time, when it's all over?"

Lotie hurried out of the room. "It's no use," she cried, "it's no use, she'll never see reason. I'm not going to have anything more to do with her. She might as well be dead, for all I care. You'll be marrying an orphan."

Nahum tried to calm her. "When we're married and settled down and she's got grandchildren to play with, she'll be a different woman."

"Grandchildren? I won't let her near them."

He found the whole situation painful and embarrassing. He hated scenes, raised voices, recriminations.

"I love my mother, but you don't know how I hate her when she upsets me like this. I once nearly got into bed with one of the black servants when she upset me, only I was afraid Father would have the poor boy lynched. I hate her."

They were joined some minutes later by the father.

"I'm sorry about that," he said. "My wife isn't an easy person and she's been unwell, but I've called the doctor, and he's calmed her down."

"What with," Nahum wanted to say, "an axe?"

Nahum had been away from Glasgow for two weeks, and he had made provisional arrangements to return on the third, but he cabled Colquhoun that he had had to delay his departure.

He and Althouse had been able to convince Lotie that, as her mother was fairly seriously ill, they should dispense with a formal engagement, and certainly the engagement party, and should concentrate their attention on the wedding, arranging that it should take place in some six months' time, at the end of the year. Then somebody pointed out that the weather was always bad at the end of the year, and if they hoped to make use of the lawns and the gardens for the ceremony or reception, they should have it in the spring or summer, and they finally settled on the following June. In the meantime, Nahum and Lotie were involved in several meetings with lawyers because of the numerous trusts involving her affairs.

"I've been left money by my grandparents, uncles, aunts, but I never see a penny of it," she complained. "It's all tied up, and as far as I can see, most of it goes to the lawyers."

While these meetings continued, they stayed in New York, and at Lotie's request he asked Esther and her family to come to see them. Nahum had been apprehensive about the encounter, and his apprehensions were fully justified by events.

When Esther appeared, Lotie rushed forward to embrace her, but, sensing coldness, she immediately recoiled into a pained silence. Arnstein in the meantime tried to maintain a conversation.

"I hear you're from Philadelphia."

"Yes."

"Lovely city."

"In parts."

"Your people in business?"

"Yes."

"What did you say your name was?"

"Althouse."

"Althouse? The—"

"The—"

Which left him in awed silence for much of the afternoon, and he kept throwing glances in Nahum's direction which seemed to say, 'Some people always land on their feet.'

In the meantime, his daughter, a lively, irrepressible child with red hair and green eyes, ran riot around the hotel, and on the rare occasions when something like a conversation developed, it was cut short by the sound of crashing palms or breaking glass. Eventually, Lotie complained of a headache and rushed to her room.

"Not bad for a boy from Volkovysk," said Arnstein. "Who said America is no longer the land of opportunity? You going to stop in Philadelphia?"

"Why should I?"

"Because her father owns Philadelphia—though they say the mother has the money and the brains. He's as rich as Rothschild. You want an Atlantic liner? He can buy you a whole fleet—from the petty cash. You should see the store. It's not a store, it's a city. Everything you can imagine, anything your heart can desire, it's all there under one roof, and all you need is money. In fact—"

"Will you shut up for a minute?" his wife interjected. "They're not married yet."

"I haven't said a word all afternoon."

"Then keep not saying it." She turned to Nahum. "She's very pretty, but very delicate-looking. Are you sure she's in good health?"

"With all that money, she should have good health as well?"

"Will you shut up?"

"I said nothing."

"She's got her difficulties," said Nahum, "but they've nothing to do with health."

"She's also rather shy."

"She isn't, usually, but some people bring out the shyness in her. As a matter of fact, I thought you were rather unfriendly."

"Unfriendly?"

"Yes."

"Me?"

"Yes."

"What did you expect me to do, throw my arms around her? In any case, I wasn't quite sure about the precise nature of your relationship."

"I told you she was a friend that I particularly wanted you to meet."

"There are friends and friends, but, if you must know, I was not particularly taken with her. She seems precious and spoilt and used to having her way."

"What Jewish daughter isn't?" asked Arnstein. "Why do you think so many Jewish fellows marry *shiksas?*"

"I mean, if it's money you're after, she may be the ideal choice, but you know the old Yiddish saying, the wife with money costs money."

"Whatever she'll cost," said Arnstein, "she'll bring more than you'll ever be able to spend."

"Can't you shut up?"

"That's another reason why so many fellows marry *shiksas*. With a Jewish wife, you never get a word in."

"Money isn't all that important to you, is it? It wasn't to Father. I mean, you may not mind making it and having it, but do you actually want to *marry* it? That's making money the hard way. But look, if you're set on marrying her, don't ask my opinion—after all, I didn't ask yours. I'll come to the wedding, I'll bring a present, I'll even buy a new dress."

And she gathered up her child, who at that moment was plucking the tassels from an expensive rug, and fled.

Nahum felt relieved as he watched her receding back that he had only his sister in New York and not his mother. The following morning as he was packing to leave, a letter arrived from his mother to say that she was widowed again, that there was no one left in Volkovysk and that she was making arrangements to move to Glasgow.

CHAPTER XIII
MOTHER

NAHUM SOMETIMES WONDERED AT HOW LITTLE HIS MOTHER EN-
tered into his thoughts. Her marriage to Grossnass had certainly
induced a certain distance between them. She had not consulted him
on the marriage (which he felt she should have done), and he would
not have opposed it if she had, but he did not cherish the thought of
Grossnass as a stepfather, especially after Yechiel as father, and once
he had heard of the marriage, his contacts with her became more and
more attenuated. He sent her a brief and not very informative letter
on the approaches to Passover and the New Year, telling her how he
was doing and asking how she was, and she replied in kind.

Then, after his encounter with Esther, he sent her first a telegram,
saying that Esther was alive and well, and then a letter, describing
how he had come to meet her, what had been happening to her (omit-
ting some of the more squalid details) and how she was doing. He also
described the appearance and vivacity (though not the destructive-
ness) of her first and, so far, only grandchild, and while writing—as
if the discovery of the stray member of the family had somehow drawn
them closer—he went on to describe his own situation in rather greater
detail than usual, and the problems which had brought him to America
and which he was fairly confident he would overcome.

After meeting Lotie, he wondered if he should write to tell his
mother about her prospective daughter-in-law, but he found it difficult
to put pen to paper, as if it was too intimate a subject to discuss with
her and he decided to write to her after he got back to Glasgow and
the wedding arrangements had been finalised. He hoped she would
be able to attend, and if Grossnass should be unwilling to pay for the
price of a ticket, he was willing to send her one.

Her unexpected letter, with its even more unexpected news, had an
oddly upsetting effect on him, for it meant that he would be beginning
married life with his mother as a permanent guest.

He discussed the matter with Lotie, who said: "But of course we
must have your mother staying with us, where else? Only I hope she's
not like my mother or, for that matter, your sister—but it does mean

that we'll probably want a bigger place than we first had in mind."

"Mother'll only need a room."

"And a bathroom, and it'll mean an extra maid."

He arrived back in Glasgow unannounced, and the moment he set foot in his house he was overwhelmed by an odd sense of relief, like a traveller returned to earth after an excursion to some exotic but enervating planet. He settled himself in an armchair in his front room and gazed out the window at the terrace across the way. There was a sound of children at play, which faded as the sun set and the day darkened. It was a calm, unhurried universe. In the distance he could hear the clatter of trams. Familiar sights, familiar sounds, familiar people—a wholesome, ordered, workaday world. New York, Philadelphia, Castle Althouse, Lotie, all seemed improbable, unreal, like a dream. He had been perfectly happy in the world he had devised for himself in Glasgow—he thought so now, even if he had felt otherwise in America—and it seemed threatened by his encounter with Lotie. He didn't even feel himself to be the same person in Glasgow that he had been in Philadelphia. Althouse had understood his desire to remain in Glasgow and had reconciled himself to it, but Nahum felt threatened, not only by his wealth but by his size. Everything about him had seemed extravagantly large, and he wondered how long, with Althouse as his father-in-law, he would remain master of his own world. He could not wait to get back to his office and the familiar morning routine, his meetings with Colquhoun, his mid-morning coffee amid the dark panelling of Cranston's tearoom. The shoptalk, the visit to the docks, the conferences with the shippers and agents. He particularly relished the occasions when he was told that something could not be done, and he would demonstrate that it could. He, for example, felt that the ships were spending too much time in dock, and when he was told it could not be otherwise, he travelled to the different ports, injected a little extra money at strategic points, changed some personnel and proved his point. He had satisfied himself that a move to New York was not out of the question, but was this what he really wanted?

Mrs O'Leary had been in while he was away to clean the house and had restocked it with basic necessities. He made himself a small meal and was preparing for it, when there was a knock at the door and Tobias and Katya appeared. Both were in black.

"I saw the light on and was wondering if you were back," said Tobias. "When did you get back?"

"Earlier this evening."

"Well," said Katya, "aren't you going to kiss your aunt?"

He kissed her on the cheek, and she grasped him with both arms and kissed him on the mouth.

"You taste different," she said, "and look different."

"What do you expect him to taste of, vanilla?"

"I don't suppose you've heard," said Katya.

Nahum's heart sank. "Heard what?"

"Why do you think we're dressed like this? We've just been to a *shiva*, dreadful affair."

"Who died?"

"A fellow Volkovyskian—Miri's husband."

"Yerucham dead?"

"And how!"

"He died in a fire two weeks ago."

"And the *shiva*'s only now?"

"It was no ordinary death."

"Don't tell him," said Katya. "I don't want to listen, it makes me sick to hear it."

"He was in bed with two great, fat whores, and Yerucham—I don't know if you've seen him lately—was no skeleton himself. When the firemen got to them, they were a charred, molten mass. Their fat had fused, and they were uncertain where Yerucham finished and the whores began."

"A fitting end, if ever there was one," said Katya.

"I don't believe it."

"It's all over town."

"How is Miri taking it?"

"With composure," said Katya. "She may have wanted him to go in a less dramatic way, but you may be sure she's glad he went. There's a suspicion of arson, by the way, that's why the funeral and the *shiva* were delayed. Wouldn't surprise me if she organised it, and I wouldn't blame her if she did. His business was in a mess, but he was insured for a fortune. She asked after you, by the way, and when I told her you were in America, she said, I'll bet he'll come back with a wife. You *do* look different, you know."

"So would you look different if you'd just returned from America and you had an obstreperous aunt belabouring you with nonsense," said Tobias. "Come on, let's go."

The minute they were gone, he put on his coat and rushed over to Miri. She was in her dressing gown in the kitchen, making herself a drink. Her face brightened at the sight of him.

"I thought you were in America."

"I've just come back, and I heard."

"Who from?"

"Katya."

"Don't believe a word she said."

"But Yerucham is dead."

"He's dead all right, couldn't be deader, but I would take the embellishments with a pinch of salt. But tell me about yourself. Did you find what you were looking for?"

"And what was I meant to be looking for?"

"What does an eligible bachelor with a prosperous business generally look for when he goes to America? Did you find yourself an heiress?"

"I may have done."

"Which means you did. I suppose the wedding'll be in America, but I'll be there, provided I get sufficient notice. Can I kiss you by way of *mazeltov*?"

"That may be premature."

"I'll kiss you all the same." And as she did, her daughter Sophie entered and quickly withdrew.

"You know, I get the feeling that that child is spying on me. She moves around the house like a shadow."

"How have they been taking it?"

"It's difficult to say with her. She's been tight-lipped and silent, but then, she always is. She hasn't shed a tear. Alex was rather shattered, but Hector has become the school hero. Wherever he goes, the boys crowd around him for details, and I suspect that some of the embellishments you may have picked up from Katya probably originally came from him. Father took it badly, though. This all happened in Edinburgh, and somebody had to go over to identify the remains. I was perfectly willing to go, but Father wouldn't let me and went himself. He's seen quite a few things in his life, but I don't think he was quite prepared for what he saw there. I shouldn't have let him go, him an old man. When he returned, he was on the point of collapse. He was too ill to go to the funeral and hasn't been out of bed since. He worshipped Yerucham." She looked at Nahum fondly. "You must be exhausted."

"Rather less so now than I was, earlier in the evening."

"You've lost weight. You should keep on losing it, the lean look suits you."

"I was seasick most of the way across the Atlantic and didn't eat."

"You should cross the Atlantic more often. What's she like? Is she very pretty?"

"Very, but look, not a word to anyone for the time being—my own mother doesn't know."

"Not a word. I'm very happy for you."

He returned to an immense mass of papers and had brought another mass with him, including the merger proposals drawn up by Kurtzhammer. He had spent the Atlantic crossing, with a large jug of coffee by his side, going over them in detail. They seemed every bit as favourable as Kurtzhammer had suggested, but he regarded them with less enthusiasm than he had done in New York, and he ascribed his change of heart to his meeting with Althouse. If the merger took place, he would almost certainly have to move to America, and he feared that once in America, he would be sucked into the Althouse maw. He closed the file, put it into a bottom drawer for later consideration and turned to cope with his domestic problems.

His mother was about to arrive, and Lotie overwhelmed him with an almost daily deluge of letters and telegrams. The letters were long and affectionate, the telegrams short and reproachful, demanding why he hadn't written, and when he replied that he also had a business to look after and that he was searching around frantically for a suitable house, he would receive long and recriminatory letters which usually ended: "But, of course, if your business is more important to you than my happiness, then you needn't write at all, and I'll let your silence speak for itself," and there were moments when he was tempted to do just that.

The house was a problem. He had to have something which would accommodate Lotie, himself *and* his mother, and which would afford something of the spaciousness which Lotie was accustomed to. On the other hand, as he had told her, he had no desire to live in a Castle Althouse. Neither, she assured him, had she, which solved one problem. The other was the distinct possibility that, the merger aside, once he had his management problems ironed out—which might take three or four years—he might want to move to America. He retained his very mixed feelings about the idea, but he was aware of an indefinable force pulling him westwards (which possibly had something to do with his inability to see Lotie settled in Glasgow), and he thought that, in the circumstances, it might be best to rent a house rather than buy one, and he left the matter in the capable hands of Jessie Colquhoun, at which point he had to let Colquhoun into his immediate plans.

"I'm delighted," he said, "but why are you treating it as a dirty little secret?"

"Because Mother doesn't know, and I don't want her to hear it from a second-hand source." Though he wondered if one of the reasons why he was so secretive about it was an unspoken hope that it might never materialise. He could not understand his lack of elation. Was he not about to marry the girl of his dreams—a beautiful young woman of good family, graceful, accomplished and wealthy? He should have been walking on air; instead, he felt as if doomsday was in sight. Was he afraid of marriage itself, or was he worried about the revolution in his circumstances which would come with marriage? Or was it not the marriage which worried him so much as the thought of his mother coming?

His mother had originally planned to come on *The Tikvah* and he had reserved the best cabin on the ship for her, but the weather was stormy and she decided to come by train instead, and he travelled down to Victoria to meet her. Her hair had turned a silvery grey and it made her look distinguished, and she had put on a little weight around the chin and neck; otherwise, she had changed little since last he had seen her.

She stood back to have a good look at him. "You've lost hair," she said, "but the moustache suits you."

They breakfasted at the station and then took a cab to Euston to catch the morning train to Glasgow. He still had not told her about Lotie, and his secret pressed upon him like a badly digested meal. He thought he would tell her in the train home, but they spoke mainly about Esther; then she fell asleep, and when they reached Glasgow his secret was still intact. He wondered if he ever would tell her.

They were greeted at Central Station by Tobias, his two young daughters, Katya and Lazar, and conveyed home to a meal consisting of stuffed pike, duck soup and dumplings, smoked tongue, roast duck with potatoes and vegetables and stewed fruit.

"That was not a meal," said the guest of honour, "that was a wedding feast. You haven't forgotten how to cook, Katya."

"I might as well have forgotten, for all the use it's been. My husband is trying to lose weight, or, rather, I am trying to make him lose weight, and I could also lose a pound or two. Lazar's too busy to eat, and the girls peck at everything but eat nothing. Remember the meals Mother used to make? She'd think nothing of having twenty people at table."

"Mother had servants."

"And we were so poor."

"We weren't *so* poor. The poor don't have twenty people at table."

"We were poor compared to Yechiel or Grossnass, and very poor compared to your son. You've got a rich son, you know, and he hasn't got one servant, only a cleaning woman."

"What do I need servants for?"

"Servants aren't a matter of need, they're a matter of social standing."

Nahum, anxious to change the subject, asked his mother about Volkovysk.

"Now that I'm out of it," she said, "I don't know how I could have stayed so long. It's like shrugging off a long, long night."

"Is there anybody left?"

"Those too broken to move, and those too rich to want to move."

"Wasn't it always like that?"

"No. In the past—and, of course, I was younger in the past—but in the past, you somehow went to bed with the hope that things would be better in the morning. There was a feeling of continuity. You moved among the same people, the same faces. Now there are gaps everywhere, and gaps beget gaps. You can't imagine the feeling of desolation you get when you see people you've known for years moving in droves in every direction—Argentina, South Africa, America, Engand—but all moving. There have been no pogroms in Volkovysk, but you don't need a pogrom. What makes Jews move is the sight of Jews moving."

"But you wouldn't have moved if Grossnass had been alive."

"We were preparing to move, but it wasn't easy. Channan had so many fingers in so many pies, and there were the daughters to marry."

"Aren't they married?"

"Well married, thank God, but their husbands, nice young men from good family, were penniles. We had to set them up in business when Channan's own business was running down. It's been a difficult time. People buy as much as will see them through the day. Everybody's afraid to hold stocks. You may not believe this, but Channan died almost penniless."

It was clear from the faces around the table that no one did. She did not look like the widow of an almost penniless man.

Katya was serving tea when Nahum mentioned, almost in passing, that he was about to get married. The glass she was holding fell with a crash, and everyone cried, *Mazeltov*.

"I've been waiting for this for twelve years," said his mother. "Why couldn't you have told me earlier? Where is she from?"

"America, obviously," said Katya. "I'll bet she's rich. What does her father do?"

"He's a shopkeeper."

"What sort of shop?" asked his mother. "What does he sell?"

"Everything."

"Where are they from—her parents, I mean."

"Her father's from Vienna, her mother's American."

"American American?"

"Yes."

"My. Is she Jewish?"

"Just about."

"Do I have to get everything out of you like blood out of a stone?" she cried with exasperation. "Sit down and tell us who they are, what they are, how you met her, where you are going to live."

"He's going to be a millionaire and won't have anything to do with us," said Katya in a glum, resigned voice. And then she brightened. "Has she got a sister? Lazar could do with a rich wife."

Jessie eventually found a red-sandstone house standing in its own grounds, with a sizable garden and greenhouses and a good view overlooking the River Cart and the prospect of distant hills. It wasn't quite his idea of small, for it also had three public rooms, a billiard room, a conservatory and servants' quarters, but he could not imagine Lotie settling for anything smaller. He paid a deposit and telegraphed Lotie to come over and see it before he finalised the contract. He anticipated that she would take three weeks to a month to get over and left for Poland to cope with a crisis which had developed with Schwartzman in Danzig.

One afternoon Katya was having tea with her sister when there was a knock on the door. She opened it and found a tall, elegantly dressed young woman smiling at her apologetically.

"I'm sorry to bother you, but I'm Nahum's fiancée. You must be his mother, I can see the likeness." Katya was too voiceless to answer, and all she could do was to gesture to her to come inside.

"I know this is unexpected. I was in Paris seeing my couturier and I was going to come over eventually, but Father cabled to say you had found a house and I felt I couldn't wait. I had to see it at once. I should have cabled, but I thought I'd surprise him. I suppose Nahum's still in his office."

"He's abroad," said Katya, at which Lotie's face fell, but she brightened when she was introduced to his mother, and, after a moment's hesitation on the part of them both, they fell into each other's arms.

"You are a good-looking family," said Lotie. "All Nahum's womenfolk seem to be handsome, even his sister. His little niece is beautiful."

The house was a short distance away. They walked around to see it, and Lotie pronounced it "beautiful," and "exactly, but exactly what

I wanted. It's a storybook house, just out of my dreams." And she went excitedly around each room, making notes and measurements and discussing her plans with them. She said she would have a four-poster in the master bedroom, "the real thing. It doesn't have to be something Queen Elizabeth slept in, but it's going to be real Tudor." She found the garden a trifle small, "but," she added brightly, "perhaps we can buy the house next door and knock it down. But you mustn't tell them, will you, otherwise they'll push the price up."

They hoped to persuade her to stay on for a few days until Nahum was back, but she had to be back in Paris; otherwise, she said, her trousseau might not be ready for the wedding, and she left in the morning train. "I'll be back in a week or so," she said; "in the meantime, he can get me at the Crillon."

She sent Nahum a telegram to that effect, and he received it as he was about to board a ship. He caught the Berlin express instead and from there took the night train to Paris. When he reached the Crillon, she was gone.

"She must leave quickly," a clerk explained. "Her mother very ill."

When he reached Glasgow two days later, he learnt that her mother was dead. He remained at home long enough to have a night's rest and caught the first available ship to New York. When he got to Philadelphia, Lotie was ill in bed. She looked oddly sallow and shrunken. Her eyes were swollen.

"I didn't want you to come," she cried, "I didn't want you to see me like this. Why did you come?"

"Because I know how you felt about your mother."

"I killed her, you know. I killed her as if I'd done it with my own hands. We can't marry, now or ever, we were never intended to marry. Poor Mummy."

Nahum saw no point in trying to argue with her while she was distraught, and he sat patiently by her bed, holding her hand.

"I was the only one who meant anything to her. Father didn't care for her; he did at the beginning, but not now; Edgar hardly spoke to her. She only had me, and I abandoned her. She was in a coma when I went off to Paris. 'She's only shamming,' Edgar said, 'she'll be all right.' I killed her."

"It needs time," her doctor told Nahum, "give it another week." But a week passed, two weeks, and there was little change in her condition. Nahum brought breakfast to her on a tray, and she sometimes came down to lunch, leaning heavily on his arm, and in her calmer moments he mentioned that some difficulties had cropped up in Glasgow, but it never occurred to her to suggest that he should cut his visit short and get back to work. She obviously presumed that he could remain indefinitely.

Schwartzman had embezzled large sums, and it seemed to Nahum that he could not have done so without gross incompetence or collusion on the part of someone in the Glasgow office, and he was anxious to get to the bottom of the matter himself. But, apart from his business worries, he found his very inactivity depressing. He slept badly, rose early, had coffee, bathed and took a long walk around the estate before joining Lotie for breakfast, but he got little joy from her company, her conversation, or her tears. Perhaps it was proof that he did not really love her, but she was not the same person, or perhaps this was her true self and the Lotie he had fallen in love with was a persona she acquired on special occasions, except that his mother had also fallen in love with her, was enraptured by her. "So gay," she said, "so lively, so beautiful, so graceful, so regal. All you told me was that she was rich, you didn't tell me that you had found a queen. She glows, do you know that? The house lit up when she set foot in it." There was no glow about her now. She was lifeless and wan, wallowing in remorse and self-pity and even a trifle demented, and, instead of getting better by the day, as the doctor hoped, she seemed to be getting worse.

Althouse told him, "It's happened before, it'll happen again, I shouldn't worry," which was hardly a source of comfort. Then he vanished suddenly on what he called urgent business and left Nahum alone amid the echoing spaces of the vast house. He began to hate the servants, who, for some reason, regarded him with amusement, and he found them insolent and not infrequently drunk.

There were occasional visitors in the afternoons or evenings—some were relatives, others were friends—but Lotie, for some reason, chose not to introduce him, and they thought he was some sort of servant, and he began to feel like a servant, especially after Lotie had a bell connected from her room to his.

One afternoon Esther came on a visit, and he was so delighted to see what he called "a normal face" that he almost wept. She didn't stay long. "The girl's mad," she said, "and if you hang around much longer, you'll go mad yourself."

The next day was unbearably hot. He went down to the lake which was in a secluded part of the estate, took off his clothes and went in for a swim. But for the view of the castellated roof of the house, he could have been back in their Volkovysk *dacha,* for he had never bathed in the nude since; there was even a screen of silver birch trees running almost to the edge of the water. He swam on his front, on his back, dived, frolicked, went under water and, for the first time since he arrived, felt carefree and relaxed. Then, as he surfaced, he noticed that he was not alone. Lotie was also in the water, in her nightgown, with her hair bedraggled like a drowned Ophelia.

"Why didn't you tell me you were going swimming?" she said.

"I hadn't planned to go, but the morning was hot, and I went in on an impulse."

"And left me all by myself?"

"You never come down in the mornings."

"If I had known it was so hot, I would have come down."

"If you had let me open the curtains, you'd have known what sort of day it was. You cover yourself in darkness."

"You sound angry."

"I'm not angry."

"You look angry."

"Lotie, darling, I think you should leave Philadelphia and leave this house, you won't recover until you do. The house is a tomb."

"I was born in this house. My Mummy built this house. Uncle Willie was the architect, but it was almost her design, how can you call it a tomb?"

"It's gloomy enough as it is, and you never let light into the place."

"The light hurts my eyes."

"Let's go away, just for a few days, and you'll see what it'll do for you."

"I can't travel. I'm too unwell. I get dizzy. And I think you should put something on. I wouldn't want the servants to see you like this."

That night he received a telegram: POLICE ENQUIRY URGENT YOU RETURN.

He showed her the telegram the next morning and told her that he would have to get back to Glasgow without delay. He expected a scene—tears, recriminations, perhaps even a collapse—but she said to him in a calm, matter-of-fact voice which surprised him: "If you can't stand my company, then go, by all means."

"You know it's nothing to do with that."

"I only know that when Mummy was ill, Father never left her side."

"You saw the telegram."

"I'm sick of your telegrams."

Nahum felt there was nothing more to be said, and went upstairs and packed.

CHAPTER XIV
THE FIRST MRS RAEBURN

NAHUM RETURNED TO A BUSINESS AND DOMESTIC CRISIS. THE BUSI-
ness crisis arose out of a system of rebates, which he himself had
introduced for party bookings of twelve or more. His Danzig agent,
Schwartzman, a brisk, bald-headed little man with pointed ears, there-
upon grouped disparate individuals, who had paid the full fare, into
so-called parties and pocketed the difference himself. And then, finding
that he was getting rich only slowly through this piece of chicanery, he
entered into a conspiracy with the purser of *The Tikvah* to admit passengers beyond the ship's capacity on tickets which he had printed himself. The over-crowding came—or was brought—to the attention of the
authorities, and a police investigation followed. Nahum was able to
show that he was the victim of a conspiracy, to which the judge retorted: "A well-run company does not leave itself open to such conspiracies," and fined him ten thousand pounds for presenting a false
manifest.

But what distressed Nahum more than anything else was the fact
that young Cameron, Colquhoun's protegé, who was by then head of
the Leith office, had passed the purser's papers without querying them,
and, although they had no proof that he had been part of the conspiracy, there was little doubt that he was implicated.

"I know that he's able, quick and intelligent," said Nahum, "but I've
always found him a bit too quick, and, not only that, I always had the
feeling that he was laughing at me. I can now see he had something to
laugh at."

Colquhoun was almost broken by the discovery. "Perhaps we piled
him with too many responsibilities and exposed him to too many temptations. He's still very young, you know. Perhaps we should give him
another chance."

"I would," said Tobias. "If you've caught someone with his fingers
in the till, you've got a slave for life. He's an able youngster, he could
come in useful."

"If that's your philosophy," said Nahum, "it makes me wonder what
sort of legal practice you must be running."

"It's the sort of thing that happens when you grow too fast too soon," said Kagan. "It is fortunate that you failed to establish your trans-Atlantic link; otherwise, you could have gone under. I don't know what other plans you may have had to expand, but this should put them out of your mind for the foreseeable future."

The whole affair, including the legal fees, had cost him some twenty thousand pounds, and in an odd way he blamed Lotie for it all. Schwartzman had begun his career of embezzlement and fraud some years before, but Nahum prided himself on having a nose for irregularities, and he was convinced that, but for his meeting with Lotie, he would have been able to root out the mischief before it got to the attention of the police. As it was, by the time he got to grips with it, the damage had been done. But, as he told himself, this could have been worse: he could have had the débacle *and* Lotie on his hands.

In the meantime, he had his mother on his hands. When he returned from New York with the news that his relationship with Lotie was finished, she dropped into what looked like a dead faint, but she soon— too soon for Nahum's peace of mind—recovered, and she was as near to tears as he had ever seen her.

"The fact that she's rich is the least of it. You felt better for looking at her, she's out of this world. Losing a mother is a serious thing—although you may not think so—and she may be out of her mind with grief, but that's no reason why you should be out of *your* mind. Wait another few weeks, a month, and then go and see her. She'll want you. I know how a woman's mind works."

"But you don't know how my mind works," he said. He wasn't sure he knew himself, but there was no doubt about the feeling of relief, which, with all his troubles, he felt when it became clear that his relationship with Lotie was finished. Perhaps his mother was right, perhaps Lotie was out of this world, in which case he clearly preferred to be in it and was happy to be restored to his pre-Lotie workaday self. His mother, disappointed and aggrieved, began to sulk. She was a good sulker, and once she began she could keep it up for months and, if necessary, years. Her sister, a frequent visitor, joined her, either out of sympathy or contagion.

"We could have done with a bit of class in the family," she said. "You've let us all down."

When his sister wrote to say how glad she was that the affair was at an end, his mother retorted: "Who is she to advise anyone about anything? Do you want to do with your life what she's done with hers?"

The end of his relationship with Lotie finally brought to an end his Atlantic ambition, which convinced him that the two—whether he knew it or not—had been connected in his mind. He had thought himself genuinely in love with Lotie, but clearly her money had played a part in his affections. Her mother hadn't been entirely wrong. He, of course, hadn't known she was rich when he first met her, but it was fairly certain that anyone—and especially an American—appearing in a Kagan family group had to be very rich indeed.

One *Shabbat*, Nahum was in synagogue when he was startled by a commotion in the front row. Someone had fallen or fainted, and there was a rush of congregants trying to help, amid shouts of, "Don't panic," "Clear the way," "Let him breathe." Eventually an ambulance arrived, and Nahum was shocked to see the prostrate form of Moss Moss being carried out on a stretcher. He died that night.

The funeral was a large one, for Moss Moss's Gorbals house, which had been a meeting place for newcomers from the year he arrived, had continued as such until the day he died. One could tell at a glance the old settlers—with their bowler hats, their trimmed moustaches, their well-cut coats and their polished boots—from the new, and Nahum was clearly among the old; he was pointed out as such by the new—the local *gevir,* the penniless Volkovysk boy, who had been able to pay a ten thousand pound fine and continue in business as if nothing had happened.

Nahum felt deeply affected by Moss Moss's death, for the old man represented Nahum's humble beginnings in Glasgow, his struggling days as a shy, speechless foreigner; he recalled Moss's house, with its all-pervasive aroma of chickens, where his overworked, harassed wife dispensed imprecations and tea to all and sundry. With Moss Moss dead, something of Nahum's past had fallen away. He felt that he had lost his status of foreigner and exile, and, more than that, of a promising young man (which is how people had frequently described him). He had been chastened by the Schwartzman affair and had no further plans to expand, thinking that he had probably gotten as far as he ever would in business. He felt oddly middle-aged, and, indeed, he sometimes wondered (as did his mother) if he would ever marry.

Miri took her father's death stoically.

"We knew he hadn't long to go," she told Nahum, "and he shouldn't have been out of bed, but we couldn't keep him out of synagogue. I think he was always hoping to die on consecrated ground, and he had his way."

When she saw him to the door she said: "The last time you were here was when Yerucham died. You needn't wait till someone in the family drops dead before you come again, you know."

He saw her fairly frequently after that and made friends with her children and, during the school holidays, took them on outings to Edinburgh and elsewhere, and even on a short cruise on one of his boats.

"Seeing a widow is one thing," warned his mother, "but when you start taking out her children, she may begin to think things."

Nahum was aware of the danger but not at all perturbed by it. She was thirty, and, in spite of the trouble she had had with her husband and occasional bouts of ill health, she still had her lively personality and her coquettish good looks. She stemmed largely from the same world as he did, and, although her background was less cultivated, she had become a lady of taste and fashion, which he ascribed less to the influence of Yerucham than to that of his rich friends. He and Miri had, in their different ways, risen in life, and they had many similar experiences to compare, many mutual acquaintances to talk about, and their relationship did not involve him in a wild leap into the unknown. If they married, he would continue to enjoy the same rather pleasing world he had come to know. He liked her three children—a girl and two boys, who had come in quick succession and wcre now thirteen, twelve and eleven—and he was sorry when she told him that she was planning to send the boys to boarding school, for he had grown particularly fond of the younger boy, Hector, blond and angel-faced, who, even with all the good will he could muster (which wasn't much), could rarely keep out of mischief.

"I want them to be everything their father wasn't," she said.

"That's asking a lot of a child," said Nahum. "And what about Sophie, don't you want her to be a lady?"

"I need her company—though I'll send her to a finishing school when she's seventeen. I'll never forgive Father for marrying me off when I was sixteen. You'd have thought I was in the family way, or something."

"As far as I remember, you didn't protest. I couldn't imagine you doing anything you didn't want to do—even when you were sixteen."

"Of course, I didn't protest. Yerucham was a very good-looking man, and I wanted to have him in bed, and as far as I knew then, marrying a man was about the only way of doing it."

Nahum was mildly shocked by her remarks but felt encouraged to ask: "Did you never want to have me in bed?"

"From the day I set eyes on you, but after you'd been with us for about a year and never laid a finger on me, I began to wonder if you were up to that sort of thing. I mean, everybody else did—the pluckers, the packers, the drayman, the shopman, even the *Shochet*, Reverend Hochmay, remember him? A tall man with long arms like a gorilla. He would put an arm around me in a friendly avuncular way and manage

to grasp both breasts with one hand. What happened to him? I sometimes think he must have become an all-in wrestler."

"Was Yerucham a good grasper?"

"No, he was a pusher, or rather, a rubber. We could be in an empty
room with ten feet between us, but he somehow managed to rub against
me on his way in or out, and it's amazing the number of times he'd go
in and out, but after a week or two, he went beyond that and made a
frontal assault. Did you ever hear me call him 'Thumbs'?"

"Thumbs?"

"That was my nickname for him. He came up to me once and pressed
one nipple and then the other, as if he were calling for an elevator, and
every time he did it I put out my tongue, and it soon became a little
private game between us, but not private enough, for Mother caught
us once, but she's a bit short-sighted and confused, as you know, so she
probably didn't know what we were up to. Then we varied it a bit, and
he asked me to press his button."

"Which one?"

"I'll leave it to your imagination—and I shan't tell you what he stuck
out."

"He didn't!"

"He did—and asked me to hold it."

"The dirty dog, and then, I suppose, you went on to prepare chickens
without washing your hands. Good God, I'm glad I've stopped eating
chickens. But look, if you went that far, what made you think you had
to marry him before you could get him into bed?"

"What do you mean, 'that far'?" She sounded mildly scandalised.
"How far do you think we went? He stuck it out, he didn't stick it in.
I wouldn't have let him, he wouldn't have dared."

Nahum wasn't too sure about either point, but he leant forward and
pressed her nipples, not with his thumb, but his forefingers.

"Why didn't you do that fifteen years ago?" she asked.

"It's never too late to err."

"Well, not now, the children are still about. Can't we go around to
your place?"

"That wouldn't help, my mother is still about, but look, she's going
to her sister's for supper tomorrow night."

"Tomorrow's another day. You've started something and you're
going to finish it." She took him by the hand. "The maid's out and she's
got a lock to her door, let's use her room." They rushed upstairs on tip-
toe, like scampering mice, dashed into the maid's room and locked the
door. Miri threw herself on the bed, kicked off her slippers and pulled
up her skirt.

"Don't start with thumbs or forefingers, and don't start undressing. I'm too impatient for that. Come right in and quick."

Nahum was about to do just that when he heard the door-handle turning, then an Irish voice said: "Is there anybody in there?"

Miri let out an exclamation which he hadn't imagined could be heard from a woman, grabbed him by the lapels and rolled over on top of him.

"I'm sorry," he said. "I can't perform like this."

"Yerucham could. Yerucham did. He preferred it in the maid's room to our room. He even made me wear a lace apron."

They eventually adjourned to an hotel. As they were going out, arm in arm, Miri said to him: "Do you know what I was thinking while we were together?"

"That I wasn't half as good as Yerucham."

"On the contrary, you were much better, but then, I suppose, you've been saving it for a rainy day. I felt as if you were exploding inside me. Isn't it unhealthy to keep it back for so long?"

"Who says I've been keeping it back for so long?"

"Go on, you'll be telling me you've been keeping a mistress next. You, your mother and her, a *ménage à trois.*"

"I haven't been keeping a mistress, but I haven't been a saint, either," and, as if to confirm his claim, he tweaked her nipple.

"Be careful. Once I'm started, I can't stop."

"You could—or you said you could—when you were fifteen."

"Yes, but I'm thirty now. Let's go back to the hotel."

"Do you mean it?"

"Shall we have to pay again?"

"We might."

"Then it can wait. To think of it, I've got a house with about ten rooms, and you've got a house with eight, but we have to rent an hotel room if we want a minute of privacy. What a waste."

"What do you think your maid will say?"

"She'll tell Sophie—they're as thick as thieves, Sophie and her. You'll have to make an honest woman out of me now."

Three months later, they were married.

CHAPTER XV
THE GOLDEN YEARS

THERE IS A PICTURE OF THE GROUP TAKEN IN MIRI'S BACK GARDEN.
Miri, with her slightly slanted eyes, jet-black hair and slender
build looked like a porcelain figure. Nahum, beside her, with his black
moustache and thinning hair and large, dark eyes, looked handsome
and distinguished but slightly gone to seed, as if his best days were
already behind him. He was flanked by his mother in a large hat,
formidable, statuesque and glaring into the camera with displeasure,
as if she disapproved of the whole affair, which she almost certainly
did. Katya, on the other hand, was all smiles, and, at the end of the
line, erect, with hands down his sides as if on parade, was the skeletal
figure of Lazar, in thick glasses and a well-cut suit. He had just become engaged, which was perhaps why his mother was wreathed in
smiles. His fiancée, a plump, gap-toothed girl, pressed against his arm.
A white-haired woman with a haggard face, who looked as if she
might be a kitchen hand who had strayed in among the guests, stood
next to Miri. It was her mother, and next to her stood Sophie, with
large, dark rings around her large, dark eyes, her face downcast.
Tobias, standing a little apart from the rest with hands behind his
back and looking rather stern and downcast, completed the line. Before them, with legs crossed, sat four children—Alexander and Hector
and Tobias' two children by his previous marriage, Arabella and Caroline. Alexander, dark-haired and with glasses, and Hector, blond, with
one eye shut against the sun, both looked intensely bored. Arabella,
with a small face, all eyes and ringlets, scowled into the camera. Caroline, looking oddly like a miniature version of the bride, was smiling.

Nahum liked to quote a Russian sage who said that no one was
entitled to more than two or three golden years in a life-time. He would
claim seven or eight, from the year he married until the outbreak of
war in 1914. The marriage was not devoid of storms, but the family
grew, the business prospered and the world seemed happy.

The first thing Nahum discovered after his marriage was that his
business did not require nearly as much attention as he thought and

that his tendency to stay late in the office and spend half the year rushing around Europe might have arisen less out of the strict demands of the company than the emptiness of his personal life; his office was usually less bleak and less troublesome than what he had called home. He was now always home by seven, hardly ever worked at week-ends and was never away on business for more than three or four weeks a year.

The three children Miri brought to the marriage were joined by three others, who followed in quick succession—Yechiel Yaacov (named after his father, but who was to be known simply as Jacob), Victoria and Benny—and, as the family expanded, they moved out of Miri's old house in which they had begun married life to a substantial property with a large garden near Queen's Park.

Nahum's relationships with the children of the first marriage were at first not too easy, and he found it particularly difficult to amuse or gain the affection of Sophie, who, for no reason that he was aware of (unless it was something the maid had told her), had made up her mind that she did not approve of him and, while always obedient and polite, was always distant. The boys were rather less difficult. Alex, a studious youngster, showed a lively interest in everything and constantly plied him with questions about his ships and their various ports of call, and showed some impatience with his inability to answer them.

"Is it possible to run a shipping line and know so little about ships?" he finally asked.

"It's possible to run anything, as long as you can afford to hire people who know," said Nahum.

With Hector, he always had the apprehension that he was up to something he shouldn't be, for there was a constant glint of mischief in his pale blue eyes. Miri assured him that he was born with the look, "which doesn't mean he's *not* up to mischief," she added.

Miri had intended to send her boys to Fettes, a famous Edinburgh public school. Nahum wasn't entirely happy about the idea of sending them away at all.

"Why not?" asked Miri.

"Won't you miss them?"

"No—and, in any case, they'll be home often enough."

"What about their Jewish education?"

"Why, do you want them to be rabbis?"

"No, but I want them to be Jews. Alex will be *bar mitzvah* in another few months."

"We can arrange something with the local rabbi."

"It's not good enough. At least, if they go to a local grammar school, they come back to a Jewish home of sorts, but there they'll be away from it all, no *Shabbos,* no *Yom Tov,* nothing."

"Look, Nahum. Yerucham and I decided on this shortly after they were born, and whatever you may think about him, Yerucham was, after all, their father. It doesn't have to be Fettes, but they are going to a public school. He even left a trust fund to pay for it."

"I'm not worried about the money—"

"I know you're not, but they are still going to a public school."

It was Tobias who came up with the idea of Clifton, a celebrated public school near Bristol, which had, and still has, a Jewish house. Nahum and Miri went down to visit the school, and they were impressed with the buildings, the grounds, the general atmosphere, the staff and, especially, the Reverend Polack, head of the Jewish house; they enrolled the boys there and then, but they agreed to keep Alex back until after his *bar mitzvah.*

They had engaged a rabbi to prepare him for the occasion, and the rabbi, by a twist of fate, turned out to be the very man who had gotten the job for which Yerucham had applied, but Alex complained that he was a stupid, pedantic and ignorant man, and Nahum decided to take his Jewish education in hand himself.

It was sixteen years since Nahum had left *Yeshiva,* and he had made no attempt to maintain his learning since, but he was amazed how almost everything came back to him the moment he opened a learned tome. He was even more amazed at the pleasure it gave him. He did not for a moment believe it was holy writ given by God to Moses on Sinai, yet the moment he began to sway to the ancient chants, he began to feel the hair stand at the back of his neck and that he had been caught up in a mystical experience, and when Alex complained that he saw no point in it and didn't believe in it, Nahum replied that he wasn't sure if he believed in it himself, but it did something for him which he found hard to describe.

"Brings back memories, nostalgia?" suggested Alex.

"No, more than that, an oddly comforting feeling."

"You feel God smiling down upon you."

"In a way, yes."

"Can't say I feel it. I can't imagine the sort of God you've been talking about, smiling."

Nahum, even as a small businessman, had been fairly generous, and his munificence had grown with his means, though on occasion it could become a source of domestic friction.

"It's not the money I mind," Miri insisted. "I don't care if you give every *schnorrer* who comes to the door five pounds, ten pounds, I wouldn't even mind if you gave them the house, but I do mind being laid under siege. We can't sit down to a meal without having some snivelling old sod with a straggly beard and whining voice coming to the door for some little something, or, rather, some not-so-little something, to get his daughter married. If he has to go *schnorring* around doors to get her married, he'd be better off sending her on the streets."

"These snivelling old sods, as you call them, are the source of my fortune. Who do you think travels on my ships? German barons? English milords? American millionaires?"

"All right, marry their daughters, bury their fathers, feed their wives, but I don't want them here."

And to avoid further friction, Nahum appointed a young man, a recent immigrant, to act as almoner, and he arranged to receive callers at the office during fixed hours.

His commercial success and his generosity, even as a bachelor, had pushed him to the fore of communal life, yet the fact that he was still unmarried and therefore, in Jewish eyes, still not quite a complete person, could not be overlooked, and he had not been drawn into the inner circles of the commuuity. Once married, however, the last barrier to eminence fell away, and he was regarded as one of the lay leaders of Glasgow Jewry. Thus, when Alex was *bar mitzvah,* he felt compelled to rent a large hall and invite half the town to the celebrations. And Alex acquired, by way of presents, a library of Bibles, prayer books, hymn books, rabbinic legends, biblical commentaries, Talmudic extracts and other works of holy and quasi-holy writ, which remained unopened from that day even unto this. Four different rabbis had been invited to make speeches, another four pulled Nahum aside to ask if they could say a few words and a fifth, who wasn't called, thought he had been and addressed the large gathering—which grew noticeably smaller as he continued—for nearly an hour. Alex, who had prepared a speech, felt he could not add to the miseries of his guests and remained silent. He later claimed that any shreds of Jewishness which he might have harboured were purged by his *bar mitzvah.*

Nahum avoided office on synagogue boards but served on a couple of charity committees, and he became active in the Zionist organisation.

In 1909, he was a member of the Scottish delegation to the ninth Zionist congress, which was held in Hamburg. He was frequently on business in the city so that the venue was particularly convenient, but the congress itself was a disappointment. Much of the business was taken up with attacks on the president of the Zionist organisation, David Wolffsohn, a prosperous timber merchant with whom he had had some dealings and whom he knew and admired, and he could not see how an organisation so involved in in-fighting could achieve anything useful. He was particularly unhappy to find his idol, Weizmann, among the detractors, and, after hearing him attack Wolffsohn for running the Zionist organisation "like a business enterprise," he rose to speak.

"Perhaps," he said, "I should apologise for opening my mouth at all, because, like our esteemed president, I, too, am a businessman, not, unfortunately, as successful, but I try to see that by the end of the year, or at least by the end of three or four years, I earn rather more than I spend, and that if any part of my business still makes a loss I close it down and turn to something better. Is there anything wrong with that? I know that you cannot run a political movement on quite the same lines, but does that mean that it need take no account of practicalities? Our president, it would seem, has been too much of a businessman and too practical. If that is a sin, I wish that others were guilty of it, for in the meantime all I can hear on every side is wild dreams and wilder schemes."

He sat down to loud applause. He had not said anything original, but, unlike most of the other speakers, he had said it briefly and in decent English; the sound of his own voice and the applause were so uncommon to his ears that he found them intoxicating. He was also flattered by the attention he received from Wolffsohn, Ussishkin, Sokolov, Weizmann and other leading figures of the Zionist movement, and, in spite of his disappointment with the congress itself, he felt elevated by the experience. When he returned from Hamburg, he reported on the congress in a speech—in Yiddish and English—lasting nearly an hour. Later that year, he bought several acres of orange grove overlooking the Philistine coast near Ashkelon.

His business continued to prosper. There was a decline in passenger traffic, but he had anticipated the trend and had acquired two cargo vessels, which he employed as tramp steamers and which managed to build up a considerable clientele in the Baltic timber trade. By 1909, he owned three vessels totalling over eight thousand tons, and he could speak of his fleet without sounding absurdly grandiose. *The Tikvah,* which was still devoted to immigrant traffic, continued to do well and to provide steady business for what he called his "overland interests," which is to say the transfer of household goods and other baggage from Leith to Glasgow, and he expanded his fleet of vans to move goods to and from Glasgow and London and other towns; it was said at the time that no Jew could move ten yards without adding to the company's fortunes.

The company might have grown faster but for the restraints imposed by its bankers. Nahum was no longer as dependent on Kagan as he had been and was able to obtain extensive facilities from the Scottish banks in Glasgow and Edinburgh, but they were not as extensive as he hoped, and they always came with cautions and warnings which he found increasingly irksome.

"They're as bad as Kagan," he said, and Colquhoun suggested that they go over their heads.

"Over their heads?"

"To the public. There are very few companies doing so well with so little capital as ours. We've had our thin years, but we've hardly ever made an actual loss, and we're an established successful firm. Why not, instead of going cap in hand to the bankers every time we need a penny, go straight to the public?"

"You know, I never thought of that. You've got yourself a Jewish brain."

"Not at all, it's you who should get yourself a Scottish one."

When Nahum brought the idea to Kagan, the latter claimed that he had been pondering over such a scheme himself.

"But, of course," he added, "it would be premature to go to the market right now."

"But I need the money right now."

"Don't we all, but supposing, for argument's sake, you raised a million, it doesn't mean you'd have a million available for use. You'd want to retain at least half the shares to assure control of the company."

"Not if the rest were sufficiently scattered," said Colquhoun.

"That's playing with fire. Scattered shareholders can get together and often do. You are, if I may say so, too stretched, far too stretched, to go public at the moment. The balance sheet doesn't look healthy."

"It's never looked healthier," said Nahum.

"Income is healthy, but all your assets are tied up, and you have no reserves for unforeseen contingencies. We live in a troubled world with small wars here, there and everywhere, which could turn into big ones. And then there's the small matter of the mishap."

"The mishap?"

"*The* mishap. The Schwartzman affair."

"That was years ago, we took that in our stride. Nobody suggested that we were being dishonest."

"It's easier to forget dishonesty than negligence. If you were to wait a year or two, it would fade further from the memory and allow reserves to pile up; you'll get a better price, a much better price. At the moment, it looks as if you actually need the money, and you must never give the market a suspicion of need."

"What you are trying to tell me is that I should go to the market only when I can manage without."

"It almost comes to that."

"I would rather go now."

Tobias tended to agree with Kagan, he nearly always did.

"What would you expect from a lawyer?" said Colquhoun. "Caution clogs their bloodstream."

"Better caution than whisky," said Tobias. "We're an odd ragbag of things. We don't know if we're shippers, carters, depositors, property men. If we're short of cash, we should sell off some of our side interests and—"

"Our side interests give a better return on capital than our main ones," said Colquhoun.

"Then sell off the main interests and reorganise your assets. That's the whole point I'm making. We just wouldn't look good on a prospectus."

"When somebody reads a prospectus, he looks at the profits. He's not interested where they're coming from."

"Institutions are interested. They don't like ragbags."

"They like profitable ragbags," said Nahum. "I think we should risk it."

"But why? You've got assets you haven't even touched. You've got freeholds scattered across Europe which you could convert into ready cash and then lease back from the buyers. To me this is just a bit of vanity. You want to go public because you're impatient to become a public figure and to head a publicly quoted company. That's all it is, vanity."

"I'm still prepared to risk it."

"I don't know why the hell you want me on the board if you don't take my advice."

"Because he doesn't know if he's doing the right thing till he's sure you're against it," said Colquhoun.

There were further arguments about at what point to fix the price.

"It isn't a company with pedigree," said Kagan; "we mustn't expect too much."

"There's no pedigree better than a good profit record," said Colquhoun; "we don't have to give the shares away."

Kagan's view, however, prevailed, though Colquhoun was proved right by events, for the issue was oversubscribed, and the shares went to a sizable premium.

They had a small reception to celebrate the result at which the whisky flowed fairly freely, and in the course of it Colquhoun danced over to Tobias and said: "And whaur's your ragbag noo?" at which Tobias whipped off his glasses, which Nahum recognised as a sign of wrath, and walked out.

He came around to see Nahum later in the evening and told him he was resigning from the board.

"You're doing what?"

"You heard, I'm resigning from the board."

"Just because you had words with Colquhoun?"

"I had more than words. I can't take that drunken yok."

"He was entitled to a drink. The whole idea was his, and he saw it through from beginning to end."

"He's an anti-Semite, you know that, don't you?"

"Now look here, Tobias, there is a limit to the nonsense I'll take, even from you."

"He makes little digs at Jews all the time, you haven't even noticed."

"He makes digs at lawyers—"

"He makes digs at Jewish lawyers."

"Most of the lawyers we deal with happen to be Jews. I'd trust my life to the man. I'd have gotten nowhere without him."

"*Nowhere?* You're one of those Jews who feel flattered that *goyim* talk to them at all. You picked him up from nowhere. I remember when he joined the firm. He was wearing a second-hand suit and looked as if he hadn't eaten for a week. He was nothing. Now he has a house in Kelvineside, a place in the country and a yacht, and he's talking of buying himself a car."

"And what was I when I started? What was Goodkind? He's earned everything he's got, and more."

"I'm much older than you, Nahum, and more experienced, and I understand people better. Mark my words, one day you'll regret you ever set eyes on that drunk."

Nahum was half hoping that his spirited defence of Colquhoun might induce Tobias to make good his threat of resignation. He was sorry he had ever taken him onto the board, for, quite apart from the clash of personalities, his advice was nearly always negative. He was useful when Nahum wanted support for not proceeding upon a certain course, but whenever they sought to embark on anything even mildly hazardous, he could produce a hundred reasons why they shouldn't. When Nahum first knew him, he had always given the impression of brightness and alacrity, but he had lost both. The death of his wife was possibly one cause; his marriage to Katya was perhaps another. He was also nearly sixty, and although Nahum had been brought up to think that years meant wisdom, he was discovering too many exceptions to the rule to believe it, for he was finding Tobias deficient even as a lawyer, and were it not for the fact that he was now also his uncle, he would have removed him from the board and taken on a new lawyer.

Sometime later he heard that Lazar, who had been made a partner, had left Tobias to set up on his own and had taken some of his most important clients with him. The news didn't surprise Nahum. It nearly killed Tobias, and even Colquhoun felt drawn to commiserate with him

Lazar had married about a year before, and Katya ascribed the move to the influence of her daughter-in-law Hilda, who, she said, "was scheming and ambitious and was driving the poor boy in all directions at once."

A few months after Goodkind-Raeburn became a public company, Nahum received a letter in a familiar hand, which he at first hesitated to open. It was from Lotie:

Dearest Nahum,

Congratulations on going public. Kagan said you have the Midas touch and advised me to buy your shares, which I did, thousands and thousands of them, so that I must almost own you by now. What is it like to make your first million? I suppose one day you'll arrive in New York on your own trans-Atlantic liner.

I suppose you've heard that Richard Kagan and I are to marry.

Nahum had met Richard, a very tall, very haughty, very silent figure, with bushy, black eyebrows, who worked in his father's bank. He couldn't recall ever exchanging a word with him.

They married a few months later, and he received the news with relief as if, while single, she was an unexorcised spirit who might one day return to haunt him, for there had, in fact, been no formal break between them. He had walked out without a word, and for all he knew she could still have been waiting for him to return. The gay tone of her letter had reassured him, but he was not entirely at ease until she married.

She sent him and his mother invitations to the wedding, and, much to his surprise and perhaps even his alarm, his mother decided to accept.

"I never knew you felt so close," he said, "you only met her once."

"The once was enough. I've felt closer to her than I feel to anyone. And besides, I want to see Esther before I die."

She stayed away for a month and came back claiming that she had never had such an exciting time in her life, but looking strangely distressed, and finally, when she was alone with Nahum, she broke down and cried.

"It was like a royal wedding," she sobbed. "Lotie was like a queen."

"But what's that to cry about?"

"I saw her coming up the aisle, amid the assembled guests—the cream of American society, the cream. I couldn't help thinking that if you hadn't been so stupid you could have been the man on her arm, and she could have been my daughter-in-law. Instead, you marry the daughter of a poultry dealer, a middle-aged widow with three children."

Her voice gave way to a flood of tears, but she gradually collected herself. "And your sister's as bad. If it wasn't enough to marry Simyon, she makes things worse by marrying that nothing. She's running a hotel and making a good job of it, but she's making the money and he's spending it. I don't know where I got such children."

Some weeks later, Lotie wrote that they would be in Scotland and that they hoped to come in to see them, and one evening, when they were about to sit down to dinner, she appeared unexpectedly on her own (Richard was nursing a cold in their hotel). Nahum shook hands with a fully extended arm, as if afraid to let her come too near, but she fell upon his mother's neck, and they were locked for a time in what seemed to be an inextricable embrace. Miri watched the scene with a smiling mouth and anything but smiling eyes.

They asked her to stay to dinner, but she said she had to hurry back to poor Richard.

Miri hardly touched her food when they finally sat down to dinner, which Nahum knew was a sign that she would hardly sleep when they got to bed, and, in fact, she remained silent the whole evening until they were in bed. Then, when the lights were out, she said: "She's very beautiful, isn't she?"

"Who?"

"You know very well who. I can't understand why you didn't marry her."

"It's a bit late to ask that after four years of marriage and three children."

"But why not?"

"Why not what?"

"Why didn't you marry her?"

"It didn't work, we weren't happy with each other."

"You looked happy enough with each other earlier this evening."

"I'm not married to her now, am I?"

"You weren't married to her then, were you?"

"Look, she's a happily married woman, and I'm a happily married man, it's all over."

"Is it? You should have seen the way she looked at you. She'll be back." And with that, she turned over on her side and began sobbing quietly in the darkness.

The three children by Miri's first marriage were so different in appearance, character and temperament that it was difficult to believe they had the same parents.

Sophie was generously built, with long, jet-black hair and large, kindly, almost beatific eyes which made her look like a well-fed madonna, but she radiated a feeling of simmering resentment which often puzzled Nahum. She was academically brilliant, which both he and Miri regarded as a mixed blessing in a daughter, and had immense physical energy, but, as Hector put it, "Nobody is perfect, and the trouble with Sophie is that you couldn't keep her out of synagogue, or her nose out of prayer books. She not so much worshipped God as laid siege to Him, and must have forced Him back into His uttermost Heavens." She was, he added, "good to look at, but there was too much of her to take in at a glance." She also taught herself Hebrew and even began to study the Talmud, a book traditionally closed to womankind. If Nahum watched her with wonder, Miri watched her with alarm—for a girl to study the Talmud was, in her eyes, tantamount to growing a beard. "She'll never marry if she goes on like this," though, in fact, as she grew older, she had to thrust her way through an admiring throng of eligible bachelors after Saturday morning service.

"They're all after my money, or, rather, your money," she told Nahum. "If my prayers were answered, we would be poor tomorrow."

"Be careful with your prayers," her mother warned. "You never know with God, He could be listening."

"What makes you so sure they're after your money?" said Nahum.

"What then, my looks?"

"Why not?"

"There's nothing wrong with being after money," said Miri, "as long as you've got something to offer yourself. Take young Samuelson, a good-looking boy and a medical student. In another year he'll be a doctor."

"And in another two years he'll think Father'll set him up in practice. Or young Michaelson, a lawyer, who thinks Father will buy him a partnership, or young Steinman, who has a small business and who thinks Father might buy him a big one, or young Shulman—"

"A picture of a boy, from a good family—"

"But who is nothing in particular but who thinks Father will take him into business. They're all the same. They look at me and see money-bags."

"You're not doing yourself justice," said Nahum. "You're intelligent, you're well educated, you're of good—"

"Good family," she chorused. "That's all I hear, good families. What's so good about our family—or any of the other so-called good families? What was my grandfather, a broken-down poultry dealer? And what was my father? Or shouldn't I ask? It seems to me your definition of a good family is somebody who's been able to make a bit of money without landing in jail—and if they've made enough money, it doesn't even matter if they've been in jail!"

Sophie's religious phase, which began when she was about fourteen, did not survive much beyond her eighteenth birthday, and when she joined Glasgow University she stopped going to synagogue, stopped praying, abandoned her Jewish studies, and it was as much as they could do to persuade her to get out of her workaday clothes before she came down to dinner on a Friday evening.

Nahum was inclined to ascribe the cause to the influence of University, but her younger brother Alexander (or Alex, as he was generally known), explained that the process had begun earlier when Sophie found that she could not penetrate the Talmud on her own and had sought the guidance of a young rabbi, who sympathised with her efforts but said he could not spare the time to help her and had passed her on to an older colleague. The older colleague, who hardly spoke English, at first thought she had some sort of spiritual problem, but when she went on to explain in Hebrew that she actually wanted to study the Talmud, he rose, led her by the elbow to the door and said: "Go home, my dear, get married, have children, and leave the Talmud to your brothers."

That experience, said Alex, began a chain of thought which eventually led her out of religion.

Alex, tall, lean and unsmiling, was both brilliant and industrious, and there was hardly a year in which he did not come home with prizes testifying to his academic excellence. "The rest of us," said Hector, "were never quite forgiven for not being Alex."

Miri took immense pride in him but wished that he took more pride in his appearance and showed a little more life. "He's so scruffy and dried up," she said, but Nahum found in him all that one could wish for in a child. He himself had left school at thirteen and spoke of Alex as 'my University," for he found it an education to talk to the boy. Alex gave an impression of extreme physical frailty, as if he might be blown over by any passing wind. He wore large spectacles which made him look owlish, though he had the build and jerky movements of a stork. He had no friends and was often set upon in the playground or street (Sophie once came to his aid and fell upon his tormentors with such fury that for years later they fled at the sight of her).

Nahum was sorry that he couldn't persuade Miri not to send the boys away, for he missed Alex and feared he would be bullied (which he was —until he was joined by Hector), but he was frequently home on holiday, and Nahum took him to the office and introduced him to Colquhoun and the staff, and to Leith to visit his ships as they came into harbour. They were in Leith one morning when *The Tikvah* docked, and they stopped to watch the passengers disembark.

"They look so pale and crumpled, as if they've never seen the sun," said Alex.

"Well," said Nahum, "that was me, twenty years ago."

"And is that how you came, with a few parcels under your arm?"

"Almost."

"And you built up this whole organisation from scratch?"

"Well, Father left me a bit of money, though by the time he died, I already had a sizable business. With his help, things went a bit quicker than they might have done. Do you know the name Ballin?"

"Ballin?"

"Albert Ballin."

"Isn't he the head of the Hamburg-America line?"

"His father was a Danish Jew who settled in Hamburg and built up a small shipping business—well, not so small, it was, in fact, a bit bigger than mine. He was also mainly engaged in immigrant traffic, but his son, using the father's company as a base, built it into something much larger and eventually absorbed Hamburg-America."

"And are you hoping to do something similar?"

"No, not myself. I'd be content with the role of Ballin's father, but if you would like to come into the company, you could be Ballin himself."

When he was eighteen, Alex won a scholarship in oriental languages to Magdalen College, Oxford. He asked his parents to visit him, and they travelled down one week-end in December. It was a cold afternoon with the sun a reddish blur in the gathering mists, and they had tea in front of a blazing fire in his rooms overlooking the park. They then took a walk through the park, with Alex giving a running commentary in his rapid, staccato voice on the great men who had stayed in the college and pointing out the rooms they had occupied. Suddenly he fell silent. It had grown dark. There were church bells ringing in the distance, and from the chapel there came the sound of choir practice. It was some three weeks before Christmas, and they were singing carols. The voices, floating on the cold night air, seemed disembodied. Nahum thought he had never heard such a heavenly sound in his life, and at that moment he felt as if he were being grafted to the very soul of England.

Hector, the third of Miri's children, was an enigma. There was, first of all, his appearance. He was tall, ash blond (which made him look prematurely grey in photographs), with blue eyes, chiselled features and a particularly handsome profile with a tiny cleavage at the tip of his nose. There was no one else in the family who looked remotely like him, and it was jokingly suggested that he was a changeling, to which his mother added, only half jokingly, "and I got the worst of the bargain." She once said, "The trouble with Hector is that he thinks he can get anywhere and do anything with good looks." To which Nahum added: "And what worries me is, he may be right."

Hector was an instant success among his contemporaries at Clifton without being particularly good at anything except English, tennis and amateur dramatics. He was soon being invited at week-ends to the stately homes of his newly found friends. His parents saw little of him, and the Reverend Polack noted sadly that "his adherence to Jewish observance leaves something to be desired," to which Hector replied, "My sister atones for my sins," though by then she was doing nothing of the sort and was well past her religious phase.

One summer, the whole family was invited to the wedding of a fellow immigrant who had become a prosperous merchant. It was a fairly lavish affair, with a dinner followed by a ball, and Nahum noticed in the course of the evening that Hector, who was in evening dress and joking about something with Katya, suddenly leaned over and pressed her nipples.

Nahum could almost see the ghost of Yerucham as this happened. He had always worried what effect heredity might have on the children, and he presumed their lack of religiousness was one of them. Now he discovered another, and he immediately hauled the boy out of the room and demanded to know what he meant by his behaviour.

Hector blinked at him. "What behaviour?"

"You know very well what behaviour. What do you mean by pushing Aunt Katya on—on—by pushing Aunt Katya?"

"Oh, that. I was just illustrating a principle."

"Then don't illustrate your principles on Aunt Katya's bosom. You're drunk."

And Hector, whose voice was slurred, did, in fact, look rather the worse for drink. Nahum thought that he had seen signs of inebriation in him before. Now he was sure of it, and he ascribed it all to the influence of his non-Jewish friends at Clifton.

He discussed the incident at length with Miri and wondered whether they should withdraw him from the school.

"But he's only sixteen, and I haven't known him to behave like this before. I suppose he's beginning to grow up."

"Beginning? If this is only a beginning, can you imagine where it'll end."

"These tight dresses Katya wears, she asks for it. She's forgetting her age."

"I don't feel responsible for Katya's behaviour, I do for his. He was tottering on his feet, his voice was slurred, he was *drunk*. Is that what we send him to Clifton for, to teach him to drink?"

The younger children, as yet, posed no problem. Jacob—or Yechiel, as Nahum still called him—showed a deep religious streak which he might have inherited from his grandfather and would often be late for breakfast because he spent half an hour over his morning prayers. Hester, an elderly servant who used to work for Moss Moss as a plucker and now looked after the younger children, called him her little saint. Miri might have worried about it, but the precedent of Sophie made her confident that he would grow out of it. His sister, Victoria— dark-haired, blue-eyed and with an upturned nose—on the other hand, threatened to turn into a female Hector. Nahum insisted that all the six children were the same to him, but Victoria—or Vicky, as everyone called her—could twirl him around her little finger, and she had only to whisper a wish into his ear to have it fulfilled. It was at her behest that he bought his first car. He had toyed with the idea of doing so, but he did not have the time to learn to drive and was a trifle nervous of machinery and machines, so that getting a car meant also getting a chauffeur/mechanic, and he was not convinced that the expense would be justified, until Vicky complained.

"But *everybody* has a car," and she mentioned a neighbour who had recently acquired one. "And he has only two shops," she added, "while *everybody* knows that you're practically the richest man in Glasgow."

"You're going to have another Esty on your hands," his mother warned. Some outhouses were converted to make room for the car, the chauffeur and his wife, and a few months later the car arrived, a gleaming black monster with brass trappings. Miri and the other womenfolk watched apprehensively through the kitchen window, half afraid that it might run amok while the chauffeur took it through its paces. A few weeks later, Nahum nearly lost the car and his three younger children when Vicky, with her two brothers seated at the back, climbed into the driving seat, lowered the brake and the car started moving slowly downhill towards the main road. The driver, however, came into view just then and managed to dive into the driving seat and stop it.

"He dared me," said Vicky, pointing to her younger brother, a plump, breathless little lad who wouldn't have known what a dare was.

Katya's two step-children, Arabella and Caroline, also spent more time in Nahum's house than their own, especially when the boys were on holiday from Clifton, and they not infrequently brought their friends, and at week-ends the place was over-run with young people; Nahum would sometimes stand on the terrace and watch them—some on the tennis court, some on the swings, some playing tag or treasure-hunt in the shrubberies—and glow with a sense of achievement which even the sight of his ships (or the returns from them) failed to give him. He could sometimes hear his mother slam her bedroom window against the noise, but the sound of children at play, echoing on the balmy summer air, was music to his ears. They had played the same way in Volkovysk—he, Lazar, Uncle Sender's children and others—but every time there was some unexpected sound, the thud of hooves, or the boisterous cry of a drunken peasant, they froze. Who was that? What was that? The unexpected was menacing. Perhaps their fears had been exaggerated, but they had lived with their ears cocked. Children were never quite children, and childhood was never quite childhood in Volkovysk. He had come out of bondage and had found himself in a country where even the adults were sometimes like children. He did not regard himself as a particularly religious man, but at such times he found himself uttering the words of an old prayer under his breath: "Blessed art Thou, O Lord, who has kept us in life, and hast preserved us, and enabled us to reach this time."

He only wondered how long it could last.

CHAPTER XVI
TROUBLED WATERS

ON JULY 18, 1911, A GERMAN GUN-BOAT, THE *Panther,* ARRIVED at the small port of Agadir on the Moroccan coast. Nahum had never heard of the *Panther,* or Agadir, and had only a hazy idea of the exact whereabouts of Morocco, but the incident nearly ruined his business. The boat, it was said, was meant to protect German interests threatened by French expansion. Britain feared that the Germans were planning to gain a foothold close to the Straits of Gibraltar, and on July 21, Lloyd George, who was then Chancellor of the Exchequer, told a public gathering in the City of London that if the *Panther* were not withdrawn it could mean war.

Nahum read the speech at breakfast the next morning and immediately phoned Colquhoun to ask what should be done.

"Nothing, I would say," said Colquhoun.

"What do you mean, nothing? Every ship we've got is in the Baltic, two of them in German ports. Can you imagine what would happen if there was war?"

"Aye, I can, but I don't think there'll be war, all the same."

"Didn't you see the papers?"

"Yes, but that's Lloyd George. And even if there should be war, it's not likely to come overnight. *The Tikvah* will be in the North Sea in another day, and the rest will have left port within the week. We'll be all right."

Nahum cabled Goodkind to come to London for consultations, and he arrived slightly bemused by the commotion.

"What do you need me for?" he asked. "To hold your hand?"

"Do you think there's going to be a war?"

"Yes, if Lloyd George wants to make it, but, you know, Morocco's not part of the British Empire, not yet, nor the Atlantic."

Goodkind had recovered his bulk, but it was not a buoyant bulk. He had become thick-set and heavy, and he had acquired a Wilhelmian moustache, with the two ends pointing upwards aggressively.

"We're spread right out over Europe," said Nahum, "and if there's a war, we're finished."

At that moment the phone rang. It was their broker. About eighty thousand pounds had been wiped off the value of their shares, and they were still falling.

"Well, what do you think of that?"

"That's what happens if you go public," said Goodkind. "If you had asked me—which, I may remind you, you did not—I would have advised you against it."

"We have been making paper gains, and these are only paper losses," said Colquhoun; "the real value of our assets remains the same." He had made enquiries about what action other shipping lines had in mind and gathered they were treating the matter calmly.

"They can afford to," said Nahum. "They've got ships all over the world. Ours are all locked up in the Baltic."

"What do you suggest, then, that we order them to turn around without taking on passengers or cargo?"

"It's not the first international incident, and it won't be the last," said Goodkind. "If we turn tail every time Lloyd George opens his big mouth, we'll soon be out of business."

The matter died down for a time, only to erupt again two months later. War seemed imminent, and ships everywhere hurried for home ports. *The Tikvah* was about to dock in Hamburg en route for Riga when she was ordered to turn around. At the same time, the very gravity of the crisis had caused a rush for tickets at all her ports of call, and when notices were posted that sailing was cancelled, there were ugly scenes, although all fares were promptly refunded. In Danzig, where the company's agent was rather less prompt, there was a riot, the office was torn apart and staff were manhandled before the police restored order. When the crisis was over and *The Tikvah* eventually did appear, it was faced with a virtual boycott. Its reputation for reliability, so painfully built up over the years, had suffered, and for several months the number of passengers carried was barely sufficient to pay the crew.

"We're sailing in dangerous waters," said Nahum and proposed closing their Stettin office and cutting down the size of their Hamburg operation. Goodkind was aghast at the idea and hurried back from Germany to argue his case.

"You're mad. Germany's the country of the future. It's got the most hard-working, intelligent population in Europe and vast natural resources. We'd be making a good investment, even if we didn't pick up a single passenger. The installations, buildings and sites are themselves worth three times the amount we paid for them."

"Which is as good a reason as any for selling," said Tobias. "Nobody becomes bankrupt from taking profits."

"Supposing there's a war?" asked Nahum.

"Between Britain and Germany? Germany would win. And if France came in on the side of Britain, Germany would still win, and if Russia came in, the Austrians wouldn't stay out, so they'd win again. There's no beating the Germans."

"The whole discussion's academic," said Colquhoun. "There isn't going to be a war."

"And we're not pulling out of Germany altogether," said Nahum, "we're only cutting down the size of the investment."

On this occasion, Nahum was glad to have Tobias at his side, for he supported him to the hilt.

Goodkind stormed, threatened to resign, tried to form a consortium to buy out the company's German assets but failed, and finally he returned to London looking a little crestfallen, with the ends of his moustache pointing downwards.

About the same time, Tobias came up to Nahum and offered his services as a full-time director; he was thinking, he said, of retiring from the law, though Nahum was aware that the law had virtually retired from him, and he was glad to have Goodkind's return as an excuse not to take up the offer. Goodkind's return, however, brought other problems, for he resented the dominant place that Colquhoun had assumed in the company.

"When I left, I was a partner; now I'm an underling. It's Colquhoun this, Colquhoun that. Nothing happens without his nod. He seems to be king of the castle."

"I've had to delegate a good deal to him. Don't forget, when you left, I was a bachelor. Now I'm a married man with six children."

"I'm surprised you didn't delegate that to Colquhoun as well. The way he goes around the place, you'd think he owns the bloody company."

A few days later, Goodkind drew him aside again. "He's an anti-Semite, you know. Don't forget, I've worked in Germany, and I know anti-Semitism when I see it."

The voice was the voice of Goodkind, but the sentiments were the sentiments of Tobias, and Nahum accused Goodkind of being anti-*goy*.

"You were happy enough to have him as a clerk, but now that he's come up in the world, you can't take it. You of all people should know how hard he's worked for the firm."

"There's a dozen people in this building who have worked every bit as hard but have got nowhere."

"They haven't got his ability."

"No, and they haven't got his wife, either."

Nahum looked at his swollen cheeks, his great underchin which gave an aggressive thrust to his face, his drooping moustache.

"You great, bloated swine," he began but broke off, for at that moment there was a knock at the door, and Colquhoun appeared. He looked from one to the other and said: "Am I intruding?"

"No, you're not," said Nahum and turned to Goodkind. "Say to Colquhoun what you've just said to me."

"I'm sorry," said Goodkind in a contrite voice. "I don't know what made me say it, I didn't really mean it," and he walked past Colquhoun with averted eyes.

"That, I suppose, was the Goodkind-Tobias axis at work," said Colquhoun.

"So you know about it?"

"I can't help knowing, and I've been asking Jessie what to do about it."

"It's difficult to be angry with Goodkind when you know what he's been through."

"No, but by the look on your face when I came in, you were managing. I had the impression you were about to hit him."

"I nearly did. I don't know what's happening. We used to be such a happy team."

"Tobias is what's happening. He's been putting poison in his ear."

"Tobias is also difficult. You've been taunting him; you never miss an opportunity to taunt him."

"Aye, perhaps, but I've no time for the man. He's the worst sort of failure, the sort who's had a bit of success. We *goyim* take failure in our stride, but if a Jew doesn't make it, he becomes embittered and thinks the world's been conspiring against him."

Nahum opened his mouth to say something but couldn't, and for the first time he wondered if Tobias wasn't possibly right. His thoughts on the matter were cut short by a torrent of telegrams. War was imminent in the Balkans. They had two tramp steamers off Malta heading eastwards, and Nahum's first inclination was to recall them.

"War's always imminent in the Balkans," said Colquhoun. "I'd let them go about their business."

"But supposing war does break out?" said Nahum.

"We'll have to risk that." Goodkind agreed with Colquhoun.

The next day, war did break out. Nahum spent a number of sleepless nights but kept to the original decision, less out of bravado than a weariness of spirit. The ships emerged unscathed.

"Congratulations," said Goodkind, "you've become an Englishman."

"If this happens again," said Nahum, "I'll become an invalid."

And it happened again the following year—first skirmishes, then threats and counter-threats, then a period of suspense and, finally, war. Nahum, who had arranged to take his family on holiday, had to cancel his arrangements and was closeted in endless conferences with Colquhoun, Goodkind, Tobias, his insurers, his lawyers, studying maps and the disposition of his ships, especially in the Aegean with its many islands, for no one was quite sure where the war zones began and where they finished. The matter was not academic; it was by no means clear if his ships were covered for misadventure in war zones. Every time a cable came or the phone rang, he braced himself for disaster, and he recalled the advice given to him by Wachsman many years ago; he wondered whether shipping was, after all, a likely trade for a Jew, especially if he wanted to sleep at night. He had aged visibly in the past year or two. His one consolation was that talk of wars always quickened the flow of passenger traffic, and the receipts from *The Tikvah*, which had slumped disastrously in the wake of the Agadir incident, now picked up dramatically.

Tobias urged that they sell off some of the ships while prices were favourable.

"And do what with the money?" asked Colquhoun.

"Invest in building, property—in this country."

"You wouldn't get the same returns."

"But they'd be safe. Nothing's safer than houses. You could sleep at night."

"Aye, and by day. This happens to be a shipping company. All our experience has been built up on ships."

"All *your* experience has been built up on ships."

"And mine," added Nahum.

Tobias waved a finger at him. "You'll sink with your ships, mark my words, you'll sink with them." And he was about to rise from the table, when he sank back in his chair, ashen-faced. Small bubbles were forming on the corner of his mouth. Goodkind rushed out to get a glass of water; Nahum phoned for a doctor, but Tobias insisted he was all right. It had happened before, he said. All he needed was a rest.

If things were difficult in business, they were not all that easy at home. Miri became ill and spent much of the winter in bed. The doctor suggested a change of climate, and Nahum decided to take her to Menton.

Because his previous year's holiday had been disrupted, he had planned to compensate himself and his family by taking a large villa in Menton for the summer (the Riviera, in those days, was principally a winter resort, so that the summer rates were comparatively inexpensive), and they therefore advanced their plans to leave by some six weeks. Sophie arranged to go with her mother, and as Nahum, in any case, had some business to attend to in Paris, he decided to spend about a week with them before returning with the rest of the family in July. In the meantime, he left the household in the charge of his mother, and they set off together for Central Station.

"You know," said Miri, "I feel better already at the thought of the sunshine."

"We'll have a second honeymoon," he whispered to her.

"A third, if you come to think of it," she whispered back.

He was about to board the night train, when he heard his name being called and saw a figure running towards him along the platform. It was Lazar.

"Tobias," he said breathlessly. "Tobias is dead."

Miri felt that they should all go back, but Nahum insisted that she and Sophie continue on their journey, and he drove back with Lazar.

"When did this happen?" asked Nahum.

"About an hour ago. As you know, he was ill last week, but he seemed to be fine the last day or two and ate a hearty supper tonight, but he complained of being chilly and they made a fire for him in the living room, and he sat down for a nap. He must have been sitting too near the fire, for after about half an hour his trousers began to smoulder, and Mother shouted to him to wake up. He didn't stir. She called the doctor, then called me. He was dead. He must have had a heart attack."

They drove on in silence, then Lazar said: "I suppose you think I killed him."

"Walking out with half his clients couldn't have done much for his health."

"They'd have left him, in any case. I was doing half his work, as it was. I wasn't prepared to carry him for the rest of his life. Though, of course, I had no idea he was a sick man."

"No, neither did I. I suppose, in our different ways, we all helped to hurry him to his grave."

Tobias had an older sister who was not on speaking terms with Katya and who was convinced that he had been poisoned by Katya and/or Lazar, and the funeral was delayed for a post-mortem, which, in turn, delayed Nahum's departure for Menton, but then, as he was about to set out again, there came news of the assassination of the Archduke Ferdinand at Sarajevo.

"It's a bloody conspiracy," he said; "every time I pack a case to go away, this sort of thing happens."

"It'll all blow over like the other things did," said Colquhoun.

"And even if it doesn't," said Goodkind, "your presence here won't change things."

"You look as if you could do with a holiday," said Colquhoun.

"I feel as if I could do with a holiday."

"Then stand not upon the order of thy going, but go," said Goodkind.

Nahum hoped he was only imagining it, but he was beginning to have the feeling that the Goodkind-Tobias axis against Colquhoun had given way to a Goodkind-Colquhoun axis against himself, and that they were trying to get rid of him.

"Don't be facetious," he said.

He was of a mind to recall all the ships to home ports, and he felt that he had had a little too much of Colquhoun's breezy reassurance.

"If we panic now," said Colquhoun, "we'll never pick up another load, apart from the fact that we could be sued right, left and centre for breach of contract."

Nahum was by no means convinced that this was the case, but everyone else seemed to be carrying on business as usual, and he did not take the matter further.

Miri was, in the meantime, belabouring him with telegrams to know when, if ever, he was coming. Schools were due to break up in another few weeks, and he saw no point in going ahead of his mother and the children, especially as Vicky was quite a handful, and he was not sure how his mother would cope with her on her own. He also warned Miri that their company would be rather larger than they anticipated because Hector wanted to bring a friend with him, and he felt that, after what had happened, his Aunt Katya was in need of a holiday, and she would be coming down with her step-daughters, Arabella and Caroline. To which Miri replied: "Bring anyone you like, but I'm coming back to Glasgow."

He wasn't at all sure that she was joking, and, until the day he left, he was afraid she might turn up, but when he got to Menton there were no recriminations, partly because there were too many people with him (though that in itself wouldn't have stopped Miri from speaking her mind), but mainly because she was aghast at his appearance.

"Have you been ill?" she asked.

"I've had problems."

"You've always had problems, but you've never looked like this."

"I've never had problems like these."

But after a few days in the sun, his problems no longer seemed so many and grievous, for his main problem had basically been one of exhaustion. Once rested, he was able to see people and events in perspective. In the last days before he left, he had smelt treason and conspiracies on every side. He began to regard everyone in his office as a potential Schwartzman, and he was half afraid that when he returned, his business would no longer be there. By the time he left, he was so weary that he no longer cared if it was or it wasn't, but after a week in Menton, he almost felt moved to write to Colquhoun and Goodkind to apologise for the feelings he had harboured about them. He was enjoying the holiday, and he had enjoyed none before. Towards the end of the month, they were joined by Alex and Hector and a very tall blond school friend called Cyrus. Lazar was on holiday in the vicinity and would sometimes drop in with his wife, and there were evenings when he counted nearly twenty people at table. He recalled the descent of relatives on his father's *dacha* in Volkovysk and the pleasure he took in the massed cousins, nephews and nieces; he almost saw himself as his father revived.

Katya had surmounted her second experience of widowhood with aplomb, and she and his mother were delighted with the villa, the grounds, the view, everything. To them, Menton was a sort of upper estate to which the elite graduated in their moments of glory. They looked about them with the awed faces of pilgrims, and as soon as they were settled in, they rushed down to the Hotel Windsor where their older sister had stayed and from which she had sent them descriptions of the paradise in which she had found herself. The hotel had been renamed the Royal, which was one disappointment, and no one there remembered their sister, which was another. They did, however, remember a cousin, a rather nondescript woman who suffered from bronchial ailments and who had, they were told, since settled in Grasse, and they planned to visit her.

"I should like to die here," said Katya.

"I doubt if we'll be stopping here that long," said Nahum.

He liked to have people around him, but Miri was rather less fond of crowds, and sometimes, to escape their many guests, they dined together quietly in their room which overlooked the garden.

"I think this is the nicest holiday I've ever had," said Nahum.

"It would be nicer if Katya and her scraggy daughters hadn't been here," said Miri. "Did they have to come?"

"But what's wrong with them? Katya's a good cook, and the girls are very pretty."

"Oh, there's nothing wrong with their looks, but the older one's a tart, and I don't like the way she's latched onto Hector."

"Hector's old enough to look after himself."

"I don't know if he is. She's so thin, and with those slant eyes and large teeth, she reminds me of a she-wolf."

There was something slightly vulpine about Arabella, but that was because she was tall and slender, but he found that Miri, who, after six children, was neither one nor the other, tended to take an instant dislike to such people. He, on the other hand, took a liking to Arabella, even if he disapproved of her. She could be moody, sulky and withdrawn but was as often pert and lively, and had a sort of disarming *chutzpah*. One afternoon he was reading in the garden, when Vicky came rushing out to him in a paroxysm of tears.

"She told me to go to hell!" she screamed. "She told me to go to hell!"

"Who did?"

"Arabella did."

He took her by the hand and went inside at once. "Arabella, did you tell this child to go to hell?"

"Did I? I may have done, but I'm sure I had good cause to if I did."

"But you can't speak like that to a child."

"If I can't speak like that to a child, who the hell can I speak to like that?"

He was also told that she smoked and drank. He had never seen her smoke, but they usually had wine with their meals, and he noticed that the bottle tended to stay near the end of the table occupied by Arabella and Hector.

They often had their evening meal outside on the terrace, and Sophie, Alex, Hector, Cyrus and Arabella and her sister would remain at the table long after everyone had gone upstairs, talking deep into the night. Their voices came floating up on the balmy air, and Nahum listened to them with envy. This was a phase of life he had missed. He had come to Glasgow when he was a year or two younger than Hector, and had thrown himself immediately into the business of earning a living, grubbing away for a few shillings a week, without time to read or to study or even friendship, and without any opportunity to meet anyone who had studied or read. His transition from boyhood to manhood had been brutally abrupt, while there below him sat the gilded youth, all from good homes and good schools, some at University, relaxed, unconcerned, certainly about such minutiae as a livelihood. Cyrus was a keen musician and played the piano beautifully, and Arabella, among her many gifts, had a fine voice, and they would sometimes give an impromptu recital—Schubert, Schumann, Brahms, Wolf, Mendelssohn, names that meant little to Nahum, for he had never been to a concert.

It had not occurred to him that either the piano or the human voice could yield so sweet and delicate a sound. He felt he would remember those evenings long after he had forgotten everything else, but, as always, when he experienced something close to ecstasy, he wondered if it could last.

One evening, he was taking a walk by the shore, when he saw a huddled figure in a battered straw hat being pushed along in a wheel-chair. There was something vaguely familiar about that figure. He stopped to have a closer look and recognised Wachsman. He greeted him, and Wachsman looked up and scrutinised him over his glasses.

"Do I know you?"

"I'm Raeburn, Rabinovitz, from Volkovysk."

"Ah—ships, isn't that right?"

"Yes, that's right."

"You're still in ships?"

"I am."

"Then you're in trouble. But who isn't? It's all over, my friend, everything. I thought when I retired—I've been very ill, you know, very ill, it's a miracle I'm alive. I had a heart attack, and they were already saying *kaddish* for me, but anyway, here I am, alive, in a manner of speaking, but when I retired, I thought I'd be finished before the world was, but here I am, still in one piece, but the world is going to pieces—finished. Have you heard the news?"

"You mean about Austria and Serbia?"

"Austria's sent Serbia an ultimatum it can't possibly accept. It means war."

"Yes, but that's hardly news. How many wars have there been in the Balkans in the last few years?"

"But this is more than the Balkans, my friend. You've got the Hapsburgs in—and start with the Hapsburgs, and you finish with the devil. Russia will go to the help of Serbia, and then Turkey will attack Russia. Before you know what's happened, Germany will be pulled in, and then France and England. They've all gone mad, even the Germans, the nicest, the most civilised, the most sensible people in Europe. Mad, all of them. What a tragedy, especially for us Jews. We've only just found our place in the world, and what happens? The world itself falls apart."

When he got back, he found Sophie, Alex, Hector and Cyrus discussing the news on the terrace.

"The clouds have been gathering for years now," said Cyrus; "nothing like a scrap to clear the air."

"It's an odd way to talk about war," said Sophie.

"War's a fact of life," said Hector.

"Everything's a fact of life if people choose to make it a fact," said Alex. "There's nothing inevitable about war."

"Can't see how they'll stop this one," said Cyrus.

"Plain common sense, provided there's enough of it about, should do the trick," said Alex. "Britain hasn't fought against a major European power for sixty years. If she gets pulled into this, she'll get knocked to her knees."

"Britain?" said Hector.

"With her navy?" said Cyrus.

"To her knees," repeated Alex.

When he came upstairs, Miri was already in bed.

"This hasn't been much of a honeymoon, has it?" she said.

"It would have been, but for the bloody Serbians."

"And bloody Katya, and bloody Arabella and your bloody mother and bloody everybody else."

"It's a large villa, there's plenty of room for everybody."

"Except you and me. You didn't come near me in Glasgow—"

"You didn't want me to come near you."

"I was ill in Glasgow, but I'm better now, but you've spent more time with the youngsters than with me."

"I'm sorry. I left home at sixteen and didn't know any youngsters when I was young. There was Shyke, but I haven't seen him since I left Volkovysk. There was Colquhoun, who is only a year or so older than me, but who, for some reason, I have always regarded as much older—"

"And who is a *goy.*"

"What difference does that make?"

"It shouldn't make any difference, but you've never learned how to get on with *goyim,* and you never will. You don't quite know how to take them. But forget about the *goyim* for the moment. Pull the blinds and put on the light."

"But I like to feel the evening breeze."

"And I like to watch you undress."

"I'm nearly forty and getting fat."

"I know you are, but I'm not getting thin. Bulk unto bulk. Thin people don't really know how to make love."

She didn't wait for him to pull the curtains but got out of bed, pulled them herself, put on the light and began to undress him.

"I generally take my shirt off first," he said.

"You can keep your shirt on," she said and unbuckled his belt with one hand, while she reached into his trousers with the other.

Just then there was a knock on the door.

"It's a telegram," said Sophie.

Nahum turned for the door, but Miri held on.

"Not now, you don't," she whispered.

He let the telegram wait, but it impaired his performance, and Miri went to bed in tears. It was from Colquhoun.

HAVE ORDERED SHIPS TO HOME PORTS. ENJOY YOUR HOLIDAY.

He had been inclined to give such an order himself after speaking to Wachsman, but he wasn't too sure how far Wachsman was in touch with events. He had sounded slightly senile, and Nahum hoped that things might blow over as they had done before, but if Colquhoun himself had felt compelled to take action, without even waiting to refer the matter to him, then there was something to worry about.

Early the next morning he ordered everyone to pack but had, in his anxiety, forgotten that Katya, his mother and some of the children had gone to visit their relative in Grasse and would not be back for another day. Nahum at once dispatched Alex to fetch them, but they returned too late to catch the evening train. They did, however, manage to leave the following morning, and as the train moved slowly—very slowly, it seemed to Nahum—across France, the wildest rumours spread through the crowded compartments and packed corridors—that Austria had declared war on Serbia, that Russia was about to declare war on Austria, that Germany was mobilising. When the train stopped at Lyons, Nahum was able to confirm that the first of them was true, and he cabled Colquhoun to let him know the disposition of all craft at the Hotel Scribe in Paris, which he hoped to reach the following morning. When he reached Paris, it was clear that they had acted too late. Germany had declared war on Russia. But that was not the worst of it. Two of the ships were in Riga, and amidst the general chaos and congestion, it was not certain when they would be able to raise anchor, and *The Tikvah,* his flagship and by far the biggest source of revenue, had developed engine trouble and had just been towed into Stettin. There was no question of her moving out under her own steam. Miri watched him as he read and reread the cable with shaking hands: he seemed to age before her eyes.

"Looking at your face, you'd think it was the end of the world," she said.

"It is, it is the end of the world."

"There have been wars before. It'll all be over in a matter of weeks."

"No, not this time. Start with the Hapsburgs, and you finish with the devil. My whole business was built around *The Tikvah*. The other ships made us seem big, but it was *The Tikvah* which brought in the profits. Engine trouble would have been a disaster at any time, but now we're finished, finished."

"Don't keep tearing your hair and wringing your hands."

"I'm not tearing my hair."

"You would, if you had enough hair to tear. That's when you really get to know a man, when he's in difficulties. Anyone can be nice and fine when everything's nice and fine. You remind me of the way Father would go on every time he was stuck with a chicken he couldn't sell."

"A ship's not a chicken."

He recalled a warning Tobias had once given him.

"Mark my words, you'll be sorry you ever set eyes on that *goy*." There was the suggestion that Colquhoun might rob him. Colquhoun didn't, and Nahum had never—except when verging on a nervous breakdown—for a moment believed that he would, but he was a little too phlegmatic in the face of a crisis, and Nahum felt that because he himself was comparatively jittery, he was inclined to accept such phlegm as a form of wisdom in its own right.

He saw nothing ahead except ruin.

CHAPTER XVII
WAR

THE FAMILY WAS TOO EXHAUSTED TO CONTINUE THE JOURNEY AND spent the night in the Scribe. Nahum continued on his own, reached London early the following morning and went straight to Kagan's office. It was not the calm, composed place he had found on earlier occasions. Everything was in turmoil, with clerks rushing in all directions, and Kagan was nowhere to be seen. Nahum, however, managed to grab hold of him as he came in, almost furtively, through a side entrance.

"Not now, please, Mr Raeburn, I have an important meeting up-stairs."

"And I have a train to catch in an hour."

"Then catch it, by all means. I haven't a minute."

"Do you know I'm ruined?" he said.

"You're not, and I doubt if you will be. Whenever there's trouble, shipping's at a premium, and serious trouble means a high premium."

"Unfortunately, half my fleet is trapped in German waters, and *The Tikvah* has engine trouble."

"*The Tikvah?* In a German port?"

"Stettin."

"That's most unfortunate, but that, if I may say so, is what I meant by unforeseen contingencies. I don't know why the devil you come to me for advice when you never take it. You were always dangerously stretched, dangerously stretched. Whenever you found yourself with a shilling in hand, you went out and bought a ship. Now I suppose you want emergency credits. So does everyone. Unfortunately, I am not in a position to find them, and I don't know if I would if I were. But why ask me? You've got shareholders, why not ask them? Now, if you'll excuse me."

Nahum managed to catch his train as it was pulling out of the station, reached Glasgow late in the evening and took a cab to Col-quhoun's house. Jessie was preparing for bed when he arrived, and she was shocked at his appearance.

"My God," she exclaimed, "what's happened to you?"

"Never mind what's happened to me. Do you know what's happened to the fleet?"

"I know what's happened, but you needn't shout at me. It's not my fault, I'm not the Kaiser."

She poured him a glass of whisky to calm him down. Colquhoun was in London.

"In London? I was in London. He could have told me he was coming."

"He sent a telegram to your Paris hotel; presumably you didn't get it. You think it's his fault, don't you?"

"Whoever's fault it was, the damage is done."

"The decision was yours, you know. You asked his opinion, and he gave it. You didn't have to take it."

"What's he doing in London?"

"He was hoping to speak to you about that." She paused as if to deliver a shock. "He's joining the navy."

"The navy! At his age?"

"What do you mean, 'his age'? He's only forty. He's been a sailor all his life and was in the volunteer reserve. He's hoping for an active commission, though in all probability he'll be given a desk job."

"He can't leave me like this, not with all this chaos. I don't know what's happening."

"That's what I told him, but he can't see the whole thing lasting more than a month or two."

"If he's away for a month or two, there'll be no business to come back to, you can tell him that."

The navy was, in fact, not all that quick to make use of Colquhoun's services, and more than three months passed before he left.

The company, in the meantime, had to be reorganised from top to bottom, for the immigrant traffic on which it was largely based had stopped almost completely, and no one was certain when, if ever, it would be resumed. They did not anticipate any difficulties in finding work for their remaining ships, their horses and vans, but the ticket and forwarding agency of Goodkind-Raeburn, from which their whole business had sprung, was redundant, and when it became clear that the war would continue for years rather than months, Goodkind was required to wind it up. It took him some weeks to do so, and then, when the job was complete, the last man paid off and a new home found for the office cat, he went home and died.

Nahum could not believe he was dead, not when he was told the news, not when he embraced the weeping Jessie by his bed, not even when he saw the ample form of his partner laid out in the front room. His face was completely white, except for his nose and ears, which were a dark bluish red; it reminded him of the clown's face he used to put on for the parties they gave for the children of employees near Christmas, and he half expected him to turn on his side and wink. But he remained immobile with his big toes—each the size of a potato —protruding from under the white sheet, looking as if they had turned to stone. It was those toes which somehow brought home the truth of the situation. Goodkind was, indeed, dead, and he sat down and wept as he had not wept since he was a child.

Jessie sat down beside him, put an arm around him and kissed his neck and ear, but he would not be comforted. He could not understand his own distress, for he and Goodkind had not been as close in their later years as they had been in their early ones. As Goodkind had grown older, Nahum had found flaws in his character he had not noticed before—petulance, envy, suspicion, even, he sometimes felt, deceit. He had not expected Goodkind to be wholly consistent, because people never were, but there were times when he underwent complete changes of personality and even appearance. Nahum found it perfectly possible to work with a curmudgeon if he knew him to be one, but it was rather more difficult to work with a man who was curmudgeon one day, and genial, generous, hail-fellow-well-met the next. He had been under medical treatment for some time, and perhaps the medicines he had been taking had had something to do with it, but in recent years Nahum had never been quite certain which Goodkind he would be meeting when he came into the office, though now that he was dead, he felt overwhelmed. Perhaps he was mourning for Goodkind-Raeburn, rather than Goodkind. He was not at all certain that his business would survive into the new year, and what worried him was not so much the imminence of the ruin as the feeling that he was about to let everyone around that table—to say nothing of his employees, whom he often spoke of as a family—down.

His employees proved less of a difficulty than he feared. One of the things he dreaded in business was the occasional need to dismiss an incompetent or, worse, a redundant employee. He did it eventually, but always with a heavy heart, and when he realised the full effect of the war on his company, he did not know how he would be able to bring himself to dismiss the greater part of his work-force. In the event, it was done for him, for hardly had the first shot been fired when there was almost a stampede of personnel rushing to join the navy, the army, the highland regiments, the lowland regiments—almost every able-bodied man and a few who had struck him as less than able-bodied. And they all went, boisterous with excitement as if they were off to a ball. Nahum had for years been trying to understand the pleasure grown men took in shooting at birds; it had never occurred to him that they could carry their passion to the point of shooting each other.

Hector, too, had intimated that he intended to go into the army. His school reports had been almost uniformly dismal, but he had been active in the school cadets and, according to his commandant, "had the natural makings of an officer." They had read the report with some gratification at the time they had received it, but they now recalled it with consternation. However, they drew some comfort from the fact that the boy was only seventeen, and by the time he was old enough for army service, the war might be over. In the meantime, his eyes lit up at the prospect of military action, and it seemed to Nahum that he was not only a natural officer, but, with his hunger for battle, a natural *goy*.

Alex, on the other hand, who was getting taller and thinner and slightly bent, was decidedly not officer material, nor did he impress one as even private material. He did not expect to leave Oxford until 1917, and no one—certainly not Nahum—imagined the war could continue till then.

In some ways, Sophie was his greatest cause of consternation. She had failed to marry even during his years of plenty—how would she marry during his years of famine? News of misfortune—especially financial misfortune—travelled fast, and he could not help noticing that the crowd of young men who thronged around Sophie at *bar mitzvahs* or weddings, or on the rare occasions she appeared in synagogue, had thinned considerably. He would have liked to know what her plans were, but he had always been diffident about tackling her, and his business difficulties had increased his diffidence. Prosperity had given him a certain amount of self-assurance. He might not have had the wide reading or intellectual depth of Sophie or Alex, or the easy manners and social verve of Hector, but he was a good businessman, with a sound sense of timing, successful, prosperous, a man whose opinion counted for something and whose counsel was widely sought, so that he was on the executive of numerous charities and a vice-president of the Zionist Organisation of Great Britain. Now all that had changed. The least that a businessman could do was to make money, and if he failed even in that, what was there to be said for him? Nahum was not required to resign any of his offices, but he was no longer called upon to grace platforms or address meetings with the same frequency. When a leading Zionist figure visited Scotland, he came and went, and Nahum was not even informed he had been there. But more painful than the diminution in his public standing was the decline in his authority among his employees and his own family—his wife, the older children and even the younger ones. He had to shout to be heard and even then was not infrequently ignored. In a matter of months, he had changed from magnate to *nebbich*.

The day of Goodkind's funeral (which had been delayed because they were waiting for a sister to come up from Brighton), his mother came to his office and, looking around to make sure they were alone, leaned over his desk and whispered breathlessly: "Why not write to Lotie?"

He looked at her as if she was crazy, and there was, indeed, something a trifle crazed in her manner.

"I know you're in difficulties, everybody does. Lotie'll help you out. A million dollars is nothing to her. She'll do anything for you—she's a woman, I understand her."

"You may understand her, Mother, but I don't understand you," and, taking her by the elbow, he led her firmly out of the office.

After the funeral, Lazar offered him a lift home in his car (Nahum had sold his own some weeks previously), and, as he drove, Lazar said to him: "I suppose things will be difficult without Goodkind."

"They weren't that easy with him."

"But I daresay things will pick up soon."

"That's what everybody keeps telling me, but in the meantime I keep negotiating loan after loan, mainly to pay for the money I've already borrowed. I'm borrowing long and I'm borrowing short, and if things go on as they are, I'll soon be in the hands of the money-lenders. To be honest, when I saw poor Goodkind lying there quietly in his grave, I was half-envious."

Lazar was silent for a time, then he said: "Have you thought of selling?"

"Selling?"

"The company."

"Everybody thinks of selling if he is offered the right price, but who would want to buy it?"

"I might be able to find a buyer."

"*You* might be able to find a buyer?"

"I might."

"You wouldn't by any chance be the buyer yourself?"

"That's surely beside the point."

"It isn't beside the point if you bring the matter up in a casual conversation and make me run down my own stock."

"Look, Nahum, I'm not looking for bargains. You'd get a realistic price."

"My boy, you'll never in your life be able to afford a realistic price.

I may be in difficulties, but I'm not on my knees. Will you stop the car?"

"We're not home yet."

"I want some fresh air."

He had given his cousin a thousand shares in Goodkind-Raeburn as a wedding present; he thought he might one day regret his generosity, and he did. Presumably he also had charge of Tobias's shares which Katya had inherited, in which case, he controlled about 15 percent of the equity. But he, Nahum, owned nearly 50 percent, and Colquhoun owned another 12, and Lotie owned about 10 percent, so he did not feel in danger; he was as much amused as chagrined by his cousin's *chutzpah*.

"A funny thing happened on the way from the funeral," he told Miri. "Someone offered to save me from my creditors."

"What's so funny about that?"

"You haven't heard who it was—Lazar."

"I still can't see the joke. There are no flies on Lazar—fleas, maybe, but no flies. He's done well for himself, that boy."

"What do you mean, boy? He's nearly my age."

"You're jealous of him, you always have been. You arrived before him and went straight into business, while he managed to get himself an education, go to University, take a degree, become a lawyer, marry an heiress."

"Look, if I had had a daft cousin on whom I could sponge, I, too, could have gone to University and become anything I wanted. I don't know how long he stayed with me—free house, free board, without paying a penny."

"His mother kept house for you, that was worth something. You used to like Lazar, or so you said."

"When?"

"When he was dependent on you. What you can't forgive is that he's gone out on his own and, what's more, is doing well."

Nahum wondered if he imagined it, but it seemed to him that since his difficulties had begun, Miri seemed to challenge almost everything he said, and he couldn't say good morning to her without provoking a rebuttal.

His situation improved as the dislocation which had accompanied the early part of the war was overcome. A fund was established to help companies with assets in enemy hands, and the ships still at his disposal were in constant use, but he could not any longer maintain his old life-style and, as the pressures increased, would not have felt justified in doing so even if he could, especially as servants were becoming hard to get and expensive to keep, and, in the summer of 1915, he moved back into the house in Carmichael Place he had occupied before he married.

"There," said Miri to her older daughter, "you've always been praying that we should be poor, now you've had your prayers answered. Happy?"

"All the world should be so poor," said Sophie.

They might not have been poor, but they were cramped, for they had only four bedrooms, and, apart from Hester—who was sinking into old age and becoming something of a liability—there was Thelma, a huge, black bitch whom Sophie had found in an almost dying condition and had nursed back to life, but who was now fat, old, almost blind and all but incontinent and lumbered about the house, bumping into people and things. But any suggestion that she should be put to sleep was resisted by Sophie with the cry: "You'll have to put me to sleep first," which, to Hector's ears, at least, sounded like a reasonable proposition. When he and Alex were home on holiday, the two younger children had to sleep on a folding-bed settee in the front room. Alex, who usually brought a small library with him, complained that there wasn't a quiet corner in the house.

Hector was more vehement: "Good God! Do people actually live like this? It's not our permanent billet, is it?"

Nahum and Miri regarded Hector with a mixture of pride and despair —pride in his appearance, manner and bearing, despair about his prospects and the feeling that he was not quite theirs. They both thought it had been a mistake to send him to Clifton, for, although it offered a good education (which he did his best to avoid), it had placed him, if not above his station, then at least above theirs, especially now that they had come down in the world, and he spent much of his free time with his "grand friends," as Miri called them. They had hesitated to move house for some months because they could not quite see Hector in Carmichael Place, but, as Miri said, "We don't have to ruin ourselves to keep up with his lordship's taste."

Nahum, who had regarded the move with a certain amount of apprehension, felt curiously happy once it was made. He had not felt quite himself amid the opulent surroundings and spacious grounds of his previous home. It always seemed full of people who, even if they were servants, sometimes made him feel like an intruder. Moreover, it seemed to him that Miri was never particularly good at controlling their servants. The maids kept getting pregnant, the gardeners kept getting drunk and they all kept giving notice, so that he had hardly gotten used to one set of faces and persons (and caprices) than he found himself faced with another. He and his wife had once spent a week-end with the Kagans, and Mrs Kagan had told Miri: "The secret to a stable household is a good, reliable butler. A butler to a household is what an RSM is to a regiment; without him, the servants become an unruly mob," and Miri did broach the matter of a butler when they got back, which Nahum promptly rejected on the grounds of cost.

"I'm fairly well-to-do, but I'm no Kagan, not yet," but the real reason was that he was intimidated and awed by butlers, certainly Kagan's butler, and he could not have lived with such a personage under the same roof. Indeed, he was half-intimidated by his cook, and he was glad to be back to an almost servantless house.

What surprised him, however, was the delight that Miri expressed with the move, but that was simply due to the fact that Nahum's mother had taken one look at the place and had decided, for the time being at least (for she came and went as her mood took her), to move in with Katya. He looked back on the four different homes he had occupied since he had come to Glasgow, and in some ways he found Carmichael Place the most satisfying. If only there had been no war, he would have been content even in his reduced circumstances. Perhaps he had finally found his true level and had been presumptuous in trying to go beyond it.

The war filled him with anxieties and foreboding. All the papers were filled with stories of victories and advances or, at worst, with strategic withdrawals, but nobody seemed to be getting anywhere, and there was no end to the slaughter. And every day the papers were filled with column after column of men killed in action. He had heard the expression "oriental resignation," but it did not compare to the occidental sort, at least as he saw it in Britain. He met people who had lost sons, brothers, fathers, but who went about their work with expressionless faces, as if nothing had happened.

Hector left school the summer they moved, and early in the following year he was commissioned in the Enniskillen Fusiliers, and Nahum could not quite make out the system whereby the English-educated, Scottish-born son of a Russian Jew should have been commissioned in an Irish regiment, except that he felt that it was vaguely appropriate that he should. At the same time he regretted that he was not in a Highland regiment. Hector looked magnificent in uniform with his Sam Browne belt and ceremonial sword, but Nahum felt he would have looked even better in a kilt.

Hector was posted abroad shortly after he was commissioned, and before he left Nahum gave a small party. Nahum felt a pang of regret that they were not in the old house, for he thought the new one was not sufficiently worthy of such an occasion, but the party turned out to be very small, indeed; a deep fog descended on the city which made movement almost impossible, though Arabella somehow managed to turn up.

"She would," whispered Miri. "I won't be able to sleep once he's out of the country," she said to Nahum, "but, honestly, I'm less worried about the Germans or the front than about her. I liked Tobias, but I wonder what sort of mother the girl had, she's poison."

When she came downstairs the next morning, she found Arabella making breakfast.

"Were you here all night?" asked Miri.

"Why, did you expect me to walk back in the fog?"

"If you walked here, it shouldn't have been impossible to walk back. I'm sure Hector would have been happy to escort you."

"To be sure, but I was worried about him walking back on his own. Such a pretty boy, anything could happen to him."

He left by boat—by paddle-steamer, in fact—from the Broomielaw. He was in high spirits, as was everyone on board, and, but for the grey skies and the khaki uniforms, they might have been off on a pleasure trip. Nahum and his wife stood at the quayside until the boat was out of sight.

"I don't know where he's going to," said Miri, "but he'll be safer there than he was here."

"What sort of mother are you? For all you know, he's on the way to the western front. What do you think his chances are of coming back alive, especially as an officer? And all you can worry about is his girl friend. He's eighteen, he'll have a hundred girl friends before he settles down."

"Not if she has her way, and she's the type who generally does. Do you know she spent the night with Hector under our roof and didn't even try to hide the fact? When I came downstairs, I found her making breakfast as if she owned the place."

"There's a war on. Who knows when he'll see her again, if at all? You have to make allowances."

"Not for people like Arabella. She makes allowances for herself."

Nahum could not continue the exchange indefinitely, though Miri was in a mood to do so. He had to rush back to the office, and as he came into his room, he found Jessie Colquhoun waiting by his desk. She had been there for the past half hour. He was always delighted to see her, but she was a rare visitor to the office, and there was something about her appearance which alarmed him. He took her hand in his.

"Is there something the matter?"

Her eyes filled up and she nodded. "Kenneth is missing," she said in a choked whisper.

"Missing?"

"He went down with his ship."

CHAPTER XVIII
LAZAR

Nahum was stunned. He still had a letter in his pocket he had received the previous day, in which Colquhoun had discussed his post-war plans. "I'm sure that the end is near," he wrote, "not, unfortunately, because victory is in sight, but because both sides must come to realise that they have killed out the better part of a generation and that they have both lost. When it's all over," he added, "the whole world (or what's left of it) will be on the move, across continents and over the oceans. Anyone in shipping, in transport, in travel will have opportunities they have never dreamt of, so whatever your difficulties, hold on to any ships you have, and buy any hulk you can find."

Colquhoun never mentioned what he was doing in the navy, and whenever Nahum asked Jessie about him, she was not particularly forthcoming.

"He's either in something hush-hush, or he's ashamed to tell me," she said, though Nahum presumed that, given Colquhoun's age, he probably had some safe desk job, but, in fact, he was serving on a cruiser which sustained a direct hit in its magazine and went down in the North Atlantic with all men on board.

There was a memorial service in his local church, and when Nahum arrived, he found to his surprise that he was sitting next to Lazar.

"What are you doing here?" he whispered.

"You had better ask Mrs Colquhoun."

He did not think this was the occasion to do so, but some weeks later Jessie told him: "He's our family lawyer. We used to have an old man looking after our affairs, but he became a bit doddery, and when he died, Kenneth thought he'd get himself a good, young, bright Jew lawyer, and, I must say, he's marvellous."

A few months later, Lazar asked if he could come and see him. Nahum said he was busy, but Lazar advised him with a slight hint of menace in his voice that it would be in his interest to find the time.

Nahum did not find it difficult to guess what it would be about. Lazar was trustee of Colquhoun's estate, which gave him control of about

25 percent of the equity, apart from the shares he owned in his own right, and Nahum presumed he was not too satisfied with the running of the company, which was understandable. Other shareholders had made adverse comment. He was himself aware that, since the death of Colquhoun, his heart had gone out of the business. Goodkind had been blow enough, but he had valued Goodkind less for his judgment than for the fact that he had been his partner in his early struggles. Colquhoun, on the other hand, had been his sounding board. He was never quite sure about the reasonableness of an idea until he had tried it out on Colquhoun, who could always reduce it to its component parts, arrange the advantages on one side and the drawbacks on the other, and enable him to reach a prompt decision. There was a lot of small print to the shipping trade, and Colquhoun could glance at a page of small print and pounce on its snags.

Nahum, moreover, regarded his gentile staff with a certain diffidence. He thought of his company as a family, and he would attend the weddings of his employees and the christenings of their children, and he would make a large party for them every Christmas, but he was never particularly at ease with them; he sometimes had the feeling that they laughed at him, and when Colquhoun was away, he always sensed a slackening of effort. Colquhoun was what Mrs Kagan would have called the butler of his establishment. Nahum valued the friendship he had built up with him and his wife, and if he knew any other gentiles in the shipping trade at all, it was largely through him. Colquhoun had been his passport to the wider Scotland, and with his death, Nahum feared a reversion to the ghetto.

He had been sustained in the difficulties he had encountered in the early stages of the war by the thought that, once the fighting was over, they would make a fresh start, and, with the fleet released from German hands, they would make an attempt to break out into the Atlantic; as the months passed, he saw his main function as keeping the machine ticking over until the new dawn. With Colquhoun dead, he was overcome with something like despair. He did not particularly care to do business with Lazar, but if he was seriously interested in gaining control of the company he would, given a reasonable price, have been ready to sell. Goodkind was dead, Colquhoun was dead, and Goodkind-Raeburn no longer had much meaning for Nahum.

Lazar, however, had other plans. He wanted a nominee on the board, to which, given the number of shares he controlled, he was perfectly entitled. But that was not all.

"The trouble with you and your people," he said, "is that you know the Baltic and not much else, and with the Baltic closed, you feel there's nothing you can do. But there are still the neutrals, the Scandinavians, the Dutch—"

"We used to do quite a bit of business with the Dutch."

"But it's all stopped. Now, I have an associate, a Dutch chap, actually, name of Zaiderbaum, who knows the trade inside out and has contacts everywhere. Now, if you were to install him as managing director—"

"*Managing* director? And what would I do?"

"You could continue as chairman."

"You mean you don't want to buy me out, but at the same time you want me to retire?"

"Nothing of the sort. You're a respected name, and Goodkind-Raeburn would mean nothing without Raeburn. You'd be concerned mainly with long-term policy. That was always your forte, wasn't it, long-term planning?"

"That was in the days when there was a long term to plan for, but what can you see ahead now except darkness?"

"It can't continue forever. You were always bored by day-to-day details, even when you were in a small way of business, and you left those things to Goodkind and Colquhoun."

"Unfortunately, there aren't enough day-to-day details to justify the cost of an executive director."

"He would generate new business, don't you understand? That would be the whole point of taking him on, while you could concentrate on post-war plans. And, of course, if you find after a year that he does not generate new business, you can always drop him."

Put that way, the scheme sounded attractive, but he felt uneasy about it for no reason that he could describe. It might simply have been due to the fact that it had emanated from Lazar in the first place, but everyone consulted agreed that the company could not be allowed to flounder on as it was and it was perfectly possible that Lazar's scheme could revitalise it, but he agreed more out of weariness of soul than conviction that he was doing the right thing.

He was unhappy with the new order almost from the first day. It was true that, as Lazar suggested, he was generally bored by the day-to-day details of business, but he liked the hurly-burly of the business day— messengers, callers, telegrams, the mails, phone calls, the comings and goings of managers and clerks, the occasional overseas visitor. Things had quieted down since the outbreak of war, but now he found himself isolated even from the little activity that remained, a prisoner in his own office. He would sometimes get up and wander into Zaiderbaum's office and ask a few questions, which Zaiderbaum, a fat man with thick glasses and a bald head, answered politely but briefly and was studiously careful not to enlarge on any point Nahum raised.

The fact that he had little to occupy him in business also made his domestic problems seem more acute.

Miri had developed some circulatory trouble in her leg and was finding it difficult to move about. She had always been a brisk and animated little woman but was now considerably less energetic, inclined to put on weight and to sleep late in the morning. Old Hester made breakfast for the family and, as she suffered from palsy, was inclined to slop cold milk and boiling water over everything and everybody. The younger children fought and screamed, and their mother screamed back from her sick bed that if she was compelled to come downstairs she would murder them all. Thelma proved more awkward than ever and once, when Miri tripped over her while she was asleep on the landing and nearly fell headlong down the stairs, she threatened to poison her. When Thelma died naturally in her sleep a few days later, Sophie was convinced Miri had done just that, and a violent quarrel ensued which did not quite peter out until Nahum arranged for a post-mortem.

Nahum's previous years had not been without their domestic troubles, but he could escape them once he was immersed in business, but now there was hardly any business in which to be immersed.

On top of all this, there arrived a long and unexpected letter from his sister in America which made his own difficulties seem insignificant:

Dear Nahum,

You may have heard, because these things travel fast, but we're in trouble.

You may remember that with the help you so kindly gave us some years ago, we set up a small lodging house which over a time became a big one, and we built up enough capital to buy a small hotel. The hotel didn't do brilliantly, but it paid for itself and left a bit of profit until a fire last month which burned the place to the ground, but I assure you that it wasn't just another attempt to pick up a quick dollar from insurance, because the insurance cover lapsed on December 31, Arnstein forgot to renew it, and we were burned down on January 2, and unfortunately though everything went up in flames, Arnstein did not. Everything we had is in ashes and we haven't a kopek, but that is only one of our difficulties. The other is that there were fourteen people in the place (or maybe more) who were burned to a cinder, and their families are cross about it. Arnstein was nearly lynched but the police managed to rescue him, which is a pity, for his own insurance hadn't lapsed (and I shall see to it that if there is to be any lapsing in future, he lapses first), and we are being sued for about four million dollars (I haven't totted up the figures, perhaps it's only three). But that too isn't all. It also looks as if we've infringed about every fire regulation going, and not a few that I thought had already gone. The regulations are so many and complex that anyone who tried to keep half of them would go out of business, if not out of his mind. I don't suppose many people try, and nobody is found out until there actually is a fire. Anyway, Arnstein has been up before the courts (happily, the hotel was in his name) and is now out on bail and is due to appear again in another few weeks.

I shouldn't imagine that things are as easy in Britain as they were four or five years ago, but if you should find it possible to lend us two or three hundred dollars, you'll save our lives. Frankly, I don't know if they're worth saving, or at least mine isn't and Arnstein's certainly isn't (the first thing I'll do when we're out of our present difficulties is to cut his throat), and if it wasn't for our little girl, who is no longer so little, I wouldn't have bothered you at all.

The first thing Nahum did was to arrange for five hundred pounds to be sent to New York by telegraphic transfer. He also wrote to advise her not to spend a penny on lawyers, to let them hang her husband and to come to England with the child.

Months passed without a reply, and he eventually wrote to Lotie, mentioning his sister's difficulties and asking whether there had been anything in the papers about the trial. She replied by cable:

NO TRIAL STOP ARNSTEIN JUMPED BAIL STOP FAMILY INCLUDING CHILD VANISHED

His mother seemed curiously untroubled by the news.

"One evening you'll hear a knock at the door, and there outside will be Esty and her daughter and that awful little man she's picked up. She's always been an impossible child, and I have never been able to do anything with her—and the fact that she was the apple of your father's eye didn't help—an impossible child, but I feel she's got her own private guardian angel who sometimes falls asleep on the job but who, on the whole, sees her through. That's why I wasn't in the least surprised when you wrote to say you'd found her. I knew she'd come to no harm the first time she vanished, and she'll come to no harm now."

Nahum did not share her optimism. He recalled how his father used to add the words *kein-ein-horeh* to every positive utterance. The children? Marvellous—*kein-ein-horeh*. My health? Fine—*kein-ein-horeh*. The business? I'm managing—*kein-ein-horeh,* the expression being a formula to ward off the evil eye. It was not a formula which he ever used himself, but he began to wonder if the evil eye had not, in fact, cast its evil gaze on him, or perhaps upon the whole universe, for so many things were going wrong that he began to doubt that anything would ever go right again.

One evening, Sophie announced that she was going to be an auxiliary nurse.

"A *nurse?*" said Miri, aghast.

"An auxiliary nurse, just for the duration of the war."

"And carry bed-pans and things?"

"Somebody has to carry them."

"Is that what we sent you to University for, to carry bed-pans? I never had an education at all. I left school at thirteen and didn't have all that much schooling even before that, and I hoped that my children at least might enjoy everything I missed."

"I did enjoy it and am grateful for it, but there *is* a war on, you know."

"Hector's in the army, an officer."

"But men are being wounded by the thousand, every day, people like Hector—"

"Heaven forbid."

"And they haven't enough hospitals, they haven't enough nurses, they need auxiliaries."

"What do you know about nursing?"

"Not a thing, but I'm willing to learn."

"It wouldn't have been so bad if you had taken medicine and had volunteered as a doctor, but a nurse?" She turned to Nahum, who had listened to the exchange in silence. "Did you hear her? A nurse."

"They need nurses."

"But why her? A girl with a university education."

"Her education will never come amiss."

Later that evening, Sophie came over to him with a smile, which was a rare occurrence.

"I never expected you to take my side. I was afraid that you'd take up the typical Jewish attitude that a daughter's place is in the home and that she should only leave to marry and have children."

"That is exactly my attitude, only you don't happen to be that sort of daughter, and I suppose this isn't that sort of home."

When she left to undergo training at a hospital in southern Scotland, she embraced him with a warmth that quite startled him and surprised her mother.

As the war progressed, a fuel shortage developed, and as a rule they would have a fire in only one room even in the depths of winter, and they would all crowd around it. His mother, who insisted on a certain minimal spaciousness, often walked over to Katya, where circumstances were less cramped. Then one night someone in an adjoining street was raped, and his mother was afraid to set foot out of the house after dark, which Miri found amusing.

"I think if I was your age, I would feel safe," she said.

To which his mother replied: "And I think if I had your appearance, I would feel even safer."

Vicky overheard the conversation and chirped in with: "Round one to Grandma," at which Miri turned on her like a fury and boxed her about the ears.

Nahum waited until his mother was out of the room before he remonstrated with her. "You know, that was uncalled for."

"*Uncalled* for?" said Miri. "You may take such insolence from your children, but I shan't, not even from your darling little Vicky. God knows what she'll turn into. She's got the makings of another Arabella."

"I wasn't talking about Vicky. It's what you said to Mother."

"What *I* said to Mother? Did you hear what she said to me? And you sat there in silence without a word. You let her insult me."

"You started it."

"I was just making a little joke, in bad taste, perhaps—but a joke. God knows we could do with a bit of laughter in this house. And she turns and insults me."

"You insulted her first."

"*Insulted* her? It's no insult to say someone's old—though I hope to God I'm dead before I get to her age—it *is* an insult to call someone ugly, and that's what she called me, ugly, and all you could do was to sit there in silence."

He sighed.

"Is that all you can do, sigh?"

"What do you want me to do, cry?"

At which she burst into tears, and he leaned over, put her on his knee and rocked her gently, humming an old Russian melody, until she fell asleep.

His one source of comfort during those bleak days was that Zaiderbaum was every bit as able as Lazar had said he was; for all the handicaps of war, the business was improving, but he got little joy out of it, possibly because the improvements arose out of Zaiderbaum's efforts rather than his own, and he still found the future too doubtful and the possible outcome of events too uncertain to engage wholeheartedly in long-term planning.

One bleak afternoon during what would normally have been his busiest season, he happened to pass a cinema showing a comedy film, and on an impulse he went inside. The comedy was not very comical and he was not very amused, but he found the darkened hall—even with the piano twanging by his ear—and the flickering images relaxing, and thereafter he went to the cinema at least once a week, and occasionally two or three times, always in the afternoon. He came and went furtively and never spoke about it, for he felt guilty about his addiction. There was a war on. Men were dying by the thousand, everyone was being urged on to greater effort, and there he was, a man in his forties, spending half his working week in cinemas.

One evening he came home to find Miri hobbling around on her one good leg in a state of great agitation.

"Where have you been? I phoned your office, they've been looking for you everywhere. I've just got a telegram from the War Office. Sophie's ill, seriously ill, in hospital. Will you go to see her, or shall I? Can you look after the children?"

"No, of course I'll go."

He took the night train to London and got off at Lockerbie, but it was morning before he found a conveyance to take him to the hospital, a large country house set in spacious grounds which had only recently been converted to hospital use. He found Sophie in a corner bed in a small ward, very white with dark patches under her eyes, breathing heavily and fast asleep.

He sat by her bed for a while, gazing out through the windows at the misty autumnal scene. Eventually, he found himself in conversation with an elderly woman in the next bed.

"They say it's the food," she began. "Well, it couldn't be, could it? I never touch it, the food, I mean. I'm the cook, you see, and if I was to start eating, I'd never stop. Not that I'd have the time for it in the first place, at least, not for a proper meal. I just have a bit of this and a bit of that as I'm going along, and maybe a cup of tea. You get out of the habit of eating if you're a cook—well, almost. No, I never touched nothing, but they blame it on me all the same. They say I poisoned them and that I should volunteer as a cook in the German Army. Well, if I poisoned them, how is it I'm down with it myself?"

It was not the sort of question to which Nahum could volunteer an answer, and she changed the subject.

"This lady your wife?"

"My daughter."

"Daughter is she? Deserves a medal. The nurses couldn't cope, you see, so she was at it—day and night, she was at it—for the better part of a week. Not surprising she dropped, is it? They couldn't cope, no, none of them."

"Cope with what?"

"Well, there was this outbreak, you see, everybody vomiting and coming out in a rash and dropping dead. You've never seen anything like it. Half the nurses themselves was down with it, even the doctors. You'd think it was all my fault, the way they went poking their noses into my pots and pans. But if I poisoned them, how is it I'm down with it myself?"

"How long has she been in hospital?"

"Your daughter? Three or four days, maybe five. You know, you lose all sense of time being here. She was taken bad last night—or was it the night before? They put the screen around her, and they were trundling machinery and doctors rushing. You've got to be pretty bad before you can see a doctor these days. Mind you, it's not so bad here. Where my late husband was, you had to be dead for a week before you could even see a nurse. But I did get worried when they put the screen up. They're like conjuring acts, them screens. Up they go, and the doctors and nurses come rushing in. Then they remove it, and, presto, nobody's there, and the bed's made and looks as if it's never been slept in, in the first place. I was relieved when I saw she was still there, not only for her sake, but for mine. You know how it is, you begin to think it's your turn next."

Sophie was beginning to stir. She opened her eyes, looked at him without recognition and with something like bewilderment, then a smile began to spread slowly over her face like sunshine breaking through a misty morning. For a moment, Nahum thought she looked beatific.

"How long have you been here?" she asked. Her voice was so weak, he could hardly make out what she was saying.

"I've only just arrived."

"It's a very long way."

"It isn't, you know. It's not all that far from the main London line, and I enjoy a train journey."

"How is Mother?"

"Fine."

"Is her leg better?"

"It's not the sort of thing that gets better, but it's not getting any worse, thank God. She sends her love. We couldn't both get away."

"I didn't expect to see you here, either. Can you take a day off, just like that?"

"Unfortunately, I can even take a year off, just like that."

"Is it as bad as that?"

"We're not what we were. We're not really a shipping line any more; we're dabblers, importing this, exporting that, turning our hands to anything which will bring in an honest penny."

He could see that she was speaking with difficulty, and he urged her to lie back and rest, which she did, and in a minute she was asleep again.

"Doesn't look too good, does she?" said her neighbour.

Nahum got up and searched around for the doctor, and eventually found him as he was making his ward round—a lean, harassed-looking young man in a white coat several times too large for him. His face and neck were covered in boils, and he looked as if he hadn't slept for a week. "Pneumonia," he shouted to Nahum over his shoulder. "She's past her crisis, but it'll be a day or two before she's out of the woods."

Nahum booked into a hotel in a nearby town and remained there for the next four days. He visited Sophie twice a day, and she seemed to gather strength with each visit, and they were able to converse with an intimacy and ease they had not experienced before; for the first time, he felt he had gotten to know his step-daughter.

She asked him about Miri.

"You asked me yesterday, and I said she was fine."

"Forgive me, but I have the feeling she isn't fine."

"Well, there's her leg."

"And only that?"

"You're trying to sniff something out; unfortunately, as far as I know, I have nothing to hide."

"You remember Mummy and I went together to Menton?"

"Will I ever forget?"

"And you know how she hates to sleep alone. I shared her room, and we spoke together late into the night. And she told me that she was very proud of you and complained that I wasn't nearly proud enough, and I said to her—forgive me for saying this—I said to her, 'But what is there to be proud of?' Which made her sit up. 'What is there to be proud of? He came here as a penniless immigrant, not speaking a word of English, and now owns a shipping line and is one of the most prosperous and respected citizens of Glasgow.' 'Oh,' I said, 'you mean he's rich, but I know lots of rich people.' And she said, 'You may do because of what your father is. He didn't, I didn't. We both came up from nowhere.' I'm afraid success means a lot to her, and she hasn't been able to take the decline in your fortunes with grace."

"Who can?"

"You can. I thought you were going to pieces on that nightmare journey from Menton, but you collected yourself, and you're the person now you always were, in some ways more, but Mother isn't. I'm afraid it isn't only the leg. She has visions of herself spending her old age plucking chickens." Her eyes filled up.

"Your mother will be all right," he assured her.

"She will if you will. Her health is tied to your fortune."

"As a matter of fact, I'm not doing too badly."

"Too badly isn't good enough, not for Mother. She has to be the wife of a shipping magnate."

He would have liked to pursue the subject further, but it seemed to distress her, and when he returned the next day, he asked what she hoped to do after the war.

"*After* the war?" she said. "Is there ever going to be an *after?* It's beginning to seem as distant and improbable as the hereafter. Don't you ever get the feeling that war and slaughter are the natural order and peace is an aberration? It all makes for callousness and amorality, which I suppose is a form of callousness. We had some girls down with food poisoning. Everyone blamed the poor cook, though, as a matter of fact, it was traced to a bottle of sauce someone had brought into the canteen. Seven young girls died. They were hardly more than children, but there was hardly a tear. There's been so much death, so much slaughter, that another seven young lives seem to count for nothing. And the way people live, without a thought for tomorrow, without a sense of responsibility, without a sense of decency. There're hundreds of us here, most of us away from home for the first time, in dormitories, miles from anywhere. We try to arrange all sorts of occupations and amusements—choirs, concert parties, games—but the most popular amusement—even among married women with husbands at the front—is fornication. They'll grab at anything in trousers. Some of the poor soldiers hardly have a chance to recover before they have them at their backs. One poor boy came in with half his side shot away. We managed to patch him up, but before he was on his feet he was down with syphilis."

"How did you manage to land in a place like this?"

"What do you mean? I volunteered. It's a job which has to be done. You're a Russian Jew who's had all sense of concern for others knocked out of him by persecution. I was born here. This country means something to me. It's bleeding to death, and I wanted to do something to help. Don't you feel the same?"

"To be honest, I'm so dazed by what's happening that I don't know what I feel. At the beginning I was so immersed in my own worries—the whole business I had built up was tottering—that I didn't have a mind for anything else, but then, as the war went on and on, I began to wonder what was happening. It didn't occur to me that anyone could take on this country and last for more than a year—even the Germans. I swore by everything British—the British Army, the British Navy. But look, the war's in its third year and there's no end in sight, and it seems to me they're prepared to sacrifice every young man alive for the sake of something they call victory. Of course this country means something to me, it means a lot to me, only I don't understand it."

The next afternoon he had a few hours to spare before his train home and he thought he would go to a cinema, but there was none in the town, though he found a theatre which was no longer in use; for the first time since the outbreak of war, he felt a stirring of business instinct. He sought out the local estate agent, enquired about the condition and price of the defunct theatre and took out an option to buy it. He then arranged to have it surveyed, and a month or so later they exchanged contracts. It was difficult to get the labour and the building materials to make the necessary conversions for the time being, but this was his first investment in the future and he kept it separate from his shipping concern, but as soon as the war was over he would open his first cinema. There was little in the external situation to make him hopeful about the future, but the very act of investing in it had in itself somehow made him more hopeful. Or was it the fact that he had found himself away from the heavy, perspiring presence of Zaiderbaum, where he could exercise his own initiative?

Sophie made a fairly rapid recovery and was soon out of hospital, but in the meantime Miri became seriously ill. The trouble with her leg proved rather more acute than either she or Nahum were led to believe. She had complained frequently of having to drag it around like a lump of lead, and eventually her doctor ordered her into hospital. "We hope to save her," the doctor told Nahum, "but there is no hope for the leg."

Miri took it all with remarkable composure. "You've no idea how glad I'll be to be rid of it. I began to hate the leg as if it was something nasty which had latched on to me and had never belonged to me in the first place. But imagine me with a wooden leg? Thump! Thump! Thump! Won't I look comical?"

Nahum was less composed than Miri and less reconciled to the thought that the leg must come off. He discussed the matter with his doctor and wondered if there was any point in travelling down to consult medical opinion in London.

"Frankly, I don't think your wife could make the journey. In any case, Britain isn't Russia. Not everything is concentrated in the capital. The medical skills available in Glasgow are as good as anywhere in the world. And there's a war on, you know. The London hospitals are choc-a-bloc with mere boys who have had their legs shot from under them."

It was not at all certain, given the general state of her health, she would survive the operation, and Sophie and Hector came home on leave and Alex came up from Oxford. She, however, proved more resilient than either her doctor or her family could have imagined. Her leg was removed below the knee, and a few days later she was holding court in bed, with her family seated around her.

"Seeing you all gathered like this makes me feel as if I'm on my deathbed."

"Heaven forbid," said Nahum.

"Well, I've already got one foot in the grave."

"You know," Nahum said to Sophie later, "I think you were doing your mother an injustice. She's a remarkable woman. I wouldn't have her courage. I feel more broken about her operation than she does."

"She's very good in extreme adversity. Did she ever tell you about Father and—" she hesitated.

"Father and who?"

"It strikes me that if she hasn't told you, I shouldn't have mentioned it."

"But you have mentioned it."

"Don't press me, I had no right to. In any case, it makes me sick to think of it. She was very much in love with Father—at least I think she was—and something happened which would have driven most women out of their minds, but she acted as if nothing had happened, and, for all I know, she may have convinced herself that it hadn't."

"You mean she found him in bed with another woman?"

"No, she was used to that, but please don't press me."

Some months later, Alex graduated from Oxford with a double first in oriental languages. The joy with which he and Miri received the news was tempered by his announcement that he was about to go into the army. They already had Hector in uniform, and they jumped every time the phone went or there was a knock at the door, and they went through agonies of consternation in the long gaps between letters. But Hector exuded such airy self-confidence that he left an impression almost of invulnerability, and whatever worries he excited in his absence, every time they saw him they felt that—amid all the death and destruction—he, somehow, would emerge unscathed. Alex, on the other hand, with his slight physique and lachrymose features, gave an impression of extreme vulnerability. Hector had told them, "They're beginning to scrape the bottom of the barrel, but I can't see them taking old Alex," and Nahum could not imagine him in uniform, but Alex passed his medical without difficulty, and a few months later he was on an officers' training course. Nahum began to wonder if he could look forward to seeing his son Jacob, who was then nine, in uniform.

Early in 1917 he was in London on business and was told that Vladimir Jabotinsky would be addressing a meeting in the East End. Jabotinsky, one of the legends of the Zionist movement and its ablest orator, had enlisted in the British Army with a number of followers and was now trying to raise a Jewish Legion to liberate Palestine from the Turks. Nahum was unable to attend the meeting, but he was able to get to a reception for him in the private house immediately afterwards. The place was packed with a motley collection of individuals and loud with the babble of Russian, Yiddish, Hebrew, German, French and even English. Jabotinsky, a slight figure with thick glasses who reminded him slightly of Alex, was in one corner of the room, surrounded by a dense throng of admirers, but as Nahum pressed towards him he noticed a tall, red-faced figure in uniform, with a glass of tea in his hand, talking to a young woman. He stopped as if turned to stone. If it wasn't for the fact that the man was in the uniform of a private in the British Army, he could have sworn it was his boyhood friend from Volkovysk. He pressed towards him until he was almost next to him, at which point the figure looked up, looked at him and dropped his glass with a crash.

"It's Nahum," he shouted.

"Shyke!"

CHAPTER XIX
THE SOLDIER'S TALE

THEY EMBRACED WITH SUCH VIOLENCE AND AROUSED SUCH A COM-
motion that the babble stopped and people looked around to see
what was happening.

"What are you doing here? You in the British Army? What are
you up to? Aren't you a bit old for that sort of thing?" Nahum found
the questions pouring from him in an uncontrollable torrent.

"What do you mean, old? I'm the same age as you are."

"You're even older."

"All right, so you're forty-one and I'm forty-two, but have you got
a birth certificate? I haven't. I told them I was thirty, as if they care.
As long as you're strong enough to handle a rifle, they'll take you."

They found it difficult to talk in the crowd, and they went out in
the hallway and sat on the staircase.

"What's been happening to you? I've heard all sort of stories about
you on and off—that you owned a shipping line, that you were a millionaire—but I couldn't believe them, not the Nahum I knew, a dozy
little twerp, without push or go, who, I thought, had all the makings
of a rabbi. Are you a shipping magnate?"

"I was, and a small one, as magnates go."

"What happened?"

"The war."

"But most people seem to be doing well out of the war."

"There you are, I'm doing badly."

"Ah, you're still the *shmerl* you always were."

"But what's happened to you?"

"What hasn't?"

"How do you come to be in the British Army?"

"It's a long story."

"I've got a long time."

"I suppose you know that I left Volkovysk not long after you and
went first to Odessa. What a town! Ever been there?"

"My mother's parents lived there. I was there as a child but don't
remember it."

"It's a city with a hundred and fifty thousand people, more than a third of them Jewish, but different Jews from the sort we knew in Volkovysk. They were emancipated, not only from Russia bondage (which you can always evade by scattering rubles here and there), but *Jewish* bondage, which, in Volkovysk, at least, seemed inescapable. My objections to the sort of teaching we received in *cheder* and *Yeshiva* was purely intellectual; it offended common sense. What had not occurred to me was that it could also be debilitating. Those *tefillin* you and I had to bind around the arm and head (I take it that you still do) strangle initiative, energy, courage and leave us supine, timid and helpless. There are still, unfortunately, any number of *tefillin* Jews in Odessa, but the majority have thrown them off, and the result is a metamorphosis, and instead of the quivering ninnies hudding in dark corners at the first whisper of violence, we have sturdy, virile Jews—Jews with bones, *cossacks*—who, if bitten, bite back (some even bite before they are bitten).

"I was also overwhelmed by the cultural riches of the place. Do you remember our studies in Volkovysk, the constant regurgitation of stale thoughts, with commentary heaped on commentary and a gloss upon gloss, and never a new idea, a fresh expression, a diversion from the weary old treadmill? I was thought of as an *ilui* because I could recite whole tracts of the Talmud by heart—a skill which should have become redundant with the invention of printing. It was all right for the Yeruchams—what's happened to him, by the way?"

"Yerucham?"

"You know who I mean—'Holy, Holy, Holy.' He was going to marry your sister."

"He didn't marry my sister."

"I'm not surprised. I couldn't understand how she latched onto him in the first place; she was an intelligent, educated girl. Wait a minute, didn't she—"

"She did."

"Good for her. And 'Holy, Holy, Holy'?"

"He's dead."

"Well, that's something in his favour, I couldn't stand him. Where was I, now?"

"Odessa."

"Ah, yes. In Odessa, for the first time, I came upon novelty and the possibilities of creation—poets, writers, thinkers, some of them writing in Russian, some in Yiddish, some in a Hebrew so beautiful that it would not have been out of place in the Psalms: it was as if a window had suddenly been thrown open, letting in light and air.

Works poured from the presses, not all of them of equal merit, but providing a feast for the mind. There was a flourishing Yiddish theatre.

"Emancipation, of course, can have its drawbacks. The apprehensions we had in Volkovysk imposed their restraints. In Odessa, with restraints thrown off, there is—or at least there was—a flourishing Jewish underworld with Jewish gangsters, Jewish brothels, Jewish pimps and Jewish whores, and, in fact, I was once beaten to within an inch of my life because I had spent a night with a tart and did not have the money to pay for it (I thought she had importuned me for my good looks). But an underworld is not too high a price to pay for emancipation, and, in any case, one of the reasons why places like Volkovysk are so peaceable is because the unruly elements, which might have acquired roots there, are drawn off by places like Odessa.

"I remained in Odessa for about ten months, doing various jobs—including kitchenhand in one of the brothels (I was paid in cash and kind). I saved enough to get a ship to Jaffa, but I took ill with I don't know what the moment I set foot on holy soil. I was carried to a doctor, who came to the door wiping blood from his hands on a grubby towel, and I suddenly recovered my vigour and fled. I eventually found refuge in some sort of hospice and was nursed back to life by nuns. I found work as a farm labourer in Petach Tikva but could not compete with the local Arabs, who, it seemed to me, could live for a month on a handful of olives and a hunk of bread, and I moved on to Galilee, where I became ill again. And again, I was not sure what it was, for it was none of the familiar killers like malaria, cholera or typhus, but I could hardly hold food and was too weak to stand up. The most memorable thing about that illness was the intense yearning I felt for Russia—not so much for my father's house and the comforts of a well-to-do home, but for Russia itself—the vast spaces, the great forests, the plains. It was March or April, the time of the year when the snows and Volkovysk begin to melt and the rivers to flood, the fields to emerge from their grey wrapping, and the earth softens. The term, Mother Russia, is very apt, you know, for Russia in the spring somehow reminded me of my own mother, a large, grim woman (she had a lot to be grim about, poor thing), but who in a relaxed moment could break into a smile which seemed to warm every corner of the house. Which reminds me. How is your mother?"

"Don't say you didn't know?"

"Know what?"

"That she married your father."

"Yes, but that was years ago, she's buried him since—poor man.

What did she see in him? He was a considerable scholar, but that's not the sort of thing your mother went in for. And as for his money, he had all my sisters to marry. You haven't seen any of them, have you?"

"No."

"I heard Sorke was in England."

"Sorke in England?"

"So I heard. I also heard she was in France. Her name keeps cropping up everywhere, but I've not come across anyone who's actually seen her. Anyway, there I was, dying in Palestine and dreaming of Russia. All the Russian folk tunes I had ever heard went running through my head—*Polushka, The Red Poppy, The Birch Tree*. I also yearned for Volkovysk. Remember the bath nights and the bath days, Thursday nights for women and small children, Friday afternoons for men and boys? Water everywhere, pink, slithery figures splashing in all directions and shrill voices muffled by steam. I learned to recognise the womanhood of Volkovysk by their pubic hairs. The rabbi's wife's was as luxuriant as her husband's beard; my aunt's was heart-shaped; your Aunt Katya was blond on top but red below, how was that? Yankelson's wife was protuberant and spiky, as if she had a hedgehog between her legs. I was precocious. One Thursday night, the rabbi's wife looked down at me and gave a shriek. My mother, rushing to the source of the commotion, gave a louder shriek and threw a towel around me. I could not have been more than seven, and thenceforth I went with the men. It was like being exiled from paradise. The men, twice-bearded and well hung, had less interesting shapes. I was, however, proud of my father's physique—like a Turkish wrestler—and when he jumped into the *mikvah*, the waters burst their banks. The smells of the place came wafting in to me—the smell of the logs which fired the boilers, the smell of the steam, of the decaying timbers, and, above all, the smell of the birch twigs—the *besums*—with which the men flagellated one another till their flesh tingled, and you emerged, as Father said, not only with a new body, but a new soul. This yearning was the nearest thing I suffered to actual pain. Have you never felt it?"

"Often."

"What is this pull Russia has? Is it the size of the place? Its dark depths? Its whispering forests? Its great plains? Was it perhaps the winters? Do you remember the silence which descended with the snows? The clatter of wagons stopped, and the familiar ring of hobnailed leather on cobbled stones. Voices seemed oddly muffled, and the sound which still echoes in my ears is the crump-crump of footsteps in the snow, and this continued for almost half the year. The only colours which met the eye—certainly the only colours which I remember—were black and white, white and black. The forests sighed and creaked with the snow and did not show their greenery till the spring—white branches and black trunks, except for the silver birches, which were all white. I should imagine that the extremes of colour must have affected attitudes, so that those, who, like me, did not become religious fanatics turned anti-religious (I doubt if I would have remained Jewish at all but for my stay in Odessa, which showed that you could remain Jewish without becoming a fossil). I made a slow recovery, and, because I lacked the energy to do anything else, I began writing and had a few things published—not enough to earn me a livelihood, but enough to make me attempt to earn a livelihood —and nearly starved in the process. Now, believe it or not, I live mainly by the gun. After my recovery, I went through a long period in which I couldn't sleep and decided to cash in on my disability by learning to use a rifle and getting a job as a night watchman. Most of the other watchmen in the area were Circassians, and my job, mainly, was to watch them. They were, I may add, perfectly reliable, but most of the people around there have not been out of Russia long enough to trust *goyim*, even non-Christian *goyim*. In the meantime, I learned Arabic and French and was published fairly regularly in an Aleppo newspaper."

"Aleppo, of all places."

"Aleppo, of all places. I happened to be there with nothing much to do when I noticed—in Aleppo, of all places—a branch of Wachsman's bank. Wachsman was a friend of my father, if you remember."

"He seems to have been a friend of everyone's father."

"Anyway, when I saw that name I went in with a proprietorial air, asked for the manager, mentioned the many languages I spoke— which by then were five—and asked if I could be of use. I also, needless to say, played on the Wachsman connection."

"Everyone plays on the Wachsman connection."

"Not in Aleppo. Anyway, I got a job and worked my way up fairly rapidly. I was about to be transferred to Beirut when the war broke out, and instead I transferred myself back to Cairo."

"You still haven't explained how you happen to be in the British Army."

"I'm coming to that. I had an instinctive feeling once the war broke out that, whoever wins, Turkey would lose, and it would be the end of the Ottoman Empire. That exactly was the feeling of the great Vladimir. In 1915, he formed the Zion Mule Corps to aid the allied cause. I was amongst the first to join. We served in the Gallipoli. When that was wound up, he joined the British Army. I followed suit, and here I am."

"It was as simple as that?"

"As simple as that."

"Are you married?"

"I'm a widower."

"I'm sorry to hear that."

"You wouldn't be if you had met my wife. And you?"

"Yes, with six children."

"That's what I call married. I suppose I must have a couple of dozen, including two by my wife—I think."

"You haven't changed."

"Why, do you think I should have done?"

"No, everybody's so altered that I'm glad to find somebody who is what he always was. Are you working with Jabotinsky?"

"After a fashion. He's working in the *Yeshiva shel ma'alo,* so to speak, and I'm in the *Yeshiva shel ma'ato.* He's trying to persuade the British government that if they would only establish a Jewish Legion, God would be on their side and the war would be over in days, and I'm trying to rally the Jewish masses to the flag. Believe me, he has the easier job. They're worse here than in Volkovysk. They don't want to fight for the Tsar, and I don't blame them, and they don't want to fight for the King, which is rather less understandable, but they don't want to fight for the Jews, either. They just want to get on with making a living and leave the dying to others. They won't get away with it, they shouldn't get away with it. I don't know what's happening to us Jews."

"You've been mixing with the wrong sorts of Jews. There've been thousands of Jewish volunteers. Look, I've got three children of military age, one's a nurse and two are in the army—officers both."

"Officers!'

"Both of them."

"Kein-ein-horeh. Even the great Vladimir is only a sergeant, and look at me, Shyke, a leader of men if ever there was one, a private. Our C.O. is young enough to be my son, and for all I know he might be. Yechiel's grandsons officers in the British Army? Gad, there's a land of opportunity for you."

"As a matter of fact, they're not Yechiel's grandsons. They're Yerucham's sons."

"Yerucham's?"

"I married his widow."

"Ah, so you've acquired a family the easy way, leaving the dirty work to poor old 'Holy, Holy, Holy.' "

"Not quite, I have three children of my own."

Nahum suggested that he come up to Glasgow with him and meet the family.

"Just like that? I'm a soldier, a private, I've got to be back in barracks by midnight. So has the great Vladimir. He had tea with the Foreign Secretary this afternoon. Among us Jews he is king, but back in barracks he is plain Sergeant Jabotinsky."

"Couldn't he persuade the crowds to join the Jewish Legion?"

"Oh ho. You've never seen anything like it. The hall was packed. There must have been about a thousand people there, with others milling around outside; they clapped, they cheered, they stamped their feet. Many were in tears. There was a new king in Yeshurun. When he finished, they wanted more, and when he gave them more, they wanted still more, and they cheered every word. But you know how it is. We treat a speech, no matter how cogently argued or forcefully delivered, as a pleasure in its own right and not a call to action. It was an evening's entertainment. There were nine or ten of us in the hall to take names and addresses. Between us, we collected just over a hundred names, and how many of these do you think will actuallly join the Legion?"

Nahum returned to Glasgow on the overnight train. It was crowded, but he managed to find himself a corner seat after some passengers alighted at Rugby, and he soon fell asleep. When he woke, he could not quite believe that his encounter with Shyke had taken place and thought he must have dreamt it all, for, although he could imagine Shyke in almost any conceivable situation, he could not quite see him as a private in the British Army, but the more he recalled of their conversation, the more he became convinced that it had actually taken place, and a few weeks later he became involved in a controversy on the very issue raised by Shyke.

In the early stages of the war the British Army was manned by volunteers, but after the carnage on the western front, the volunteers proved insufficient, and in 1916 conscription was introduced. Most of the Jews living in Glasgow were Russian aliens and thus not affected by the conscription laws, but in the following year, legislation was introduced compelling Russian citizens of military age who were unwilling to serve in the British forces to serve in the Russian Army. A protest meeting was organised against the measure, and Nahum was invited to join the platform party; he agreed to do so without enquiring too closely what the meeting was about—it was also some time since he was last called upon to grace a platform, so that perhaps he was also flattered by the invitation—and it was only when the first speaker had finished his tirade that he realised what it was about. He at once rose and, without invitation or warning and to the dismay of the chairman, he walked to the front of the platform and addressed the meeting:

"Ladies and gentlemen. I wasn't invited to speak, but as I was invited to a place on the platform, I hope you will excuse me if I say a few words.

"Like all of you here in this hall, I came to this country during the past twenty–twenty-five years. Like some of you, I've prospered. I've had my ups and downs, but I live in a decent house, I eat regular meals, my children have been to good schools—and something we didn't dream of in *der heim,* University—and I do not go to bed at night worrying what might happen the next day or even that same night. I am not saying that people here welcomed us with open arms, and I shall never forget some of the articles I read in the papers about the 'alien scum'—the alien scum, that's you and me—who were flooding the country. But for all that, it's an open country, a free country and, on the whole, an honest country, and even if it's not paradise, you know and I know that we have moved from a place of darkness to a place of light—and it is being threatened.

"This country has been struggling now for three years, wading in blood. It's not so long since I lost my closest colleague—a man of my ship in the North Atlantic. I used to have just over a hundred people working for me before the war. More than half rushed off to join the own age—who volunteered for the navy and who went down with his minute war broke out. Fourteen of them, most of them boys, children, are dead. Two are crippled. There is hardly a family which hasn't lost a father, a brother, a son, sometimes all three. Supposing you were caught up in a war which went on year after year—"

At which he was interrupted with shouts of, "We wouldn't be! It's only *goyim* who can be so crazy!"

He waited for the noise to subside before he continued:

"Supposing you were caught up in a war which went on year after year in which your brothers and sons—the cream of their generation —were slaughtered by the thousand. And supposing there were among us strangers—not complete newcomers, but people with steady jobs and growing businesses—who were going about their work as if the war was none of their business, enjoying all the benefits of citizenship but accepting none of the dangers. Would you not—especially if you were mourning the loss of a brother, a father, a son—hate them? And if so, can you blame them if they should begin to hate us?

"I can understand why no Jew in his senses should want to fight for the Tsar. What I can't understand is how any Jew with self-respect who has made his home in this country can refuse to fight for the King."

At this there was pandemonium. Some sections of the audience stood up and cheered, others shouted and jeered. The chairman asked Nahum to resume his seat, but he refused.

"I shall be heard," he shouted above the chaos; "if it's the last thing I'll do, I shall be heard." The chairman pulled at his coat, but Nahum pulled himself free. "You will not shut me up. I shall be heard, even if I have to wait all night, and I shall be heard because you know in your hearts, as I know in mine, that what I'm saying is true. I shall be heard." And the chairman, unable to subdue the speaker, attempted to calm his audience—with rather more success—and Nahum continued in a more controlled voice:

"Can I ask you a question, Mr Chairman? Why was I, of all people, asked to sit on this platform? I have two sons in the army—one volunteer, the other a conscript—both of them officers. My daughter is a nurse—again a volunteer—in a military hospital, and you invite me, of all people, to a meeting to demand the right not to perform any national service at all, neither in Russia, nor here, neither for the Tsar, nor for the King, and to let others do the dying. Why did you invite me? I'll tell you why. Because you think I'm a *heimishe Yid*—which I am—who can understand the feelings of other *heimische Yidden*—which I do, but *rabboisei,* not every attitude we bring from *der heim* is healthy or wholesome. Some are poisonous, and the most poisonous of all is the belief that what happens to the *goyim* is no business of ours. That may have been justified in Russia or Poland; it is *not* justified here, and we have no right to demand to carry on business as usual while the country is bleeding to death.

"A few weeks ago I was privileged to meet one of the greatest Jews of our time, Mr Vladimir Jabotinsky, who is trying to raise a Jewish Legion, so that Jews can rally under their own flag and show that the spirit of the Maccabees is still alive. But will you rally to his flag, will your sons? Or do you all believe that the whole business of life is business?"

Again there was uproar, but by now he felt he had made his point and strode out. As he turned to leave, he was pulled aside by a burly figure who said to him: "You don't remember me, do you?"

"I'm afraid not."

"I came here on one of your boats. So did half the people in the hall, but now that you're carrying troops instead of customers, you've turned patriot. You've found a better customer."

Alex came home on leave shortly after in the uniform of a lieutenant in the Royal Corps of Signals. He did not, even in uniform, look quite the soldier, and Miri confessed she almost laughed when she saw him, for, with his trousers ballooning out of his tight puttees, his thin legs and huge boots, he resembled a concert-party comedian rigged up as an officer, but Nahum was more in awe of him than ever. He spent most of his leave in reading. Sometimes when Nahum walked into a room and found him alone with a book, he would sit opposite him and cogitate on a likely topic of conversation, but whatever the topic, it usually petered out fairly quickly.

"The war isn't going too well."

"Sorry?"

"The war isn't going too well."

"Not well at all."

"The soldiers are all right, but I don't think much of the generals."

"Neither does anyone, I'm afraid."

Silence.

"What sort of work do you do in the signal corps?"

"We're not really supposed to say."

"Sorry."

"Not that I know much about it."

Silence.

"Do you think they'll make Hector a captain?"

"Wouldn't surprise you if they did."

"Don't you think he makes a good officer?"

"Frankly, no."

"Why not?"

"He's so indifferent to death himself that he's likely to endanger his men. There are too many officers like him in the British Army. The last time I saw him, he complained that he had never even been nicked."

"Never even been what?"

"Nicked, wounded. The way he put it, you'd have thought he'd been passed over for promotion."

"He's a brave man, though."

"He's fearless, which is not quite the same thing. Only cowards like me can be brave."

"You a coward?"

"My goodness me, yes. I get terrified every time I hear the sound of gun-fire."

"But you didn't try to get out of the army."

"I was too much of a coward even for that."

Nahum told him about his now infamous speech, and, to his surprise, Alex took the side of the immigrants.

"I can't blame these chaps for staying out if they can. People like me are pushed in by social pressure. There's no such pressure in their circles, and, in any case, you can't imagine what the army's like to an immigrant. There were a couple of chaps in our unit when I was doing basic training. Everyone ragged the life out of them. If you have a bullying sergeant—and who hasn't—you know him to be a bully and a thug, but I should imagine, to a newcomer from Poland, he must seem like another Haman. People like Hector rushed into the army because they saw it as an extension of public school, with a good chance of being a prefect, but it's an alien world to these people and one, moreover, in which you have more than a passing chance of being killed. If you've been chased around from pillar to post for two thousand years, you're inclined to hold onto dear life while you've got it."

"That's no argument," said Nahum, "not at a time like this."

By a dreadful irony, he received a telegram the next day to say that Hector had been seriously wounded in action.

He immediately got in touch with the War Office to ask if he could visit him. The elderly officer on duty was taken aback by the request.

"He's at a base hospital in Belgium, not far from the front line," he said. "There've been thousands of casualties. If every parent put in such a request, the front line would be over-run with civilians. There's a war on, you know."

"I know, but he's severely wounded."

"That may be the case, but it will take you nearly a week to get to Belgium—"

"A week?"

"Mines. It's not a pleasure jaunt, you know. There're mines in the channel. It takes three days to get to Dieppe, and goodness knows how long to get across northern France. The poor chap could be dead by the time you get there."

Nahum asked to speak to his superior. When that proved difficult, he got in touch with his M.P. and eventually got the necessary papers for the journey, which took him what he later described as the eight longest days of his life. The sea was rough, and the vessel zig-zagged across the channel, and, as he had been warned, what would normally have been a crossing of a few hours took nearly three days. In France it was almost impossible to move at all. There was chaos and confusion; waggon trains; pack horses; mule trains, laden and unladen; and endless columns of soldiers on horseback, on mules, on foot. The railways were disrupted and torn, and he continued on much of his journey by horse-drawn waggon. It was almost like being back in Volkovysk, except that, as he moved across northern France, the green of the landscape changed to a muddy brown, with mile upon mile of churned-up soil. There was hardly a blade of grass to be seen, or a tree intact. When the waggoner pulled into the courtyard of a shattered farmhouse to rest, Nahum found another who was setting out northwards, and he continued to journey with him. But when he reached the hospital, Hector was no longer there.

"Why?" cried Nahum in alarm. "What's happened to him? Is he still alive?"

"Good question," said the medical officer. "I'm new here, unfortunately, but it shouldn't take me a minute to find out." It took him ten minutes, by which time Nahum was himself ready for a hospital bed.

"Sorry for the delay," said the officer cheerfully. "Care for a drink, by the way?"

Nahum did not care for anything.

"There's been a bit of shelling, can't think who from. The Fritzes are supposed to be thirty miles away, but, anyway, they moved the chaps they could patch up. He couldn't be too bad if they were able to move him."

It was dark by then, and Nahum could not continue the journey. He woke up in the early hours of a grey morning to the rumble of what sounded like distant thunder, and when he went out into the courtyard, he could see black clouds of smoke and dust where the shells landed.

A medical orderly took him by car to the hospital, which was about thirty miles away, and they drove for nearly an hour before the sound of guns finally faded from their cars; they pulled up in the grounds of what had once been a château. There were beds everywhere, in the halls (which had been stripped of their furnishings), in the corridors, in the outhouses. He found Hector in a long hut which had been built on the back terrace. He was sitting up, thin, white, with broad, red rings around his eyes and sores around his mouth. He seemed to grimace rather than smile when Nahum appeared.

"What the hell are you doing here?" he asked.

Nahum grasped his hand and squeezed it with grateful relief. "So what's happened to you?"

"Been perforated, like a postage stamp. A bullet or two came in here"—he pointed to an area below his chest—"and went out there. I suppose, if anyone had cared to look, he'd have found daylight coming through me. I don't think they hit anything which won't mend, but I lost a lot of blood, gallons of it. It was pouring out like water from a burst pipe. This was my last thought as I passed out, 'Good God, I never thought I had so much of it.' "

Nahum was given a bed in a converted greenhouse and remained in the hospital for nearly a week; he made himself useful as a hospital orderly, moving beds, making beds, moving bed-pans, making tea and occasionally helping out in the morgue. He had never felt so usefully engaged since the war broke out. The effort gave him an extraordinary sense of fulfillment, and he began to understand why Colquhoun and the others had rushed off to the war as soon as they could. There was an intensity to living near the front line—even if it took the form of emptying bed-pans—which was not to be found elsewhere. He was too old to have been conscripted, but he was sorry not to have volunteered. With a sick wife and small children it would have been impractical to do so, and it was unlikely at his age that he would have been posted anywhere near the front line, but it would have been something to have been in uniform at all. Everything he had been engaged in, even if it was now drawing a profit, seemed oddly irrelevant compared to the war.

He also found, as he had found with Sophie, that he could communicate more easily with a sick Hector than a sound one, as if one needed the proximity of death to open out. On Nahum's first visits, Hector had been too weak to talk to him at length, but on his last day in hospital they had spent the better part of two hours together.

"You know," said Nahum, "I could never understand how you, the Jewish son of a Jewish father, could have volunteered for the army. But now I can. There's something about soldiers and soldiering, and guns and battle, so that even I, a plump, middle-aged Russian Jew, am beginning to feel like rushing to arms. I wouldn't have believed it."

"Are you sure I'm the Jewish son of a Jewish father?" said Hector.

"What do you mean?"

"You know that Sophie has strange theories about our likely parentage, don't you? She is sadly convinced that Father is her father—she wishes he hadn't been, but she is convinced he was—because she looks like him. Alex and I don't. She also mentioned that Father was away fairly frequently when she was a small girl, and that you were a frequent visitor—"

"I was a friend of the family. I have known your mother since she was fifteen."

"There's no need to apologise or explain. Sophie has never quite been able to forgive Mother—or the world, or mankind—for the fact that she is the child of her father and feels it is a stigma she'll never outgrow. I didn't mind the old man; if anything, I admired him. Alex speaks of him as if he was an ordinary human being like you and me, who might, if the occasion arose, indulge in something shady, whereas Sophie looked upon him as the complete villain, who would not knowingly be found doing an honest thing if there was a dishonest way of going about it. His religious observance, his synagogue going, his pretence of piety, were all, she thinks, intended to give an extra dimension to his villainy, an extra layer to his deceit. He deceived and robbed his wife, his father-in-law, his customers, his suppliers, his workers, customs and excise, even his lawyers—and think, finally, of the manner of his going. Who cannot admire such a man? Sophie, who always looks for hidden motives—or, rather, very hidden motives, motives so hidden that one doesn't know one had them in the first place—thinks I joined the army because I hated mankind, and I hated mankind because I hated my father."

"Why did you join?"

"Because it was the thing to do, but there were times when I had my regrets. I was based in some muddy estuary in Norfolk with nothing for company except wild geese and drunken soldiers, with stores piled high everywhere and nothing moving. Somebody, possibly myself, must have mentioned that my family was in shipping, for I was driven to a small port, and my C.O. said to me: 'Things are in a bit of a mess round here, Rabinovitz—er—Raeburn'—that's almost my accepted name, by the way, Rabinovitz-er-Raeburn. 'Things are in a bit of a mess round here, can you get them moving?' And got them moving I did, even if it meant commandeering every waggon and ship in sight and dumping civilian cargo—inadvertently of course—into the sea. However, the danger of doing anything with minimal competence in the army is that you're stuck with it for life. I was given an extra pip and moved to France, but there I was faced with a more formidable situation—larger port, heavier congestion, greater urgency and a sullen, depleted and thieving work-force. While men were dying at the front, they complained that the loads were too awkward or too heavy, that the hours were too long, that the weather was too wet or too dry, that the holds were too slippery, and, amid all the holdups, cargoes kept vanishing without trace. I sought permission to take a few of them—not more than a dozen or so—and have them shot *pour encourager les autres,* you understand, but the C.O. said you can't do that, they're not our people. There was also, as always, some civilian cargo tied up amid the general confusion, with the owners tearing their hair and shrieking of ruin. I got a few of them together and suggested I could possibly get things moving with the help of a small fund, and the fund was quickly organised. I did not have to bribe the whole work-force, only their leaders, who suddenly remembered their country was at war, and things began to move."

"But if you were only involved in transport, how were you wounded?"

"My C.O. wanted to know the same thing and told me that I would be court-martialled if I recovered. Well, when we got things moving at the port, we went on up the line to ease congestion at the railhead. At that point, we were helping an artillery brigade organise the flow of ammunition. We were not near the front line to start with, but the Germans advanced by night and surprised us all and wiped out a supply column. The gunners found themselves short of ammunition, and I quickly organised a column of my own men to keep them supplied; and it was while heading the column that I stopped the bullet. It hadn't occurred to me the Germans were that near. It could have been a sniper, though I shouldn't be at all surprised if I was shot by one of my own men."

"One of your own men?"

"Happens all the time. I'd been driving them a bit hard. Odd thing is, it hardly hurt at all, though it felt a bit draughty. I was on horseback at the time and found my saddle getting wet and sticky. I got down to see what was happening and collapsed under the horse, but things wouldn't have been too bad if the horse hadn't collapsed on top of me."

"It's a miracle you're alive."

"It was touch and go for a bit—which reminds me. Cyrus—remember Cyrus, tall fellow, he was with us in Menton? He saw me a week ago, or was it two weeks ago—you lose all sense of time in hospital—when I was in pretty bad shape. He said he might be in Scotland, in which case he'd be looking Ara up, and I'm afraid of what he might tell her. You'll be seeing her, I suppose?"

"Of course, I will, and I'll tell her you're fine."

Fine was an exaggeration, and Nahum would have liked to stay on until Hector was better, but he was becoming anxious about events at home. Alex would have left by now, and he presumed that Sophie would also have gone back, and, although old Hester was still around, he was not too happy at the thought of Miri and his mother being thrown too frequently together.

It took him ten days to get back, and the nearer he got to Glasgow, the stronger grew his sense of foreboding that something had gone badly wrong.

When he got home, two large men in trench coats were waiting for him in the front room. They both rose as he entered, and one of them pulled an identity card from his pocket.

"We're from the police," he said.

The next morning he was arraigned before the city magistrates under the Trading with the Enemy Act and released on bail. Warrants were also out for the arrest of Lazar and Zaiderbaum, but they had both vanished.

CHAPTER XX
TRIALS

"IGNORANCE IS NO DEFENCE IN LAW," SAID KROCHMAL, HIS LAWYER. "And, in any case, there are innumerable documents with your signature implicating you to the hilt."

"Who reads documents? I only read the figures and couldn't always make head or tail of them, either, but I can see now why they were anxious to have me as chairman. I said to Lazar only a few weeks ago: 'You know,' I said, 'there's so little to do I'm hardly earning my keep,' and he said, 'On the contrary, you're invaluable.' They needed somebody to take the blame."

"You do yourself an injustice," said the lawyer. "They needed an established name to give respectability to their effort. But tell me, if the others got wind that the police were making enquiries, why didn't you?"

"And supposing I had, what could I have done about it? Where could I have run to, and what for? And, in any case, what can they do to me?"

"In this climate, almost anything. We'll be seeing counsel tomorrow, but it seems to me that the most obvious course is to tell the story exactly as it happened. The fact that the others ran for it and you did not is in itself in your favour and may suggest that you were the victim of a conspiracy, rather than a party to it. And of course, you could point to domestic worries—children in the army, son injured, wife gravely ill—as reasons why you were unable to pay sufficient attention to the company."

"I wasn't paying sufficient attention because the business was largely out of my hands. I had no idea what they were up to."

"So you keep telling me, and, of course, I believe you, but you should have taken greater care in signing papers. You were chairman of the firm, they were your co-directors. You should have made it your business to see what they were up to. Didn't the improved trading figures arouse your suspicion?"

"No, why should they have done? The whole point of reorganising the company and taking on Zaiderbaum was to improve the figures.

If they had gotten worse, then I would have wanted to know what was happening, but the natural thing in business is to leave well alone. I can see now I was a fool, perhaps even a greedy fool, and a fool and his money are soon parted. The only thing that upsets me is that a business which I've spent twenty-five years building up, and which at one time counted for something in the shipping world, should end in this way."

"Anyway, the damage is done. The best thing we can do now is to drag things out a bit till the war's over——"

"And have this thing hanging over my head for goodness knows how many years? No, thank you. When I've got something nasty ahead, I want to get it over and done with. I'm innocent, you know, I'm innocent, God knows I'm innocent, but if there's no way of proving it, then let's plead guilty and have an end to it. Apart from anything else, it'll save on legal costs."

"You're forgetting the atmosphere in which we're living. You'd be found guilty—not only of being a felon, but a foreign felon——"

"What do you mean, a foreign felon? I've been a British subject for years."

"Which only aggravates the offence and makes you a traitor. The public is in a hating, hateful, rabid mood, and even the courts are affected. If they should find Rabinovitz guilty of trading with the enemy, you could be hanged, drawn and quartered, so that the longer we can delay things, the better."

Nahum felt rather less troubled about the whole affair than he thought he should be. He had pangs of regret about the collapse of his business and his livelihood—his shortsightedness, his gullibility, his stupidity—but they did not compare to his domestic worries. His business worries were a dull ache, his domestic worries, a sharp, gnawing pain.

Hector had been awarded the MC (the irony of the fact that his son was a war hero and that he was being charged with trading with the enemy was not lost on Nahum), but his recovery was a good bit slower than anticipated. "The damned thing about being in hospital," wrote Hector, "is that there's no knowing what wretched plague you could pick up from the others who are brought in—there's no telling where they've been," and Nahum feared that if Hector ever did recover, he could be an invalid for the rest of his days.

He was worried about Alex. Six weeks had passed since they had last heard from him, and he seemed so thin, frail and vulnerable that they did not know how he would face up to the stresses of army life, let alone actual fighting. He looked as if he might disintegrate at the very sound of gun-fire.

He was worried about Sophie, who seemed to show a growing reluctance to spend her leave at home and had found an excuse to stay away even over Passover. She was now nearly twenty-three and rarely met a Jewish soul from one end of the year to the other, and he began to wonder if she would ever marry.

Above all, he was worried about Miri. The operation on her leg had not been a complete success. She suffered from considerable discomfort and was in and out of hospital for further examination and further treatment.

The surgeon explained that they were experiencing some trouble containing the infection.

"Do you mean," said Miri, "that you'll have to cut off another bit?"

"That may be necessary."

"Then why don't you cut my throat and be finished with it? What do you think I am, a roll of salami?" And it was only then that she broke down and cried. Nahum was at once moved and reassured by her tears, for hitherto her fortitude had been such that he first marvelled at her and then began to wonder if she were human. When she had to enter hospital for a second operation, her spirit collapsed. She remained six weeks in hospital, and when she finally came home, she was a different person—shrivelled, shrunken, her skin in loose folds, her eyes lustreless, her head to the side. Those who had not witnesssed her gradual deterioration gasped when they saw her, and Nahum had to warn visitors of the change. He tried to cheer her up with any good news that came their way, but Allied victories in Palestine, Mesopotamia or even the western front left her unmoved. Jacob, their first "joint product," as he liked to call him, now nearly eight—a fat, silent, red-faced lad with awkward ways, who spent most of his free time marshalling toy soldiers on the living-room floor—had, to the surprise of everybody, won a scholarship to Clifton, but she received the news without enthusiasm. The news that the end of the war was at last in sight did occasion something like a sparkle in her eyes, but when Nahum added that Sophie and the boys would soon be home, she said: "Where will they all sleep, especially now that your mother's moved in for good?"

His mother had talked of moving to Katya's, but when it became clear that Miri was permanently crippled, she remained, and her presence became an obsession with her daughter-in-law. One evening, as Nahum was getting ready for bed and Miri was sitting upright in bed watching him undress, she said: "You know, you've been neglecting yourself. Look at yourself, all fat and flabby. Your trousers are baggy, you've got stubble on your face, your moustache is drooping like a rat's tail. You're not even fifty, and you're beginning to look as if you're seventy. Lotie'll never marry you now."

He felt there was no point in reminding her that Lotie was happily married and that he had virtually lost contact with her, but he was curious to know what had made her think of Lotie at all. He soon found out.

"I could see your mother's face light up when she heard I'd have to go back to hospital. I could read her mind: 'That'll be the end of her,' it kept saying. 'Another week, another two weeks, another month, and he'll be free to marry his Lotie.' Oh, she's been very helpful, I know, but every time she comes into my room, there's that same sorrowful look in her eyes—the thought that her son, her only son, could have married an heiress and ended up instead with the widowed, crippled daughter of a poultry dealer. In a way, I don't blame her, I would have felt the same myself, but I could feel the poison in her look. My stump begins to smart every time she looks at me, as if she's rubbing salt into it. I wish she'd go away, leave the house, even if it means I'd have to hop around on my lone leg. I don't say anything because I don't want to upset you—you have enough to worry about—but she poisoned me with her looks as surely as if she had put arsenic into my food—which she would have done if she had had half the chance. Your mother was never really a religious woman, was she? Yet I saw her praying before I went in, and I'm sure that it was for only one thing, that I should never come out. It was that which kept me going even in my fever; when they thought I was finished, one thought kept me going—that I'll outlive her yet."

His mother's behaviour had, in fact, been a revelation to him. He had always thought of her as spoilt, self-indulgent and pampered, but as soon as Miri entered the hospital, she rolled up her sleeves and took over the household—cooked, cleaned, washed, scrubbed, darned socks, polished shoes, tended the house plants and the garden and came padding up and down the stairs to look after old Hester, who was now almost paralysed. He had never seen her work so hard or so cheerfully, and when Miri came home, she looked after her like a nurse. He could hardly tell her to go now when she was needed more than ever, but, on the other hand, she was preying on Miri's mind, and he asked her to keep out of sight. Even that didn't help, for Miri began complaining that she could "feel" her presence—"she's like a dark spirit brooding over the place."

Miri was, by then, not in a condition to be reasoned with. He explained the situation to his mother, who understood it perfectly and packed her bags and returned to Katya. At the same time, he wrote to Sophie, who obtained leave and returned to keep house.

As Miri's condition continued to deteriorate, he moved her bed to the front lounge. The house smelt like a hospital, and everyone moved on tip-toe and spoke in subdued voices not to disturb her She had a small bell by her side, and they ate their meals in silence in case her bell should go unheard; Nahum would sometimes bring in his meal on a tray and join her by her bedside. She ate pitifully little and was in almost constant pain. They got a day nurse and then, as she kept waking in agony, a night nurse, and finally she was taken back to hospital.

A date had in the meantime been set for the trial. Krochmal said he could have it postponed without difficulty.

"No," said Nahum, "for God's sake, don't. Let's get that over and done with, at least."

The trial lasted less than a week. His counsel made much of the fact that both his sons had been commissioned in regiments of the line and were on active service, that one of them had only just been awarded the MC for gallantry and that his client had been distracted by concern about their safety and by domestic worries from paying sufficient attention to the conduct of his business. Moreover, the absconding directors had been at pains to keep all knowledge of the illicit transactions from him, knowing full well that he would never have been a party to them; they had falsified accounts; drained assets; and reduced a prosperous company to a mere shell.

The court appeared to be impressed by the argument, and the judge, in his summing-up, said that, in view of all the circumstances, he proposed to take a "lenient" view of the case, at which Counsel nodded across to Nahum, as if to say, "We're all right, boy." He was fined fifty thousand pounds.

The sentence took their breath away. If this was leniency, thought Nahum, what might a harsh sentence have entailed? Fifty thousand pounds! He doubted if the assets at his disposal would bring in half that sum, and the legal costs could probably amount to a further five thousand. Yet the whole trial had seemed oddly irrelevant and unreal and had left him with an odd sense of anticlimax. He had somehow expected something more dramatic. He recalled the old Yiddish expression, *abi gezunt*, which, roughly translated, meant nothing mattered while one was in good health. It also worked the other way around. The thought of finding fifty-five thousand pounds, and the fact that his business was in ruins, seemed trivial, compared to the thought of Miri writhing in agony.

As he was coming out of court, he was handed a note asking him to come straight to the hospital. He stopped a cab and was there within minutes. When he got to the ward, he found a screen around Miri's bed. Sophie was on a bench in the corridor.

"She's having difficulties with her breathing," she said; "they're giving her oxygen. How did the trial go?"

"Does it matter?"

"No, I don't suppose it does."

"How long have you been here?"

"Two or three hours. They phoned this morning."

"Why didn't you let me know earlier?"

"What could you have done? I told them to wait till the hearing was over. I've contacted the War Office, but I can't see much chance of either Alex or Hector getting here in time."

"Why not? Your mother'll pull through. You don't know your mother, she's been through a crisis before."

"She wanted to live before, she doesn't any more. It's the last thing she said to me: 'They keep reviving me,' she complained, 'what for? I want to sleep, tell them to let me sleep.' "

About an hour later, the doctor came out and told them that the crisis had passed and that she was sleeping. "She should pull through," he added, "she's fundamentally sound."

They went home and had supper, which they ate in silence and with difficulty. Later, Nahum went upstairs to have a bath, and as he sank into the hot water, he thought how nice it would be if people could only dissolve as easily as bath salts. Everything about him was dissolving or had dissolved. His business was at an end, his marriage was almost at an end, the world he had known was at an end. By chance he had only that morning read of the death of old Wachsman. He recalled his words. "Shipping isn't a business for a Jewish boy. Start with ships, and you finish at the bottom of the sea," which was approximately where he was. He recalled Kagan's warning against growing too big and, indeed, his own hesitation on the same score. He should have listened to his inner voice. He might not have grown so rich so fast but would not have fallen so far and would never have become entangled with Lazar and Company. Katya had pleaded with him not to blame everything on her poor son. "And, in any case," she added, "he's probably dead now, and you mustn't speak ill of the dead," to which Nahum remarked, with rare bitterness: "I don't know if he is dead, but if I should get hold of him, he'll wish he was."

He had no idea what he would do with himself or how he would feed his family in the coming months. He was well insured, and the happiest solution for everyone, he thought, would have been to drop dead. Had he been a really dutiful Jewish father, he thought, he might have gone out and hanged himself, but he was only forty-two, and, although he was not particularly anxious to stay alive, he did not feel he should strive officiously to be dead. He would have to sell his terrace house in Carmichael Place and move back to the Gorbals. He would be back where he was twenty-five years ago, but with a crippled wife and six children and none of the optimism of youth. And tomorrow the papers would be full of his trial. Nahum Raeburn, né Rabinovitz, *der heiser patriot,* the flaming patriot, had been found guilty of trading with the enemy. And he, the very same Nahum, an esteemed public figure, who had represented Glasgow at Zionist congresses in Hamburg and Vienna, who had mixed with the mighty, who had graced public platforms, whose success stories had been printed in Yiddish papers the world over and to whose door an endless succession of *schnorrers* had beaten a path, would himself be reduced to the status of *schnorrer.* To be poor was never pleasant, but to be poor after having been rich was nasty.

There was a knock on the door, and he sat up in alarm. It was Sophie. The hospital had called. Miri was in a coma.

They sat silently by her side through the night. Then, as day was breaking, her eyes flickered, opened, gazed at them without recognition and then closed again. Minutes later, she was dead.

When they got home, there were three policemen outside their door and a small crowd on the pavement opposite. Every window in their house and not a few in the adjoining houses was shattered. Hedges had been uprooted, and glass, bricks and clods of earth were strewn about the road. A mob had descended on the street in the early hours of the morning with shouts of "Jewish traitor" and "alien scum." Nahum's mother, who had come over to look after the children, had put her head out of the door to see what was happening and was immediately attacked. Neighbours had come to her help, and someone had called the police. There were shouts and scuffles. Several heads were broken by flying stones and others were injured by broken glass. The police had managed to evacuate Nahum's mother and the children to safety in a van, but Hester, who could not be easily moved, had collapsed and was rushed to hospital in an ambulance. There were several torn newspapers amid the rubble in the street. One of them carried the head-line: RUSSIAN JEW FINED FOR TRADING WITH HUN.

"You see," said Nahum, "you don't have to be in Russia to have a pogrom."

But it didn't really hurt. Nothing seemed to hurt, as if he were suffering from a leprosy of the emotions. His wife, only forty, after years of discomfort and months of agony, was dead. His children were orphans. His step-children had grown to maturity, but Jacob was only nine, Vicky was eight, Benny was six. His business was in ruins, his name in tatters. Where he had been a source of pride, he had become a source of reproach. And yet it didn't seem to matter. He didn't even cry until Hector appeared unexpectedly, like a ghost of his former self, white-faced and leaning on a stick. He rose to embrace him and fell back into his chair in tears, and he suspected that he was crying for Hector, rather than Miri or himself. He had been inordinately proud of him, not only as a step-father but as a Jew, for Hector seemed to display all the qualities which he thought had become atrophied in the Jew. He was martial, fearless, erect, and Nahum took such pleasure in the sight of him as to overlook the unfortunate fact of his parentage, but now even Hector the indomitable seemed broken.

Nahum had lapsed in many Jewish observances, but he kept a full week of mourning, with his children sitting by his side, and the house was filled with milling crowds from morning until night; what distressed him more than anything was the sight of his small sons saying *kaddish* and the sound of Hector stumbling over his Hebrew in his attempt to do the same.

The war came to an end during the course of that week and there was the sound of jubilation outside, but Nahum was as little moved by the good news as he was by his own misfortune, beyond reflecting thankfully that Alex, at least, had come through unscathed.

Miri had slept alone since her operation so that he had had time to get used to his large, cold double bed, and they had not, in fact, slept as man and wife since her leg had begun troubling her. "It's like having a foreign body beside me," she used to complain, and pain-killing drugs had dampened her sensuality. Her sensuality had been perhaps her supreme quality as a wife, for even when she was a slight little woman, like a porcelain figurine, she flared with lust, and he sometimes wondered how she contained herself on the frequent occasions he was away.

"I've been a *good* girl," she had always assured him when he got back, as if he had had any doubts on the matter, which, as a matter of fact, he had, but these only kindled his own feelings, and, although she could be shrewish and peevish and occasionally reverted to the foul-mouthed poultry dealer's daughter, he thought his marriage had been as happy as a marriage could be; if he had any regrets, it was that he didn't get in before Yerucham, but even there, he wondered if he could have sired three children quite as exceptional as Sophie, Alex and Hector.

Almost everyone he had known came to call in the course of that week. Katya and her two daughters more or less took over the running of the household, and with the to-ing and fro-ing of visitors, something like a party atmosphere developed as the week progressed. One evening he looked up and saw Jessie Colquhoun in the crowd. She felt and looked slightly out of place, and he got up and went over to her. It was nearly two years since he had seen her, and she had then been talking about joining some women's army corps, but he hadn't taken her seriously.

"Oh, yes," she said, "I am in the army now, and an officer, too, so you had better salute."

She had lost weight and seemed to have grown taller as a result, but she was as lively and bright-eyed as ever. He asked her what she was going to do after the war.

"It is after the war."

"Well, after after."

"I don't know. I'm just back from Malta. I love Scotland, but it's given me a taste for sunshine."

His mother later asked him who she was, and he told her.

"She's very attractive, isn't she?"

"Do you think so?"

"Very. Is she Jewish?"

CHAPTER XXI
BEGINNING AGAIN

"FROM THE GORBALS TO THE GORBALS IN ONE GENERATION," SAID Nahum as he pushed open the door of his flat. He felt strangely glad to be back, as if this were his natural domicile (though he had vague recollections of feeling the same when he returned to Carmichael Place). It was small but sufficient, and easy to keep warm. Victoria and Benny shared one room. Sophie—who kept house for him—occupied another, while he slept in an alcove in the kitchen and used what they called "the big room" as his office.

There had been no absolute need to dispose of Carmichael Place, the cost of which, compared to the overall scale of his debts, was small, but he sold it when it became clear that, as Sophie predicted, neither Hector nor Alex would be returning to Glasgow.

When the war finished, Nahum presumed that they would both be promptly demobilised, but over six months passed before that happened, and Hector decided to sign on for a further period of service. He had by then made an almost complete recovery, and Nahum thought that, with his war record, every door would be opened to him, but he had no clear idea what he wanted to do. Nahum was not in a position to make him an attractive offer, and the army seemed to be the most likely option.

"Do you mean to say you're going to be a professional soldier?" asked Nahum incredulously. "I mean, the war is over."

"*The* war may be over, but there're little wars all over the place, and quite a big one in Russia, which may get bigger."

"What about Ara?" he wanted to ask, but he did not quite feel it was any of his business, and Sophie suggested that Hector was going back into the army to keep out of Ara's way, which did not strike him as a particularly satisfactory answer, because whenever he saw them together, Hector seemed very happy in her company.

"Is he never going to marry the girl?" asked Katya.

"Would she want to be an army wife?" asked Nahum.

"Who would? But who says he has to go into the army?"

"What would he do if he didn't? I've no money to give him."

"Her father left her a bit."

"Can you see those two living on a bit?"

"So what's going to happen to her?"

"I don't know. She's a big girl, he's a big boy. They'll have to work it out for themselves."

With Alex, the situation was more straightforward. He was offered a job on the staff of the governor of Jerusalem, Sir Ronald Storrs.

"With your qualifications," asked Nahum, "couldn't you get a job here?"

"I daresay I could, but I would rather be there."

"I didn't know you were a Zionist."

"I'm not sure what a Zionist is, but I find it difficult to reconcile myself to the prospect of Glasgow when there's a chance of living in Jerusalem."

Kagan had sent him a long and sympathetic letter on Miri's death and had asked him about his post-war plans, adding: "Presumably, in the light of your experience, you may find shipping a particularly unrewarding line of business." When Nahum replied that he was thinking of going into the cinema trade, Kagan told him that this was so far outside his experience that he would hesitate to offer advice. What was more to the point, he hesitated to offer money, and Nahum turned instead to *lantsleit,* various small Jewish traders who stemmed from the Volkovysk area, whom he had helped in their early struggles and who were only too eager to help him. The sums involved—compared to the scale of his earlier operations—were so small that he was almost embarrassed to approach them, but he wanted to renovate the old theatre he had bought in southern Scotland, to convert it into a cinema and hire a manager to look after the place. The total amount necessary would not have met the Goodkind-Raeburn wages bill for a week.

The cinema was an instant success. The war was over; people were tired of grey reality without the dramas that had accompanied war. They sought escape, and the cinema was the nearest refuge. By the end of his first year, he had accumulated enough capital, not only to repay his debts, but to invest in another cinema in a small mining town in Lanarkshire, some twenty miles south of Glasgow. By the end of his second year, he acquired a third; by the end of the third, a fourth; using one building as collateral for the next. By then he had acquired an office again, a manager, a secretary and a bookkeeper, and he was pleasantly surprised to discover how far one could prosper on so meagre a capital outlay.

His new prosperity did not, however, restore him to his old status. A cinema owner was not a ship owner, but if he was not in the same class of business, neither did he have the same class of worries. He was not troubled by international crises—of which there were many in the post-war years—storms at sea, mutinous sailors, suicidal passengers, corrupt agents, predatory bankers. He could sleep at night, but he missed the sense of importance which came with the constant descent of international telegrams, the meetings in panelled rooms with bankers and ship owners, the invitations to embassies and consulates, and, although he had resumed his donations to Zionist charities (if not on their previous scale), he was no longer elected to attend Zionist congresses or to grace Zionist platforms. He had ceased to be a public figure and had not entirely reconciled himself to the taste of anonymity. He no longer had business dealings with Kagan, but since he and Miri had been Kagan's week-end guests at his country estate, he had been under the impression that their relationship had progressed beyond business to a personal level, and he had thus invited him to Jacob's *bar mitzvah*. Kagan's secretary replied with a formal little note regretting that pressure of work would not allow him to come, which Nahum accepted as a formal intimation that their relationship was at an end.

He missed Miri deeply, or, rather, he missed the opportunity to discuss the turn in his fortunes with her. His decline in business had coincided almost completely with her decline in health, as if the one had brought on the other, and the admiring gaze which he thought he had seen in her eyes in their early years of marriage had gradually hardened to contempt. She thought she had married a success—"the catch of the century," as his mother had put it—and he had proved a failure. "Everybody seems to be making money out of the war," she complained, "while you seem to be losing it." Not everyone, of course, was in shipping, and in so volatile an area of shipping as immigration, and he could hardly be blamed—certainly he did not blame himself—for failing to foresee the war. He did blame himself for falling in with Lazar, but he felt vindicated as a businessman by the success of his new venture, and he was sorry she was not alive to witness it.

He had developed a good relationship with Sophie and found it easy to talk to her, but there were two topics in which he could never engage her—business and money. She was an excellent housekeeper, but rather sharp with the children and particularly short-tempered with Vicky, whom she found lazy, wilful and insolent.

"She's only eleven," Nahum reminded her.

"A girl of eleven isn't a child," Sophie retorted. "She has to be made to understand that you are no longer a rich man, that I'm not her servant and that she'll have to make her own bed."

For ten days Vicky's bed was left unmade, and then, one day, Sophie looked into her room, and behold it was made.

"Happy?" asked Nahum.

"No," said Sophie, "I think you made it."

"*I* made it? I don't even make my own bed."

"I know, but you'd make hers."

And she was right.

What worried him most about her, however, was the fact that she was twenty-six and still single. She used to say when she was much younger that the young men who laid siege to her were less interested in her than her father's money, and she was proved right by events, for the siege was raised when his money vanished, but then, she had also grown older and harder, though—in Nahum's eyes, at least—no less attractive.

His mother, who had settled in permanently with Katya, said to him: "She's a very earnest girl with a strong sense of duty and very English. The English don't attach the same importance to marriage as we do. She feels obliged to keep house for you, and you won't get her off your hands till you marry."

A few days later his mother happened to be looking at pictures of a charity ball in the *Tatler* or *Sketch* and came upon a photograph of Lotie, dancing with her brother Edgar.

"Why is she with her brother?" she asked.

"Why shouldn't she be?"

"People usually attend such functions with their husbands."

"Perhaps her husband lost a leg in the war and she's dancing with her brother, how should I know?"

"She could be divorced."

"Why should she be divorced?"

"Americans often are, especially rich Americans."

"Then perhaps her brother's divorced. I mean, why isn't he dancing with his wife?"

"Perhaps they're both divorced."

"Fine, then I'll marry his wife. I've always fancied Kagan as a father-in-law."

"The trouble with you, Nahum, is you never take me seriously. Sophie will never marry while you're unmarried. She thinks you need her."

"I'll get a housekeeper."

"You try it. Sophie wouldn't let her step over the threshold."

On that point, at least, his mother was right, for, as his situation improved, he wanted to move to a larger house and get a housekeeper, but she wouldn't hear of either.

"But I can afford it."

"How do you know your good fortune will last?"

"Why shouldn't it last?"

"Because it hasn't lasted before."

"I was robbed before."

"You could be robbed again."

He sometimes felt that she took positive pleasure in their reduced circumstances and that she wouldn't really be happy until they were living in a but-and-ben.

If Sophie was a cause of worry, Alex was a cause of joy. Shyke, after various adventures and misadventures—none of which, to Nahum's chagrin, had brought him to Glasgow, was now in Jerusalem, working with Barclay's Bank, and he had met Alex at a garden party given by the High Commissioner.

"Everyone from the High Commissioner downwards thinks the world of him," he wrote. "He's bright, articulate, hard-working, gets on marvelously with the Arabs—better with the Arabs than the Jews, as a matter of fact. Give him another ten or fifteen years, and he could be High Commissioner himself."

Hector was posted to Egypt from which there came news of recurring turmoil, but he claimed he was spending much of his time perfecting his polo. He managed to get out to Jerusalem from time to time, and he was able to confirm much that Shyke had written about Alex. "I need only mention I'm his brother, and every door opens."

Nahum had always made a point, when regarding his family, not to think in terms of children and step-children, yet he could not help comparing his own progeny with those of Yerucham, and finding them wanting. Vicky, though a headache, was a source of reassurance, and, if she lacked Sophie's questing intelligence, she had something of Hector's personality and good looks (though she was much less even-tempered). Jacob and Benny, however, had neither looks nor personality, and he had to keep reminding himself that they were only young boys and might in time acquire both. He sent them to Clifton, and he allowed himself to hope that, even if neither would ever be a Hector, one of them could conceivably emerge as an Alex.

When Benny left home, he felt oddly distressed. He still had Vicky staying with him, but Vicky never had had the innocence of childhood, even as a child. She was fourteen now and had something of the appearance and many of the expensive tastes of a young woman. While Benny was around, Nahum, even if middle-aged, had passing feelings of youthfulness, but now that there was no longer a piping voice echoing about the house or the paraphernalia of childhood—the bats, the balls, the stumps, the toy soldiers—he began to see himself as his father, and he had always recalled his father as an elderly man, though he died only at fifty-six.

Vicky, who went to an expensive girls' school in the West End, complained that she could not bring friends home while they lived in the Gorbals, which, said Sophie, was as good a reason as any for living in the Gorbals, but by then Nahum had more or less made up his own mind to move and, without raising the matter with Sophie, bought a house almost next door to where Miri had lived in Polokshields. When he had exchanged contracts, he mentioned it casually over supper. Sophie looked at him as if she had misheard.

"Did you say a house?"

"A house."

"You don't mean it."

He pulled the contract from his pocket and put it on the table.

"But whatever for? Even this place is too big, there's only the three of us here."

"I think we should move," chirped in Vicky.

"Nobody's asking you."

"I also happen to be a member of this family."

"And a particularly messy one."

But once faced with a *fait accompli,* she did not argue further and equipped herself with a large collection of wallpapers and fabrics. Money, she often said, meant nothing to her, and she made out her orders as if money was no object; she spent almost as much on furniture and furnishings as he had spent on the house itself, but by the time she had finished, it was a showplace.

Relatives abhor a vacuum, and, as soon as the house was finished, his mother found that Katya had "become impossible in old age" and moved in with them.

The garden was large and secluded with high hedges, and his home became a favourite venue for charity garden parties, and he was glad to notice that Sophie was again receiving the sort of attention from eligible bachelors she had received before the war, and that she did not recoil from them as she had done in the past.

"If you had moved house a year or two ago," said his mother, "she would have married by now."

His new house, however, was nearly his downfall. Nahum now had five cinemas, all of them conversions of old theatres or obsolete chapels, and he had always dreamt of acquiring a cinema which had actually been built as such. About the same time as he bought the house, he acquired a site in a holiday resort on the Ayrshire coast and engaged an architect to build a cinema which would incorporate all the latest wonders of the trade. Building operations, however, had hardly begun before it became clear that the final costs of the scheme would bear little relation to its original estimates. He searched around frantically for loans, but his bankers believed that so costly a venture could not be made viable, and the sums involved were no longer the sort he could borrow casually from acquaintances and friends.

His lawyer, Krochmal, a portly, grave-looking man with the flopping jowls of an overfed bloodhound, had advised him to form each of his cinemas into distinct limited-liability companies, so that if one collapsed it would not pull the others down with it, but Nahum thought the arrangement too complicated. He hated paperwork, and bridled at the legal fees, but he now saw that Krochmal had been right, for his new cinema threatened to swallow everything he had accumulated from the old. But then, as he was tearing his hair in desperation, an angel, as he called her, suddenly appeared—Jessie Colquhoun. She was lean and tanned and had dyed her hair a dark red, which made her look slightly tarty, but he had never regarded tartiness as an unattractive quality.

She had been stationed in Malta during the war and had taken an immense liking to it. She had returned there after the war and, with the help of an army colleague, had invested in a small hotel which had prospered, but, she said, she was tired of coping with drunken sailors, obstreperous naval officers, lecherous colonial officials and treacherous Maltese and thought there must be an easier way of making a living. She had accumulated some capital and wondered if Nahum wanted a partner in his cinema business. It was, said Nahum, like asking a drowning man if he wanted a life-belt.

She proved her worth almost immediately. She moved into the coast town to supervise the building operations which had been lagging badly behind schedule. Her army experience proved useful, and she had an energising effect on the site manager. Nahum travelled down one day to see how the work was progressing and offered to take her out for a meal.

"No," she said, "you're coming back to my place to taste my Italian cooking."

She had rented a small house, which was about a five minutes' bus ride from the site. They were too impatient to wait for a bus; they couldn't find a cab, and they decided to go on foot, at first walking casually, then breaking into a trot and finally a gallop.

As soon as the door was closed behind them, Nahum began clutching at his tie.

"No, no," said Jessie, kicking off her shoes, "there's no time for that," and as they sank to the floor, he felt almost as if he were making love to Miri, though Jessie knew a few tricks with which even Miri had been unfamiliar, and the musty smell of the carpet somehow added flavour to the occasion.

Later, as they were sitting on the stairs smoking, Jessie said: "Age does not wither her, nor time stale her infinite variety."

"Who are you quoting?"

"An old admiral, but it's from Shakespeare originally."

"How old was the admiral?"

"He must have been nearly eighty."

"Which gives me hope."

"Which gives us time."

Thereafter, he travelled down to Ayrshire almost daily, and as he watched his splendid Picture Palace emerging from the surrounding chaos, he saw it almost as a symbol of his reawakened emotions. It was five years since Miri had died, and he had never given thought to another woman, not out of loyalty to his wife's memory, but because— with the exception of occasional stirrings when Arabella was around —no such thought had ever come to mind, and he took it to be a consequence not so much of bereavement as of age. He was nearly fifty. He was aware of the Bible stories about ancients who kept begetting sons and daughters when well into their nineties, but he wasn't living in biblical times and suspected that the stories were written by old men to cheer themselves in old age. He did not think that he had had a deprived manhood, for he regarded his twelve years with Miri as rich in companionship as most men derived from a life-time. Besides, there had been the brief encounter with Lotie, and the more lasting one with Katya. He had had his share, perhaps more than his share, of carnal pleasures, and he had reconciled himself, fairly cheerfully, he thought, to the inevitability of decline, until Jessie's sudden arrival. Once, when he was a small boy, a visiting relative from Odessa had brought him a box of English chocolates, and he remembered his inexpressible delight when, on finishing one layer, he had pulled back a piece of paper and found an identical layer beneath. He had experienced something similar with Jessie. She had exposed a new layer of emotion.

Sophie was quick to notice the change in him.

"What's the matter?" she said. "You keep buying new clothes, new hats, you've got a carnation in your buttonhole. You don't walk, you dance."

"He's in love," said Vicky.

And she wasn't entirely wrong.

The question of marriage was never broached between them, but he had often given thought to the possibility, and what stopped him from discussing it with Jessie was the ghost of his father, and the presence of Sophie. In the meantime, both he and Jessie were preoccupied with the final arrangements for the gala opening of their picture palace, which they had decided to call the Imperial. It was to be the greatest event in the recent history of the town. The Provost would be there, the Lord Lieutenant of the county and various other public figures. They would open with the Scottish premier of *Golden Nights*, starring Miss Leonor Langton, and Miss Langton herself would grace the event with her presence. The producer of the film, Victor Cassel, also promised to be there. Nahum sent invitations to all his relatives and friends and assured Sophie, Alex and Hector that he would send them tickets for the journey. All three sent their apologies, but Shyke, who was also invited, replied that he hoped to come. He had expressed such hopes on so many occasions that Nahum no longer took them seriously, but Shyke had to be in London on business, and he used the opportunity to come to Glasgow. When he eventually materialised, a leathery-looking figure in a well-cut suit with a small grey moustache, Nahum could not quite believe it was he.

"You look so distinguished," he said, "so prosperous."

"The distinction is natural," Shyke said, "as for the prosperity, it's a sham. It's part of my job to look prosperous. I'm working for a bank. But if it comes to that, you don't look as if you're doing too badly yourself."

"You've caught me on a gala occasion. You should see me on an ordinary night. But why have you waited all this time before coming? It must be eight years since I've seen you."

"I know, I know. I've been trying to get here for years, especially when I heard you were in films. I expected you to be surrounded by beautiful temptresses. Where are they all?"

At that point, they were joined by Arabella, who looked as if she were clad in a collection of black chiffon handkerchiefs, which parted here and there every time she moved to reveal alluring glimpses of leg and thigh.

"Ah," said Shyke, taking her hand, "you must be Leonor Langton."

"Actually," said Nahum, lowering his voice, "she's much prettier."

"And more talented," said Arabella.

A few minutes later, Jessie, who had been busy behind the scenes, emerged from her office.

"I've been looking for you," said Nahum. "I want you to meet a very old friend of mine," but even as he was speaking, Shyke pounced on her. They had met before. He had stayed in her hotel. From the stray remarks Jessie had made about her hotel, Nahum had acquired a certain vision of the place, and when Shyke mentioned that he had been a guest there, he had a sinking feeling that his partnership with Jessie was about to expire. Shyke, however, spent most of the evening with Arabella, keeping an arm first around her shoulders, then around her waist and finally around her thighs, and Nahum felt compelled to take him aside and point out that she was almost engaged to Hector.

"Oh, I know all about Hector. She told me. And, as a matter of fact, I know Hector. Fine young man."

Nahum had to travel to London the next day. Shyke had initially planned to travel down with him, for he knew that they would have little opportunity to talk amid all the commotion of the gala, but he now decided to stay on another few days.

"I want to see Scotland," he said, "everybody tells me it's a beautiful country," and Nahum set off on his own.

He usually enjoyed a train journey, especially on one of the crack expresses. He generally had an early lunch with a bottle of wine. He would then read and doze off till tea-time, go over some of his papers, and before he looked up, the train would be slowing down and he was in London. This time, the journey seemed endless, and when he sat down to lunch, he could not stomach the food. He didn't know what disturbed him more, the thought of Shyke as Jessie's "guest" or the sight of Shyke with his hairy hand on Arabella's thigh, though he couldn't quite understand why he should be distressed at all. What had happened with Jessie had happened long before her return to Scotland, and she had never tried to hide the fact that she had been a fairly merry widow. As for Arabella, she was neither his daughter nor yet his daughter-in-law. He didn't see why he should feel such a protective attitude toward her, and he ascribed his distress to the fact that Shyke was probably doing what he had always yearned to do himself. But if so, how true were his feelings for Jessie?

He recalled how he and Shyke used to sit in the back row of Volkovysk *Yeshiva* with huge volumes of the Talmud open before them, shaking back and forward as if in study, while Shyke recounted his exploits out of the side of his mouth. Nahum had lived vicariously on them, even if he had suspected they were imagined; now that he could see they were real, he was almost sick with envy.

When he got back to Scotland a few days later, Shyke had already left. There was no sign of Jessie, either, but she phoned to say she was visiting an elderly relative in Perth. He would have liked to talk to her about Shyke but did not feel this was the occasion to do so. "Hurry back," he said, "I'm missing you." And he paused, hoping for some reciprocal sentiment, but there was none.

The next day Arabella came to see him. She wanted a letter of introduction to Victor Cassel.

"Whatever for?"

"Didn't you know? I want to be an actress."

"Can you act?"

"I can sing."

"I know you can, and I enjoy your singing, but films are silent, you know, and a good voice isn't of much help."

"Singing involves acting, especially in operatic roles."

"Have you been in opera?"

"Small parts."

"I didn't know that."

"There's not much about me that you do know. Will you introduce me?"

"Why don't you marry and settle down? I was a close friend to your father, a very close friend, and I know what he would have wanted for you."

"My father's been dead for nearly ten years. I don't know what he would have wanted for me, but I do know what I want for myself, and I want to be in films."

"Didn't you meet Cassel when he was here for the gala?"

"I did, but he may have forgotten."

And he put his hand on hers. "My dear child, if he met you, he couldn't forget, but I'll give you a letter all the same." While he was writing it, he couldn't resist asking her what she thought of Shyke.

"He's all right."

"That's all?"

"He was trying to put his hand up my dress and into it, but one gets used to that. I think he was rather taken with Mrs Colquhoun."

Jessie returned a few days later, and there was something to her appearance that said she had not spent all her time tending to an aged relative.

"How was the honeymoon?" he asked.

"Honeymoon?"

"You and Shyke."

"Ah, is that what you think we were up to? He asked me to show him something of Scotland."

"Is that all you showed him?"

She threw her arms around him and kissed him all about the face.

"You're jealous," she laughed, "like a schoolboy. It almost makes me feel young again. Oh, he's a bit of a lad, your friend, and he tried the usual, but he tries it on everyone."

"I know."

"But he didn't stop there. He asked me to marry him, and I said surely you know I'm *shiksa*, and he said it would never have occurred to him to marry anyone else. Can you imagine it, me, Mrs Grossnass? I must be daft. I said yes."

The race was to the swift.

Later, when Nahum congratulated Shyke, he said to him: "I seem to be doomed to relive my life. I only hope you're not doomed to relive Yerucham's.

"What do you mean by that?" asked Shyke.

"It's a private thought."

CHAPTER XXII
THE VISITOR

WHEN NAHUM'S SISTER AND HER FAMILY DISAPPEARED FROM NEW York, he wrote to everybody who might conceivably have had knowledge of them for news of their whereabouts, but he heard nothing of them until early in the war, when a sea captain told him that they, or a party like them, had been seen in Odessa. Nahum immediately made further enquiries through the British consul and shipping companies with business in Odessa, but he drew a blank.

Then came the Russian Revolution, which, as far as the Jews were concerned, was the best news to come out of the war. The hated Tsar had fallen. Jewish disabilities had been removed with a stroke of the pen, and Nahum allowed himself to hope that if his sister, Arnstein and their child (who must by then have been sixteen) were still alive, they might, in the new situation, be able to contact him, but as one revolution gave way to another, and the second revolution to a bloody and prolonged civil war, attitudes changed, and a friend wrote in a letter to Nahum:

"The Whites kill you and the Reds rob you (and sometimes kill you into the bargain), so all in all it's better not to be here in the first place, but what can you do if you're stuck here without money and every road is closed? And even where you can move you're afraid of moving, because no matter how bad things are, the chance is that in the next place they'll be worse." And apart from the ravages of war, there were hunger and disease, with thousands dying of cholera and typhus.

Then, towards the end of the war, Nahum heard that Hector's friend Cyrus was with a military mission in Russia and he was immediately seized with hope that he might soon hear news of his sister, but Cyrus found himself in Murmansk, in the Arctic circle, which, as he wrote, is "further from Odessa than London and infinitely more isolated from it or from anywhere else, for that matter."

Nahum did, however, establish contact with a colleague who was being sent to Odessa. Over a year passed before he heard from him, when he wrote to say that he had met a family called Arnstein, but they did not tally with the description he had been given. And there, for the time being, Nahum had to let the matter rest, for as his mother said to him: "There's no war now. They know where you are, you don't know where they are. If they're alive they'll contact you sooner or later, and, if I know my daughter, they're alive." Nahum was not so sanguine.

During the twenties there was a trickle of newcomers from Lithuania, Latvia and Poland and even the occasional individuals from Soviet Russia, and as soon as they showed their faces in synagogue or in any of the many Jewish shops which crowded the Gorbals, they were surrounded by people anxious for news of *der heim* and showered with offers of hospitality.

Nahum now went to synagogue more frequently than he used to, partly out of a sense of thanksgiving for the restoration of his fortunes, partly because there was less pressure on his time and partly because he was no longer regarded with open-mouthed awe like a visitor from another planet. No one crowded around him to grasp his hand or to offer him prayer books or prayer shawls; he could relax and be a *Yid* among *Yidden,* a Jew among Jews, and, like other congregants, he not infrequently brought a visitor home for lunch.

One day he noticed a white-faced, skeletal figure in a sagging threadbare suit and a cloth cap at the back of the synagogue. There was something familiar about him which Nahum couldn't quite place. He went over to him after the service, and as soon as he opened his mouth he knew what it was—his teeth, large and regular like those of a horse. He had seen those teeth before. Nahum asked him where he came from.

"Warsaw."

"And before that?"

"Everywhere and nowhere."

"And before that?"

"Volkovysk."

"Ah." Nahum grasped his hand. *"Sholom aleichem.* You're the son of Yankelson the *shammos.* You look just like him."

"And you?"

"Don't I remind you of anyone?"

"You've got a well-fed face. There weren't many well-fed faces in Volkovysk."

"I'm Nahum, Yechiel's."

"Yechiel Rabinovitz? I knew him, everybody knew him. He held me on his knee. Finest man in Volkovysk."

Nahum brought him home. Usually, when he returned with such a visitor, Sophie would throw up her eyes and sit at the table drumming her fingers with boredom, suppressing yawns.

"I'm not inhospitable," she would protest, "and I like company, but whoever you bring home, you always go on about *der heim,* and always in Yiddish and always at length, and I can never understand a word."

On this occasion, though the conversation was still in Yiddish, everyone around the table, and especially Sophie, followed with rapt attention, as if their visitor had broken through the language barrier.

Like many of his Russian Jewish contemporaries, the visitor had been in *Yeshiva* when the war broke out, but by the end of 1914 he was in the army and so harried by bullying soldiers and Jew-hating sergeants that he was almost yearning for a confrontation with the enemy as an end to his torments, "though I don't know what I would have done if I had met a German or an Austrian or even a Turk face to face," he added, "because they were much less of an enemy to me than the Russians."

He was stationed near Kovno, and early in 1915 they began moving west, heavily laden and covering about fifteen miles a day.

"The supply columns did not always keep up with us, or were re-routed, or lost. We were nearly always hungry, and some of the soldiers fell by the way. Others deserted under cover of darkness and lived off the land, and it seemed to me that our division—which I'll admit was not one of the crack units—would disintegrate long before we came within sound of gun-fire. We had been on the move for about ten days when we received reports of an advancing army and took up defensive positions. We were still digging in when it became clear that we were facing not an advancing army, but a retreating one, our own, which had been shattered by the Germans at Tannenberg and was falling back in disarray all along the front, like a broad river which had burst its banks. The sight of the broken soldiers, wild-eyed, tattered, did nothing to raise our own depleted spirits. For a day or two there was utter chaos. Then came orders to retreat, but too late, for we had been out-flanked. Our line disintegrated, and so we did our own retreating, in ones and twos. I fled under cover of darkness, throwing my rifle behind me, and found shelter in a hay barn. The next morning I put my head around the door in the farmhouse and sniffed around for what food I could find, which was very little. The place was deserted, but in the stable I found a man about my size, who had hanged himself—or been hanged—from the rafters. I lowered him down, changed his suit for mine and fled. Everywhere I moved, there were Germans, but I felt safer among them than among Russians.

Whenever I was stopped, I threw open my mouth, threw up my eyes and pretended to be an idiot, which wasn't too difficult for me. I managed to get work with farmers or peasants who were all short of hands, sometimes acting as a deaf-mute, sometimes as an idiot, sometimes as myself, and not always certain which I was meant to be when, but, if nothing else, I had a roof over my head and I didn't starve."

He broke off as his voice was getting parched, and Nahum passed him a glass of vodka, which he downed in a gulp, and continued.

"I envied the peasants. They lived a hard life but an assured one, with its own inevitable continuity. Whatever happened, cows had to be milked, fields plowed, crops reaped. The identity of the overlord was a matter of indifference. 'In my grandfather's day,' one ancient told me, 'it was the Poles. Yesterday it was the Russians, today it's the Germans. Tomorrow, who knows? Who cares? A curse on them all.'

"I might have stayed on as a farm labourer to this very day. I liked the life, I liked the security, which is to say there was always something, not much, but something to eat, but I was worried about my family and knew they would be worried about me, and I tried to make my way back towards the east, and that was where my troubles began. I made for Latvia first, where I had relatives, but found that whole Jewish communities had been uprooted by the Russians—they were afraid they'd collaborate with the Germans—and moved east. There were ghost villages everywhere—emptiness, desolation. Here, too, there were Germans. I had almost no idea what was happening in the outside world and had the impression that the Germans had over-run the whole of Russia, but eventually—by then I must have been on the move for nearly two years—I found myself behind the Russian lines. I didn't get far before I was picked up by military police, and again I tried to play the idiot, but it didn't work, maybe because being an idiot is no excuse in Russia."

He opened the side of his mouth and pointed to three teeth, broken, jagged and saw-edged. "One crack across the teeth restored me to my senses. I gave them the name of my unit, explained that we had all been ordered to fall back but that we were cut off by the advancing Germans, and that I had been trying to make my way back to my unit ever since but kept being overtaken and held by the Germans.

" 'And I suppose,' said my interrogator, 'that you expect us to give you a medal.'

"I was court-martialled, found guilty of desertion and sentenced to be shot the next morning. This was the Russian Army, thank God, and not the German, and when I was taken to the cells, I found several prisoners who had been sentenced to execution weeks ago and looked as if they were more likely to die of cold and malnutrition. 'They can't spare the bullets,' said somebody, which was a comforting thought, but a few days later I was awakened by the sound of rifle-fire. Ah, I thought, this is it. I said the *shema,* something I had failed to do during the previous year or two. Then my cell was flung open, and I was embraced by a large soldier who kissed me on both cheeks and invited me to step out into freedom.

" 'The revolution has come, comrade,' he cried, 'the revolution is here.'

"He seemed to be drunk, which I thought was a bit much. The least you can expect when you are being led to your execution is a degree of sobriety, but he kept ranting: 'It is here, the revolution.' Finally I said, 'Which revolution?'

" 'The workers', comrade. You're free, we're all free. The Tsar has fallen.' I staggered out into the open compound, still unsure what he was talking about, half expecting to be stopped by a bullet between my eyes.

"From the age of eleven till the age of nineteen I had been in *Yeshiva,* a hermitage cut off from the outside world. From the age of nineteen I was sealed up in my own world, concerned only to stay alive. The word 'revolution' had floated around for as long as I could remember, rather like the word 'Messiah' among us Jews, but it seemed to represent a vague aspiration, rather than a probable event. There had been what they had called a revolution in 1905, when I was ten, but, revolution or not, Russia was still the Russia that it had always been—the police were as tyrannical, the officials as corrupt—and I had no reason to think that this revolution would be any different, but I was grateful enough for the changes it had brought for me, and as soon as I actually found myself out in the open, I fled before things could get back to normal and I was thrown back into prison and shot.

"And so I wandered around for I don't know how long, until I came to a small town. It was dark. There were lights in the windows, but the streets were empty. I heard the vague sound of singing and suddenly realised, with tears in my eyes, that it was Passover. I knocked on the first door I came to. The singing suddenly stopped, and I could hear the hubbub of anxious voices.

" 'It's me, a Jew,' I shouted. Someone pulled a curtain aside to take a look. Then someone else, and the door slowly opened, just an inch, and a pair of anxious eyes scrutinised me carefully. It opened wider, more eyes, more anxious confabulations, and then, when they were satisfied about my *bona fides,* the door was flung open, and I was greeted as if I were Elijah and invited in to join their *seder.* The *matzos* were grey and had the appearance and texture of asbestos, but I had never tasted anything so delicious in my life. For once they were more than a symbol—you could feel the flavour of freedom on the tongue. Apart from the *matzos,* there was little to eat and drink, but we feasted on hope, we were drunk with it, because they were all convinced that a new day had finally dawned for Russian Jewry. In the past years they were bondsmen; in the coming year they would be free. I was merely glad to be alive, and I couldn't quite understand what the fuss was about, and when they gave me to understand, I was still not convinced that there was anything to fuss about, but I joined fully in the spirit of the occasion.

"I remained in the *shtetl* and found work with a scribe turned distiller. He never let me into the secrets of his alchemy, which is to say I never discovered what he distilled or, rather, what he used as raw material, because there was none available—no grain, no potatoes, no sugar. There was a bit of straw about, and I supposed he used that, and old socks. He offered me a drink once, overfilled the glass and burned a hole in the tablecloth. My job was to push, fetch and carry, for his horse had died of starvation—and had probably been cut up and distilled along with everything else he could lay his hands on."

He paused while Nahum poured him another glass.

"As I said, my job was to push, fetch and carry, but as the weeks passed, it became clear that I was being measured up for a more arduous function—to marry his daughter. She was young, but she grew fast, and as soon as she approached marriageable age, or at least marriageable proportions, I fled.

"By then, the first revolution had given way to another, and you could hear exultant voices cheering the new, new dawn, and emaciated little Jewish cobblers and hat-makers pulled you aside to tell you that their sons were generals, admirals, commissars. But if there had been hunger in the spring, there was starvation in the winter, and I came upon a house occupied by seven people, including four children, all of them dead. No one knew what had killed them, hunger, cold, disease, perhaps all three, no one cared. If you saw people moving, you suspected they were moving from pockets of famine to pockets of plenty, and you moved with them, but I was still anxious to find my family, and eventually, after many other adventures, I reached Volkovysk. How long had I been away, three years? It couldn't have been more, but there was hardly anything or anyone there I could have recognised. There had been a fire. There always were fires. Summers were hot and long, and by August the houses were like tinder, but there had always been fire-brigades. But some of the firemen were in the army, some were dead, others had left, and when the fire broke out, it consumed half the town, and the other half was falling apart. But there was food in Volkovysk, bread, even potatoes. A new king had arisen in Volkovysk, a pocket Trotsky, with pince-nez like Trotsky, and a tiny beard. Guess who it was? Selznick."

"Not Rabbi Selznick," said Nahum.

"His son. He was in *Yeshiva* with me, but he didn't remember me, or pretended not to. Anyway, here he was, king of Volkovysk, in the guise of commissar of the local soviets. I had made my way back to Volkovysk to see my family, and there was nothing and no one to see. My mother had died in the fire, and my father died in bed a week later. My two sisters—they were only fourteen and fifteen—had disappeared, nobody knew how or when. They didn't even sit *shiva* for Father. They vanished the day he was buried. I made what enquiries I could and continued to make them everywhere I went, but nobody knew anything, or perhaps they knew and were afraid to tell me. Anyway, as soon as I could get on my feet, I staggered on, not quite certain where I was trying to get to—not that it made much difference—until I was press-ganged into the Red Army."

"When you were in Volkovysk," Nahum asked, "did you come across anyone from my family?"

"Who was there left? Your Uncle Sender? There was no sign of him or his family. And he had moved from Volkovysk, hadn't he?"

"I was thinking of my sister."

"Esty? Wasn't she in America?"

"She was, but I heard she had made her way back to Russia."

"She couldn't be that crazy. She certainly wasn't in Volkovysk. Anyway, I was telling you, there I was, in the Red Army. The advantage of being in the army is that you were assured your slice of bread, and sometimes even of your plate of cabbage; the disadvantage, in that particular war, was that you were never quite sure who you were shooting at, or, what was more to the point, who might be shooting at you. The war with Germany was over—that much even I knew—but there were German soldiers still popping up all over the place, and there were, of course, the Whites, plus a number of small and not-so-small private armies all over the place—Poles, Latvians, Lithuanians, Estonians, Finns, even Czechs—sometimes fighting with us, sometimes with each other, and ready to have a shot at almost anyone who passed. Enemies turned into allies and allies into enemies, and you were never quite certain who might turn out to be what, when you might stop a bullet or whose bullet it might be, and you had an odd feeling of triumph when you could settle down at night with your limbs intact and your body in one piece.

"After an endless march in which we lost a good part of our fighting force—when we set out, we had about a rifle between every two men, by the time we reached our destination, we had rifles to spare—we came to a railhead, and there we piled onto a train—cattle-waggons, I may tell you, not the drawing rooms on wheels you have here—and headed for the north. There were rumours that we might be fighting the English and French, who, as far as I knew, were, or until recently had been, our allies and who had landed somewhere in the Arctic, and we also had to keep a lookout for the Czechs—nobody had any idea what they could be doing so far north, though they could not have been more lost than I was. Anyway, whatever our destination, we didn't get there, because before we got very far our engine broke down, and while we were waiting for another we were attacked, though I'm not quite sure by whom. We repelled the attack, but the railway line on either side of us was blown up, and, engine or not, we could neither go forward nor turn back. Just then the first snows of winter began to fall. A number of detachments were sent out to look for billets and to forage for supplies and establish communications with the outside world, and I quickly detached myself from my detachment, which was not a very sensible thing to do in a Russian winter. I got frostbite and had my big toe amputated—you must have noticed my limp—by a village *shochet* with the knife he normally used for killing chickens. 'It means the knife isn't kosher any more,' he said, 'but it's months since I've seen a chicken, and I don't know whether I'll ever see one again.' I didn't know you could have such trouble over one blighted toe. It was weeks before I could walk again, but he welcomed my company, for we could study the Talmud together. He had, he said, been praying to heaven for a *chavruso,* someone to study with, and I had appeared as an answer to his prayer, to which his wife retorted that it would have been better if he had prayed for a chicken, for they were both on the verge of starvation and they had little to spare for me, though, even so, they somehow managed to find something. Her specialty was *schavil,* a weed which she made into a soup; she could make anything into a soup. I was sure if I stayed on, she would make me into soup. Anyway, I moved on again, first through Lithuania, then to Poland, and I've been on the move since."

"When did you get here?" asked Nahum's mother.

"Two days ago."

"Have you got a room?"

"I've got a bed."

The word *bet* in Yiddish sounded much the same as bed in English, and Sophie said immediately: "We've got plenty of room here. I'm sure Father would be delighted if you stayed with us."

Nahum translated her offer without much enthusiasm, but their guest wouldn't hear of it.

"No, no, no. I'm comfortable where I am. I don't like walking and I don't like travelling, and I've had the offer of a job just around the corner from where I live."

"What do you do?" asked Nahum.

"For a living? I stay alive, which up to now has been a full-time occupation, but tomorrow I start in the slaughterhouse, putting seals on kosher chickens. I seem unable to get away from chickens and slaughter, slaughter and chickens, and, as a matter of fact, I get phantom pains in my toe every time I eat chickens or chicken soup."

Sophie had become an infrequent visitor to synagogue, and Nahum was therefore surprised when he looked up to the women's gallery the following Sabbath to find her sitting in her mother's old place in the front row. She was there again the week that followed, and on each occasion he found her in conversation after the service with Yankelson, she exercising the few words of Yiddish she had picked up, he his few words of English.

Nahum had to go to London on business and was away the better part of a week. When he returned Sophie was out, but he was greeted by a beaming Victoria who said: "You know, I do think our Sophia has found herself a young man at last."

A week or two later, Sophie called at his office and asked if she could see him alone.

He gazed at her across his desk and noticed a becoming softness in her eyes. He would have liked to embrace her. She looked happy and excited and rather bashful, like a young girl who had only just become aware that men were interested in her.

"What would you say," she began, "if I were to marry Yankelson?"

"What could I say? You're a big girl now and free to do as you wish."

"Would you be happy about it?"

"Frankly, no."

"I'm surprised."

Nahum was a little surprised himself at his reaction, which came out almost involuntarily, for he had taken an immense liking to Yankelson. There was a grandeur about him mixed with pathos. He was indestructible and, for all he had been through, devoid of self-pity. On the other hand, he could not overlook the fact that Sophie was, after all, Miri's daughter, and there was something possibly in his subconscious mind which had made him react as Miri would have done.

"What have you got against him?"

"Nothing at all. I like and admire him, he could be an example to us all, but I'm not sure if he's the right man for you. Think of your background, and think of his. His father was a *shammos,* a synagogue beadle, a nice man in himself, but everybody's servant—broken, half-blind, a *nebbich.*"

"And who was my father? And who, for that matter, was my mother?"

"A remarkable woman, Sophie; never underestimate your mother."

"She was pretty, she was lively, but she was empty and she was a snob—though God only knows what she had to be snobbish about."

"Her children, for a start. She may have been only the daughter of a poultry dealer, but look at her children. How many Glasgow Jewish families sent their sons to Clifton. How many went through Oxford—with first-class honours? How many became officers and rose to the rank of major? How many won the Military Cross? But never mind your brothers, think of yourself. You're a well-read woman, a University graduate, cultivated—"

"I've had the opportunities to study, to read; he hasn't. All you're telling me is that we've been luckier than he has."

"But he must be thirty. He's got no sort of qualifications, what'll he do for a living?"

"He's not interested in becoming a professional-son-in-law, if that's what you mean."

"Yes, but what are you going to live on, his wages as a poultry sealer?"

"Yes, if necessary, but it won't be necessary. He intends to be a farmer."

"A what?"

"A farmer."

"A farmer?"

"You know, someone who plows, sows, reaps."

"I know what a farmer is, but do you know what a farm costs, even a small farm, and has he any idea what's involved in running a farm?"

"He knows something or is willing to learn more, and he won't need much money because he's starting out in Palestine. Some friends of his have started a *moshav*—a cooperative settlement—and we're planning to join them."

"In Palestine?"

"You make it sound as if it's on the moon. I thought you were a Zionist."

"I am a Zionist, but it never occurred to me that you were."

"I wasn't until I met Yankelson, and I'm not sure if I am now, but the idea of living in the country and working on the land certainly appeals to me. I thought you'd be pleased, but you somehow look disappointed. Is it because we won't need your money?"

Nahum was disappointed. He was, of course, aware of the direction of the relationship between Sophie and Yankelson and its probable outcome, and he was equally aware that there was nothing he could do to stop it, and, whatever Miri's feeling might have been on the matter, he did not, once he had voiced his/her reservations, particularly want to stop it, but he had been confident that whatever else her marriage to Yankelson might bring, it would bring a partner to his business. His rapid expansion had given him staffing troubles. He had lost Jessie and had found nobody of the calibre of Colquhoun or Goodkind to join him, and when it became clear that his sons had no plans to enter his company, he thought he might benefit from a son-in-law, but now even that was not to be the case.

"Suddenly everybody's going to Palestine," he said, "but I'm very happy for you."

She leaned across the desk and kissed him on the forehead, at which he leaned forward and grasped her in an embrace, sending inkwells, pens, papers flying in all directions.

"Never mind who your mother and father were," he said, "I'm no great believer in heredity. You're someone very special in yourself, and you've found someone worthy of you. I'm only sorry you'll both be two thousand miles away, instead of just around the corner."

"You'll have to come with us, won't you?" she said.

They were married a few months later, and the entire family, including Alex and Hector, assembled for the occasion.

It was a large wedding, and, as Nahum said later, "It almost cost me the price of a cinema," but it was as much an act of thanksgiving as anything else, for his business was continuing to prosper, and the more he thought about it, the happier he was with the match. Fond though he was of his step-daughter, he had had dark visions of her drifting into middle age, growing larger and possibly sullen and embittered, for Jewish women, at least from traditional Jewish homes, did not accommodate themselves readily to spinsterhood. She had, since the arrival of Yankelson, gained warmth and lost weight, and was a beautiful and radiant bride.

Nahum had only six children, but he had a bad memory and could not always remember their ages or disposition, and it needed something like a wedding to enable him to undertake a comprehensive review of his family.

Benny, his youngest, was fifteen by then, a slightly built youngster with thick glasses, a cheerful disposition and a toothy smile, though with little to be cheerful about, and Vicky spoke of him affectionately as "the family dud." He wasn't quite a dud. One had only to glance at him to appreciate that he was no athlete, but his thick glasses gave an impression of academic excellence, which was entirely misleading, for he was bad at everything except Jewish studies. He was also, said the Reverend Polack, "a young man of exemplary character, pious, studious and helpful in the running of the synagogue and the organisation of religious services," and Nahum reconciled himself to the thought that he might be a rabbi.

Vicky, who was sixteen, was alternately a cause of pride and despair. She was a taller version of her mother, pert, pretty, insolent, with considerable natural intelligence but any disposition to work sapped by the demands of her social life. He would have liked her to enter University but could rarely prevail upon her to open a book, and even when—as sometimes happened—she tired of company and settled down with reading material, it rarely had any bearing on her school studies, and, as she was later to say: "I am well read but badly educated." She spoke of being an actress, which he ascribed to the influence of Arabella, and although he was devoted to Arabella, he was far from happy with the effect she had on his daughter, and he told her so, at which she protested: "But Nahum, darling, what's wrong with being an actress?"

"Nothing, only I wouldn't want my daughter to be one."

"But surely you don't expect her to settle down in marriage like all these other little Jewish girls?"

"Why not? I sincerely hope she does."

"I think you're going to be disappointed, my love."

And he was rather afraid she could be right.

If he had been asked to imagine the exact antithesis of Vicky, his mind would probably have conjured up someone like Jacob, then nearly eighteen, who was as stolid as Vicky was effervescent. Stout, red-faced, breathless and with large glasses, he was nicknamed Podge at school and was frequently bullied. He was, for a time, so unhappy there that Nahum had contemplated bringing him back to Glasgow, except that by then Benny was also at Clifton and reasonably happy there (though Nahum could not imagine him confessing to being unhappy anywhere), and he did not want to leave him on his own. As he grew older and bigger and too large to be bullied, Jacob also became more self-possessed. He was always beautifully spoken. He tended to remind Nahum of Goodkind, except that he had an odd habit of ending everything he said on an interrogative note. He was doing rather well at school, and when Nahum asked him casually if he would be interested in joining his firm when he had finished, he said: "Rather a waste of good education, don't you think?"

"So what do you want to do?"

"Don't think a few years in Cambridge would do me much harm, do you?"

"And after Cambridge?"

"Doesn't do to probe too far into the future, does it?"

He hoped to have Hector in the company but was rather diffident about making a direct approach, and he asked Alex—who had lately been appointed Assistant District Commissioner in Galilee and was regarded with deference by all the family—if he might possibly have a word with Hector on the subject.

"I wouldn't have suggested it four or five years ago, when it was a little business of no account, and four or five years ago I didn't need help, but I do now," and he described how he had had to dismiss one manager because he had falsified accounts and embezzled funds, and another because, in the words of the police charge, he had permitted "lewd and unseemly behaviour" on his premises. His general manager, a withered little figure by the name of Bintovsky, who, but for his beardless chin and atheistic beliefs, might have come from a rabbinical seminary and who had taught him all the rudiments of the trade, had taken to the bottle and was not in command of his faculties by two in the afternoon. Colquhoun had also been a heavy drinker, but he rarely showed the effects of it before nightfall, and then he was a *goy,* while his general manager was a Jew, and the least he expected of a Jewish colleague was sobriety.

Alex listened to his troubles impassively and said: "What makes you think Hector would be any better?"

"He wouldn't get drunk."

"I'm not even sure about that."

"You're talking about a man who's been ten years in the army, a major, an MC."

"With respect, Father, Hector was born for war and lives for war and is not much good at anything else, so that in peace he is apt to create small wars around him, and I am not really sure he'd be good for you, or you for him. But he may be available."

Nahum's hopes soared.

"Is that so? Is he thinking of leaving the army?"

"He may not have much option on the matter."

"What do you mean?"

"I'm afraid I can't say more. If anything, I've already said too much."

Towards the end of the evening, after most of the guests had left and the musicians were packing their instruments, Katya came over to him and pointed out Hector and Arabella who were sitting together in the corner of an ante-room, he with legs stretched out on a chair, she leaning on his shoulder and apparently nibbling his ear, and both looking slightly the worse for drink.

"What do we do about those two?" she said despairingly. "What do we do?"

"What can we do?"

"Are they going to go on like that all their life?"

"If they want to, there's nothing you or I can do to stop them."

CHAPTER XXIII
ARABELLA

HECTOR AND ALEX LEFT THE DAY AFTER THE WEDDING, AND Nahum waited for the bombshell to fall. It didn't. He waited for letters, telegrams, but they didn't come. Then one day, about a month after the wedding, Arabella came dancing into his office, kissed him by way of greeting and said: "Guess what? Hec is coming back—for good, he's leaving the army."

Nahum pretended surprise.

"Did he say why?"

"Because he loves me."

"That everybody does, what I can't understand is why, with you about, he should have wanted to leave Glasgow in the first place."

"Because I had no intention of getting married until I had built up something of a career."

He left his desk, took her by the hand and led her over to a couch at the back of his office, and, still holding her hand, asked her: "Arabella, my pet, how old are you now?"

"Ancient."

"I have been in the film trade now for seven years, so I know a little about show business. First of all, you are more beautiful than any of those little sluts they have in the films; second of all, you are more talented; third of all, you are more intelligent; but those little girls start when they are seventeen or eighteen, and—if you'll forgive me for saying so—by the time they get to your age they're on the scrap-heap."

"But that's because they haven't got my talent. Don't forget there was a war on when I was seventeen or eighteen, and I was stuck out here in the provinces with a sick father and a crazy step-mother, and I spent many, many years training my voice. I'm to have a large part soon in the West End."

"Are you? I thought Victor Cassel was going to help you into films."

"But he wanted to help me into bed first, and he's such a hideous-looking creature, don't you think?" She stroked his hair as she spoke and kissed him on the lips.

"Don't do that please, Arabella. I love you, but I want to talk to you seriously. Did Hector tell you why he's leaving the army?"

"I told you, because he loves me."

"We're talking in circles now. He's always loved you."

She stroked his hair again.

"Are you cross with me?"

"I'm not cross, but it's impossible to talk seriously to you. Let's start again. Hector is leaving the army, correct?"

"Correct."

"But what's he going to do?"

"For a living, you mean? Oh, he's going into engineering."

"Engineering? What does he know about engineering?"

"Not a thing, from what I can make out, but an army friend of his is setting up in business, and he's going into partnership with him."

"Are you getting married first?"

"That's a detail."

"It's not a detail. Neither of you is getting younger. You want to have a family, don't you?"

"Do we? I am not at all sure that we do."

"You may feel like that now, you won't feel the same when you're a bit older and when it may be too late. I've built up a fairly good business and I've had to work pretty hard to keep it going, and no day passes without its headaches and heart-aches, but I'm prepared to make the effort because I've got children to work for."

"But then, dear, sweet Nahum, you're one of those people who live for others, whereas I'm one of those people who live for themselves; there's quite a number of us around, you know."

"And is Hector like that?"

"I don't really know."

"Don't you ever talk to him seriously about serious things?"

"Do you?"

"He doesn't talk to me about anything. The only time I've spoken to him at length about anything was in hospital in Flanders. He didn't tell me he was leaving the army or why he was leaving, that he was setting up in business, or in what business, or even that he was getting married."

"Oh, we're not getting married quite yet."

"What do you mean, not quite yet?"

"Nahum, darling, are you raising your voice at me?"

"I'm sorry, but you two seem to think that time stands still."

"We're not in a hurry. He wants to set up the company first, and I've got this musical, it could run for years."

"*Years!* So you're not, in fact, getting married."

"Not immediately, no. Why are you so anxious to see us married?"

"Because I want to see you happy and settled, that's why."

"Is that the only reason?"

"What other reason could there be?"

She leaned towards him and stroked the back of his head.

"You could be afraid of me. Have you never wanted to marry me?"

"Marry you? I could be your father."

"I was using a euphemism. Wouldn't you like to fuck me?"

"Wouldn't I like to do what?"

"Fuck me."

He jumped up and put his hands to his head.

"Ara, Ara, Ara, you're about to become my daughter-in-law."

"And have fathers-in-law never slept with their daughters-in-law? About the only thing I remember from the Bible is the story of Judah and Tamar."

"Your memory is imperfect. Tamar was widowed."

"And I'm not even married." She stretched herself out on the couch. "Aren't you dying to touch me?"

He sat down beside her and kissed her gently on the lips.

"You'd better lock the door first," she said dreamily, "though I don't mind if you don't."

He went to the door but, instead of locking it, threw it open, ran down the corridor, down the stairs and out into the street. It was pouring, but he continued to run until he was drenched and exhausted. When he returned to his office some ten minutes later, trailing water with every step, Arabella was gone, but her perfume was still in the air like a presence. He sank down in his chair and remained for some minutes with his face in his hands. Then he happened to look down at his pad. Scrawled across it in lipstick was the word *coward,* at which he broke into a smile. He took the pad home, had it framed and hung it above his bed.

A few weeks later Hector returned home, looking like a commercial traveller in a not particularly profitable line of goods, who had alighted at the wrong station and had left his samples behind. Arabella was by then in London where her show had gone into rehearsal.

"Yes, I heard all about it," said Hector. "She should do very well. She's finally found herself."

Nahum didn't like to say so, but he had the feeling that Hector had finally lost himself. He said nothing about why he had left the army or what he planned to do in civilian life, and Nahum hesitated to press him for the time being. He had obviously suffered some major setback, and a man was entitled to nurse his wounds in private.

He had been home for about two weeks, sleeping late, picking up an occasional book, going for a stroll, but otherwise doing little and saying less, when he announced that he would be leaving Glasgow.

"You're going on holiday?" asked Nahum.

"No," he said, "I'm going for good. My main base will be in London, but I'll be travelling rather a lot."

Such reticence was excessive even for Nahum, and he decided to take the bull by the horns.

"I know I'm only your step-father," he said, "but I was married to your mother for twelve years, and I had some share in your upbringing and perhaps more than my share of worries when you joined the army, but you have always kept me at arm's length, and whenever you told me anything—and that was rare enough—it was as a *fait accompli*. You have never discussed anything with me or sought my advice. You signed on as a professional soldier without telling me why. You left the army without telling me why. You came back here without a word. You've been going around with Arabella for twelve or thirteen years now. Everybody thought you'd marry, but you've never said anything, and now you tell me you're leaving, but never a word as to why or what. Don't you think I have a right to know?"

"You ask too many questions at once."

"Right, then, let me deal with them one by one. Why did you leave the army?"

"I was cashiered."

"Cashiered?"

"I was forced to resign. There was some mishap, but I'd rather not go into details."

"What are you going to do in London?"

"Business."

"What sort of business?"

"Machine tools—distribution, mainly."

"Have you enough capital?"

"I think so."

"Can I be of any help?"

"No, thank you."

He was very unhappy about their conversation. He had thought a straightforward heart-to-heart talk might clear the air between them, but it had taken the form of an interrogation, and he was particularly pained by the curt, parting "no, thank you." He felt that, instead of being drawn nearer to him, they had become more estranged, and it was too late to do anything about it.

He wrote to Arabella about the conversation, and she wrote back to say that he hadn't mentioned it, "but he loves you," she added, "everybody does," which made him feel slightly better.

In the meantime, he found himself with another, more pressing issue on his hands. One day he was summoned by Vicky's headmistress for what turned out to be a short but unhappy meeting. It appeared that Vicky was not only unwilling to do any work herself, but that other girls were following her example, and, said the headmistress, she was "an unwholesome and disruptive influence."

When he told Vicky of the meeting, she said: "The old hag doesn't like me, she doesn't like any of the Jewish girls, she's an anti-Semite."

"Do you expect me to believe that?"

"Why not? It's true."

"You know, when Sophie was your age—"

"Sophie, Sophie, it's Sophie this, Sophie that, I'm sick and tired of Sophie. Sophie's herself and I'm myself, and that's how we're going to stay."

"I'm not going to continue paying school fees if you're not going to make the slightest effort—"

"I have been trying."

"You have *not* been trying," he shouted. "You're out every evening. I can't remember when I last saw you open a book."

"Daddy, something's upset you, because you don't normally raise your voice to me."

"Then perhaps I should. Your mother warned me that I was letting you get out of hand, and she was right, absolutely right. Well, my dear, there's going to be a new regime in this house—no more evenings out, no more hours on the phone. You're going to be upstairs in your room doing homework, and I shall make a point of being home early to make sure that you do."

And for a month or two she was a different child, but Nahum could not always be home early in the evenings, for he was frequently out of town, and he decided finally to remove her from school at the end of the term.

"You should marry if only for her sake," his mother said, "a girl of her age needs a mother." Then, about the time she was due to leave school, it began to look as if the Vicky problem might solve itself.

She had always had many admirers, and at week-ends, especially, Nahum had gotten into the habit of flushing young men out of the different corners of the house before going to bed. They were so numerous and seemed to change so frequently that he never paid particular attention to them, but gradually one figure began to crystalise amid the unidentifiable mass, partly because he was older and more mature-looking than the others, and partly because he was taller and of a fairly striking appearance, with jet-black hair, a handsome profile, a pencil-moustache, immaculate clothes and impeccable manners. His name was Bruce Flemyng, and he had lately qualified as a barrister. It transpired that Nahum had been introduced to his mother when she was single, and she was now the wife of a prosperous skin-merchant called Flambaum.

"You might have been brother and sister," he told Vicky.

Nahum was pleased with their friendship, not only for Vicky. It seemed to him that young Flemyng was just the man he needed for his company, for he could have done with a trained lawyer on his staff. The young couple had been going out together for some months when Nahum asked Vicky if it wasn't about time that the two families got together.

"But I thought you already knew them."

"Yes, but I mean a formal get-together."

"If you want. It'll be a terrible bore, though."

It was not so much a bore as a disaster.

Nahum's mother, who was very taken both with the young man and his family, came down in a red-velvet dress which had been the cynosure of Volkovysk in the early years of the century, but she had been half her size at the beginning of the century, and he wondered how she had gotten into it, or, indeed, how she would get out of it, for it fitted her like a corset. Hector happened to be home that week-end. He had spent most of the time in bed and was not disposed to get dressed at all. Instead, he undertook to keep out of the way.

"You can't keep out of the way," said Nahum with exasperation. "They all know you're here, they've all heard about you, they'll want to see you." And Hector finally went upstairs to change, but he omitted to shave.

At table, everyone was anxious to hear of his war experiences, but he parried each question with monosyllables.

"What was it like at the front?"

"Wet."

"Wet, did you say?"

"And muddy."

"How did you win your MC?"

"Luck."

"Luck?"

"Bad luck, I stopped a passing bullet."

The evening seemed a very long one to Nahum, and when the guests were gone, he turned upon Hector with heat.

"You know, I sometimes think you go out of your way to upset me. This was an important evening, and I almost had to go down on my knees to get you to put on a suit, but look at yourself even in a suit—you haven't shaved, your shirt is crumpled. And then, at table, you were afraid to open your mouth. I've read whole books by people who haven't been through half what you've been through, and all you could do was grunt. What will they think of you?"

"I can't imagine, but then the chap's marrying Vicky, not me. He seems a pompous young Jack, but he's doing well for himself. A girl with Vicky's looks and personality and money is entitled to have a skeleton in the family cupboard."

"I didn't say you were a skeleton in the cupboard."

"Well, a fly in the ointment, or whatever, you know what I mean."

When the young couple had been going out together for a further six months, Nahum asked Vicky if it wasn't about time they got married.

"But what's the hurry?" she said. "We're having fun. Marriage might spoil things."

"You're beginning to talk like Arabella. Shouldn't you get engaged, at least?"

"But we are engaged, more or less."

"I don't like the more-or-less bit. I like things to be formal and cut and dried."

The boy's parents felt the same, and Nahum suggested a meeting to discuss what he called the final arrangements. Vicky overheard the phrase.

"What do you mean, the final arrangements? You make it sound like the last rites."

"When to make the announcement, where to make it, what to say, and then, of course, there's the business of the marriage settlement."

"The what?"

"The marriage settlement."

"What sort of marriage settlement? You don't mean *nadan,* do you?"

Nahum laughed. "What's wrong with *nadan?* I've put a bit of money aside for all of you, but instead of passing it on when I'm dead or dying—as the *goyim* do—I want you to have it while I can still see you enjoying it. Sophie didn't want to hear anything about money, but when I pressed a cheque into her hand, she didn't throw it back at me."

"Sophie happened to need the money."

"She didn't, you know, or said she didn't."

"Bruce doesn't need it, either."

"Not now, maybe, but once he has to buy a house and furnish it, and he has to provide for his children and pay school fees—"

"Then he'll have to earn it, won't he?"

Nahum put an arm around her. "It's all right, my dear, I'll look after him."

Vicky didn't say anything but went out of the house with a purposeful look on her face, which left him troubled. She didn't return until very late, but he waited up for her, growing more and more anxious as the hours passed. When the clock struck two, he went to bed but didn't fall asleep until he heard her rapid steps on the stairs some time later. He had an uneasy feeling that her relationship with Flemyng was over.

She wasn't down for breakfast the next morning, and he phoned her from the office, asking her to meet him for lunch in town. He studied her face carefully when she arrived. If she was heartbroken by the events of the previous evening, she showed little trace of it; he felt a good deal more upset than she looked.

"What happened?" he asked.

"Nothing's happened. He's a money-grubbing little shit, that's all. I asked him what all this talk of a marriage settlement was about, and he laughed and said I should leave that to the men, but I wasn't prepared to leave it to anyone, and it seems that you promised him half of Glasgow."

"*I* promised him?"

"Well, if you didn't, it's what he expects. You said you'd expect him to take over your company."

"*Look after,* I said, you misunderstood him."

"No, if anything, he misunderstood you, but I don't think he did, because he brought in his father, who's in the skin trade, as you know, and who looks as if he might skin anyone alive if it would bring him an extra half-crown, and his father said that you gave him a clear undertaking, to which I said to hell with your undertaking—"

"In those words?"

"In rather rougher words. It stunned them for a bit, then Bruce said, 'But don't you expect to live in a certain style?' and I said, certainly, when you've earned it. His father, who reminds me of an overfed crab, then interjected and said, 'Don't talk to her, she's only a schoolgirl, she doesn't know what life's about. I'll talk to her father.' To which I retorted that I may not have known what life was about, but that I was learning fast."

"As a matter of fact, his father did phone me this morning; he sounded very upset. He explained how he had given his son-in-law a start in life—"

"Bruce doesn't need a start; if anything, he needs a stop. That's what gets me. I wouldn't have minded so much if he had been a penniless student or something like that, but they're stuffed with money, it's coming out of their ears. I wouldn't have minded if you had slipped me a cheque after the wedding, as you did with Sophie, but to talk about settlements and preconditions and shares as if the whole thing was a business merger was more than I could stand. I walked out. So here I am, eighteen and on the shelf."

"I think you may have been a little rash, my dear. It's usual for a man in my position—"

"To buy a husband for his daughter?"

"Don't put words into my mouth."

"But that's what it comes to."

"I've been fortunate enough to make a bit of money, but who do you think I made it for?"

"Not for Bruce Edward Flemyng, né Flambaum, M.A., L.L.B., L.S.D. If you want to shower him with gold, that's your business, but I don't want to have anything more to do with him. Have you noticed him in profile? With his long, thin neck, large bow-tie, lean build and slightly bent posture, he's beginning to look like the pound sterling. Actually, Arabella warned me about him."

"Arabella?"

"Didn't you know? He's one of her cast-offs."

Nahum and Hector had been sent tickets for the opening night of *The Queen of Hearts*, the new musical which, Katya claimed, would establish Arabella as an international star, but Nahum was too busy to travel down and Hector was unwell—or said he was unwell—and Katya travelled down with Arabella's sister Caroline. She returned the next evening almost in tears.

"It was too awful," she said. "Caroline walked out after the first act. I sat through the whole thing because I thought it might improve. I wanted to talk to her, but I didn't know which way to turn. She sang and danced beautifully, but the words they put in her mouth—I didn't think they allowed such things on a London stage. She played the part of an expensive trollop, and I'm sorry to say she looked it. She was half-naked half the time—I'm surprised she didn't catch her death of cold. I'm glad I didn't know anyone there, and even then I felt too embarrassed to look around me, but that's not the worst of it. The impresario, or whatever you call him, is a dark-skinned Oriental with a pocked face, called Azulay, and she's living with him—"

"How do you know she's living with him?"

"He was there in her dressing room when she was dressing. Look, I have a nose for situations, and if I tell you she's living with him, she's living with him."

"And if she is, is there anything you can do about it?"

"I can't, but she's got respect for you. I would like you to see the musical and that awful Azulay, and see for yourself the dreadful situation in which the poor child has landed herself. She's not my child, and she's not yours, but I keep thinking of her poor dear father and what he would say. It breaks my heart. You will see her, won't you?"

It was not a difficult promise to extract, for Nahum had every intention of seeing the musical at the earliest opportunity, but Katya's lament made him approach the experience with eager anticipation. He was in London about two weeks later and managed to get a seat in the front stalls with distressingly little difficulty; he was sorry to see that the theatre was half-empty. As the evening progressed, he could understand why. The music was thin and sickly sweet, the plot was banal, the dialogue improbable, but he found the sight of Arabella delightful and indeed took such pleasure in following her movements that he was inclined to overlook the deficiencies of the play as a whole. He certainly did not share Katya's feelings that it was a lewd and disgusting spectacle, but he found it a sensuous one. He had tended to associate sensuality with bulk, but Arabella was an exception, for she was so thin and bosomless as to be almost boyish. The contrast of white skin and black silk, however, the décolleté dresses, the glimpses of shapely undraped limbs were almost overpowering, and when he went around to her dressing room after the show, he was half afraid to go near her, but she fell upon him with a shriek of delight and draped herself around him.

"Don't tell me what you think of the show, I know it's too awful," she said. "It's closing at the end of the week, thank God. But listen, I'm going into films. What do you think of that? No more traipsing back and forth between London and Glasgow. I'm stopping here for good, and then, maybe, who knows—Hollywood." She was changing out of her clothes as she spoke, almost oblivious of his presence.

He looked around for someone who might answer to Katya's description of Azulay, but there were no Orientals there, pock-marked or otherwise.

She hadn't eaten. He took her out for dinner, and in the taxi he asked about Azulay.

"Azulay? How do you know about Azulay? Katya must have told you, the bitch. I know what you're thinking, but don't. He couldn't get an erection if he was to put it in splints. He's my guardian angel, though I'll admit he doesn't look like one. He's setting up—has set up —a small production company, and they're starting work this summer. He's already found the story he wants, and the director."

"Has he made any films before?"

"No, he hasn't staged any plays before, either. He's a financier."

"And he's doing it—"

"Out of pure admiration for my art."

"How did you get to know him?"

"He got to know me. He saw me in a small part in an operetta, and he came backstage and said I was far too good for such a small part, and, of course, he was right."

"You are good, but I don't think much of the rest of the show."

"Neither does anyone else."

"What makes you think he'll choose the right film for you?"

"He probably won't, but one thing leads to another."

"And your marriage?"

"I knew that would come up. We're as good as married as it is, we're living together, you know. Does that shock you?"

"No, my dear, it does not. I've lost all capacity for shock where you are concerned, but why don't you make the whole thing kosher and finished with?"

"Time, darling, time. I'm dying to get started on the film, and Hec is hardly here, in any case. He's away now, as a matter of fact." She took his hand. "Want to come back with me?"

"You know, I sometimes think you're making fun of me."

"Fun of you, darling? I love you, but I am amused by your inhibitions. You are a terrible puritan."

"The way you pronounce the word, you'd think it was a bad thing to be a puritan. There's nothing wrong with being a puritan. Unfortunately, I'm more of a dirty old man."

"Then why don't you come back with me?"

"You know very well why not. Are you going to be like this after you marry?"

"I'm not sure."

"Then why get married?"

"That's one of the reasons why I haven't."

"I'm beginning to think you and Hector are bad for each other."

"I know I'm bad for him, but what makes you think he's bad for me?"

"If it wasn't for him, you might have married years ago."

"Never."

"And he might have done something with himself, gone to University, built up a career. I haven't much faith in his machine-tool business. What exactly does he do?"

"I'm not sure what he does, but he's doing very well out of it. But you're changing the subject. Are you coming back with me?"

"No."

"Coward."

She was in Glasgow a few months later for the marriage of her sister Caroline to a diminutive figure called Erich Krochmal, the son of Nahum's lawyer and himself a solicitor. It was a small wedding because it was a small family, and Katya, in any case, felt she could not afford anything larger. Nahum found it a joyless occasion, for Katya's daughter-in-law, Lazar's wife, had died a few weeks previously, and her passing had cast a shadow over the whole affair.

The fact that Lazar had vanished without divorcing her had left her an *agunah* (a "chained wife") in Jewish law, neither a widow, nor a divorcée, and therefore unable to marry. Her father had spent much of his fortune in sending private detectives to different corners of the globe in an attempt to trace Lazar, but the old man had died earlier in the year, and his daughter followed him to the grave some months later. Katya claimed to be grief-stricken and wore a black crepe dress for the occasion in which she looked quite striking.

A few days later, Katya told him she was putting her house on the market. "It's far too big for me on my own."

"Where are you—" Nahum began, and, realising the answer his question would elicit, he left the sentence in mid-air, but too late.

"Where am I going to live? I was hoping you might have a room to spare until I find a place. It shouldn't take me long, not more than a week or two."

It took her more than a month or two, by which time, not being able to find anything to her complete satisfaction, she became a permanent member of his household.

There was no shortage of space. Victoria had left for an extended holiday in Palestine and was staying with Sophie. Hector was, of course, in London. Jacob had left Clifton and was now in Cambridge. Benny

277

was in his final year at Clifton. His mother, however, was still with him. She was becoming hard of hearing, cantankerous and eccentric, especially in dress, and the more she advanced in years, the further she reverted to the fashions of her youth, and whenever there was a formal occasion to attend, Nahum half expected her to emerge in a bustle and crinolines. He noticed with surprise how old she had suddenly become, especially when sitting next to her sister, who was only six or seven years her junior but who looked infinitely younger and who, although in her sixties, still had a firmness and vivacity which one did not always find in women half her age. She stirred temptations in him which he at first ascribed to memories of their earlier encounters, but when they persisted, he took them as a measure of his loneliness. The fact that he could not look at his aged aunt without yearning to slip his hand into her bodice suggested to him forcibly that he was badly in need of a woman, and for the first time since Jessie, he began to think actively of remarriage.

Arabella phoned him one evening to say that her film was finished. Would he like to come down to a private viewing? He said he would do so at the first opportunity, but as he put the phone down, doubts overwhelmed him. They would sit together in the darkened cinema, celebrate the film (whatever its quality) with drinks and then go to her flat, and the inevitable would follow. The thought of the missed opportunity, enshrined in the framed blotting-pad above his bed, gave him pangs of yearning almost every night, and he anticipated that they would continue to bother him while he had blood in his veins; he began to wonder whether he should sleep with Arabella and get it over and done with. He was by now convinced that Arabella and Hector had only played at the thought of marriage but had never seriously considered the possibility, that they would ever marry, certainly not each other, and possibly not at all. Why, then, should he not give in? She was, after all, only a single woman, and even the Talmud, so strict about so many other things, had made allowances for this. Single women were fair game, and it occurred to him that the real reason he held back was not moral or ethical, but because he feared that his fairy princess, once slept with, would turn into a pumpkin, or a monster, or a toad, or just another common-garden woman. That, indeed, might have been the consideration with Hector, except it seemed to him that Hector had never evinced real interest in any woman except Arabella, which was unusual in a man so attractive. It might, of course, have been a simple matter of loyalty; if so, it was unrequited, for Arabella had no inhibitions about liaisons with other men.

He often thought about the matter, especially when alone in bed, but late one night his speculations were cut short by a phone call from Hector.

"I thought you'd like to know that we're getting married," he said. "Ara and I, that is."

He didn't quite know how to take the news, but his response was automatic: "I'm delighted!"

Arabella came on the phone. "Well, are you happy?"

"Never mind if I'm happy. Are *you* happy?"

He heard her talking to Hector: "Hec, are we happy?"

"Yes," said Hector.

"He says yes, we're happy."

"Then I'm also happy. Hold the line, I'll get Katya. I only hope for your sake and mine that you're not joking, because if you are, she'll cut your throat and mine."

Katya, who was sitting up reading in bed, was alarmed by the knock on her door and even more alarmed when she was told she was wanted on the phone. It was nearly midnight. She came down in her night-clothes, her bosom billowing over the top of her gown.

"It's all right," said Nahum, "it's good news."

"People don't phone at this time of the night with good news."

She received the news calmly but without enthusiasm, while Nahum was still too confounded to know what his true feelings were.

"I don't know what to make of it," he kept saying. "I just don't. Why, after all these years? Why now?"

"She could be pregnant. No, she couldn't."

"Why not?"

"Because the Arabellas of this world don't have to stay pregnant if they don't want to. She's had any number of doctors sniffing around her. She could have an abortion at the drop of a Dutch cap. But it doesn't answer your question. Why now?"

Vicky came with what she claimed was the answer a few weeks later. She had stayed with Arabella on her way back from Palestine.

"Ara has just finished her film and is about to become a film star, and spinsterhood doesn't go with stardom. A film star has to have a husband, and the right sort of husband—attractive, dashing, a war hero, an officer and a gentleman. Hector does have all the necessary qualifications. What I would like to know is, what's in it for him?"

"A rich wife," said Katya predictably, "she must be earning fortunes as a film star."

"She's not, you know, not yet, but he's making fortunes in his business."

CHAPTER XXIV
BLACK YEARS

KATYA WANTED A LARGE WEDING. "I HAVE SO MANY FRIENDS AND so much to celebrate," she said, "and, given my age, I can't see many other occasions ahead for celebrations."

In the event, it turned out to be a good deal larger than she could have imagined. She had spoken to Nahum about the possibility of having the wedding in his garden. He was delighted with the idea and offered to pay for the cost of the reception. He was to be spared the money.

Arabella announced that Azulay had kindly made his house, a large mansion on the outskirts of London, available for the wedding, and when Nahum arrived with Katya, his mother, Vicky and his two younger sons, he found that the affair had been taken over by Arabella's publicity people, and it seemed to him that, as Vicky had suggested, the whole wedding was a publicity stunt. Arabella's first film had been launched amid great fanfare a few months before, and when she and Hector got engaged, the papers were full of their pictures with such headlines as: STAR TO MARRY WAR HERO. The wedding, it seemed to him, was but a further stage of the same campaign, and he was surprised that Hector should have lent himself to it.

The whole of the film trade was there—film stars, producers, directors, distributors. Cameramen and reporters weaved in and out among the crowds, grasping at glasses, importuning the more famous and being importuned by the less famous, and before the afternoon had gone far, some of the guests were already fornicating in the shrubberies, and others had emptied their innards over the Rodins on the terrace.

Nahum, Katya, Arabella and Hector were lined up in the entrance hall, while a bemedalled toastmaster with the harsh voice of a sergeant major announced each guest as he appeared. After an hour or so, Nahum's hand, arm and then his whole body began to ache. He knew some of the guests and recognised some of the others from their films or publicity stills, and at first he greeted them with a show of animation, but after a time the faces became a blur, as if they were all a film which had been jerked out of focus, and then suddenly he heard a name and saw a face which made him jump to life. It was Colquhoun's protegé, young Cameron, and, although it was twenty years since he had last seen him, he did not—with his lean figure, cleft chin, dimpled cheek, sandy hair and freckled face—look all that old, even now.

Nahum at first hesitated to shake his hand, but he couldn't quite believe it was *the* Cameron, and he asked him: "Are you also a film star?"

Cameron laughed: "I wish I was. Didn't Hector tell you? I'm his partner."

There were still people arriving, and Nahum, by now in something of a daze, continued to pump hands and bare his teeth in what he thought was a smile, but as soon as he could conveniently disengage himself from the line, he pulled Hector aside.

"Why didn't you tell me about young Cameron?"

"Young who?"

"Cameron."

"Oh, Eddy, my partner. Why, what is there to tell?"

"Didn't he tell you that he once worked for me?"

"He did. I met him in the army and had known him for years before he realised you were my step-father."

"And didn't he tell you he once worked for me?"

"Oh, it's all right. I know everything about him, and he knows everything about me."

"And you're not afraid to do business with him?"

"Not in the least. What's more to the point, he's not afraid to do business with me. He's got a very good war record."

"A war record isn't everything. Do you know about his peace record?"

"I told you, I know everything. Can you imagine him hiding anything from me, once he discovered I was your step-son? You can say what you like about Eddy, but he's no fool. He came up from the ranks, you know, no public school, no cadet force, no OCTU. He started as a private and finished as a major. That takes a bit of doing in the British Army. People often tell me it's difficult for a Jew to get far in the army, which it is, but it's infinitely more difficult to get anywhere if you're working-class. His father was a docker."

"What sort of business are you in?"

"Didn't I tell you? Machine tools."

"Yes, but what sort of machines do your machine tools make?"

"Light engineering. Springs, coils, tubes, that sort of thing. We don't make them, by the way, we sell them."

"Can I come and see your business?"

"Of course, if you want, though there's nothing much to see. It's a converted warehouse. Just Eddy and me, a couple of technical people, some secretaries. Not more than a dozen of us altogether."

"So how come you've done so well so quickly?"

"Who says I have?"

"Vicky."

Nahum looked around for Vicky and found her in conversation with Arabella and a very tall, round-faced figure in rimless glasses whom he recognised as Arabella's producer, Kapulski. He hesitated whether to join them, for he had taken an instant dislike to Kapulski, but Arabella gestured to him to come over, and as he did so, Kapulski put an arm around his shoulder. He didn't like being embraced by a comparative stranger, and he did not like standing too near Kapulski, for his great height made him feel small.

"We are discussing Vicky's future," said Arabella.

"You didn't tell me you had such a pretty daughter, Nahum," said Kapulski. "What's a girl like that with looks like that and a shape like that doing in a godforsaken hole like Glasgow? She's made for the movies."

"Think of her poor father," said Arabella. "He already has a daughter-in-law in the trade. Spare him his daughter."

"But perhaps his daughter would like to be in films," said Vicky.

"My dear, you don't know what you're letting yourself in for. You'd be better off on the streets."

Those, indeed, were Nahum's own sentiments.

Nahum was later to look back on Arabella's wedding as the beginning, if not the cause, of what he called his *schwartze yoren*—his black years (which sound a good deal blacker when pronounced in Yiddish); almost everything which could go wrong did go wrong.

Shortly after Vicky had returned from Palestine, he held a reception to celebrate the opening of a new cinema—his first in Glasgow—in one of the suburbs. It had been purposely built, and again a film star came down to open it, and to make sure that it opened under the very best auspices, he had a rabbi down to bless it and affix a *mezuzah* to the door.

The idea of the *mezuzah* was Michael Mittwoch's, the manager designate of the new cinema, the son of penniless immigrants who Nahum took on as an act of charity, but who quickly proved himself to be a young man of outstanding ability; when it became clear that none of his sons had any interest in the business, he began to look on Mittwoch as his heir apparent. Mittwoch was rather coarse in utterance and manner, but Nahum knew very few people in the cinema trade who were anything else, and there were some who regarded his defects as qualities. He was brisk, presentable and alert to the point of being impatient. Nahum had only to start a sentence before Mittwoch thought he had gotten the message, and the constant refrain to their conversation was: "Will you let me finish?" He would have liked him and Vicky to meet, but he had a distaste for organising the necessary conspiracies, which might have derived from the years, not so long ago, when he was himself the victim of them, and, in any case, knowing Vicky, he was certain that she would have nothing to do with the young man precisely because he had arranged their meeting. However, the gala was a perfectly natural occasion for them to meet, and when they did, they formed the immediate attachment Nahum had hoped for, and Katya warned him: "You'll soon have that young man as a son-in-law, if you're not careful."

"Careful? It would be the answer to my prayers."

Katya looked at him as if he was out of his mind.

"The child's only nineteen. I know she's a handful, but she could do *much* better than that. I know his family. His father could never make a living."

"His father's dead."

"Then he certainly can't make a living. His mother's a corsetière—she looks after me."

"Then she does a very good job, by the look of things."

"It's not as if Vicky's on the shelf. She's got young men round her all the time, and even when she was away, I spent half the day answering telephone calls and taking telephone messages from Nat, Schmat, Basil, Henry, Gavin, Herbert, Malcolm, Stephen, Duncan—I can't even remember their names—doctors, dentists, architects, lawyers, young men with good prospects from good families. Why pick on him?"

"I didn't pick on him, she did, and I can tell you he'll do better than any of your Nats and Schmats."

"With your money, maybe."

"I could spend money on worse things."

Then came the wedding, and Nahum felt that Mittwoch was partly to blame. He said that his new cinema had teething troubles, and he couldn't get away. "You're too conscientious," Nahum had told him (though it later occurred to him that he might not have wished to come to the wedding because his mother had not been invited). In the main, however, he blamed Kapulski. Nahum was aware of Vicky's defects, but he had always thought of her as level-headed, and even if he was upset when she ended her relationship with Flemyng, he had admired her attitude; it showed that in some ways she had more sense than he, yet Kapulski had only to whisper the poisonous word "movies" in her ear, and she immediately began to think of herself as a film star, another Arabella.

He tried to remonstrate with her: "Look, Vicky. You know how devoted I am to Arabella. I love her and would do anything for her, but if I could have put her into a convent to stop her leading the sort of life she leads, I would have done it."

"And would you do the same to me?"

"I would, if only there was such a thing as a kosher convent, which unfortunately there isn't. Is that the limit of your ambition, to be another shadow on the screen?"

"I should be so lucky. Unfortunately, I haven't got Arabella's poise or lack of scruple, but I'm twelve years younger than her, and better-looking—"

"You're beautiful, my child, and a pleasure to look at—on those days when you take the trouble to put a comb through your hair—but no one is better-looking than Arabella."

"You *are* besotted with her. She's misshapen. She has no body. She's all arms and legs—her thighs go all the way up to her nipples—and she has no breasts to speak of, but she has the poise to carry it off, and obviously she's carried it off with you. Look, I don't know if I will be a film star, I am not even sure that I'd want to be one—does that satisfy you—but I'd like to have a try."

"What about young Mittwoch?"

"What about not-so-young Mittwoch?"

"I thought you were, well—"

"Well, we're not, but if he's half as interested in me as he is in making you rich, then he knows where to find me."

"So you're going?"

"I am."

"But I need you here."

"What for? You've got two women in the house. Katya's a good housekeeper and a marvelous cook. Or are you afraid she's going to eat you?"

She was a good deal nearer the truth than she could have imagined, for he was afraid to be alone with Katya. He was not quite alone, but his mother spent most of her time in bed. While Vicky was around, Katya felt obliged to behave with a certain amount of circumspection, but when Vicky was away, she roamed half-clad around the house. Sometimes she would inveigle him into her bed, and not infrequently she would climb uninvited into his, almost as a right. A wife, he thought, would have been more hesitant. He had no idea that lust could persist to such an age in a woman.

He sometimes asked himself why he didn't throw her out of bed, but there was a chivalrous streak in him, and he found it difficult to insult a woman, especially a woman of his mother's generation who also happened to be her sister. And there was the matter of usage. She had by now been in his bed so often that she could claim squatter's rights, but possibly the main reason was that if he told her to go when he didn't want her, she might refuse to come when he did.

For the first time, he became aware of how large and gloomy his house was. Sophie had furnished it in what she had thought of as the height of fashion, but that was shortly after the war, when provincial taste was still dominated by Edwardiana; now, with its clutter of heavy, useless objects, the place was part obstacle course and part museum, though the pungent perfumes in which Katya doused herself gave it the slight whiff of an expensive brothel.

He had two sources of consolation during the dark days which followed. When he sent Sophie an invitation to Arabella's wedding, Vicky said: "You're wasting your time. She won't come. She's big with child"—and added characteristically—"not that she's small, otherwise, but she's big, very big with child, perhaps even children," and a few days after the wedding, he received a telegram that she had had twin boys. The birth had apparently been a very difficult one, but Shyke, who had been at the *brith* (the circumcision), said that Sophie was making a good recovery, that Yankelson was as well as could be expected and that the twins were splendid, or, as Jessie put it: "Gorgeous little buggers."

The other source of consolation was the boys. Jacob had taken a good degree at Cambridge and had been offered a job in an Edinburgh grammar school, so that Nahum would be able to see him frequently, and Benny, to everybody's surprise (including his own), had managed to get a place in the medical faculty of Glasgow University, so that Nahum could look forward to company at home and perhaps even some protection from Katya.

He had been careful after he married Miri to treat all her children as his own, and he had, in fact, gone so much out of his way to make sure that Alex and Hector should not feel like step-sons that he had, in some ways, neglected Jacob and Benny. It was clear from their earliest days that neither of them would be an Alex or a Hector, who, though the sons of an immigrant father and grandsons of a flea-bitten poultry dealer, had almost broken through to the ruling circles of

England. Hector had become something of a disappointment, but he was only thirty-two and could possibly resume his upward course, while no one had any doubt that Alex would be a colonial governor and a knight—if not higher—before he was much older. He couldn't see either Jacob or Benny approaching such eminence, nor could he imagine either of them as officers in the British Army. He had been told that the most important part of an English public-school education was the self-assurance and poise it gave to its pupils, but if Jacob and Benny were anything to go by, it gave poise to the poised and self-assurance to the self-assured. When Jacob and Benny came to Arabella's wedding, they sat in a corner in their badly cut dinner suits (Nahum had, in fact, taken them to a good tailor, but they had the sort of figures on which everything seemed badly cut), blinking at the scene with bewilderment and dismay, as if trapped in a nightmare.

When Benny returned to Glasgow to begin his studies, he was not quite as companionable as Nahum could have wished, and, if anything, he reminded him of Lazar.

He had had hopes of the house filling up with young people again, with the sound of music and records and laughter, but Benny was a friendless young man and extremely industrious; when supper was over, he was impatient to get back to his books and his room, which left Nahum once again a prey to his aunt. As a result, whenever he visited some of his more outlying cinemas, instead of driving back to Glasgow he would stay overnight, though when he did, he sometimes wondered if Benny was safe.

He was also deeply concerned about the nature of Hector's business, as, indeed, he had been from the minute he was introduced to Hector's partner. He could not imagine Hector being involved in anything shady; on the other hand, he could not imagine Cameron being involved in anything else. He certainly seemed a personable young man, perhaps a little too personable for Nahum's tastes, but he could never forgive someone who had betrayed a trust, and, if he had betrayed him, Nahum had no doubt that he would, in time, betray Hector. On the other hand, he had to remind himself that Hector had left the army under a cloud (the nature of which he had still not discovered), and if he had never, in fact, been publicly charged with an offence, neither had Cameron, so that in some ways they were a likely pair, but still he remained troubled, and one day he made an unannounced visit to their company. He found their entire enterprise in a shabby little warehouse on the edge of Epping Forest, and his unexpected arrival caused obvious embarrassment and consternation. Both Hector and Cameron were in town; they were hurriedly summoned by an apprehensive-looking secretary who kept him in an outer office and discouraged him from exploring the place.

The partners eventually arrived in a huge Bentley and ushered him into a comfortably appointed inner office, where Cameron busied himself with drinks, while Hector explained that Nahum had caught them at an inopportune moment, for they were about to move to new and larger premises.

"Can I see the sort of equipment you're selling?" asked Nahum.

"Surely," said Hector and immediately whisked him off to a warehouse near the London docks where machinery was being crated; the crates did bear the name of the firm, which reassured Nahum a little, for a suspicion had been growing in his mind that they were engaged in smuggling whisky to America.

That night Hector took him out to dinner, and they were joined by Arabella, Vicky and Cameron. It was a splendid meal in a splendid setting. Arabella, swathed in furs, looked more beautiful than ever, the wine flowed freely and Nahum did not know which was the more intoxicating—Arabella or the wine; he found it difficult in the convivial atmosphere to maintain the antagonism he had harboured against Cameron, though he was troubled by the familiarity which seemed to exist between him and Vicky. Vicky herself looked troubled about something, and she lacked the radiance he would have expected of a budding film star.

He asked her how her career was progressing.

"Ask Ara," she said.

"She's got a small part in my next film," said Arabella.

"A *very* small part," said Vicky. "I play the part of a scullery maid who is strangled in the first frame."

"But she plays it beautifully," added Arabella.

When he returned to Glasgow the next evening, he was surprised to find the house in darkness. He called for Katya and Benny, but neither of them seemed to be about, and eventually an upstairs door opened and he heard the heavy shuffling tread of his mother; she came slowly downstairs in her dressing gown with a heavy walking stick in her hand.

"I wasn't sure if it was you," she said. "You went away and left me here on my own."

"I was in London, didn't you know?"

"What difference does it make if you're in London or China, if you're not here, then I'm on my own. Anything could have happened to me. Somebody knocked earlier on, but I was afraid to answer. Anything could have happened to me, a defenceless woman all on my own. And the phone's been ringing."

"The phone?"

"It hasn't stopped."

"Then why didn't you answer it?"

"Because by the time I got to it, it stopped ringing. It happened three or four times, up and down, up and down. And there was somebody at the door, but I couldn't answer, a defenceless woman all on my own. That and the phone, I thought I was going crazy."

As she spoke, the phone rang again.

"There, what did I tell you, it's been going like—"

"Hush, Mother, it's long distance."

"What did you say?"

"Will you shut up, it's long distance." She not only shut up, she sat down with a bump on the bottom step and let her stick drop with a clatter.

It was the Colonial Office. Alex had been attacked by an Arab and was critically ill in hospital.

CHAPTER XXV
ALEX

NAHUM HAD READ IN THE PAPERS ABOUT TROUBLE IN PALESTINE —of Arabs killing Jews and Jews killing Arabs—and whenever such troubles arose, he immediately thought with alarm of Alex, but, as Hector explained, Alex was "part of the government set-up, shielded, protected and well above the fray, you've got nothing to fear." But he feared all the same, especially as the scale of the troubles increased, and now his fears were confirmed. He was beginning to feel that there was no such thing as imaginary fear: hope could be imaginary, but not fear.

When he reached Jaffa, he was greeted by a government official and a senior officer of the Palestine police. Nahum studied their faces for news, but they were both impassive.

"He's better than one might have thought," said the official. "A lot tougher than he looks, Alex. He should pull through—none of us would have thought so this time last week."

"What happened? How did it happen?"

"He was sitting in a Tulkarm café reading a Hebrew paper," said the police officer, "not a wise thing to do, if I may say so, not in Tulkarm, not at this time. They're a restless lot in Tulkarm, especially now. Chap came at him with an axe."

"With an axe?"

"They can turn nasty, the Arabs. He deflected the blow with his hand, otherwise, the blessed thing would have gone through his skull. As it was, he lost three fingers and was badly concussed."

"But what nearly killed him was the bleeding," said the official. "You wouldn't think, looking at him, that he had that much blood. The place was covered with it."

They reached Alex after a two-hour drive. He was in a hospital run by a Catholic order, set high on a hill amid pine trees, and when Nahum entered his room, Alex was sitting up smiling, though swathed in bandages with his face as white as the bandages. One hand was in plaster. Nahum rushed over to him and grasped his free hand, then opened his mouth to say something, but no words came, and he broke down and cried. He quickly pulled himself together.

"Not much of an Englishman, am I?" he said.

"A tear of two doesn't do anyone any harm," said Alex. "They're used to tears here. The place is dedicated to the tears of Christ."

"You see, in *der heim*, when you got a telegram calling you to a sick-bed, it only meant one thing, and you began saying *kaddish* in your head. I suppose I broke down because I'm so glad to see you're alive."

"I was cross when I heard they'd sent for you. You needn't have come, not now. It can be very hot in September."

"And if they split your head open in September, should I come in May?"

"They didn't split my head. I lost a few fingers, but my head's in one piece—I think. The wound's superficial."

"It doesn't look superficial to me, not with all those bandages round you. What actually happened?"

"We've had some trouble in Jerusalem and Hebron, as you know. There was a dreadful massacre in Hebron, but it was comparatively quiet around here, and I'm fairly well-known, which is why it took me by surprise. I was having my usual coffee in my usual café, when a chap came at me as if I was a chopping block. Happily, it was a clean axe. If it had been dirty, there would have been no end of bother. When I came to, I found myself here with a dreadful headache and my right hand so sore and heavy that I couldn't lift it. Luckily, I'm left-handed, so I should be all right. I lost a good bit of blood and had to be topped up again—with Arab blood, I believe—which I suppose makes me half-Arab. Sophie was here the other day, and when I told her of the blood change, she regarded me with envy and questioned me at length. As you may know, she's obsessed about the character of our father, of blessed memory, and thinks that she has tainted blood. It wouldn't surprise me if she attempted to open her veins one day to have a transfusion. Have you seen her?"

"Not yet. I hope to spend a few days with her."

"She was here with the twins, lively little chaps. Drove the nuns wild—kept crawling under and up their habits. I thought I might have seen you at the *brith,* by the way. I know that an excised foreskin isn't quite in the same class as an excised finger, but there's greater ceremony attached to it."

"Don't talk to me about the *brith,*" said Nahum.

"Why not?"

"It's a sore point. The—why are you laughing?"

"The *brith*, a sore point, that's a good one, coming from you, but you mustn't make me laugh, it hurts."

"By the time I got the telegram, it was too late to come."

"It was a splendid occasion. Half of Volkovysk was there, to say nothing of Bialystock, Brest Litovsk, Kamenets Podolsk and all stations east. You'd have loved it. Yankelson's grown a foot taller since he's become a father. Natural farmer, Yankelson, truly a son of the soil, though I wouldn't say dear old Sophie is a natural farmer's wife. She looks like a lady of the manor fallen among tenants and still has the grand manner—which has, if anything, become grander. 'One must keep up standards,' she told me, 'especially among people who have none.' She's not very popular, my sister, and my presence didn't add to her popularity."

"Why not?"

"Didn't you know? I'm public-enemy number one. I'm the local Solomon—local disputes are often brought to me for settlement—and I decide on the merits of the case which, as often as not, go against the Jews, and so I'm accused of bending backwards to favour the Arabs. So was Herbert Samuel in his time, so is any Jewish official who attempts to discharge his duty with a semblance of impartiality, but I'm regarded as the worst of the lot. I'm unmarried, you see, and have an Arab servant, Jamal, a rather attractive young man, and stories have been put about—one wonders by whom—that we are living together in blissful buggery."

"In blissful what?"

"You shouldn't know of such things, but I think you've got the import. It got to the point where the H.C.—the High Commissioner—drew me aside and suggested that it might be prudent for me to find a female servant or, better still, a wife, preferably of the Jewish persuasion, to which I replied that Jamal was more than a servant but a cook, and that if he or anyone else could find me a wife, of any persuasion, who could cook half as well as Jamal, I'd marry her tomorrow. Anyway, what with one thing and another, I was taken to be an honorary Arab, and when I was found with my head bleeding and my fingers scattered about the place, there were rumours that my assailant was Jewish. Now that it has been established that he was Arab, I have been forgiven, more or less, and only the other day I was visited by a prominent rabbi, who told me that prayers were being said for my speedy recovery, which made me fear an imminent relapse. If word should get around that I'm not only well on the way to recovery but brimful of Arab blood, their attitude might change again."

Nahum visited Alex daily for the better part of a week and was delighted to see him making progress with every visit, though the coming and going of the nuns filled him with a slight sense of foreboding, for, with their white, voluminous habits and their silent movements, they seemed to float around like benign angels of death. At the end of the week, he went off to visit Sophie.

He had not seen her for over two years, and she had, for all her physical exertion, become larger and very tanned, and, because she always insisted on wearing a dress rather than trousers or shorts ("trousers, short or long, detract from the dignity of womanhood," she said), she looked like an Arab peasant woman. She and Yankelson were members of a *moshav,* which was not a kibbutz but a cooperative village in which each family farmed its own plot and tended its own livestock, but machinery was communally owned and produce was communally marketed. The thought of spending a few days in a village had charmed Nahum, but the *moshav* was unlike any village he had seen. All the houses were nearly identical, small and square, as if they had come from the same concrete mold (which they had), with white walls and red roofs, though interiors differed with the differing tastes and circumstances of the occupants. The furniture in most cases was makeshift—lopsided sticks laboriously put together from odd, sometimes very odd, bits of timber—but *chez* Yankelson was different.

Sophie had been anxious to avoid ostentation, but during their honeymoon, which they had spent touring the Scottish border country where she had been stationed during the war, she had picked up chairs and others bits of furniture in various antique and second-hand shops, and before she was quite aware of what had happened, she found herself with enough genuine Regency furniture to equip a mansion. She had also received expensive wedding presents, like a silver tea service and Wedgewood table service, and at first felt too embarrassed to take them out of their crates, but she found that the enamel plates, which were *de rigeur* in the *moshav,* tended to turn her stomach.

Yankelson said: "Why do you keep your good china holed up in crates as if they're a dirty secret? Nobody's ashamed of using their samovar if they have one. Why should you be ashamed of your silver? On the other hand, if you are ashamed of them and can't bring yourself to use them, give them away, and be finished."

And so she gradually unpacked them, and their house came to be known in the neighbourhood as *ha-armon,* the palace. But grand though it looked, the opulent appointments left little room for people, especially people as substantial as Sophie had become and Yankelson was becoming. Whenever there was an important guest in the area, he was usually entertained at the *armon*, until reports began to appear in some overseas papers that the settlers were living like lords, and the practice was discontinued.

They enjoyed an abundance of fresh fruit, vegetables and dairy produce of a quality Nahum had never tasted in Glasgow or, for that matter, in Volkovysk, though meat and fish were rare, but if they ate well, they slept badly, and there were times when Nahum wondered if they slept at all, for they were always up and about at work in the fields when he rose in the morning, and they were still at work, usually on one committee or another, when he went to bed at night. One or other or both of the twins usually cried in the night, and if they did so in chorus the rafters shook, and he would look up from his bed on the living-room sofa to see Sophie tip-toeing across the room with an infant or two on her shoulders. He found the heat suffocating, and sometimes he pushed back the rug and slept on the stone floor, until one night he was awakened by a small army of many-legged insects trampling over him, so huge and heavy-footed that he actually felt their weight. He had arranged to stay for a week and would have liked to leave after a night, but he knew Sophie would be upset if he left too soon, and Sophie did not take such upsets lightly. On the other hand, he was of an age when physical comfort and a good night's sleep, undisturbed by bawling infants and leaden-footed mammoths, were important to him. Sophie and Yankelson spoke together in Hebrew, and, although he knew classical Hebrew, he could not make out modern Hebrew, especially when spoken at speed, and he had the feeling that they were talking about him and that he was making himself a nuisance. Their house would have been sufficient for a modest bachelor with modest tastes and was not really built to accommodate guests or, for that matter, a family of any size at all. They would both rest for an hour or two in the afternoon. Nahum had always been careful not to sleep in the afternoon, except at weekends (possibly because his father had slept every afternoon for as long as he had known him, which was perhaps why he had always thought of him as an old man), and, as he tried to stir around the darkened house, he would knock into things, or push them over, or break things, or step on the cat, or trip over rugs, or otherwise cause a disturbance, and Sophie would rise, short-tempered and tight-lipped, and, although she never actually reproached him, her face radiated displeasure.

Things were somewhat more relaxed on Friday evenings. Candles were lit; the men donned white shirts, the women floral dresses, and

Nahum was able to stop people and chat to them about their life and their work. Sophie was rather more difficult to talk to, for she stacked up books and papers, including numerous English magazines which she said she only had time to read on Friday nights, but Yankelson became more congenial, and Nahum sat with him on the small front porch of the house, cracking nuts and drinking tea until Sophie told them to quiet down because they were keeping the infants awake.

The sight of the twins, small, plump bundles with dark skins and bright, beady eyes, gave him infinite pleasure, their sound rather less so, and when they were left unguarded—or, rather, with him as guardian—he was terrified, for they would clamber all over him, tug at his hair and moustache, tear open his fly, open his mouth, pull at his teeth, put their fingers up his nostrils or in his eyes; once, when he was asleep with his mouth open, they thrust a broom handle down his throat.

Nahum was pained and surprised by Sophie's unpopularity. She was nicknamed *Kum-kum-Kaspi* (the silver tea-pot) and was hardly on speaking terms with anyone. Her husband, on the other hand, was the most popular man in the *moshav,* an all-rounder—good with machines, good with animals, familiar with the soil, excellent in committees— and he was known affectionately as the *Mukhtar,* an Arab expression for village elders (he had, in fact, taught himself Arabic and was on very good terms with the local Arabs).

"What have they got against her?" Nahum asked him. "She's so good, so hard-working, so generous."

"She's too good, too hard-working, too generous," said Yankelson, "and don't forget, she's been very ill. She still hasn't quite recovered."

"Then why does she work like that?"

"You try and stop her. She believes in hard work. Hard work, she says, is the saving grace of this place. Without it, the people wouldn't be worth living with."

"They seem all right to me."

"They would seem all right to anybody, but she's got high standards. You and your sons must have been saints, the way she speaks about you. In a way, it's my fault, for it all began with the tea-pot; if it wasn't for me, the tea-pot would still be in the crate."

"And if it wasn't for me, you'd also be in the crate," Sophie interjected. They weren't aware that she had been listening, but she had been next door, and the walls were like paper.

"I knew there'd be trouble over the tea-pot, but I didn't anticipate the form the trouble would take. I'm not the only woman here from a comfortable home. There's a girl here from Poland who inherited a mass of expensive jewelry, which she keeps in a vault in a Jaffa bank, and I can't see her ever using it, but this tea-pot was something one could use, and I used it whenever anyone came to tea." She took it out. "Look at it, beautiful Georgian silver, see the lines? It's a pleasure to look at, and I wanted the pleasure to be shared, but as a result I was accused not only of being wealthy, which is just about forgivable, but of flaunting my wealth, which is not. I was prepared for envy, but not for envy of this particular sort, and certainly not in a community which is purporting to build a new heaven and a new earth. If it happened in Glasgow, I would have accepted it, I would have accepted it even in Tel Aviv, but not here. But that was only the beginning. Yankelson happens to be good at everything. He's a good builder, plumber, electrician, carpenter, painter and decorator—"

"What she's trying to tell you," Yankelson interjected, "is that I'm a lousy husband and father."

"In a way you are, yes, but don't put words into my mouth. We've also been having troubles with the Arabs, as you know, and he's commander of the local guard, not only in the *moshav,* but the whole neighbourhood, and he can never say no to anything that's asked of him, so that when he came home in the evenings—*if* he came home in the evenings—he was ready to drop. Once he did drop, and I said, enough is enough. Yankelson will do his share and no more than his share, and I've never been forgiven since. They hate me and commiserate with him, but I'm prepared to take that."

"The fact is," said Yankelson, "your daughter wasn't born and bred to live in a small community and be a farmer's wife."

"Were you born and bred to be a farmer?" she retorted.

"She's a cultured woman with cultured tastes, who needs cultured company," he went on, "and I can see now that we should have moved to town."

"If I wanted to live in town, I could have stayed in Glasgow," she said. "Perhaps we should all have stayed in Glasgow," she added, and broke down.

Nahum was startled. He couldn't remember when he had seen Sophie in tears.

She quickly blew her nose, wiped her eyes and composed herself. "I'm sorry. I was thinking of poor Alex. What was a frail wraith like him doing in an inferno like this?"

"He'll be all right," Nahum assured her, "he's not as frail as he looks. He was sitting up in bed talking, just like that, after somebody had put an axe in his head. If he survived that, he'll survive anything."

"I hope you're right," she said and gave him a fierce hug, kissed him on the head and went next door.

"Don't forget, she's been very ill," said Yankelson to him in a whisper.

"But you're happy here, aren't you?"

"Happy? I don't have time to think about it. People ask me if I was afraid during all those years I was on the run in Russia. I was too busy staying alive to be afraid. But wait"——he went out into the garden and came back with a handful of rich, red, golden soil, like a compound of blood and sand—"with this under my feet, I've got more than happiness, I've got reassurance, an end to running. But still, if this goes on, I'll leave tomorrow." And he lowered his voice again. "But I don't think it will go on. Don't forget, she's been very ill."

Late that Saturday afternoon, he and Yankelson went for a walk in the fields. They had slept and rested and had been treated to afternoon tea on the porch. The heat of the day had passed, and a breeze had sprung up which rustled through the pine trees surrounding the settlement. Sprinklers hissed on every side, and the moist soil sent out a rich, musty aroma which he found almost intoxicating.

"You've got a good life here," said Nahum. "You know, I nearly came out here more than thirty years ago. A pity I didn't."

"You wouldn't have a house like you have in Glasgow."

"Yes, but those things don't matter. I don't have the satisfaction from my business that you have from yours."

"You don't have the heart-aches when the crop fails, and you don't have to spend a night or two a week on guard duty. Our whole orange plantation was burned down last month."

"By Arabs?"

"By Arabs."

"I thought you were on good terms with the Arabs."

"In normal times we are, but things often turn abnormal. If things were normal, this would be paradise, but you know I have the feeling that, in the same way as some crops don't take root in some climates, the normal can never take root here. As a matter of fact, there's no word for normal in the Hebrew language, we've had to adapt it from the English. Which doesn't mean I regret coming here. We have heart-aches and worries, but at a calm hour like this, when I stop and look around at what we're doing and what we've done, the heart-aches and the worries seem a small price."

As Nahum gazed around him, he noticed the bulky figure of Sophie running towards them. He had never seen her run before, and she was moving at such speed that she sent up a cloud of dust.

"It's the hospital," she said breathlessly. "They've just phoned. Alex's had a relapse. I've telegraphed Hector."

A car was waiting for them by the house, and they drove rapidly through the gathering darkness.

"I've been dreading this since first I saw him," said Sophie. "His recovery seemed far too rapid. I've seen it often enough during the war, with men almost on their feet. A secondary infection sets in, and they're finished."

"God forbid."

When they reached the hospital, there were two doctors and a nurse around the bed, talking in hushed voices. Alex was in a coma.

"The impact of the blow had caused some clotting under the skull," explained one of the doctors, "and it appears that the clot has been growing and may continue to grow. We shall operate as soon as we can, but we are waiting for extra equipment."

The operation began at dawn and continued for most of the morning. At about noon a doctor came out to tell them: "We've saved his life, but it's too early to say whether we've done more than that."

They were allowed to see Alex that evening, but he was unconscious, and he was still unconscious when they called the next day. Later that evening he opened an eye (the other was in bandages) and looked at them without recognition.

They continued to visit him two or three times a day for the rest of the week. Each time Nahum thought he could discern some slight improvement in his condition, until Sophie turned upon him in exasperation and cried: "Will you stop deceiving yourself? Can't you see he's dying?"

They were staying at a small nearby pension. When Nahum got to his room, he asked for a Bible, and, turning to the Psalms, he began:

Happy is the man that walketh not in the counsel of the ungodly, nor standeth in the way of sinners, nor sitteth in the seat of the scornful . . .

And so on, right through until the final lines:

Let everything that hath breath praise the Lord. Praise ye the Lord.

They always read the Psalms when anyone was in serious peril in Volkovysk. He did not recall that the reading had ever helped anyone, but he felt strangely relieved when he had finished and better able to face the day which was just beginning to break. When he saw Alex again some hours later, he was convinced that he looked better, that there was more life in his eye, that he had looked at them with a flicker of recognition even though he was still unable to speak, but he hesitated to say so in case Sophie should turn upon him again.

Hector arrived the following morning, brisk, bright, breezy, marched in upon Alex and greeted him in a loud voice: "Now, what's this you've done to yourself, eh? A man could be court-martialled for less in my time—malingering."

At that moment something like life did flicker in Alex's eye, but, if anything, it was a look of alarm, and he seemed to recoil.

They remained there for about an hour, looking at him and then at each other with a growing sense of despair.

It was a blazing day, with the air so hot and heavy that it pressed upon them like a clammy hand. Hector suggested that they drive down to the Sea of Galilee for a swim.

"For goodness sake," said Sophie.

"What's the point of hanging around here all day? The sight of your sweet face hovering over him won't make him any better. We'll be back by the evening."

"There's no harm in having a short drive," said Nahum.

"Go without me," said Sophie, but on an afterthought she joined them.

The heat eased as they climbed steeply through the Galilean hills, then, as they descended, the air became progressively hotter and heavier with every downward turn of the road. Nahum could hardly breathe and thought he would collapse, but he was sustained by glimpses of the lake, which seemed cooler and more inviting the nearer they approached. When they reached the shore, the air quivered with heat, and Nahum at once threw off his shoes and socks, rolled up his trousers and began paddling in the water. Sophie went into the water fully clothed and settled among the reeds, with her skirts ballooning about her, like a water buffalo. Hector tore off his trousers and swam in his underpants, now on his back, now on his front, spitting jets of water, frollicking, splashing like a shoal of dolphins.

"He looks as if he hasn't a care in the world," said Nahum.

"You get like that after a few years in the army."

"I wish I'd been a few years in the army."

They remained there until the day began to cool and returned in silence under a sky like burnished copper. When they reached their pension, the phone was ringing.

"Is ringing all day," said a harassed manager, "is ringing for you."

Alex was dead.

Nahum opened his mouth for the traditional Hebrew formula uttered on such occasions—*Baruch dayan emeth,* blessed be the rightful judge—but the words wouldn't come.

Alex was given a state funeral on the Mount of Olives, with the High Commissioner, service chiefs and heads of the various communities in attendance. Shyke and Jessie were also there. Nahum nearly fainted in the fierce heat as the rabbi, who had never set eyes on Alex, delivered a lengthy eulogy. When it was over, everyone hurried to their cars, but Nahum turned back.

"Have you forgotten something?" asked Hector.

"Yes," he said, and began moving back and forward among the rows of tombstones, scrutinising each stone. "My grandfather, a saintly man, was buried here. He went to Palestine especially to die and be buried here on the Mount of Olives."

"But there are millions of stones here, it could take you a month to find it."

"I'm in no hurry."

They did not find it that day, but early the next morning, with the help of Shyke and a cemetery attendant, they managed to locate the stone.

"There you are, Nahum Rabinovitz. I was named after him."

"What's the rest of the writing?"

"I can't make it out, I can't even make out the date, but, for all a visitor would know, this could be my stone. You know, I feel like stretching out on this place here and now."

"You'd save on the stone, but I should point out that you're not dead."

"No, not yet, but do you know, my father died at fifty-six, and I'm fifty-four already."

"So what do you want to do, stop here for the next two years?"

Shyke, who was now head of a small private bank, put his villa at their disposal. Hector had to hurry back to London, and Nahum remained alone for much of the day with Jessie, who also accompanied him on walks around Jerusalem.

"Is there any point in going back?" he said. "Now that I'm here, I feel I should have come here in the first place, like Shyke, except that I don't know if I have his toughness or resilience. I've suffered one minor and one major betrayal—"

"And you've survived both," said Jessie.

"Yes, but I've had no real trials, not the sort of thing that Shyke's been through."

"Miri's illness was trial enough, and Alexander's death. You seem to think that unless you've suffered in uniform, you haven't suffered. You were very attached to Alexander, weren't you? I know he was very attached to you."

"Was he?"

"Very."

"You're not just telling me that?"

"He spoke about you with the deepest respect and affection."

"You see, that makes me jealous. He had time to talk to Shyke, but not to me. It was one man of action talking to another. As for me, all I've ever been good at is making money, which is something for which he's never had any respect, and, to be honest, I've not much respect for it, either. He never talked much about himself, Alex, not to me, he never talked much about anyone. Did he have a girl friend?"

"No, I don't think so."

"Ah, to think that a man like that shouldn't have had a family, but then, look at it this way. If a man like Yerucham could have had a son like Alex, who is there to say that a man like Alex mightn't have had a son like Yerucham? Still, it's awful to think that he's over and done with, finished, no more, because if you're dead without children, then you're really dead." And to his amazement, he noticed that Jessie's eyes had filled up.

"I'm sorry, I forgot."

"Kenneth couldn't have children, and we often talked of adopting one, but I suppose I was too selfish."

"I'm sorry, I'm so wrapped up in my own grief that I keep forgetting about everybody else."

When he told Shyke that he was thinking of selling out and settling in Palestine, Shyke said: "A bit of capital can go pretty far here, you'd do very well, especially if you went into cinemas, or anything like that. The place is teeming with soldiers with plenty of money and nothing to do except get drunk, and there'll be more soldiers here, I promise you."

"I don't know if I want to stay in cinemas."

"Right, don't stay in cinemas, but there are three times when you should never make lasting decisions, when you're in love"—and he waved a hand towards Jessie—"see what's happened to me? Three times when you shouldn't make lasting decisions—when you're in love, when you're drunk and when you've been bereaved. I think you should settle here. I think all Jews should settle here, but, first of all, go back, resume your normal life and then, when you're in a calm frame of mind and still think you should come, then come—but not before."

CHAPTER XXVI
IN MEMORIAM

DEAR SOPHIE,

You needn't worry about poor father. I must admit I got a shock when I met him at the station—so did Katya (who was all over him and almost carried him bodily into the house)—but he's back at work now, and his spirits have picked up a little. The only thing which worries me is that he's turned religious, which I always think is a bad sign. He says *kaddish* for poor Alex three times a day. If I remember rightly, he hardly said *kaddish* for poor Mummy at all, and certainly never on weekdays, though that may have been because she had four sons to say *kaddish* for her (though I'm sure they never did), while poor Alex has no one.

As you can imagine, we were all extremely upset at the news, even though we were prepared for the worst, except Grandma, and she, poor dear, hardly knows what's going on. Her face and neck are swollen, her movements are slow, her speech is slurred and she looks as if she's turned to stone, and to think how handsome and regal she used to look. I sometimes think that women should be put away—I certainly would rather be put away—before they turn into eyesores.

Did anyone write to you about the memorial service in Clifton? It was extremely solemn, dignified and impressive. Father didn't quite know how to dress for the occasion, and, after taking advice from various quarters, including Krochmal, his lawyer (who is getting very old and decrepit and deaf—you've got to repeat everything a dozen times to him, and I think he charges a fee for every time you repeat it), he finally wore striped trousers, a frock coat and a top hat. I must say, he looked very distinguished even in the distinguished gathering in which he found himself, and the headmaster kept introducing him to Lord this and to General that and even to Field Marshall Lord something-or-other, and he sat next to a minister of state who, a little to his disappointment, turned out to be an ex-miner with bad teeth (I suppose you know that Labour has won the general election). Reverend Polack conducted the service, the lesson was read by a bishop and the sermon was delivered by the Chief Rabbi, who spoke movingly and beautifully and had me in tears. Father, however, kept his composure throughout and only broke down when reciting the *kaddish* at the end, which brought me out in tears once more. I cheered up later, but Father remained upset. You know how he likes to think of himself as an Englishman (never a Scotsman, mind you, an Englishman) and to sport a stiff upper lip, and I think he felt he had let the side down. He looked a trifle dazed at the reception which followed and seemed to be asking himself what was he, Nahum Raeburn, né Rabinovitz, of Volkovysk doing among all those lords and ladies and bishops and deans and generals and field-marshalls and cabinet ministers, but, apart from his bewildered expression, he did not look at all out of place, and, whatever else he lacks, I must say that he has a natural dignity, perhaps even grace. Hector, of course, was in his element and treated the event as an old boys' reunion, grasping hands here, slapping backs there, exchanging stories of old times and gossip about mutual friends and showing off Arabella (who looked dazzling in black) as if she were a trophy he had picked up at a hurdles race. She certainly looked and dressed better than any wife there, but did you know she is slightly malproportioned? Still, she has the absolute conviction that she is the most beautiful thing in creation, which others seem to share; if anyone was to prick her confidence, she would become an eyesore. She is very proud of her last picture, but a friend of mine, who knows something about these things, thought that she overacted dreadfully and found the whole thing a trifling bit of work (it hasn't been shown on any of the major circuits yet, and I don't know if it ever will). She is now in the midst of a talking film, which will have the advantage of showing off her pleasant, if rather thin, singing voice but will have the disadvantage of showing off her rather piercing and exaggerated speaking voice, for, as you know, she can't open her mouth without making it seem as if she is addressing a somewhat hard-of-hearing public gathering.

Father, I need hardly add, is very impressed with her films, but, of course, he has no critical faculty whatever. If it moves, and enough pensioners and truants are willing to pay four pence a time to pack his flea-pits on a wet afternoon, then, as far as he's concerned, it's a good film. He is talking about building a new picture palace right in the centre of Glasgow, which, if you please, he plans to call the Arabella.

Her latest epic is called *Low and Mighty,* and you may, if you are alert enough, notice a familiar face in what I hope will always remain an unfamiliar situation. In other words, I, too, have become a film star, albeit in a modest and somewhat inauspicious way, for I am strangled in the first minute of the film. I was given the part by one Kapulski, a gigantic, hydrocephalic Yank, whose role in the set-up is undefined, but who is at the centre of everything and who has even offered to whisk me off to Hollywood. I might have been tempted but for the fact that he offered to whisk himself along with me. (Kapulski, by the way, was at the memorial service and offered to make the Countess of Bristol-or-somewhere a film star.)

But now I come to the interesting part. Kagan was there (he is a governor of the school). His beard had thinned out, and he was looking a trifle decrepit and worn, and so, for that matter, was his son, a tall, pompous-looking man with gleaming black hair and dark rings around his eyes, as if he had been suffering from constipation since puberty, and with him was a woman other than the fabled Lotie. She looked a bit like him, and I thought she might have been a relative, but she was introduced to us as Mrs Kagan, which means that the beautiful Lotie (whom I have never met but about whom Grandma—in her coherent days—never stopped talking) is either dead or divorced, and as people of her class do not usually die if they can help it, I can only presume that she is divorced. One could not, of course, ask the younger Mr Kagan what had happened to his first wife (though I nearly did), but I made it my business to find out, and I have discovered that she is, indeed, divorced and living in New England, though, as the divorce took place more than a year ago and as events move quickly in America, she may have remarried. I told the news to Grandma as soon as I got back, and she said in her slow, slurred voice: "Lotie? Not Nahum's Lotie?"

"She wasn't quite Nahum's Lotie, Grandma, though she nearly was."

"I'm talking about your mother."

"What about her?"

"Didn't she die in the war?"

Quite gaga, poor thing. I also told Katya, which was a pleasure, for her face, which always looks supple and well-fed, suddenly became deflated. Oh, how I loathe that woman! She has more or less taken over the household, you know, and sits herself at the head of table, opposite Father, as if she were Mummy. When she was much younger and more attractive—and I will admit she has a certain coarse appeal, even now—she used to dress with a brassy flamboyance which was almost tasteful in its bad taste and was certainly her, but now that she's getting on, or, rather, has got on in years, she dresses like a young woman in her first blush of maidenhood and looks grotesque. Yet she still has charm, and no one believes that she has one foot in the grave (would that she had both). I know exactly what people see in her, and I suppose it's a tribute that at her age she should still be in a condition to display it, but frankly, as long as she's around, I fear for Father, and I sometimes have the dreadful feeling that my fears may have already been fulfilled.

Should I write to Lotie? If so, how do I go about it? "Dear Lotie, you may not know me, but had you married my father you'd have been my mother. I gather you are now free to marry again; so is Father, and has been for the last twelve years. Would you care to meet? Yours truly." I somehow don't think it would work. There was a young widow on your *moshav* I would have liked him to meet. I know you thought she was common, which she may be, but not more so than Katya, and, of course, she is very much younger. Did you introduce them? I am not one of those Jewish daughters who regard marriage as a panacea for all ills, but it would solve many of his problems, and not a few of mine. Which brings me to the main point of this letter.

You may remember when we were at Shyke's, I was introduced to a very attractive young Scotsman called Eddy Cameron. I saw quite a bit of him in Palestine and have seen more than a bit of him since, and we are now living together. We would like to get married, and I was bracing myself to tell Father my news, when he received the news about Alex. Even before Alex died, Hector said to me (he is Hector's business partner): "You can't do it to the old man, it'll break him." Now that he is broken, I certainly can't do it. I know that his best friend Shyke "married out," and that, according to you, were it not for the fact that he was pipped at the post by Shyke, he might have done the same. I find that hard to believe, but in any case he is a different man now, for, as I suggested earlier, he is reverting to the ways of his father and is aided and abetted by Jacob who, as you may know, has taken on a job in a Glasgow grammar school to keep him company. With Father it may be—I hope it is—a temporary aberration brought on by grief. With Jacob it appears to be the real thing, and he seems to spend half of his life in synagogue.

I suppose, if you were in my position, you would have given up Cameron, but then, had you been in my position, it is unlikely that you would have formed such a relationship in the first place. Well, let me tell you that I tried. When I met Father as he got off the boat-train at Victoria, I was so shocked by his appearance that I decided to cut Cameron out of my life there and then, and I travelled up to Glasgow with Father and stayed with him for the better part of two months, which I think, is the nearest thing to a sacrifice that I have ever made. I didn't write to Cameron, I didn't phone him, and he, for his part, understood the situation and did not try to contact me, but I found myself going to pieces. You've no idea how depressing things were. Grandma like a concrete ghost, Father looking into his food without being able to take it and sometimes breaking into convulsive sobs, Katya trying to make cheerful conversation about her various admirers (now all dead), Benny, a dear, sweet, hard-working dolt and very short-sighted, slurping his soup and pouring half of it over himself and half over the tablecloth, and I was afraid if I stayed on in Glasgow much longer I would strangle Katya, burn the house down and kill myself; finally, when Jacob moved to Glasgow, I felt free to go back to London and my "career."

But my problem, of course, remains.

My only hope of marrying, as far as I can see, is to get Father married first. He was fifty-five last week, and I came up to Glasgow specially (you must be asking yourself, "What's been happening to little Vicky?") and made him a small party and baked him a cake (so, needless to say, did you-know-who) with the figures fifty-five in pink icing. He looked at the two fives for a long time, then, almost as if he were talking to himself, said: "You know, my father died at fifty-six," and he either hopes or expects that the same will happen to him. He told me that he had a burial plot booked on the Mount of Olives next to Alex. As far as I know, he also has a reserved plot next to Mother in the Glasgow cemetery. Does he expect a second coming? One shouldn't laugh, but he is full of morbid thoughts, and marriage might put an end to them (though it could, of course, induce others). But, in the meantime, what does one do? What would you do?

Please give my love to Yankelson and the twins (Father doesn't stop talking about them, and I am not exaggerating if I say that the thought of them has probably kept him sane during the past few months).

Love,
Vicky.

CHAPTER XXVII
LOMZER

NAHUM RETURNED TO A SEA OF TROUBLES.

There was a slump in the cinema trade, or at least in his quarter of the trade, and even his newer houses, most of which had been showing a handsome profit, were just about paying their way; his older ones, the converted theatres, church-halls, chapels, barns and a fire station on which his business had been initially based, were making a loss. He owned eleven cinemas and had marked the location of each with blue-headed pins on a map of Scotland, which greeted him on his office wall as he arrived in the morning, and he would contemplate their growing number with pride as a man might contemplate the growing size of his family; the thought of closing one was tantamount almost to arranging a bereavement.

He had been negotiating the sale of three of his older cinemas before he left, but, as business declined, the negotiations broke down, and, after inviting and failing to obtain further offers, he eventually had to close them. A fourth, which had been showing a profit, was condemned as a fire risk by the local authority, and he was required to install new doors, hoses, valves and water points. But when that was complete and he was required by another branch of the same authority to install new urinals and—as they were called in the locality —"arsenals," he suspected the machinations of a rival or anti-Semitism, or both, but when some of his patrons, who were, in the main, elderly, began to relieve themselves in the darker corners of the building rather than resort to the lavatory, he decided to cut his losses and close the place.

Amidst all this came the uncalled-for boon of talking films. He had done well out of silent films and was content with them, but the larger circuits were all going over to "talkies," and he was aware that he would soon be out of business if he did not follow suit, but the necessary equipment and conversions were expensive, and the difficulties he encountered in raising capital reminded him of his early days in the shipping trade. "I don't have to study my accounts," he said, "I can tell exactly how I'm doing by the way I'm received by the bank managers," and he was received without enthusiasm. He was able to borrow some money, but not as much as he wanted or on the terms he hoped for, and he was compelled to sell a cinema which had been making a fairly consistent profit. "And then there were six," he said ruefully as he surveyed his map. And even then he was not quite out of the wood, for with the new equipment in place—a process which took him well over a year—he needed a far larger turnover to pay his overhead, and it was slow to appear. He had been worried for years about who would take over his business; now he was beginning to worry if there would be a business to take over.

One of his difficulties was that he hated to raise prices. Low prices had begun as a policy and had hardened into something like a principle, for he regarded the cinema as a boon to mankind and himself as a public benefactor cheering drab lives with a bit of colour, and he preferred a full cinema at sixpence a head to a half-empty one—or, for that matter, a half-full one—at a shilling. Full cinemas, moreover, were less expensive to heat and gave a sense of occasion to even the most banal film. He also found that the sight of crowds converging on a cinema excited others to follow, and there was nothing like a full house to attract full houses. Moreover, people tended to get up to mischief in empty cinemas. Katya and his mother were on the coast one day and rushed into the local cinema—which he happened to own—to get out of the rain, and Katya claimed to be aghast at what they saw "not on the screen, but in the back row—I couldn't believe my eyes."

"You shouldn't have looked," he said.

"Look? I couldn't help looking. The whole place was quaking. And you'd have thought it was a pair of young lovers letting their passions run away with them. Nothing of the sort. It was a white-haired old goat with one of the usherettes, wheezing and spluttering like a broken-down steam engine."

Nahum, while he tried to make light of the episode, was troubled by such reports, for they were symptoms of decline, and there were colleagues in the trade who argued that to keep the cinema respectable one had to charge a respectable price. "Cheap seats," said one, "invite cheap conduct."

By way of experiment, therefore, he raised prices by a quarter in one of his houses, and, although attendance declined a little, his revenue rose, and he felt encouraged to do the same with the rest, and again the revenues improved, and for the first time in years, Nahum could once again think in terms of expansion.

During the year that he was saying *kaddish* for Alex, he became friendly with an elderly widower called Lomzer who was saying *kaddish* for his wife, and during the frequent occasions they had to wait in synagogue until a quorum assembled, they chatted about family, health, politics, events at home and abroad and, inevitably, business.

Lomzer was surprised to discover that Nahum was in the cinema trade.

"I know there's plenty of Jews in the business, but I never knew the sort of Jew who dabbled in that sort of business came to *shul* three times a day to say *kaddish*."

"Why not?" asked Nahum.

"Naked women."

"What naked women, where?"

"On the screen, naked women."

"Where do you get naked women? I've been in the business for over ten years, and I haven't seen a naked woman once. Half-naked women, maybe."

"But lots of half-naked women."

"All right, lots, but twenty half-naked women don't make ten naked ones. I run a respectable business. There's nothing I show to which you couldn't take your wife or daughter."

"Daughters I've never had, and a wife I ain't got."

"But if you had a wife or daughter, there's nothing in any of my cinemas that would have made them blush."

"There's nothing nowhere that would have made my wife blush—bless her—but that's another story."

Lomzer was in property. "Not in a big way, you understand, a building here, a bit of land there, but I make a living, thank God."

Sometime later, Nahum bumped into Lomzer in synagogue again and mentioned that he was thinking of erecting a cinema in or near the centre of town but was expecting difficulty in finding a suitable site at a reasonable price.

"A site?" he said. "I think I got the right site for you," and he invited Nahum to call at his office. The "office" turned out to be a back room of a small flat in the Gorbals, and when Nahum saw the surroundings—the unmade bed, the piled-up crockery, the grubby curtains, the unwashed window—he doubted whether Lomzer dealt in the type of property he was after, but Lomzer pulled a large cardboard box from under his bed and was able to satisfy Nahum that he did, in fact, have the site he wanted. Unfortunately, the price he demanded was astronomical.

"Look," Lomzer said, "God forbid that I should make a profit from my friends. If it would have cost me half the price, you'd have had it for half the price, but I can't ask for less than I paid for it, and then you've got to think of my overheads, my outgoings, my ingoings. I've got heavy expenses. You can't blow your nose in this business without a solicitor, and you know what they cost."

Nahum suggested an independent valuation.

"Valuations? They only add to your cost and mine. Let's do a deal between friends and finished with."

"That's not how I do business."

They finally agreed on a valuer, who, however, suggested a price so far in excess of anything Nahum had in mind that he felt compelled to abandon the project altogether. Lomzer, however, thought he was holding out for a lower price and phoned him daily, lowering the price with each call, and finally he demanded: "What do you want me to do with the bloody thing, give it to you as a Christmas present?"

"No, no, no," said Nahum. "Your price is reasonable, I can see that, but it just so happens that I can't afford it."

"So what are you messing me about for?" Then he added: "You know something? You don't know very much how to run a business," which needled Nahum.

"With respect, Mr Lomzer, I brought up six children on my business, I live in a nice house in Pollokshields, I have a nice office, I've got over sixty people working for me, I run a nice car. You work from a back room in the Gorbals and haven't even got a pair of watertight galoshes."

"So you're spending a lot of money. You don't have to be a genius to spend money. How much are you making on what you've got?"

"About three percent."

"You're not talking to a tax inspector, you're talking to a friend."

"About three percent."

"And you call yourself a businessman?"

"I believe in large turnovers and small margins."

"Is it written anywhere that you mustn't make large turnovers and large margins?"

"It's the small margins that make for large turnovers."

It was out of this unpromising beginning that a new partnership was born, not—initially, at least—to include Nahum's whole company, but only the city-centre project, and the first decision they reached as partners, after examining all the relevant figures, was to abandon the project in favour of acquiring a small company owning three cinemas —all of them new and one of them large—which had just gone bankrupt.

For some time Nahum wondered if he had done the right thing, not because he questioned Lomzer's business acumen, but because he had reservations about his personality. He reminded him vaguely of Lazar, who had also undertaken to put his business right, only to put him right out of business. Yet he sensed a basic integrity to the man. What troubled him more than anything else was his general bearing and *foreignness*. He had been fifty years in the country and still dressed, looked and spoke as if he'd just stepped off the boat. His English was broken and bespattered with Yiddish, Hebrew and Russian. His very smell reminded Nahum of his early days in the shipping trade when passengers crowded on deck, reeking of herring and onions, and the seamen demanded "smell money." Summer and winter he shuffled around in a black coat and homburg, both of which had seen better days, and trailing a baggy umbrella; he would arrive at his office almost daily, and always unannounced, and—without doffing either hat or coat—would settle himself in a chair, lean forward on his umbrella and ask: "How's things going?"

He had white bristle on his throat like a badly plucked chicken, and on his chin; red-rimmed blue eyes, which were always running; and a thin, red nose which was likewise inclined to drip. His cheeks were sunken, he spoke in a weak, tired voice and his appearance made the office staff giggle. Nahum found his presence embarrassing, especially when he had visitors, for his office was ornate and well-appointed, with signed photographs on the walls, and Lomzer's comings and goings tended to lower the tone of the place. He kept a fan in his office which he switched on the moment Lomzer appeared, but he grew fond of the old man and to value his judgment, and, if he turned to him initially only for business advice, he came in time to regard him as a general sage, and he would quote him so often on such a variety of topics that Mittwoch would sometimes anticipate his openings with: "Lomzer, he says . . ."

The admiration was not mutual.

"You know something," said Lomzer, "if you'd gone ahead with your fancy picture-palace thing, you'd also have gone *mechuleh*, but you've got *mazel*, and that's the long and the short of it. You're not a businessman, you don't know how to bargain, you don't know what to charge, what to pay, when to buy, when to sell, or what to do with your assets. Everything you buy you pay for, on the nail. Looking at your books, you'd think credit was never invented. I don't know how you survived this long, and there's only one explanation for it, you've got *mazel*, which is why I suggested the partnership. With your *mazel* and my ability, we can't fail."

310

Within a year of their association the company owned nine houses, all of them showing a profit, and some a handsome profit.

One misty morning Nahum and Lomzer were in a suburb of Glasgow examining the site of what was to be their tenth house. An excavator had dug a narrow trench, and Nahum was gazing into its depths.

"You know," he said, "it looks like a grave."

Lomzer looked at him. "And if it does—you want we should sublet to a cemetery company?"

"No, I'm nearly fifty-seven."

"So?"

"My father died at fifty-six."

"And mine died before I was born. So what are you trying to tell me?"

"Have you never had premonitions of an early death?"

"At my age, it's a bit late for an early death. In fact, it's getting a bit late for a late death."

"There's no longevity in my family, all the males died young."

"Your mother's still alive, how do you know you're not taking after your mother?"

"Frankly, I'd rather be like my father and dead at fifty-six than like my mother and alive at seventy-six."

"You've got no choice in these things, you'll live till a hundred and twenty."

"Who wants to live to a hundred and twenty?"

"Once you get to my age, you get into the habit of living, and you feel you could go on forever."

"Heaven forbid."

Then, suddenly, there came an event which made Nahum want to live and from the most unexpected quarter. Jacob told him he was thinking of getting married.

"You? Married?"

"Why not?"

"You never talked about it, I never saw you with girls."

"No, this was a girl I was friendly with in Edinburgh. She's from Glasgow, as a matter of fact, but she was studying in Edinburgh. Now that she's finished, I asked her if she would marry me, and she said she would. Rather pleasing, don't you think?"

"Just like that?"

"Why, how else does one go about it?"

"No, *mazeltov*, I'm very happy, but if you had told me earlier, I would have had something to look forward to."

"But I had nothing to tell earlier."

"You could have told me you were thinking about it, that would also have helped to keep me going. Still, I'm very happy. What does she do?"

"She's a doctor. Useful craft, what?"

"A *doctor*? So we'll have two doctors in the family. A pity you didn't take medicine as well. We could have opened a clinic."

The name of the family didn't mean anything to Nahum, but when they all met for dinner one evening, he recognised the mother. She was another of Black's daughters. It seemed as if his own progeny were doomed to marry the progeny of the daughters he had rejected. The mother who was a large, handsome woman, was a good deal more attractive than her daughter, who was slight, mousy and bespectacled, but she and Jacob seemed very happy with each other, and he was delighted. His *schwartze yoren,* his black years, he told himself, were finally coming to an end.

CHAPTER XXVIII
FAMILY REUNION

H ECTOR TRAVELLED UP FROM LONDON BY TRAIN AND, GLANCING out of the window at Crewe, he noticed the formidable figure of Sophie thrusting her way through the crowds. She had landed at Liverpool that morning.

He rushed down to the platform to help her, and they embraced.

"You look well," he said, when they were finally seated.

"You mean big, but I think I've lost a bit of weight in the rush to get here. God, how I hate travel."

"Where's Yankelson, and the twins?"

"The twins would have disrupted the wedding, and Yankelson's staying behind to look after them. But never mind Yankelson, where's the great Arabella?"

"In the final throes of her greatest trial, her first talking picture. I presume you haven't seen any of the other films she's made."

"As a matter of fact, I have, at great inconvenience and with no great pleasure."

"Dreadful, weren't they? And they didn't even make all that much money, but this should be different, for, although she's no great shakes as an actress, she does have a fairly pleasant voice, and it comes across rather well."

"Has Vicky also got a part in her film?"

"I'm afraid not. Vicky and Arabella get on better at a distance than they do near at hand. She's going through a difficult patch, poor child."

"Is she still living with what-do-you-call-him?"

"She is, which is the source of the difficulty."

"I could see it happening the moment they exchanged looks at Shyke's. She should have settled the matter, one way or the other, as soon as she knew her feelings."

"She couldn't, I wouldn't have let her."

"The fact that she let you interfere suggests that she didn't know her own feelings. She said she couldn't imagine me being involved in a similar situation. I was involved in an *identical* situation, in the war, when I fell in love with a young English doctor, but I knew right away the relationship had to end. I was working with him, side by side, and I asked for and received a transfer."

"Do you actually think it's wrong to marry out of the faith—even if you have no faith to marry out of?"

"Of course I don't, but my happiness was so tied up with that of Father's that I didn't give the possibility of marriage a serious thought. I certainly didn't let it drag on for years."

"But she feels Jacob's wedding may give her a way out."

"She'll announce her marriage to Cameron at the wedding dinner?"

"I wouldn't put it past her. I must admit that the glint in her eye, when she said she had probably found a solution, has made us approach the wedding with apprehension."

"I approach every wedding with apprehension. Where is she now?"

"In Glasgow, which has added to my apprehensions."

Jacob's prospective father-in-law owned a gent's outfitters in the centre of town, and he had not struck Nahum as a particularly prosperous man, but the bride was his only daughter, and he booked the principal banquet suite in the principal hotel in Glasgow and invited half the town.

Nahum tried to erase the memory of Hector's wedding from his mind as he lined up with the bride and groom and the bride's parents by the entrance to the suite to receive the guests, yet he had an odd sensation that he was reliving his past. There wasn't the same boisterousness and there weren't any reporters and cameramen, but the numbers were about as large, and as the toastmaster bawled out name after name, and as couple succeeded couple, their faces again became blurred, as if they had been jerked out of focus, until he heard a name that he thought had no right to be there; he half expected to see Cameron again (though it was not Cameron's name which was called). Instead, he found Lotie advancing upon him with open arms, and it was only when they were embracing—a little to the embarrassment of the surrounding crowd—that he finally convinced himself it was actually she.

He quickly mumbled an apology to his host and hostess and pulled her into another room.

"You've no idea how delighted I am to see you, but how do you come to be here?"

"What do you mean, how do I come to be here? You invited me."

"I—" He hadn't invited her but thought he could guess who had. It hadn't occurred to him that his mother was still up to that sort of thing; she hadn't mentioned Lotie for years. "Of course, I invited you," he said, "but I still can't believe you're here."

"To be honest, neither can I." They embraced again and kissed, and she whispered: "I'm staying in this hotel, let's forget about the wedding and go up to my room."

"And you mean, have a sort of very quiet wedding of our own? There's a rabbi next door, I'll get witnesses, I can borrow a ring, why not? Only there's an old Talmudic precept, *ein m'arvin simcha b'simcha*, you mustn't mix celebration with celebration."

"I didn't actually have a wedding in mind."

"I know exactly what you've got in mind, my love, and I have never really had it out of my mind." He felt at that moment as if the twenty-four years which had separated them had never happened. "As a matter of interest, though, are you free to marry?"

"You know very well I am. My divorce from Richard was in all the papers. You wouldn't have invited me to the wedding if you thought I wasn't. After all, this isn't the first wedding in your family, is it?"

"It's the third."

"Exactly."

Their conversation and embrace were cut short by the bride's mother, who was apologetic but gave him a look which suggested that there was a time and place for everything and that at his age he should be able to wait for it.

At the wedding dinner, Nahum, who sat hemmed in between his son and his mother, could not take his eyes off her. She had become thinner—perhaps a trifle too thin—her nose seemed a little longer and her cheekbones were more pronounced, but her eyes seemed as large and more luminous than ever, and her complexion was flawless. He also could not help noticing the look of brooding malevolence which Katya cast in her direction.

She sat at the same table as Sophie, Hector and Vicky and seemed cheerfully at ease as a member of the family, engaging even Benny in animated conversation, which Hector regarded as a feat in its own right.

Young Mittwoch sat at an adjacent table, back to back with Vicky, but they seemed to be able to converse without straining their necks unduly; when the meal was over and the ball began, Mittwoch pounced on her, and they spent most of the evening together.

Nahum had to dance the opening waltz with the bride's mother, and the next one with the bride. She seemed so slight, windblown and hard, compared to the lush abandon of her mother, that Nahum wondered whether his son had not fallen in love with the mother and had settled for the daughter by way of consolation. When he had returned the bride to the groom and was looking around for Lotie, he was seized by an arm and found himself being propelled by Mrs Mittwoch, a formidable Russian madam with the beginnings of a moustache under her formidable nose. He was not particularly fleet of foot at the best of times, while his partner, who chatted to him in Russian on the mysteries of the corsetière's craft, gave the impression that she was screwed into the floor. Moreover, she wore a long velvet gown which formed a sort of pool around her feet, over which—or into which—Nahum kept tripping and landing, nose-first, into her cleavage. It had not occurred to him that one short waltz could last so long.

But his trial was not over. Mrs Mittwoch wanted a private word, so private, in fact, that she could not utter it on the dance floor and led him by the hand to an adjoining room; as she had found his grasp of Russian imperfect, she addressed him in English.

"I don't know how good you know me, Mr Raeburn, but I'm my son's mother. He's frank, I'm frank, we're both frank, and, frankly, he's a boy in a million, and I'm thinking your daughter may be just the girl for him. Frankly, I don't think she's a girl in a million. I've got lots of clients, Mr Raeburn, they're all women and they all talk a lot—fitting a corset can take an afternoon, and they've got to do something while I'm fitting them—and they're talking a lot about your daughter—"

"I would tell them to mind their own business."

"I don't even answer them, because if you knew me, Mr Raeburn, you would know I'm not listening to low gossip—I'm not even listening to high gossip—and what I'm telling you is I'm ignoring what they're saying, and if my son wants to marry your daughter, he has my permission."

"Is that what you wanted to tell me?"

"No, that's the beginning, I am now coming to the ending." She drew her chair a little closer to his. "I've been widowed for a long time, Mr Raeburn. How long have you been widowed?"

"Twelve years," said Nahum, trying to move his chair back as unobtrusively as he could."

"Hah, by twelve years ago I had already forgotten how my husband looked like. What I'm saying is this. I'm a very conscious mother, but while my son is growing up, I wasn't thinking it was right for me to marry again—though I got proposals every week. He was a boy, I could see, who was going to do something with himself, and I'm not wanting him to have another father who would be a handicap like the first one. But now if he's getting married, I'm thinking I should start thinking about myself." She drew closer still, and Nahum drew back.

"Mr Raeburn, your friend Mr Lomzer looks as if he is needing a woman."

Nahum drew a sigh of relief.

"Haven't you met him?"

"Sure, I've met him, but I've never been introduced to him."

"Come with me."

As he led the way out of the room, he bumped into Lomzer, who was just coming out of the gent's toilet and buttoning his fly.

"Lomzer, I want you to meet a good friend of mine. Do you know Mrs Mittwoch?"

"Young what's-his-name's mother?"

"That's right."

"You've got a very clever son."

"He's taken after his mother," said Mrs Mittwoch.

"He didn't have a father?"

"His father's dead."

"Ah," at which he turned and fled, muttering under his breath: "And I bet he wasn't sorry to go."

When Nahum resumed his search for Lotie, he found her dancing with Lomzer and looking as if she was grappling with him, for they moved with arms raised, she pushing one way, he the other, and neither seemed to be getting very far. He was wearing a white tie and tails and must have starched his coat as well as his shirt, for the tails hung down stiff and erect, as if they were made of flint; clearly, he had acquired both coat and shirt when he was a more substantial, or, at least, a better-fed man.

The evening was half over before Nahum could get hold of Lotie, and by that time she was too tired to dance, and so, for that matter, was he; they found a quiet corner of the hall where they could eat fruit salad and trifle and talk.

"Who's that with your daughter?" she asked. "He waltzes beautifully."

"He works for me, a very promising young man."

"Is he going to marry the boss's daughter?"

"I don't want to speak about it, because if I start speaking about my hopes, they come undone."

"He's very good-looking."

"My daughter doesn't look too bad, either—does she?"

"She's beautiful. I can't remember her mother being anywhere near as pretty."

"Oh, she was—small, pert, very lively. Not the same colouring as Vicky, but the same sort of personality, bubbling with *chutzpah*."

"You sound as if you still miss her."

"Life isn't like that. It's twelve years since she died. You get used to what you haven't got. Her illness was terrible—long, painful and slow."

"Sounds like my marriage. People should only marry to please themselves. I married to please my mother."

"Your mother? Your mother was dead."

"We do more for the dead than the living. She always adored Richard and wanted him as a son-in-law, and in the end she got him. In a way, I suppose, he was everything a mother could want—good family, beautiful manners, beautifully spoken, elegant appearance, fine bearing, good education, but, of course, Mother didn't have to live with him. I could see in the first weeks that our marriage wasn't working and probably wouldn't work, but hope carries you through your first years and habit through the later ones. Then Father—you know, by the way, that he'd been through some difficult times."

"I heard vague rumours."

"Althouse was almost built on German goods, and once America entered the war, that was that. He wasn't completely ruined but was never again the Althouse he used to be, and I suspect he was the happier for it. Then one day he was playing golf, took a swing at the ball, missed, fell forward on his face and never got up. At the funeral, I looked up from the graveside and saw a tall, dark stranger with a black moustache standing over me. Can he really be my husband, I asked myself, he means so little to me. Instead of driving back with him, I drove back with my lawyer and asked him there and then to draw up a divorce. He tried to argue that I should wait awhile, and that I was too shocked and distressed to know my own mind, but there is, in fact, nothing like a death in the family to clear the mind. He did as I asked, and once I got the divorce, I kept wondering why I hadn't done anything about it before. Why did I wait till I was nearly fifty before starting life afresh?"

"Why didn't you let me know you were divorced?"

"What did you want me to do, put a notice in the *Times?* 'Mrs Lotie Kagan, wife of Mr Richard Kagan and daughter of the late Wilfred Althouse, has resumed her maiden name and her maiden status.' Didn't Kagan tell you?"

"Kagan? I don't have anything more to do with him."

"Poor man, nobody does. He nearly collapsed, you know."

"Kagan? When?"

"A year or two ago."

"Why don't I know these things?"

"He did his best to keep it dark, but everybody knows by now."

Nahum was overcome with a mixture of nostalgia and *schaden-*

freoude—nostalgia over his early struggles in the shipping trade when Kagan had first helped him, albeit reluctantly, to his feet; *schaden-freoude* at the humiliations he had suffered at his hands, the lectures, the chastisement, the wagging finger and the domineering tone, the social distance he had kept between them and, finally, the dismissive note from his secretary in answer to the *bar mitzvah* invitation. He thought he had noticed a touch of contrition in Kagan's face and voice when he had met him at Alex's memorial service and had almost forgiven him, for he had looked sincerely distressed by the circumstances of Alex's death, but now it seemed that he had only been sorry for himself, and not for Alex.

"Is he ruined?" said Nahum, half hopefully.

"Ruined? Not in the sense that his wife had to sell her jewels or he his real estate, but he's no longer the force he was. It was Richard who brought him down, really. Richard wanted to become a Kagan in his own right and took the bank into American securities in a big way."

"And went down with the Wall Street crash?"

"No, it was before that, a few months. The divorce came through about the same time, and naturally there were rumours that the one had led to the other, and that the bank was in danger because I had withdrawn my assets. My father had made a very generous settlement when I married, mostly in Althouse shares, but by the time of the divorce they were almost worthless. I am almost penniless, Nahum, can you imagine that, me, Lotie Althouse, almost penniless?"

"You don't look almost penniless."

"I was beginning to wonder if I would ever hear from you, for I was sure you'd have known about my divorce, and then I began to wonder whether you'd remarried or—" She hesitated.

"Or what?"

"Well, you *are* in show business."

"So what?"

"Well, you know the sort of lives show people live. I thought you might have taken a mistress."

"I'm not in that side of the business. As a matter of fact, I had heard some vague rumours that you were, or might be, divorced, but you hear these things all the time, and, in any case, divorced or not, you could have remarried. You may not be in show business, but you are American."

"I'm not that American."

"Anyway, whatever you are, I'm glad you're here and hope you can stay."

"Not for long, my love, unfortunately. I'm off to the Riviera."

"I thought you were penniless."

"My friends aren't. I'd arranged to stay with them before I knew about the wedding and am only breaking my journey here."

"Would nothing persuade you to stay on?"

"I wouldn't say nothing would, but, as matters stand, I am planning to leave the day after tomorrow."

Later in the evening, he noticed Lotie in close conversation with his two daughters, one or other of whom would look up to throw glances in his direction, and he did not have to be particularly sensitive to suspect that a conspiracy was being hatched against his person. He had lunch with Lotie the following afternoon in the Central Hotel, and as she was examining the menu she said: "It's the unanimous opinion of your family that you and I should marry."

"First things first," said Nahum, "what are you going to have?"

"Lobster thermidor."

"Then I can't afford to marry you."

They were married at a quiet ceremony about a month later. Lomzer was the best man, and he said to him after the ceremony: "As a matter of fact, I was thinking of marrying her myself, but, as I've said before and I shall say again, it's you who's got the *mazel*."

When he was making out the invitations, he had phoned Vicky to ask if he should invite Mittwoch.

"I thought you were only going to have a small family dinner."

"Which is why I'm phoning. I almost think of him as a member of the family."

There was silence at the other end for a while.

"Well?"

"I don't think you should rush things."

There were to have been fifteen guests at table, but some crisis had developed over Arabella's latest film, and neither she nor Hector were able to come. In the end there were only thirteen, and although Nahum did not think of himself as superstitious, he could not help regarding it as a bad omen.

There were only two guests from Lotie's side of the family, her brother Edgar, who was almost an exact replica of his late father, and his wife Matilda, who had lost all her radiance—as if it had depended on her father's wealth—and was now a rather gaunt-looking woman. Even her jewels seemed lustreless. Hardly a word passed between Edgar and his wife in the course of the evening, and he spent most of his time with Vicky, who did little to discourage his attention.

After the meal, Nahum asked Lotie what sort of man her brother was.

"The lecherous sort—but it takes two to letch."

CHAPTER XXIX
A NEW LIFE

THERE WERE WHAT NAHUM CALLED "WEE DIFFICULTIES" ALMOST from the start. They had agreed that his house in Pollokshields was too large and gloomy for their own needs, and Nahum planned to buy a flat in the West End, but he naturally presumed that while they were looking for a suitable property, they would be staying in Pollokshields, but Lotie refused.

"Your aunt makes me nervous. She dislikes me, and I'm sure she would like to cast a spell on me."

"She's too fat to be a witch," said Nahum.

"Who said all witches must be thin?" And they finally arranged to stay in an hotel, which annoyed Nahum, for he disliked hotels and resented the expense, and when he tried to charge it to the company, he nearly fell out with Lomzer.

They quickly abandoned their search for flats, for they found nothing which Lotie regarded as even remotely suitable. They experienced the same difficulty when looking at houses, and Lotie suggested that they buy an old, ramshackle property on a suitable site, demolish it and build from scratch.

"Have you any idea what that would cost?"

"You gave me the impression you were comfortable."

"I am comfortable, but not that comfortable."

"I suppose I could find a few thousand pounds myself."

"I thought you were penniless."

"I am penniless, but not that penniless."

"It would still be a waste of money. There're only the two of us. Who needs a palace?"

"We'd have Benny staying with us, and then one wants to have room for visiting relatives and friends."

"That's what I'm afraid of. Once you have room for visiting relatives, they don't come to visit, they come to stay. I already have a house which could be refurbished and refurnished to your taste, but you refuse to set foot in it because it already has visiting relatives in residence."

"Why don't you sell it?"

"And what'll I do with Mother, dump her in the river?"

"No, but she won't live forever."

"You don't know my mother."

Nahum finally settled the matter—or thought he had settled it—by buying a semi-detached five-bedroom house in Newlands.

Lotie liked the house, for it overlooked green fields, and it had a sizable garden, but she thought it was a bit cramped.

"Cramped? It has five bedrooms and three public rooms. How many relatives are you expecting to stay?"

"It's not the number of rooms," she said, "it's the size of them."

A few weeks later, she told Nahum that she had a small surprise for him. She had bought the adjoining property.

"Out of my own pocket," she added, "all we need to do is to knock down a wall and—"

"For a penniless woman, you've got expensive tastes," he said. "We shall live in the house I bought, but if it proves too small, then we shall begin knocking down walls."

"But what about the half I bought?"

"It isn't a half, it's a whole."

"But what shall we do with it?"

"We shall rent it out on a short lease."

She was not too happy about that, and as a compromise they decided to leave it empty for six months, in case they should require immediate possession. But then when they began to look at furniture she said: "You know, this is silly. The sort of furnishings which would be suitable in a small house would not be suitable in a large one."

"Lotie. We have bought the house, we shall live in it and if you don't want to furnish it to your tastes, I shall furnish it to mine, but I'm not going to spend the rest of my life arguing about accommodation."

She looked at him as if she were seeing him—or, rather, hearing him—for the first time. A sternness had entered his tone which she had not noticed before. She was not too sure she liked it, but she was not at the moment disposed to argue.

With that settled, Nahum experienced a period of gladness he had never known before—not even during what he had termed his golden years—and he presumed that it had somethig to do with his age and Lotie's, and that one had to reach a certain pitch of maturity before one could experience true happiness. Sometimes, when he walked home from the office through a night of chill, impenetrable fog, he felt suffused with a golden glow which seemed to melt the cold around him, and he and Lotie would often go through a litany of regrets.

Why didn't he contact her when he first heard she was divorced?
Why didn't she contact him?
Why hadn't she gotten divorced earlier?
Why had she married Kagan at all?
Why hadn't they married when they first met?

It sometimes struck Nahum that he was possibly being unfair, for his marriage to Miri, certainly in the first years, had been happy and fruitful. He had never known the serenity or contentment he experienced now, but it had been a more active, more boisterous sort of happiness, when the old were not so old, and the young were younger, and everybody was together, and death had yet to make its first inroads. And his earlier happiness had been tied to his business success. He was by no means a business failure now, but he was merely a businessman among other businessmen, a trifle richer, perhaps, but not a phenomenon, not a shipping magnate. Miri, moreover, had been in a houseful of people and had had to share his affection and attention with six growing children; he wasn't sure how his relationship with Lotie would have developed in the same circumstances.

She did not provide the same feeling of sensual fulfillment offered by Miri, but at his age he did not experience the same need to be fulfilled. Shyke had once told him that one could sleep with a queen or a skivvy, and the sensation was always the same, and that if there was any difference at all, it was probably in favour of the skivvy. There was, he found, something in that. He did not regard Lotie as a queen or Miri as a skivvy, but Miri's behaviour when they were alone together had sometimes shocked him, and the shock had added something to the pleasure. Katya, too, in their first encounters, had been more exciting, but there a sense of guilt had added an extra dimension to desire. Jessie had been in the Katya class, and partly for the same reason. With Lotie, the experience was far more tender and more delicate, perhaps too delicate. There was no wild rush of bodies seeking fusion, but, rather, a gradual consummation of intimacy, and he ascribed it less to their age than to the nature of their relationship. They had so much to give each other that sex was but a pleasure among others, and, in retrospect, the fact that sex had played so large a part in his marriage to Miri suggested that their relationship perhaps had been otherwise deficient.

Lotie began to educate him. He had lived about forty years in Glasgow and had rarely set foot in a theatre or concert hall, except during some gala occasion on behalf of a charity. She now took him to the theatre almost weekly and to a concert at least once a month, and he enjoyed both, though the fare was often demanding. Shakespeare (which he had once seen in Yiddish) was, he admitted, wasted on him, but he enjoyed Shaw and a local Scottish playwright, James Bridie. He could not take Bach but enjoyed Tchaikovsky and Mendelssohn. By way of reciprocity, he gave her a Jewish education, taught her the dietary laws and to keep meat dishes separate from milk ones. She complained that he had never mentioned such things when she had first known him, and he explained that he had been a bachelor then, and bachelors tend to be careless about such things, but his mother had kept a kosher home and so had Miri, and he was by now too used to kosher food to have a stomach for any other, at least in his own home. He also taught her how to light candles before the onset of the Sabbath at dusk on Fridays, and on Saturday mornings she accompanied him to synagogue. It was a pleasant walk through the leafy streets of Newlands and across the River Cart, and she enjoyed the service.

Nahum had never tried to define his religious beliefs. As a young man, he had been as devout as his father. In later years, he had allowed one observance after another to lapse, without consciously dropping any, and during his ship-owning years he had almost jettisoned Judaism altogether, though Miri still kept a kosher home, and he still found himself, from time to time, in synagogue for some state occasion or at a *bar mitzvah* or wedding. When Alex died, he went to synagogue thrice daily to say *kaddish*. He often asked himself why, because Alex had never, in his mature years, been a believer in any accepted sense of the word and had often expressed an indifference to Judaism and, indeed, all organised religion. Nor did Nahum himself believe that if he failed to say *kaddish*, Alex's soul would be consigned to purgatory or damnation, but he did find some comfort in being in the synagogue and uttering the ancient lines of the *kaddish*, even though he was no longer quite sure of their meaning. After the year of mourning was over, he continued to attend synagogue with fair regularity, and he was inevitably pulled into synagogue affairs, becoming first a member of the board of management and then, after he remarried, a synagogue warden, which meant that he had to acquire striped trousers, a frock coat and a top hat, but he felt good in the ensemble, and he looked good, certainly in Lotie's eyes. "You're one of the few people who can wear this sort of outfit without looking as if you're in fancy dress," she said.

There was a time when he had begun to verge on the portly, but he had suffered a loss of weight so drastic that when Sophie saw him in Palestine, she insisted that he see a doctor, but shock and worry had been the cause rather than ill health, and now that he was enjoying happier times, he began to put on weight again, until Lotie put him on a diet.

On Sundays, they would sometimes drive up to Crosshill and have tea with Jacob and his wife Gladys, who looked slightly less austere and forbidding now that she was married, and who was an excellent cook, but neither of them did justice to the plates she piled before them, for Lotie would peck at a cucumber sandwich and saw to it that Nahum had little more.

One Sunday they came for tea and found Jacob making sandwiches.

"I'm sorry, I'm a bit behind," he apologised. "Gladys's been unwell and is resting."

Lotie at once went up to see her, and when she came downstairs, she had the knowing smirk on her face which Nahum often noticed on women when discussing a condition peculiar to their gender, and she imparted the news to Nahum when they drove home.

"She thinks she's pregnant."

"What do you mean, she thinks? She's a doctor, and she should know."

"But she's also a woman, and a woman of irregular habit, if you know what I mean."

When it became clear that she was indeed pregnant, Nahum felt almost guilty about the good fortune he enjoyed and wondered what he had done to deserve it.

"All I need now," he told Lotie, "is to see Vicky happily married," at which he thought he saw something like a shadow spread across her face.

A close, almost intimate friendship had developed between Lotie and Vicky. He had to travel down to London on business about once a month, and Lotie usually went with him and spent most of her time with Vicky. She showered her with expensive gifts, and when Nahum chided her for her extravagance, she would say, "But she looks so good in good things."

One evening, à propos of nothing, Lotie asked him if it was true that he had once nearly married a gentile, and he immediately sensed that there was more to the question than the mere desire for information. He said: "You're not asking me because you want to know something, you're asking me because you want to tell me something. Out with it, then, what is it?"

She hesitated, then grabbed the phone and told Vicky to come up on the next train.

"I knew it had something to do with Vicky the moment you raised that topic," he said. "She's marrying a *sheigatz,* isn't she?"

"Marrying a what?"

"A gentile. What sort of character is he?" His voice was calm and controlled.

"A very impressive sort, as a matter of fact."

"You've met him?"

"Several times."

"Then why didn't you tell me before?"

"I was going to, three months ago, the night you came home from synagogue to tell me you'd become an 'elder of the Kirk,' as you put it. My nerve failed."

"Has she married him yet?"

"Not quite."

"What do you mean, 'not quite'? They're either married or they're not."

"They're living together."

"Phone her again and tell her to bring him up with her."

"Why? What are you going to do?"

"What can I do? I'm just curious to see what sort of man I'm going to have as my son-in-law."

"You're not going to stand in her way?"

"You've got a curiously Victorian way of putting things. How can I stand in her way? She's twenty-three—come to think of it, the age you were when I wanted to marry you, except that I'm not your mother, and I'm not going to drop dead in order to have my way."

"You seem to be taking it all very philosophically."

"I've always had the fear at the back of my mind ever since she went to London, and now that it has actually happened, it's something of a relief. In any case, in some ways the Jewish law is easier with women than men in these things. It means that her children, at least, will be Jewish."

"Even if he doesn't convert?"

"Even if he doesn't convert? Why should he convert? She's only Jewish in name, but her children could become real Jews. Ask her to bring him with her, I'd like to meet him—I've a right to, don't you think?"

"You already have met him."

"I've—?" He looked at her wild-eyed for a moment, then put his hands to his head and gave a shriek which chilled her blood. "No, not Cameron, no—not young Cameron. Tell me it's not Cameron, not Cameron, no." And before she could answer, he had sunk down to the floor with his hands still to his head, swaying backwards and forwards as if the motion might purge the hated name from his head. It took her a few moments to pull herself together to call the doctor. She could not quite believe the scene before her was actually happening.

By the time the doctor came, Nahum had quieted down but was shivering convulsively, and Lotie helped him upstairs and put him to bed. The doctor gave him an injection, and he sank into sleep.

"Shock," he said, "keep him warm and see that he has complete rest. He should be all right in a day or two. I have a case like that almost every week these days. It's the *shiksa* syndrome."

Lotie phoned Vicky to tell her what had happened and warned her not to show her face in Glasgow for the time being. She also phoned Hector.

She was making herself coffee early the next morning when the door-bell rang, and Hector and Arabella appeared. She made them coffee and described in detail what had happened.

"The bitch," said Arabella. "What did she want to get married for, she was living with him, in any case. What else does she want?"

"She wants a family," said Lotie. "It isn't an unreasonable thing for a woman to want. He took it all in his stride till I mentioned Cameron, then he went berserk."

"I was afraid that might happen."

"Then you might have warned me."

"She can't marry him, that's all," said Arabella.

"It's all right for you to say, but I've been through this sort of thing myself, and I don't think Vicky should make either the sacrifice or the mistake that I made."

"Let them move to France or some other place where these things aren't noticed and have all the bastards they want," said Arabella.

Nahum didn't stir until nearly noon, and when he opened his eyes and saw Arabella smiling affectionately at him, he didn't quite know where he was. She smoothed his hair, then kissed him on the lips.

"How do you come to be here?"

"I heard you were ill, so here I am."

"Ill? Me?" And then the events of the night before returned to him, and he put his hand over his mouth.

"What happened to me, did I have a fit?"

"Or something like it. I couldn't believe it when Lotie told me, it's so unlike you."

"Lotie? Where is Lotie?"

"Downstairs with Hector."

"Is the whole family here?"

"No, only Hector and me."

"I must have given her a terrible shock, poor dear."

"We all got a terrible shock."

"It's only when I heard the name Ca—Ca—I can't even bring myself to pronounce it."

"Then don't."

"You know, in my own way, I'm a fairly religious man—"

"I like that, *fairly* religious, you're a bloody fanatic."

"Call me what you like. I have always believed in divine retribution, but, given my habits of mind, I have let myself assume that it's something you receive in the world to come. I'm wrong, you know; retribution comes to us in the here and now in the form of our fellowmen, and my retribution is Ca—Cameron."

"What have you ever done to deserve retribution?"

"Oh, Arabella, if only you knew."

"Oh, Nahum, and what makes you think I don't know? So you fucked your aunt. It's not as if you've ever fucked your mother, though I suppose your aunt is the next best thing."

"Please, Arabella, I hate to hear such words coming from your dear sweet mouth."

"Is that why you ran for it when I invited you to fuck me?"

"I ran for it because I loved you."

"You are an incurable romantic," she said, reaching down between his sheets.

"Please, Ara," he said between gasps, "if I am, I don't want to be cured. And besides, Lotie's downstairs."

"I know, and she knows I'm upstairs. She's a very understanding woman, your wife. Besides, she's got Hector with her. She looks very fetching in her negligée." She stood up, unzipped her dress, pulled it over her head and got in beside him.

"For a sick man, you're in good shape," she whispered and eased him inside her.

Some time later, when Lotie brought him up something to eat, he was fast asleep with his hands clasped across his chest and a look on his face so beatific that she thought he was dead and quickly called the doctor.

When he thought back on the events of what Lotie was to call "Cameron night," and, indeed, the following morning, he was almost convinced that they had never happened: the one part was too painful to contemplate; the other too heavenly to be true. Later, when he asked Arabella whether she had, in fact, gotten into bed with him, she feigned shock.

"What an indelicate suggestion! What sort of woman do you think I am?" But then she put her arms around him and whispered: "You were great. If that was you in sickness, I'd be afraid to be with you in health." But then, for all the years he had known Arabella, he was never quite sure how to take her, or be certain when she was joking and when she was not.

But whether "Cameron night" and its sequel had happened or not, their effect was to purge him, at least temporarily, of his obsessive antagonism to Cameron, and a few weeks later Vicky and Cameron were married in a London registry office.

The following Passover, Nahum organised a large *seder* in his former Pollokshields home—because, as Lotie took pains to point out, none of the rooms in his own home in Newlands was large enough to accommodate all the guests—and, as if to confirm his admission to the womb of the family, he invited Cameron to come up with Vicky. Hector and Arabella also joined them, as did Jacob and Gladys. Lomzer was another guest, and, seating himself between Katya and her sister, he looked like some withered sacrificial animal hemmed in between two over-ornate caryatids. Gladys, in a green dress and an advanced stage of pregnancy, looked like one of the green hills of Somerset. Some women turn bovine in pregnancy, but she had acquired a bloom which she had lacked before. Her complexion had cleared, her eyes had softened, but, perhaps afraid she might spoil the effect by wearing glasses, she stumbled around as if she were blind. Cameron, in a large velvet skull-cap which came almost down to his ears, entered fully into the spirit of the occasion, followed the service which preceded the meal in the English translation of the *Hagadah,* asked knowledgeable questions and sang the traditional songs as if he had learned them in the cradle.

"He knows more than I do," said Vicky proudly.

"That shouldn't be too difficult," said Hector.

"I was stationed in Palestine for a number of years," Cameron explained, "and was usually invited to Jewish homes for the *seder.*"

Passover marks the exodus from Egypt and the beginning of Jewish nationhood, but to Nahum, that year it was also a feast of reconciliation. Cameron seemed so amiable a fellow that he wondered how he could have harboured such fierce animosity against him for so long, and he had to remind himself that Cameron had betrayed his trust, something which should not be easily forgiven. But *had* Cameron betrayed his trust? They had not, after all, brought charges against him because they could offer no evidence which could have stood up in court. On the other hand, if he had not been a party to the fraud, he had shown a degree of negligence which was almost criminal in itself, but all that, as Nahum reminded himself, was twenty-five years ago, which was time enough to let bygones be bygones. He was glad to see Jacob—whom Lotie had nicknamed "the Rabbi" and about whose attitude he was apprehensive—receive Cameron cordially, and even Benny, who normally had to summon courage to say "good morning" to a stranger, engaged him in animated conversation. Vicky, who in previous encounters had seemed sullen and withdrawn, looked radiantly happy. He could easily imagine what his father would have thought of the match, but they were living in different times and in a different world, and they called for different attitudes.

About a month later Gladys had a daughter, whom she named Thelma, and Nahum, so to speak, became a grandfather in his own right. Some two years later, she gave birth to a son, Aaron. Cameron came up for the circumcision and took Nahum aside to tell him that Vicky was also expecting a child, and that if it was a boy, he, too, would be circumcised. "And not one of those clinical jobs in hospital" he added, "we'll give him the whole kosher works."

Nahum found, as he had found during his "golden days," that whenever he derived any special joy from his private world, external events intruded to darken them. For many years, events in Russia had preyed on his mind. There was a short period in 1917, after the March revolution, when he, in common with most other Jews, allowed himself to think that the dark days were finally over. Then came the October revolution and the Civil War, and the massacres, the famine, the disease. Nahum lost all contact with his sister and in the early twenties, after making his own abortive enquiries, approached some leading Scottish Communists—including John McLean, the honourary Russian consul in Glasgow—to make enquiries on his behalf. They could do nothing for him, and some years later he arranged to travel to Russia to see for himself but was warned that, as he had been born in Russia, he should not expect protection from his British passport if he were arrested. Alex went instead, and he was able to establish that Esther, her husband and her daughter had been last seen alive in Odessa in 1921, that all three had left town about the same time and that nothing had been heard of them since. It was Nahum's hope that they might have found their way to Poland, or perhaps even to Germany, but if so, why had they made no attempt to contact him?

Germany had never figured in Nahum's imagination on the same level as England or America, but it still represented decency, sufficiency and order, and he would have found it easier to be a patriot during the war if the enemy had been Russia, rather than Germany or Austria. He recalled how Wachsman had urged him to settle in Germany. "It's a place which believes in hard work," he said, "it's the place to get on." He had thus followed the rise of Hitler with disbelief and was assured by the reports he read everywhere that German good sense would assert itself, but the years passed without signs of such assertions, and in 1935 he found himself out again on a platform, protesting against the treatment of the Jews. The hall was the same, the faces were mainly the same, the speeches were much the same, only the oppressor was different, and he still felt a trifle bewildered by the turn of events. Lotie felt particularly agitated, for her upbringing had been German. She had had a German governess and would fall asleep to the sound of German lullabies, and she still read German novels and poetry, and she had been rather more aware of her Germanic associations than her Jewish ones. "What happens to people?" she kept asking. An emergency committee, much like those which had existed to help Russian Jewry, was formed on behalf of German Jewry, and again Nahum found himself on the executive board. He donated two hundred and fifty guineas and induced Lomzer, who thought he was being generous when he parted with half a crown, to do the same. Lotie, who continued to insist she was penniless and about whose means he was careful not to enquire, donated five hundred pounds.

Sophie, in the meantime, assailed all the members of the family with letters urging them to come to Palestine: "If what is happening in Germany could happen in Germany, it could happen anywhere," she wrote; "if you don't come now of your own free will, you'll be chased out in another few years," and she reminded Nahum that he had been a delegate to several Zionist congresses and was spoken of as "a leading Zionist." "What is your Zionism about if you can't see your way to making your home in Zion?" she demanded. "I know you've built up a good business and you're proud of it," she went on. "There's a man in this *moshav* who owned a department store in Düsseldorf. It's still there, but he doesn't know what happened to it, and he doesn't care. He packed his bags, left and is now a farmer, and he blesses the day he came. You're too old to become a farmer, but you're still in a position to sell out. Sell now before you have to give it away. It seems to me that history evolves its own compensations, and as some areas of the globe become uninhabitable for Jews, others open up, only people don't realise it and cling to their old ways and their old places. If your father had not faced ruin in Volkovysk, you'd probably still be in Russia—provided, of course, you had survived the wars and the famine—and what sort of life would you be leading now? Do you have to wait till you're ruined to do the sensible thing?"

Nahum had an uneasy feeling that there was force in her argument, and not only because he had some pretensions to being a Zionist and was indeed regarded as one of the leaders of British Zionism (if only because he was still a considerable donor to Zionist charities). He could not forget the shattered windows of his house—his own "private pogrom," as he called it—when he was tried for trading with the enemy. He told himself that it had happened during the war and that no nation was in its right mind in wartime, but there were innumerable other incidents which, if he came to reflect upon them, made him doubt whether a Jew could ever be at ease in Britain. During his ship-owning days, he had developed the habit of going out with Colquhoun in the course of the morning for a coffee and a smoke in a nearby coffeehouse. He liked the ambience of panelled walls; the solid furniture; the smells of coffee, leather and tobacco; the friendly, convivial atmosphere; but once Colquhoun was gone, hardly anyone spoke to him, and it seemed to him that one had to have one's own private *goy* to gain entry to the *goyish* world. He also suspected—and Colquhoun thought the same—that Scottish banks treated his credit worthiness lightly and demanded the sort of guarantees which could only have been supplied by someone who didn't need their money in the first place, and it was this which had kept him in thralldom to Kagan for so long. He had also entertained various colleagues from the shipping trade fairly lavishly at his home but had never been invited back, and after forty years in the country, there was still only one gentile with whom he was on really close terms. That was Jessie, and she had become virtually Jewish, if not by conversion then at least by immersion, and she, too, had written to him in much the same terms as Sophie.

In the cinema trade he moved largely in a Jewish world, though most of his employees were gentile. He was on good terms with them and was invited to their weddings, and sometimes even to christenings, and whenever he had something to celebrate, like a wedding, he always invited them back, but they were a source of discomfort. The young tended to get drunk and boisterous, the old looked around them uneasily, a little too careful to be on their best behaviour, and he wondered what they made of the abundant fare, the extravagant dress. He was conscious, perhaps a trifle too conscious, of the probe of critical eyes.

But even if he were disposed to take Sophie's argument seriously, he was too old to change his ways, to uproot himself and start a new life, and too many people were dependent on him—to say nothing of the sums he was giving to and raising for the emergency refugee appeal—and he wrote to Sophie:

> I don't know if you're right or wrong, though I have the unhappy feeling you may be right. Did I ever tell you I actually bought a plot of land in Palestine (I paid for it and have the receipt, though no one

has been able to show me where it is), and there were a number of times when I thought of settling there before the war, after the war and again after poor Alex died, and I suppose if I'd gone out earlier, I might have done something with myself, but I've left it too late. I'm too old and too set in my ways. When things started going wrong in Russia, Father was too old—or felt too old—to go himself, and so he sent me. Well, although I didn't actually send you to Palestine, you still happen to be there, and Benny is talking about going out when he qualifies (if he qualifies—he has sat his anatomy exam five times). And, of course, poor Alex is on the Mount of Olives. So nearly half my family is already there, and more may follow. What more can you ask?

Special transports were being organised to bring Jewish children out of Germany, and Lotie asked whether they should adopt a child.

"I don't know if we're too old to have young children around the house," she said, "but wouldn't a young child be bored with two old crocks?"

"Not if they're in their second childhood," said Nahum, "and we do have the room to spare."

They did not have it for long.

If Nahum had been less preoccupied, he might have noticed that old Lomzer was shaving more frequently and with great care—so that evn his Adam's apple was free of stubble—that he changed his collar every day instead of every week (or perhaps every month), that his shirts were not too discoloured and that his trousers were pressed. It was only when he arrived one morning with a neatly furled umbrella on his arm and a brand-new hat on his head that Nahum looked up.

"Going to a wedding?"

"Somebody tell you?"

"Tell me what?"

"I'm getting married."

"*You?*"

"Why not? You think you're the only one who can get married?"

"No, heaven forbid. I'm surprised, that's all."

"What's so surprising?"

"Nothing, it's just—just that you gave no hint."

"What do you want me to do, blow a whistle and tell the world I'm thinking of getting married?"

"No, no, but I thought as your partner—"

"My business partner. For business decisions I consult, for marriages I don't have to consult."

"Look, let's not fall out over this. I'm delighted."

"And if you weren't delighted, you think I wouldn't get married?"

"Just tell me one thing, who's the lucky woman?"

"Your aunt."

"My *aunt?*"

"Your aunt, so from now on you can call me uncle."

As a result, Nahum's mother came back to live with him.

Lotie at this time was active on many Jewish and non-Jewish charities, and one day, shortly before Christmas, Nahum found himself seated next to a churchman at a luncheon in aid of one of her causes. The conversation turned to the fate of German Jewry, and his neighbour, after murmuring the usual words of sympathy, then added: "But, of course, you've got to ask yourself how much the Jews did to bring their troubles on themselves."

At which Nahum, whose eyelids were beginning to droop, sat up: "What do you mean?"

"Well, take a walk up Renfield Street or Sauchihall Street and look at the cinema posters, and go inside the cinemas if you dare, and what do you find? Profanity, lewdness, debauchery, filth. This is supposed to be a Christian country, but everything it's supposed to stand for is being undermined. My Jewish friends—I was speaking to a rabbi about it only the other day—have the very same feelings. They shudder at these things. But that's not the worst of it. There was a time when these dens of iniquity were to be found only in the centres of town, but now they're everywhere, their insidious lights blinking at every corner, and there is no way of keeping the family and children away from them. There are schoolboys—aye, and even girls—who go to these places two or three evenings a week and sometimes even play truant to go in the afternoon. They are undermining Christian tradition and family life. They are polluting the atmosphere. They are poisoning the minds of the young."

Nahum struggled to get a word in but could not.

The man, ruddy of face and heavy of jowl, with a large, angry mouth, bad teeth and stale breath, continued like a torrent: "And they're Jewish, everyone—the people who make these films, the people who act in them, who write them, who distribute them, who show them, who finance them—Jews, everyone. Oh, I have nothing against the cinema, and, of course, I have nothing against Jews. Jews have been—and the cinema could be—a boon to mankind. It could be used to elevate, to improve taste, to raise educational standards, but instead it is being used to debauch, and it offers nothing more than a diet of smut. Now, I hold no brief for Herr Hitler. He has done some disgraceful things, but one thing you do have to say for him—he has cleaned up the cinema. You can take your wife—aye, and your children—to any cinema in Germany and be certain that they will be exposed to nothing salacious or profane." At which Nahum gave up any attempt at rebuttal, rose from his place and walked out of the room.

Lotie, who had been unable to attend because of ill health, couldn't believe what he told her.

"He couldn't have known you were in the cinema trade," she said.

"But don't you see, that makes it worse. If he'd known, I'd at least have admired his frankness, and, as a matter of fact, he is right in some ways. I'm not too proud of some of the films I show—but you should only see the ones I don't show. But they're not all trash, and, even if they were, they're no worse than some of the goings-on you used to have in the music halls. I've only been once to a music hall, and it was enough. Dirty songs, dirty stories, dirty gestures, scruffy-looking characters on stage and off, and a half-drunk audience. In the cinema, at least, they're sober, and even a bad film can be something of an education. You see something of the world—a good drama, good acting, good music, sometimes. Yes, you get smut, too, but it's nothing compared to the music halls."

"Perhaps that's what he was complaining about."

"And a clergyman, too. I'm beginning to think Sophie's right."

He calmed down eventually but found the fact that he could be so upset by the stupid utterances of one stupid man extremely telling.

"A Russian Jew remains a Russian Jew," said Lotie. "He never feels secure, not even in America, and keeps looking over his shoulder and is liable to misconstrue almost anything said to him or about him." She, for her part, claimed to feel perfectly at home in Britain or, rather, in Scotland. She was in love with the scenery of Scotland—its people, history, culture—and tried to persuade the board of management of the synagogue to don tam o'shanters and kilts for ceremonial occasions, and when they looked at her as if she were mad, she said: "You're prepared to wear frock coats and top hats, which is English national dress, what objections can you have to Scottish national dress? After all, this is a *Scottish* synagogue."

"And perhaps," said a wizened little figure, "you'll be maybe wanting us to blow the bag-pipes instead of the *shofar*."

"And to toss the caber instead of shaking the *lulav?*" said another.

"And to eat haggis instead of *tzolent,*" tittered a third.

She also tried to learn Gaelic, but with limited success.

Once, after a motoring holiday in the highlands, she tried to persuade Nahum to buy a small country cottage somewhere in the hills—"something tiny, three or four rooms, at most"—and even offered to pay for it out of her own resources, but Nahum felt it would be wrong to buy a second home while there were fellow Jews turning in all directions without a roof over their heads.

One evening, on the anniversary of Alex's death, Nahum stopped off on the way from work at a synagogue in the Gorbals. Lomzer, whom he was giving a lift home, came in with him. The service lasted about ten minutes, and they were crossing the road to the car when they were set upon by five or six youths, beaten, punched, kicked. Lomzer fell to the ground and hit his head against the kerb, and, as a crowd began to collect, the youths fled. The whole incident could not have taken more than a minute. Lomzer was rushed to hospital in an ambulance and allowed home after treatment. Nahum was only bruised, but he felt too shaken to drive and went home in a taxi. When he returned the next day to collect his car, he found his tyres missing.

Lotie had been away visiting friends in London. When she returned in the evening, he told her of the incident.

"Did no one come to your help?" she said.

"No one, not a soul."

"And didn't they steal anything?"

"That's the frightening part of it. If it had been only robbery, well, these things happen, but we weren't set upon because anybody wanted our money; we were set upon because we were Jews."

"Are non-Jews never attacked?"

"Maybe in gang wars. I don't belong to a gang, and, unless I'm very much mistaken, Lomzer doesn't, either. Why don't you want to face reality? We were attacked because we were Jews. Anyway, I should be grateful for it. It's a warning."

"A warning?"

"A warning to get out. We're moving to Palestine. I know Jews are also being attacked in Palestine, but at least they're on their own soil, they can fight back."

Lotie did not argue with him. She never did when he was excited, and she was confident that in a day or two he would forget all about it, but she became alarmed when a week passed and she found that he was still not only talking about Palestine, but that he was negotiating to sell his share of the company to Lomzer.

"You're not being serious?"

"I've never been so serious in my life. He's offering a good price, almost an extravagant price. I thought I'd have to haggle for the figure I had in mind, but he offered it right away, and I wondered if perhaps he knew something I didn't, or perhaps he's getting soft in his old age, but it so happens he's in sympathy with my plans—he said he'd have done the same if he was a younger man."

"And it might have been a good idea if you were a younger man yourself, but darling, you're over sixty."

"Just over sixty. Don't make me out to be an ancient."

"But I love it here."

"You'll love it there."

"Amid all the fighting and riots?"

"They're bringing in a whole British army to quiet things down, they're bringing in the air force. I assure you, by the time we're ready to go, it'll all be over."

"But what'll you do there?"

"What am I doing here? I'll buy a cinema or build one. If I could build myself up from almost nothing twenty years ago—"

"Twenty years ago, you were twenty years younger."

"You keep coming back to my age as if I've got a foot in the grave. I've never felt better. I feel ready to start afresh. I might even go back into shipping. I can't be the only Jew who feels as I feel. If they should all start making for Palestine, there'll be plenty of business for ships. In fact, I'm going to make enquiries about it tomorrow. I've always hankered to get back into ships. They're small change, cinemas, after ships."

"What'll happen to your mother?"

"I've seen to that. Katya will be happy to look after her. Of course, I'll have to leave a bit of money aside to cover her costs—and she's a pretty sharp bargainer, is our Katya—but it's all settled."

"Are you not afraid what she might do?"

"To my mother?"

"Your mother."

"What could she do at her age?"

"Press a pillow over her face."

"She's not that bad."

Lotie was so unused to such enthusiasm or resolve in her husband that she felt unable to argue further. A few days later, while in Cooks' to work out her itinerary, she picked up a paper and found the front page filled with reports of large-scale fighting in Palestine. She showed it to Nahum.

"I've read it," he said, "and I've been listening to every news bulletin. I'm worried, but, apart from anything else, I want to see what's happening to Sophie, Yankelson and the children, but if you want, I'll go alone."

"No," she said grimly, "I'm coming with you."

CHAPTER XXX
THE LEGACY

D EAR SOPH,

All set for your visitors?

You'll be glad—or perhaps disturbed—to learn that your letters, plus one or two local incidents, have convinced Father that Britain is ripe for a Nazi takeover, and he has advanced plans to make his home in Palestine. He is on the high seas now and may be with you by the time you get his letter (presumably the troubles have been affecting the post; your last letter took nearly a month to get here). This journey is but an exploratory tour, but Father seems grimly determined to stick to his plans. There are, however, three developments, which may change them.

Lomzer is very ill. He was set upon in the Gorbals a few months ago and received a head injury, but made a good recovery. He was, however, rushed to hospital yesterday with severe abdominal pains (it wouldn't surprise me if the old witch poisoned him), and if he shouldn't pull through, the whole complex of business arrangements, which Father has made as part of his immigration plan, will fall through.

The second is that Michael Mittwoch, his protegé and right-hand man, has been offered a job by one of the cinema networks and is moving to London, though never a word to Father, please, until Michael tells him when he gets back. If Lomzer should go one way and Michael another, there can be no question of Father leaving, unless he's prepared to see his company disintegrate.

And, finally, there's trouble brewing—not for the first time—in the Ara-Hector ménage. Her first talking film, on which she had built great hopes, was fairly successful, but not so successful as to make her an international star—that is, to take her to America. She blamed all its defects (which, in fact, could be reduced mostly to her part in it) on her colleagues, and she decided to make her next film herself, and it was so complete a flop that even Father could not find a good word to say for it, and as a result the old girl is now having expensive fits in an expensive nursing home (you needn't tell Father, by the way, for I honestly believe she is the one true love of his life, and there is no need to upset him).

Father and Lotie were here for dinner before they left, and he wondered whether Ara and Hector might wish to adopt one or two German refugee children.

"It might do something for their marriage," he said.

"But think what it would do for the children," I said.

If Father is really determined, come what may, to make his home in Palestine, the solution might be for Hector to take things over in Glasgow, and let Ara rot where she is.

Love to Yankelson and the twins,

Vicky.

P.S. You may have heard I was expecting a baby. I was. I then was expecting another, but it, too, miscarried. I am now on to number three (or is it four, I'm beginning to lose count), and to make sure it completes the course, I am hardly allowed to move. I don't know who or what I'm expecting, but if it isn't the Messiah, I shall feel poorly compensated for the bloody inconvenience I'm having to suffer.

P.P.S. I should add that Lotie has no intention of going to Palestine or anywhere else, for she has fallen in love with Scotland, is usually to be seen swathed in tartan plaids and if she should die, I should imagine that she will wish to be buried in a tartan shroud. (She asked the rabbi if she could donate a supply of tartan prayer shawls to the *shul* and was rather upset when she was told she couldn't.) She is, of course, a loyal wife, and believes that if her husband wants to go to the ends of the earth, it's her duty to follow, but she has her own sweet way of getting her own sweet way, without ever raising her voice, or digging in her heels, if only because the fates are usually on the side of the very rich.

All the way across England and France, Nahum was full of plans, and Lotie kept reminding him that they were only going out on an exploratory tour.

"I know, I know," he said, "but I somehow already feel that Palestine will be my home. I can see myself there."

"Can you see me there?"

"Of course. And I'll see more of you than I ever did in Glasgow, because I may not go into business, after all. What for? I'll have enough for our needs. I've always wanted to study, and I've never had much time to sit down to read and think. It's never too late to learn, I'll catch up on my education."

In Marseilles, where they had booked a passage to Haifa, they found that their ship had developed engine trouble and had cancelled her sailing. They therefore moved on to Genoa and were one day out of port when Nahum was handed a radio message to say that Lomzer was dead. When they docked in Naples the next day, they disembarked, and three days later they were back in Glasgow.

Katya was inconsolable and old age, like an enemy which had been kept at bay, suddenly rushed in to overwhelm her. She became an old woman almost before their eyes—shrivelled, bent, peevish, lachrymose and full of self-pity.

"There's nothing for me to live for, nothing," she sobbed, "all I want to do is die."

"Was she like that when she lost her second husband?" asked Lotie.

"No, not at all, but then she wasn't too old to find a third. Now, I suppose, she'll have to give up hope."

"Anyone can lose one husband," said Lotie, "but to lose three seems nothing short of carelessness."

Nahum was not amused and thought her remark in poor taste. He had a grudging affection for Katya—her abundant build, the promise of fleshy pleasure which she seemed to exude, the glint of mischief in her eyes, the naughty air of the wilful little girl which she had carried into her old age. The older he grew and the more things changed, the more he treasured anything constant about him, and Katya was perhaps the most constant of all. She had been, throughout all her changes of fortune, much as she had been in Volkovysk. He remembered her coming to the town as a young bride, the first woman he was aware of as a woman, and there was a moist freshness about her then which she seemed to have carried through life. Now, suddenly, she, too, had changed, and he was more upset by the sight of her than the death of her husband, though he felt lost without Lomzer.

It had been the same when Colquhoun had joined the navy and Goodkind had died, and he was pained to discover the extent to which he was dependent on others. He had thought of himself as a natural entrepreneur, but it seemed to him now that what Lomzer had said was true. He did not have flair so much as good fortune, the ability to find the right guide at the right time. He had known Lomzer for less than a decade, and he did not know how he would have survived in so chaotic and competitive a business as the cinema trade without him. Before Lomzer, he had moved along in fits and starts and had measured his success by the number and size of his cinemas, rather than their returns, but it was only with the advent of Lomzer that all his assets were made to yield their fullest value, and his company was consolidated into a stable and flourishing concern.

His emigration plans were wholly dependent on Lomzer. He had received occasional bids for individual cinemas and felt fairly confident that he could have received a good price for the group as a whole from one of the major circuits, but he did not want to be swallowed up and lose the identity of a concern which he had so laboriously built up, and which was now nearly twenty years old. Moreover, Nahum had several relatives, near and distant, in the firm, and Lomzer would have guaranteed both their jobs and their likely prospects of promotion, while a takeover by an outside group could have endangered their careers.

What Nahum couldn't understand was how he, an otherwise rational human being, had not taken the possibility of Lomzer's death into account when making his plans. Lomzer was an old man already when he had first met him, and, although he never knew his exact age (it was a point on which Lomzer was discreet to the point of being a liar), Nahum guessed that he could not have been far short of eighty and might have been well over it. He was, moreover, frail and with failing eyesight. Had he thought that Lomzer would live on forever? Perhaps not, but he had assumed that he would certainly be around for a further four or five years, by which time Mittwoch would have grown sufficiently in experience and stature to take over.

The sudden death of Lomzer made him shelve his plans, not because they had suddenly become impracticable, but because he—and certainly Lotie—took his death as an omen that his plans were perhaps untimely. He did not, however, abandon them altogether, until Mittwoch announced that he was taking a job in London.

Nahum, once over the initial shock, was inclined to charge him with ingratitude, and he asked whether he thought his promotion had been too slow.

"Not at all. Many people will tell you it was too fast, but there's more scope in a larger company."

"But less chance of coming to the top. I'm over sixty, you know. I won't be around forever, and you'll be the natural person to take over when I go."

"Oh, you've got a good many years before you go."

"Lomzer thought he had a good many years, but no one goes on forever."

"No, but at your age you're hardly more than halfway to forever. But, in any case, I have signed the contracts. I have rented a flat, I have made arrangements to move and I'm moving."

As far as Nahum knew, Lomzer died without heirs, and he undertook to say *kaddish* for him. He was in synagogue one evening, waiting for a *minyan* to assemble, when he was called to the phone and told that Katya had been taken seriously ill. He drove over to her house at once and found her in a coma. She died a few days later without recovering consciousness.

The illness and death of Katya filled him with such grief that he wondered if one grew more vulnerable as one grew older. She had represented his first yearnings of manhood. He remembered Shyke talking of the woman who gave him his first start in life and describing the experience as "a carnal *bar mitzvah*—today I am a man." Katya had done the same for him, and it almost seemed as if her death also represented the death of yearning, and that he was possibly mourning less for her than for himself. Anyone in show business—even in so innocent a branch as his own—had ample opportunities to exercise his libido, especially if business took one away from home, as it often did, and he had seen decrepit, toothless old satyrs, barely able to support themselves on their walking sticks, escorting downy young nymphs barely out of their teens. He had often been tempted to go the way of most flesh himself and had, on occasion—especially after a particularly good dinner, when to return to an empty hotel bedroom would have been too much of an anti-climax—yielded to temptation, but now he no longer felt even tempted. The fare was there as alluringly displayed, but his appetite had foresaken him, and the death of Katya was an almost symbolic confirmation of the fact.

His aunt had also represented his last living link with his Russian past. His mother was still, in clinical terms, alive but showed little sign of it and was like an awkward, heavy piece of period furniture, which—instead of being dusted and polished—had to be fed, but one was otherwise barely aware of her existence. Katya, on the other hand, up to the moment of Lomzer's death had been bubbling with life and mischief, and there was about her the warmth, the abundance, the mellowness, the ripeness—bordering on decay—of late summer. He had often disapproved of her and was sometimes even afraid of her, but he was nearly always glad she was around.

Her funeral turned out to be larger than he imagined, for she had kept in touch with many newcomers of her generation, and it was almost like a reunion of the pre-1914 wave of immigrants, most of them elderly, some of them old, one or two very old.

A rabbi spoke at length of her many qualities, and there was an outbreak of coughing and spluttering when he enlarged on her "modesty, her chastity, her virtue—a woman of worth whose life was an example to every Jewish daughter."

Her death brought legal complications. He and Katya had been appointed joint trustees of Lomzer's estate, but she had died before they could discuss the matter, and he found himself sole trustee of both her estate and Lomzer's, and the experience yielded many surprises. He discovered, first of all, that Lomzer had had two sons, now living in New York, by a previous marriage. He had never mentioned either of them, and they had presumably become estranged, but, whatever the cause of estrangement he had forgiven them before his death and had settled considerable sums on both. He had also made ample provisions for his widow, but she, possibly thinking that she would live forever, had not made a will.

Her estate, after the payment of various duties, was valued at about one hundred and fifty thousand pounds, and Nahum reckoned that, by the time the matter was settled, most of that would go to the lawyers, for claimants erupted everywhere—remote cousins in remote corners of the globe, brothers-in-law, sisters-in-law, nephews, nieces, maiden ladies in humble circumstances, doddering gentlemen. Most surprising of all, his own mother, startled into temporary life either by the death of her sister or the prospect of money, also put in a claim, and a perfectly sound one at that, though Nahum could not imagine what she would do with the money if she got it. Nor was that the end of the matter, for Nahum was knee-deep in papers and lawyers when there arrived a claim on behalf of Lomzer's children and grandchildren on the grounds that—as his widow had not "really" survived to benefit from his estate—they were entitled to the residue, at the end of which he began to ask himself whether he was not entitled to a little something himself.

Nearly a year passed and the matter was almost closed, when Nahum received a call from Krochmal that yet another claimant had appeared.

"Who is it this time?" he asked. "Lomzer's mother?"

"No, but almost as close."

"Don't tell me he's got a daughter or something."

"No, but his widow had a son."

"His widow? Which widow?"

"How many widows did he have?"

"Katya?"

"Yes."

"A son?"

"Yes."

Nahum gave it time to sink in, then his voice rose to a scream.

"You don't mean Lazar?"

"Where is he?"

"Here, in my office."

"Keep him there, I'll kill him."

Nahum's hands were shaking so much he could hardly keep his car on an even course. He found it difficult to believe that Lazar, even with the prospect of a fortune, would have the nerve to show his face in Glasgow. There was probably some mistake, but he didn't know what he would do if it wasn't. He did not think of himself as a violent man, but then, he had never had cause for violence. He was afraid that, in this instance, he might lose self-control, grab Lazar by the throat and strangle him, but he presumed that they wouldn't hang him if he did. If ever there was a case of justifiable homicide, this was it.

He was too impatient to use the rickety lift in the drab building which housed Krochmal's office, and he rushed up the stairs to the top floor, two at a time; then, as he entered the office and stood gasping for breath, he was greeted by a portly figure with a rounded belly, a rounded, well-kept little beard, gap teeth and a long, thin nose. It was Lazar all right, though fattened almost beyond recognition.

He held out a hairy hand, heavy with gold rings. "Reb Nahum, it's a long time since we've met."

Nahum was too breathless and confused to talk. He didn't understand how his feelings of murderous wrath should have become dissipated in the course of a ten-minute drive across town. Was he *that* glad to see a relative? Or was it simply that one needed breath to be angry? His immediate feelings were ones of curiosity. He wanted to know where Lazar had sprung from, what he was doing, where he had been. On the other hand, he was disinclined to speak to him at all.

They were joined by Krochmal and his son, young Krochmal, who had now become a partner in the firm.

"Is he the man he claims to be?" asked old Krochmal, "namely, Lazar Elchonon Hoppinstein?"

"He is," said Nahum.

"The sole surviving son of Katerina Helena Hoppinstein?"

"Yes, yes, it's him."

"Then it settles the matter."

"No, it doesn't, not by a long chalk. He and I still have a small matter to settle between us, the matter of a shipping company, the matter of a fortune"—his voice rose to a shout—"the matter of a name. Do you know, have you any idea, what this swine did to me?"

"I'm afraid I do, but it all happened twenty years ago, and there's nothing we can do about it now. On the other hand, he may feel obliged—and I sincerely hope he does—to make an ex-gratia settlement."

"Ex-gratia?" screamed Nahum. "Ex-gratia? How can you repair a man's name with an ex-gratia settlement? He dragged my name in the dirt. My windows were broken. My children were harassed. My best friend wouldn't speak to me. I had built up a company with an international reputation. My ships were going back and forth across the Baltic and the North Sea. I was trading in the Mediterranean and the

Aegean, and I was planning to go into the Atlantic, and I would have gone into the Atlantic. I might have been another Cunard—"

At this Lazar interjected: "With respect, Nahum, if it wasn't for me, you'd have been another bankrupt."

"Bankrupt?" screeched Nahum. "Me a bankrupt?" And without a further word, he dived across the office, jumped on Lazar and grabbed him by the throat. Secretaries screamed and ran for cover. An elderly couple with a small dog who were about to enter the office quickly turned back. Lazar, taken by surprise, fell back against a couch. Nahum fell on top of him, and couch and occupants toppled backwards amid the sound of breaking timber and tearing cloth. Krochmal and several clerks rushed forward to separate them. Krochmal the elder lost his glasses in the melée and groped around, half-blind, on all fours. The clerks, however, managed to prise the cousins apart, and all five or six of them sat amid the ruins of the couch and flying horsehair, gasping for breath. A secretary, venturing her head around the corner and finding them thus pacified, entered on tip-toe and put on the kettle.

"We'll all have a nice cup of tea, shall we?" she said brightly.

"How could you do it to me?" asked Nahum, as he drove Lazar to his hotel. "How could you do it to me—especially after all I did for you?"

"I panicked. I suppose if I had been more attracted to my wife, I might have sweated it out, but I couldn't stand her, I couldn't stand her parents. I was thinking of running for it, in any case. Everything came on top of me at once, and when I found the police were making enquiries, I fled."

"Couldn't you have left a statement, a line to clear my name?"

"There wasn't time, and it wouldn't have helped. You talk about a ruined business, but if we wouldn't have dabbled in contraband, the company would have foundered."

"I would rather it foundered."

"Do you think I didn't lose anything? The money I had put into the company was the least of it. I had a profession, a flourishing practice —they're gone. Do you remember how hard I worked to learn the language, to get into University, to become a lawyer? It all came to nothing, it's all lost."

"If I could have gotten my hands on you, you'd have lost more than your profession."

"I can understand your feelings."

"Oh, you can, can you? You're a true English gentleman, prepared to forgive everyone you've wronged. I still don't know why I didn't kill you when I saw you there in Krochmal's office. That's my trouble,

I can't lose my temper for more than two minutes at a time. I should keep a gun, so that if I do lose my temper, I can kill someone while it lasts."

"Would you believe me if I told you there were times when I wanted to kill myself?"

"What stopped you?"

"My religion."

"Your religion? Your bloody religion? Your religion didn't stop you from robbing me, from ruining my name, from trading with the enemy when thousands of boys were dying on the battlefield; your religion didn't stop you from abandoning your wife, from neglecting your mother, there your religion didn't stop you. Why did it stop you from doing the one decent thing you could have done?"

"Because suicide leaves no time for atonement."

"Oh, and is that what you've been doing for the past twenty years, atoning? That's a nice suit you're wearing, good cloth, gold rings. A profitable business, atoning, by the look of things. What have you been doing?"

"This and that."

"Where have you been doing it?"

"Here and there."

"Do I detect a bit of Irish in your accent? Is that where you've been, in Ireland?"

"For some of the time."

"On the move, or on the run?"

"A bit of both."

"And you could have been a settled, respectable, prosperous lawyer. What greed does to people. Not that I'm sorry for you, sorry for you I'm not. And you needn't think you'll get that hundred and fifty thousand. About twenty lawyers have had their fingers in that pie, and Krochmal and his little boy have been in it with their galoshes on. You're not getting a penny of it, or what's left, not as long as there's breath in my body."

"Can I remind you that it's not your money?"

"Maybe, but I'm the sole executioner."

"Executor."

"I said executioner, and I mean executioner. Did you really think you were going to get away with it? You probably remember my father and think I'm as easygoing as he was, but then, my father was never robbed like I was, not by his first cousin. I'm going to take you somewhere."

Lazar's brow moistened. "Where?"

"You'll find out." He stepped on the accelerator, and after a few minutes they were among the red-sandstone terraces of Carmichael Place.

"Remember this house?"

"Yes, you used to live there."

"During the war. Things got difficult, and I couldn't keep up the big place, and I moved in here, and we were very happy till I came home one evening and found two large men waiting for me with a magistrate's warrant, and when I tried to get hold of you, you were gone, vanished. The business dragged on for months. I pleaded guilty, what else could I do? I was fined fifty thousand pounds, but that was the least of it. When I got back home, there were crowds in the street, policemen, and bits of glass all over the place. It was a private pogrom. And why? Because of you, my dear cousin. You were doing well and had married a rich wife, but you were in a hurry to be richer, and so you used my name, you forged documents, you traded with the enemy and then, when you were found out, you ran for it and left me to face the fire." He pulled the car starting handle from under his seat. "Can you give me one good reason why I shouldn't bash your head in?"

"None whatever, except that you won't."

"I won't, will I?"

"You won't."

"You tempt me."

"Go ahead and do it."

Nahum weighed the starting handle in his hand, then threw it down with despair. "You're bloody well right." He was on the verge of tears. "I'm too weak and useless. The only thing I'm good at is in making a pound here and there, in building up a business, and even there I'm not very good, but in life I'm useless. I've never been able to stand up to my mother, my sister, my wives, my children, nobody. I'm even bullied by my secretaries. There were times, many years ago when I was feeling very low, I would cheer myself with the thought of what I would do to you if I ever laid hands on you, and here you are— right beside me, large as life—and what am I doing? Acting as your chauffeur."

"You're not that weak. You'd have killed me this morning if Krochmal hadn't intervened."

Nahum perked up. "That's true, I would have. I'll have a word with Krochmal about that."

"It wouldn't have helped if you had. The money would all have gone to my wife."

"Your wife? You've remarried? *Mazeltov*. Why didn't you invite me to your wedding? I'd have sent a present. You got children also?"

"A daughter."

"And where are they living?"

"In America."

"You believe in keeping your distance, don't you? You didn't think of letting your mother know you were alive, or your wife. She died of heart-ache, your wife. So did her father. Her mother's still alive, you know. Perhaps I'll drive you around to see her. I may not have the nerve to kill you, but if your mother-in-law's the woman I think she is —and I think she is—she'll carve you up with her kitchen knife."

"Look, Nahum, there's no point mulling over events which happened twenty years ago. As I told Krochmal, I'm prepared to make an ex-gratia settlement."

"Ex-gratia, eh?" He reached for his starting handle again.

"No, not ex-gratia, a settlement."

"And how much do you think I'll settle for?"

"That we can argue about."

"Can we?" He grabbed hold of Lazar's tie and wound it around his fist. "You're going to sign away every penny your mother left."

"Do you mind?" said Lazar. "It's a new tie."

"But it's an old throat." And he continued to wind up the tie until his knuckle pressed against Lazar's windpipe. "Every penny," he said between gritted teeth.

Lazar opened his mouth to speak but couldn't. His face turned purple. He began to kick his feet. Sweat formed on his brow in quivering globules. Nahum unfurled his hand and let go his grip.

"I do myself an injustice, I could have killed you, after all, not maybe with the starting handle, I'm not a blunt instrument man, that much I can see, but I could quite easily have throttled you. And you know why I didn't?" Lazar, who was feeling his throat with both his hands, had still not quite found his voice. "Because I'm still saying *kaddish* for your mother. I've said *kaddish* for your step-father. I sometimes feel I've been saying *kaddish* for half the world, but if you don't sign away every penny, I'll be saying *kaddish* for you. No, don't thank me, it'll be a pleasure."

"She had a hard life, my mother."

"You didn't do much to make it easier."

"I did what I could. I sent her a monthly allowance."

"Did she know it was from you?"

"I presume she must have guessed, but I didn't dare tell her because my mother, bless her, was a terrible chatterbox. The only thing she could be discreet about was money—or, at least, her own money. I've been sending it for the past twenty years, that's how I knew she was dead. The bank returned a remittance."

"She was a remarkable woman, your mother."

"And yours—is she still alive, by the way?"

"In a manner of speaking. She's seen better days, poor thing, who hasn't? Would you like to see her?"

His mother was sitting upright in her chair with a face like a red Indian chieftain.

"I've got a visitor for you, dear," said Nahum; "do you recognise him?" She gazed impassively from one to the other. It was not at all certain that she even recognised Nahum.

"It's Lazar," he said, "Katya's son. Come here all the way from America."

"America," she said slowly, her lips hardly moving.

"Yes, Katya's son, Lazar."

"Katya's dead."

"She is. But this is her son, Lazar."

"He's also dead. Everybody's dead."

They ate supper quietly together. Lotie was out, and the meal was prepared for them by a maid.

"Do you remember the fifth commandment?" said Lazar. " 'Honour thy father and thy mother, in order that thy days may be prolonged.' I think it should read, 'Lest thy days be prolonged.' We wish each other long life, who wants it? I remember your mother as a young woman, the belle of Volkovysk. I'm told she was the sister my father really wanted to marry."

"There was nothing wrong with your mother."

"My mother had gaiety, yours had class. I was an immense disappointment to my mother. She wanted a daughter, to shape in her own image, and I failed her in that. And I failed as a son, for my father was apparently a dashing figure, with a Western education. Well, dashing I wasn't, and it was only when I became a lawyer that I was finally rehabilitated in her eyes. But I've never been happy with the law; my marriages have not been happy ones. Thank God money still means something to me; otherwise, I'd have had nothing to live for. You know something? People never transplant. All the happiness I've ever known in my life was in Russia, with all its hazards and all its harassments, and if I do anything now which brings me a gleam of joy, it's because it carries some echo of *der heim,* maybe a line of silver birches, bare in a wintry landscape; ducks waddling on a frozen lake; the smell of moist earth on a spring morning; the smell of dried timber."

He began singing "The Birch Tree," a popular Russian folk song, in a surprisingly pleasant tenor voice. Nahum joined him in a rather less pleasant baritone.

When Lotie returned, she found them both in tears.

CHAPTER XXXI
BLACKOUT

Nahum was perturbed by persistent reports, to say nothing of dark rumours, abut Arabella's ill health. Kapulski said she was in pieces; Vicky, rather more crudely, said she "had gone off her chump"; while Hector would not say anything at all; and when Nahum next went to London, he tried to make arrangements to see her.

"But what for?" said Hector. "The place is miles out, they have awkward visiting hours and, in any case, she'll be home soon."

"How soon?"

"Any day now."

"That's what you told me last time I was here, and that was more than a month ago. Can't you tell me what's wrong? It's not as if I'm a stranger or something."

Hector hesitated.

"Well?"

"She's had some sort of nervous breakdown, but, as always with Ara, it's a little more complicated than that, and every time she gets a visitor, it sets her back for weeks. She gets mawkish and maudlin. Why don't you wait till she gets back to London?"

"Where is she?"

Finally, after further prevarication, Hector gave him the name of the place, and Nahum travelled down that afternoon.

It was a large nursing home set high amidst pine trees in the Surrey hills, and he found Arabella alone, in a sleeveless summer dress on a white bench, gazing silently into the motionless waters of a lily pond. He sat down beside her and put an arm around her.

She started with alarm, then smiled wanly, a bleak autumnal smile, when she recognized him.

"Hector phoned to say you were coming, but I didn't expect you so soon." There were dark rings under her eyes, her complexion was sallow and her hair lank. There was a slight breeze, and she was shivering. Nahum took off his jacket and put it around her. She leaned her head on his shoulder and began to cry. He hugged her tightly and let her continue until the sobbing ceased, and he wiped her eyes and blew her nose.

"Why didn't you write to me or phone me to say that something was troubling you? You know very well I'd do anything for you."

"Nothing was troubling me," she said haltingly. "I just wanted to die."

"But why should a beautiful, talented woman like you, who has everything to live for, want to die?"

"Because my real self has caught up with me. I'm neither as beautiful nor as talented as I thought. I'm forty, which, given the sort of parts I like to play, is extreme old age, and I still haven't had the breakthrough I hoped for."

"You got major parts."

"In minor films. Kapulski once said—he was talking about another actress, but it also applied to me—if you don't make it to Hollywood by the time you're thirty, it's too late, and of course he's right."

"It's all a matter of luck."

"Maybe, but it's no consolation to know that I'm luckless, and, what's worse, I've been hampering Hector's career. He has to travel a lot but is afraid to leave London because of me. I told him to go, and that the worst that I could do with myself was to cut my throat, but that needn't interfere with his plans."

"As a matter of fact, I could do with Hector in Glasgow. Lomzer is dead, Mittwoch has left, I've no one to rely on. Why don't you both come back?"

"Hector could never live in the provinces, neither could I."

"He wouldn't necessarily have to stay in the provinces. I've just bought my first house south of the border, in Carlisle, and, in fact, I was thinking of naming it after you."

"In Carlisle? No, my darling, that's an honour I'm prepared to wait for. Call it after the Queen Mother."

"I've always had hopes of a place in London, you know, perhaps even the West End, and, if that happens, there's no reason why I shouldn't move my office to London. I'm over sixty; in another few years Hector could be in charge."

She shook her head and wouldn't discuss it further.

"Have you not been offered any parts?"

"Nothing I would look at, and nothing in America."

The next day Nahum spoke to Kapulski.

"You needn't tell me about Ara," Kapulski said. "I love her, I made her, I discovered her, she's the tops—well, maybe not quite the tops—but she's got something missing, and you know what it is."

"Mazel?"

"No, she's got plenty of that. It was *mazel* meeting me, in the first place. She's got no—how shall I put it? She's got no sense of other people. If you show her a script, she can only see her own part, and everything else fades into darkness, so she acts her part as if it's a monologue. You could get away with that in the silent days, but not in the talkies. And her talking voice jars, it's too high-pitched."

"So you mean she's finished?"

"Hell, no, nobody's finished if you're prepared to put enough money behind them."

"How much money?"

"We're talking about thousands, rather than hundreds."

"I know that."

"And tens of thousands, rather than thousands."

"How many tens?"

"We can talk about that."

"Let's talk."

Six weeks later Arabella was invited to Hollywood, and two months later she sailed in the *Queen Mary*. Shortly before she sailed, Nahum received an unexpected visit from her sister Caroline. She was normally a smiling, compact, well-composed little woman, but this time Nahum found her almost hysterical.

"You mustn't let Ara go," she pleaded, "you mustn't, you mustn't let her leave England. If she does, she'll never come back. She won't, I know she won't."

Nahum was at first slightly dazed by her outburst and tried to calm her.

"Why all this foreboding? This is her great opportunity. She's about to become a star. I saw her last week. She's a new woman."

"How long did you see her for? Ten minutes? An hour? I've just spent the better part of a week with her, and she goes up and down like a yo-yo. One minute at the top of the world, the next sunk in darkness. She's been ill, *very* ill, she hasn't recovered yet. Here at least I'm not too far away and I can get down to London fairly frequently, and, of course, she's got Hector, but in America she would be all on her own, with that awful Kapulski. I don't know if she could be trusted on a boat on her own. She could jump overboard, she could."

"Now you're being ridiculous. She's got everything to live for. She was depressed by the failure—it wasn't, strictly speaking, even a failure—by the non-success of her last film, but she's gotten over that and her best days are ahead. Her talent didn't have sufficient scope in this country. In America she'll find herself."

"In America she'll lose herself—if she ever does get to America. Can I just have one promise, that she'll not be allowed to cross the Atlantic on her own? I'd have gone with her, but I can't leave the children on their own, and I can hardly take them along."

Nahum lifted up the phone and spoke to Hector, who told him that he had never had any intention of letting Arabella travel on her own.

"I've got to be in New York on business, in any case, and when I've settled that, I hope to spend a month or more with her in California."

He repeated his assurances to Caroline.

"But are you sure you'll be going with her?"

"What do you mean, am I sure? I've got the tickets right in front of me. I hope you'll come to see us off, if not in Southampton, then at least on the boat-train." And thus mollified, she went home.

Caroline could not get to the boat-train, but Nahum was in London at the time, and he went to see them off and soon found that Caroline's forebodings were not entirely misplaced, for when he arrived at the station, Arabella was on the train, but not Hector, and she was trembling with agitation. They had been wakened by the phone in the early hours of the morning. Hector had had to rush off and told her that he might not be able to get to the boat-train; she should expect him in Southampton.

"It's not that which worries me," she said; "he's had these calls before, but when I tried to phone the office this morning, there was no reply. I then phoned Vicky, and she's in quite a state. Eddy vanished in the middle of the night without a word, and she has no idea where he is."

At that moment the train whistle blew, and Nahum urged her to delay her journey.

"I'm going," she said with grim finality. "They're starting shooting in four weeks, and I'm going to be on that set if it's the last thing I do." She gave him a long, lingering kiss. The train began to move, and, as he jumped from the carriage, he slipped and fell and bruised himself slightly. He quickly picked himself up. Arabella was by then out of sight, and he ran all the way along the platform to the nearest call-box and tried to phone Vicky. Her line was engaged. He tried again a few minutes later, and it was still engaged; he jumped into a taxi and drove to her flat. It was locked and bolted without sign of life. The porter told him that she had left an hour or so earlier.

"Did she have any baggage?"

"Not that I could see. She shouldn't be long."

He stood around in the foyer, wondering what to do next, when a car pulled up and a reporter and a photographer emerged, then another. Within minutes, the building was teeming with pressmen and photographers, all pushing bank notes into the porter's hand, and all wanting information on the Camerons. When someone got wind that Nahum was in some way connected with their quarry, they turned on him, and he ran along the road, pursued by cameramen and reporters, until he found refuge in a taxi. When he got to his hotel and switched on the evening news, he discovered the cause of the commotion. An international arms ring had been discovered operating from a warehouse on the edge of Epping Forest. Eight men had been arrested, and a further four were being sought by the police. They included Cameron and Hector. So much for their machine-tool business, he thought. But his first anxieties at that moment were for Arabella, and he ran downstairs and sent her a telegram: INSIST YOU DELAY DEPARTURE STOP AM LEAVING FOR SOUTHAMPTON FORTHWITH MEET ME AT POLYGON HOTEL

There was no train to Southampton for some hours, and he therefore hired a chauffered car to drive him there, falling asleep almost as soon as he settled back in his seat. Had he been awake, he might have noticed something erratic in his chauffeur's driving. As it was, he woke up in hospital the next day. His driver was drunk and had gone into a tree. He was concussed but not otherwise injured, and as soon as he found his bearings he phoned the Polygon Hotel to ask if there had been any callers for him; there was only a telegram which read: TO HELL WITH HECTOR AM SAILING AS PLANNED ALL MY LOVE ARA

He had some urgent business in London and hoped to leave hospital that day, but he was detained for a check-up and did not get back to the capital until two days later. The Munich crisis had come to a head, and the evening papers had come out with a special edition to bring the news; the streets were shrill with the cries of paperboys. He picked up a paper in the station but only began to read it in his hotel. It, in fact, contained nothing he had not heard on the radio a few hours earlier, and he threw it aside. Later, as he was undressing, something at the back of the paper caught his eye which for a moment made his heart stop, and he bent down to read it. It was in the Stop Press column: "BRITISH STAR IN SEA DRAMA. Film star, Arabella Raeburn, missing from the S.S. *Queen Mary*. Feared drowned. Search continues."

In an odd way, this last calamity was the least painful. For a time he allowed himself to hope that Arabella had secreted herself away somewhere in the vast depths of the vessel and might still be found, or that she had merely fallen overboard and had been picked up by another craft and was somehow still alive, but once he felt compelled to abandon all hope, he did not have the same anguish he had felt on the death of Miri or Alex, possibly because she had been so unreal a thing, so removed from all normal life, that he couldn't really think of her as actually dead. She had been a spirit who had passed his way, illuminated his corner of the globe for a moment like some ornate firefly and had passed on. He felt fortunate to have known her at all. On reflection, however, he came to suspect that there were possibly more mundane reasons for his feelings. The calamity of her death had come amid a welter of so many other calamities that he found it difficult to take them all in, for within a matter of days he had lost not only Arabella, but he had become bereft of a son, a son-in-law and a daughter. He hoped, he presumed, that they had not vanished permanently; the police were searching for them on four continents, but he had no idea of their whereabouts, or when, if ever, he would see them again.

At first he had been inclined to blame Cameron for everything, even for the death of Arabella. The man who had nearly ruined his business had all but ruined his life, and he reproached himself for not strangling him when he had first caught sight of him at Hector's wedding; if not then, when he had learned of his relationship with Vicky, but with time he returned to the view that Cameron was the mere agent of a dark deity sent to punish him for his presumption.

As external events pressed in upon him, and the possibility of war drew nearer, he began to feel that his own personal calamities were part of a wider apocalypse, and that the whole world was falling apart.

Gas masks were being distributed, back gardens were being scooped out to make room for air-raid shelters, and home-office circulars arrived with every post, advising cinema owners on how to reinforce their buildings against air attack and the steps that might be necessary in the event of a blackout. The word blackout seemed to be on everyone's lips, but he felt that—as far as his own life was concerned—the lights had already gone out.

Lotie tried to cheer him with talk of Jacob and his children, and of Benny who, after almost nine years (on what should have been a six-year course), was finally within sight of becoming a doctor and of Sophie and the twins, but he seemed inconsolable.

Then one morning he received a telegram from Mexico. It bore no address and said simply: SORRY FOR SILENCE EVERYBODY IS FINE WILL CONTACT YOU WHEN POSSIBLE PLEASE DO NOT WORRY LOVE VICKY

Three weeks later, the war broke out.

CHAPTER XXXII
MEN AT ARMS

AT FIRST NAHUM COULD NOT QUITE BELIEVE WHAT WAS HAPPEN-ing. "You'd think after what they'd been through last time, they'd wait a few generations before they started killing each other again," he said to Lotie, "but here we are, back where we were."

The immediate effect of the second war, as of the first, was to deprive Nahum of almost half his staff, and, but for the fact that he had been able to find a pair of middle-aged German refugees who knew a smattering of English and were familiar with the cinema trade, he would have faced a crisis. Although he was able to replace some of his male staff with females, it was difficult, as the war continued, to obtain or retain any staff at all, for he was unable to compete with the sort of wages offered in the munitions factories. Attendance, on the other hand, improved, and some of the outlying houses, which had just about paid their way, were, thanks to the proximity of army bases, now crammed to capacity, even in the afternoons.

Jacob was called up shortly after the outbreak of war. Nahum had hoped that, as he had been to Clifton and Cambridge, he would, like his half-brothers before him, be commissioned, but he became a mere sergeant in the Educational Corps. Benny finally qualified as a doctor in 1940, and Nahum thought he would probably escape military service both because of his slight size and poor eyesight, but he was not only called up, he was soon home with pips glowing on both shoulders as a captain in the Royal Army Medical Corps. Nahum was proud of his son and began to regard him with new eyes. He had felt that, as Sophie had put it to him, any family with six children was entitled to at least one dud, but the boy was a continuing source of surprise. He had never expected him to get into University, and, once in University, he had never expected him to qualify, but what he lacked in brilliance he had made up for in perseverance, and he became a doctor.

"And a very good doctor, too," said Lotie, "though he should be— he's taken such a long time becoming one."

Because Nahum was short of staff, Lotie sometimes worked for him as an usherette and, to her immense gratification, was rewarded on her very first night with three indecent proposals, "one of them from a mere schoolboy. I know it's dark in the cinemas, but it's not bad for a woman close to sixty."

The sudden change in the direction of the war in the spring of 1940—the invasion of Norway, the breakthrough in Belgium, Dunkirk, the fall of France—filled Nahum with despair.

"There's nothing to stop them coming here," he said. "What's the channel? A two-hour crossing."

"The last war Britain lost was the war of American independence," said Lotie, a fact from which Nahum derived peculiarly little comfort.

"That time I wanted to go to Palestine, I had a feeling about it. It was the right thing to do, the wise thing to do. Thank God Sophie and Yankelson are there."

"If Britain should lose the war, I can't see much future for Palestine or your Jewish state," said Lotie. Nahum sometimes marvelled at her composure and was at first inclined to think that she did not really understand what was going on.

The war had not yet brought any serious shortages, but some of Lotie's American relatives, thinking that the country was on the verge of starvation, began sending her food parcels, and one day, a little to his surprise, Nahum also received a food parcel, also from America. It was from Vicky. Again, it contained no address, and it came with a short note to say that "everything and everyone was fine."

Nahum wondered why she still felt the need to be secretive and why, if they were able to stay in America and even send food parcels, she could not at least have given him a forwarding address.

As the war continued, although there were—apart from minor triumphs in the Middle East and East Africa—no improvements in the overall situation, a curious feeling of euphoria came over Nahum. He had been fervently pro-British in the first world war, but his fervour had been tempered by the alliance with Russia, and he had, in spite of himself, been elated by the catastrophes suffered by the Tsarist forces on the eastern front. Now, however, he could feel involved without reservation. He had two sons in the army, and, during the Battle of Britain, his wife joined the Women's Voluntary Service. He did the occasional bit of fire watching, and he frequently volunteered his cinemas for war charities; for the first time in his life, he felt utterly at one with the people about him. Perhaps the surrounding darkness, the long winter nights, the blackouts laced with fog all enhanced the sensation, but—with all his concern about the war and the problems it brought to his life—it was intensely comforting. He had lived nearly fifty years in the country, and it took a world war to make him feel

British. The shared sympathies, the shared fears, the shared ardours, the shared efforts, the shared feelings of belonging also enriched their own relationship, and in the evening Nahum would sometimes sit by the fire with Lotie on his knee, her arms around his neck, like a young couple in the first spasms of love.

Their relationship was further enhanced by the air raids, or, rather, the prospect of them. Shortly before the war they had scooped out a substantial chunk of their garden and erected an Anderson Shelter, a crude little bunker made of corrugated iron and earth, but Lotie declared that she would rather die in her bed than sleep in a hole in the ground, and eventually they acquired what was called a Morrison Shelter, a huge table of cast iron, strong enough to withstand the weight of the house, with springs underneath wide enough to take a double mattress. It took up much of the space of their dining room, and they would crawl into it last thing at night.

They had hitherto slept in twin beds separated by bedside tables, so that the Morrison Shelter, and the ever-present sense of danger, added to the intimacy of their marriage.

One night as they were getting ready for bed, the sirens went. Nahum rushed upstairs to take his mother to the shelter but found her fast asleep and decided to leave her where she was.

"What can Hitler do to her that time won't?" said Lotie.

In previous raids, the bombs had fallen on the docks and shipyards and aero-engine factories, all of which were some distance away. This time, they came nearer. The windows rattled and the house shook, and Nahum presumed they were aiming at Weirs, a large engineering plant only about a mile from their house. They heard the drone of planes, the thunder of ack-ack, the crump of bombs and, loudest of all, the crash of collapsing buildings. There were excited voices outside and the roar of fire engines.

"They really mean business this time," said Nahum.

"I wouldn't mind going out to see what's happening," said Lotie.

"Do you want your head blown off?"

Suddenly there was a tremendous bang, the sound of shattered glass, the smell of dust and plaster, and the lights went out. Nahum grasped Lotie's hand.

"Are you all right?"

"Fine, are you?"

"My God, that was a close one." He reached for his torch, crawled from under the table, but then, as he tried to get to his feet, his legs gave way. He grabbed at a chair to steady himself.

"What's this, what's happening to me?"

"Shock, probably," said Lotie and took out a thermos she had by her bed. "Here, have some tea."

He took a sip, when he suddenly remembered his mother and rushed up the stairs two at a time, the weakness in his legs gone. She was sitting up in the darkness, jabbering excitedly in Russian.

"Is that you, Yechiel? What's happening? What's the noise? Where am I? It's very cold."

Nahum took her by the hand, helped her on with her dressing gown and led her down to the kitchen, where Lotie had lit some candles and was busy boarding up a window against the cold night air.

"Who is this?" asked his mother.

"Lotie, dear."

"Lotie? Lotie who?"

"Lotie Raeburn, my wife."

"And who are you?"

"Nahum."

"Nahum, did you say? I know that name."

"Sit down, Mother, and we'll make you a cup of tea."

"Where's everybody? Where's Yechiel? Where's Katya? Why is it so dark. Isn't there a lamp in the house? I'm very cold. What's happening?"

The lights were restored the following morning, and the windows a day or two later, and life almost got back to normal. What made things a bit abnormal was the fact that the explosion had restored old Mrs Rabinovitz to life. For the past five or six years, she had been a large, overblown object, animated enough to eat and drink and, if need be, to move, but otherwise removed from life. But now, having recovered her tongue and her use of Russian, she progressed to Yiddish and English and was soon speaking all three, sometimes consecutively, sometimes concurrently, but never stopping, as if to make up for all her years of silence. Her memory, however, was faulty, and she confused Lotie with her daughter and, more surprisingly, with her sister and sometimes even with her maid, and would attempt to send her on errands. The public had been issued with ear-plugs, and Lotie took to wearing them while her mother-in-law was about. The old woman, however, also liked to roam around the kitchen and nearly gassed the household when she turned on the gas, went to look for a match and then forgot all about it. She also once poured a cherished tin of coffee into the tea caddy and on another occasion incinerated the meat ration of the entire household by leaving it in a frying pan and recalling that she had done so only when the stove caught fire. One day, a distraught Lotie phoned Nahum at the office, asking him to come home at once or he might find his mother with her throat cut.

"She's done it again," she said, "this time with a milk saucepan. That's the second time I've had to use the stirrup-pump in the kitchen this week. She's a bigger menace than the Luftwaffe."

A few days later she died in her sleep.

The funeral was rather larger than Nahum had expected, for quite a number of people who had forgotten that she was alive were startled into remembrance by her death, and there was a sizable reunion of what Nahum called the pre-1914 crowd, but he found it a curious and, in some ways, chastening experience. At previous funerals—in fact, up to Katya's death—he was always aware of an outer fence of elders, wintry figures with white hair, who thumped around with walking sticks exchanging resigned glances in mute appreciation that their turn was next. Nahum looked around, and, though he felt in fairly sound health and had no need of a walking stick, he found himself part of the outer fence.

It was not all that long since he had finished saying *kaddish* for Arabella, and now he began saying it for his mother. He sometimes felt as if he had been saying *kaddish* all his life, and again in synagogue in the evenings he had the same sensation he had experienced at the funeral. He was among the ancients. A sad-eyed rabbi, who had arrived in Glasgow shortly before the war and who had not picked up English, gave a brief discourse on the Talmud every evening, and Nahum, who had not previously bothered to attend, joined the five or six bent figures with crumpled faces and battered hats who made up the group; he was surprised to discover how—even after fifty years —the little Talmud he had learnt in *Yeshiva* came back to him, and the pleasure he received from the hour or so he spent swaying back and forward over the yellowing pages. He could not only follow but also entered into the arguments, weaving his thumb and quoting sources to support his case, and he was regarded by the others with awe. In Glasgow, Jewish scholarship was associated with poverty, and the sight of a man who had been fifty years in the country, spoke English, had mixed with the mighty, owned ten cinemas and was married to an elegant American wife, but who could appreciate the Talmud, was alien to their experience, and he was referred to with veneration as Reb Nahum, a prefix generally accorded to scholars of standing, though Lotie protested that a man who spent as much time in synagogue as he did must hate his wife.

His mother had generally kept herself to her room and her bathroom, when not pottering around in the kitchen, but once she was dead, the house suddenly began to seem very large and empty, and there were times when Nahum was fire watching that Lotie was afraid to be left alone in the evening.

"It's not only the bombs I'm afraid of," she said, "it's the ghost of your mother. I sometimes have the feeling that she haunts this place."

"I never knew you Americans believed in ghosts," he said. "I thought that they were something created by the English."

But some weeks later, something happened which made him think that he, too, was seeing ghosts. Shortly before the war, Jacob had visited an old school friend who was housemaster at a boarding school in the Midlands and made the acquaintance of the gardener, a man called Eric, and his wife Trude, who was the housekeeper. Both were German Jewish refugees who had been fairly prosperous until the coming of Hitler. They had managed to get out shortly before the war, and the only work they could find was as domestic servants.

By chance, Jacob was stationed near the school early in the war and returned on a visit; he found the woman at her wit's end. Her husband who was considerably older than she, a broken shell of a man, had been interned as an enemy alien, which struck Jacob as absurd, and he wrote to his father:

"Does nobody know that these people fled from Germany for their lives? Even if he had been disposed to help the Germans, he is too old and broken to be of much help to anyone, least of all himself. He also suffers from diabetes and is deeply depressed, and when he got the internment order, he thought he was about to be sent off to some sort of British Dachau (though, from what one hears, conditions at the Isle of Man aren't all that pleasant, either), and, but for the fact that a master happened to be about to restrain him, he would have hanged himself. He's on the Isle of Man now, too depressed to see anyone, or to write, and, according to his wife, he just wants to be left alone to die. All of us have written to our M.P.s and are pulling what strings we can, but I was wondering if you were in a position to do anything. I seem to remember that you and Lotie once met the Home Secretary at some sort of charity do and that you were on good terms with the Lord Provost of Glasgow. Do you think you could possibly write to them? A word with the rabbi might also be useful, for, as you know, the English have great deference for clergy. His name is Eric or Erich Hauptmann, he is sixty-four, comes from Frankfurt-on-Main and his English address is Milton House, Beresford, Staffs."

Nahum was surprised that Jacob should have thought of him as a man of influence. He had regarded himself as such during his ship-owning days, but not as a cinema owner, but, once approached, he applied himself with energy and was gratified to discover how useful he could be.

A few months later, Trude wrote to him: "Erich was released from internment on Wednesday. I had hoped to meet him in Liverpool, but it is a restricted area, and I was only allowed to travel as far as Crewe, and I met him there. He looked a bit unwell at first, but he cheered up when he saw me, and he is now back home in bed enjoying a nice English cup of tea. It is his sixty-fifth birthday tomorrow, and his sister is coming all the way from Ireland for it, and one or two other friends are coming, and it should be quite jolly. I have written to your son and hope that he, too, may join us."

Jacob did join them, but the event turned out to be rather less jolly than Trude anticipated.

"Help came, but too late," wrote Jacob. "Hauptmann was released from internment last Wednesday and died two days later, in the course of the party his wife made to celebrate his sixty-fifth birthday. I was at the funeral yesterday. It was a bleak little affair. The headmaster's wife was there from Beresford, one of the housemasters, five or six crumpled, elderly ladies and myself. A rabbi, who had never previously set eyes on him, made a lengthy oration in German, which had the ladies in tears; a psalm was said, a button was pressed and rollers set in motion; a pair of curtains flew open to reveal the angry mouth of a furnace, the coffin disappeared, the curtains closed and the show was over. We then retired to a nearby house for a cup of tea, and the widow, who had been remarkably composed throughout the ceremony —and who, as a matter of fact, looked rather fetching in black—told me her whole story. It is worthy of a book, and one day I may even write it. She has an elderly sister-in-law in Ireland and one or two acquaintances in London but otherwise appears to be all on her own. I hope to see something of her when I am next on leave, but there are Christmas holidays ahead, and I was wondering if you could invite her up for a week or so to stay with you in Glasgow. I don't know if she can afford the fare, and so you might wish to append a ticket or travel voucher with your invitation."

Nahum was away on business, and Lotie arranged to pick Trude up at the station; when he returned, they were having tea together in the front room. As Lotie rose to introduce them, Nahum stood with a hand outstretched and his mouth open, as if he had seen a ghost. The young woman before him was the reincarnation of his mother as he had known her in early boyhood.

He did not even pause to exchange greeting but rushed to a photograph album and turned the pages with shaking hands.

"Have you seen this woman before?" he asked.

And this time their visitor stood, open-mouthed.

"It's Grandmother," she said. "I never met her, but Mother carried the photograph everywhere."

Nahum closed the album and threw up his hands.

"I can't believe it. It's too much like the plot of the sort of films I show. Was your father called Arnstein?"

"No, that was my step-father. My father was called Simyon Petrovitch, but I remember nothing of him."

Then she told her whole story, how she was nearly burnt alive in the conflagration that destroyed their hotel in New York and how, while her father was on bail, they fled to Canada, from where, with the help of Communist friends, they made their way to Russia shortly after the revolution. There they also found themselves among friends, and Arnstein became a member of one of the local soviets in the Ukraine, until the place was overrun by the Whites, and they made their way southward to Odessa, where they managed to find food and shelter. But as the war continued, hunger intensified, and the whole area was thrown into chaos. Their lives, and those of many thousands of others, were saved by an international Jewish relief organization, and it was there that Trude had met her future husband, who was an official of the organisation. He was over twenty years her senior, but she was attracted to him because he represented the prospect of regular meals. They married and went back to live in Germany, and she lost all further contact with her parents and everyone else.

"I, of course, tried to contact Mother and wrote to people who I thought might know where to find her, or who might know someone who knew her. I also wanted to go to Russia myself but was told I mightn't be able to get out again."

"That's exactly what they told me," said Nahum. "When did you last see your mother?"

"Twenty years ago, almost to the day."

"And you've heard nothing since?"

"Not a word."

"I'm surprised she didn't try to contact you."

"I'm not. She was very superstitious, you know."

"Your mother?"

"Very."

"I was under the impression that she didn't believe in anything."

"No, she thought she had something called the black touch and that she brought misfortune to everyone she knew—to her parents, to my father, to her friends, to everyone except Arnstein, who, I suppose, was immune because he was a misfortune himself; she told me when she saw me off that she wouldn't write. She wanted me to have a new life and thought I would be better off without her and that I should stop thinking about her."

"Which may be the reason why she hasn't tried to contact me."

"I'm sure it's the reason."

"But why didn't you try and contact me when things became difficult in Germany?"

"First of all, after all I'd been through, nothing seemed particularly difficult."

"But didn't you know you had an uncle in Glasgow?"

"Of course I knew, I even remember when you came to New York, and I mentioned your name to the refugee people here. I told them that you were a ship owner, and they made enquiries and said that you had gone under in what they called "unhappy circumstances" in the last war, which reminded me again of Mother's black touch. In any case, I wasn't too keen about meeting relatives at all, for everywhere we went, we found people with so many burdens that I was nervous of adding to them, and, to be honest, once I found a job in Beresford, I was so happy that I didn't want to move; I only wish I could have said the same for poor old Erich. When I think of him, I sometimes wonder if I haven't inherited Mother's black touch. He was an accountant, you know, and a fairly prosperous one, but when the Nazis came to power, his practise dwindled, and he took a job with the *Judenrat*, and after a time that, too, folded. The refugee people here found me a job as a cook-housekeeper in a boarding school, which was perfectly all right, but they found Erich a job as a handyman. He didn't know what the word meant, and when I explained what it was, he tried to jump out of the window. He had never handled a manual implement in his life, he said, and wouldn't know how to start. Later, he calmed down and took a more philosophical view of the situation. After all, he said, it's all a matter of knocking nails in, and he got himself a hammer and nails and started knocking nails into everything he could find, not with great success, and by the time he finished, he was ready to knock a nail into me, so we decided (though we didn't tell the school) that I should be the handyman and he the cook. He also did a bit of gardening, so it didn't work out too badly till he was interned."

Her eyes moistened, and Nahum put a comforting hand on hers.

"Anyway, your troubles are over. You don't know what it means to me to find a living remnant of the family. I'd more or less written you all off. In fact, seeing you here has given me hopes that we may eventually find your mother."

He recalled the Talmudic saying that God sends a remedy with every malady (to which Shyke retorted: "Let Him keep His remedies and His maladies"), and the discovery of his niece was, in some ways, a compensation for the disappearance of his daughter. She was just over forty and, for all she had gone through, seemed younger; looking at her made him feel that his mother had never died, that she had never even grown old. It confirmed his faith in immortality. With her fair complexion, reddish hair and grey-greenish eyes, her good looks were Slavic rather than Jewish, and she reminded him of the high-spirited, fresh-faced peasant women of Volkovysk.

She had insisted on going back to Beresford because she couldn't leave without notice, but she returned early in the new year, carrying all she had in the world in one small suitcase.

It was Passover a month or so later. Both Jacob and Benny were able to come home on leave, and for the first time since the war—which was now in its third year—Nahum was able to have a sizable family gathering at the *seder*. Lotie's brother, Edgar, was in London, as a member of a U.S. government delegation (he was very secretive about it, but it turned out that he was negotiating a contract for the supply of powdered eggs), and came up to Glasgow for the occasion.

As such meals go, it was an austere one, for wartime shortages had begun to bite and, given the quantity of wine at his disposal, Nahum was not able to offer his guests the full four cups which the occasion demanded, but it was in some ways the most memorable *seder* of his life. At one end of the table, Benny, who was working in an army VD clinic, was discussing tertiary syphilis with Jacob's wife, Gladys. At another, Jacob was describing to a not particularly enthralled Lotie the problems of attempting to educate an army which was largely illiterate.

"We've had compulsory education now for nearly seventy years," he was saying. "It's got us nowhere, it's got them nowhere; they'd have been better off going down the mines at eleven, and we would at least have had some coal to show for it, don't you think?"

Edgar—who, Nahum reckoned, must have been nearly seventy and who looked nearer fifty—was in close conversation with Trude, a hand on her knee, an arm thrown over the back of her chair. Nahum was preoccupied mainly with his two grandchildren and Jacob's in-laws. Sometimes, when he sat back and surveyed the scene, he thought he might burst with gladness and felt almost guilty—even slightly apprehensive—at harbouring so much pleasure.

Towards the end of the evening, he banged the table with a fork for silence and stood up.

"I know it's not usual to make speeches at the *seder*," he said, "but I hope you'll excuse me if I say a few words."

"We won't excuse you," said Edgar.

"He's a rabbi manqué," said Lotie. "Whenever he sees more than ten people at a table, he can't resist making a speech."

"It won't be long," Nahum assured them, "just one or two words."

"You've already said three or four," Edgar interjected, "but please continue."

At that moment, the door-bell rang.

"It's an air-raid warden to say we've got a light showing," said Lotie.

Someone went to the door and found a tall figure in a large greatcoat outside. It was a cold, foggy night, and the figure was barely visible amidst the surrounding gloom.

"A merry Christmas," he said and stepped inside. His face was red, his moustache was bushy and grey, and he had the pips and shoulder-flash of a captain in the Canadian Army.

It was Hector.

CHAPTER XXXIII
PRODIGAL DAUGHTER

DEAR SOPH,
Hi.

It's about three years since I last heard from you, and it must be nearer four since you heard from me, and I may perhaps be presumptuous in believing that you want to hear from me at all, but, as you can imagine, I've had good reasons for my silence.

You may not believe this—for it makes me sound uncharacteristically innocent and naive—but I had no idea what either Eddy or Hector was up to, and I am not even sure that I know now. I suppose, if I had had my wits about me, I might have realised that the sort of money they were making did not quite go with their shabby little warehouse, but if I didn't have my wits about me, it was partly because I was using my best endeavours to bring forth.

As I may have mentioned, I never have any difficulty in getting started but have every difficulty in getting finished, and I've lost count of the miscarriages I've had, but then, after a further try about three years ago, it looked as if the wretched thing was finally beginning to take root. It meant I had to take things easy, in fact, lie on my back most of the time, which was torture, but I was prepared to face it. Then, early one morning, the phone rang. I don't know who phoned, or what it was about, but there was the sound of the apocalypse in that call. Eddy dressed quickly and almost ran from the house, saying he would be back. He never did come back, but he phoned about three hours later to say that there was a car on the way to me and that I should leave everything and be ready to be picked up in ten minutes. I said that I would do nothing of the sort and that I was staying put where I was, whatever happened, and he said: "You be in that bloody car," and put the phone down. There was such menace in his voice that, for the first time in my life, I was frightened. I did as I was told, and ten minutes later I was in that bloody car, and bloody it was, for —what with my bewilderment and anxiety—I began bleeding there and then, though not badly. We crossed to Dieppe that day, and the following morning we sailed on a Greek coaster. I miscarried that night and was so sick and depressed that, as soon as I could summon enough energy, I tried to jump overboard. It later occurred to me that I must have made the attempt about the same time as poor Ara, only I had Eddy and Hector to restrain me, while poor Ara had no one. We laid low for a time in Tangier, where Hector heard about poor Ara. He became an old man, or at least an elderly man, almost overnight. He always looked the soldier, martial, erect, whether in uniform or in mufti, but his head went to the side and he began to sag. It hadn't occurred to me that he had cared all that much for Ara. Father, of course, loved her, and I hate to think what the news must have done to him, but I always felt that Hector had married her in the line of duty, that he never really cared for any woman, and that he took on Ara because it was expected of him. It seems I was wrong. I, on the other hand, thought I loved Eddy, but after the miscarriage I began to hate him and I would have shopped him a hundred times but didn't —partly because I was afraid of him, and partly because I didn't want to implicate Hector—but I didn't let him come near me.

After Tangier we went on to Mexico, where I spent what was almost certainly the blackest year of my life. Not that things have been particularly jolly since, but Mexico was the lower depths. We stayed in a third-rate hotel in a fly-blown little resort on the Pacific coast. The heat was intense, with dirt, mosquitoes, flies everywhere and sandstorms, hardly anyone to talk to and nothing to do. Hector and Eddy spent most of their time playing cards. I tried to engage Hector in conversation, but he has little to say at the best of times and had even less then, except last thing at night. He slept very badly, and I would come into his room, lie down on his bed, put my cheek against his, and he would put his arms around me, which we both found intensely comforting, and we would talk for hours on end.

He never mentioned why he and Eddy had had to run for it, and I have never questioned him about it, as if there was a tacit understanding that the subject was taboo. We spoke mainly about Father, whom he adores, and the regrets he felt about causing him so much anxiety, but what were the anxieties he caused compared to those brought on by me? Then, to add to my other joys, I caught malaria. My life was saved by a German Jewish doctor, who had only arrived in town the previous month, but I haven't shaken it off completely, and I get return bouts about once a year. In an odd way, I tend to look back on that year in Mexico with a certain amount of thanksgiving, as my own private purgatory, and if I have not quite been the true "daughter of Israel" Father hoped for, I think I may have paid for my sins, possibly with interest.

When the war broke out, we thought it safe to cross the border into America, moving first into Arizona, then into New Mexico, travelling furtively across America like a louse over a bedspread, and we finally surfaced in Buffalo, near the Canadian border, where we took a house and began to lead an almost normal life. My hatred for Eddy abated, and about six months ago he and Hector joined the Canadian Army. I don't know if they'd covered up their past, or if it was overlooked or ignored, but they have both received commissions. Eddy was home on embarkation leave a few days ago, and they have since been posted overseas. Where, I know not.

I have a job in a local library, send parcels to Britain, have several friends and for the first time in years, I am not unhappy, though I am a little homesick for Glasgow.

That's my story to date. What's yours? How is Yankelson? How are the twins? They must be young men by now.

Please write.

Love,

Vicky

CHAPTER XXXIV
PRODIGAL SON

NAHUM OFTEN WONDERED HOW HE WOULD RECEIVE HECTOR IF HE were ever to see him again. He was answered in a moment— with open arms. But in an odd way, his unexpected arrival shattered the euphoria of the evening. Nahum had felt elevated into a mellow, tranquil universe, and Hector had arrived trailing echoes of a turbulent past, and he looked and sounded as if he had been drinking. His face was flushed, his manner was boisterous, his words were slurred. He embraced Nahum with uncommon fervour. He kissed Lotie on her mouth and neck. He even kissed Gladys, but when he saw Trude, he stopped as if he had suddenly turned sober.

"Don't I know you?" he said.

"No, no, I don't think so."

"This is your cousin," said Nahum, "my sister's daughter."

"From Russia?"

"From Russia, America, Germany, but she's now here, with us to stay. But tell me, what are you doing in uniform? How do you happen to be here?"

"I've come to win the war."

"But why the Canadian Army? What's wrong with the British Army?"

"They're less fussy about who and what they take in the Canadian Army. At my age, I'm lucky to be in uniform at all."

Nahum asked him about Vicky and was reassured to learn that she was happy and well. There were a thousand other questions he would have liked to ask, but he did not feel this was the time for them, especially with Jacob's in-laws at table, and he had not quite finished the *seder*.

As Nahum was settling into bed that night, Lotie said to him: "Did you see the looks Trude was giving Hector? I could understand her feelings exactly. It reminded me of the time I first set eyes on you."

"I wouldn't like them to marry," said Nahum.

"Typical, typical. A couple have only to set eyes on each other, and he already talks about marriage."

"All I'm saying is, I don't like marriages in the family. I've never known a marriage between cousins to work out happily, either for the couple or their children."

"They're not blood relatives."

"I know they're not, but I would still be much happier if they married outside the family. I like the family to grow outwards, not inwards."

Hector had to leave the next day, but he was back a few weeks later and spent most of his time with Trude. He remained the better part of a week, and when he left, Lotie could not help observing that his bed had hardly been slept in.

"Either they danced all night," she said, "or they've been naughty."

"There's a war on," said Nahum.

The fact that he now had three sons in uniform made him feel that his own contribution to the war effort was grossly inadequate. He had, in fact, offered his services in various capacities—as auxiliary policeman, as auxiliary fireman, as air-raid warden—in the early stages of the war but was told that he was too old, which he would have accepted as an answer were it not for the sight of withered, white-haired ancients, ten years his senior, hobbling around in uniforms of various sorts. He wondered if the refusals he encountered did not have something to do with the fact that he was a foreigner, and a Russian foreigner at that, and he kept protesting that, though he had been born and brought up in Russia, he regarded Russia as an enemy, not only of the Jews, but of mankind. All that changed dramatically in June 1941 after Hitler invaded the Soviet Union and Russia became an ally.

Nahum spent much of his free time, and not a few of his working hours, listening to the radio and followed the news bulletins in English, German and Russian, which he knew well, as well as Polish and Czech, of which, knowing Russian, he understood a smattering. He also followed broadcasts from Germany, and he was particularly addicted to the smooth tones of Lord Haw-Haw of whom Lotie, who was equally addicted, gave a good imitation. Both of them made it a point to be at home for the sound of Big Ben followed by the nine o'clock news, and on Sunday evenings this practice became elevated almost to the level of a religious ritual, for then the news was preceded by the national anthems of Britain's allies. The use of the anthems, presumably, was to reassure people that Britain was not alone, but the effect on Nahum was quite the contrary. Although he enjoyed the tunes, especially the "Marseillaise," the anthems of Poland, Norway, Belgium, France, Holland, Yugoslavia, Greece—all of which had been over-run by Hitler—seemed more like a celebration of German victories, and the further the Germans advanced, the more rapidly the allies multiplied. But with Russia as an ally, his attitude changed, for, even as Hitler was cutting through Russia like a heated snowplow, he could not see Russia being taken, there was just too much of her. "You can wound Russia," he said, "but you can't kill her." He experienced strange stirrings in his blood when he heard the Russian national anthem, and he found himself overwhelmed with a latent Russian patriotism he never knew he possessed. It was an odd sensation for a Jew to find himself in a position to cheer Russia with a full heart, and Nahum gloried in the opportunity. He began to speak warmly of his Volkovysk boyhood—of the plains, the lakes, the forests—of the intensity and warmth of the Russian character and the resilience, the stoicism and strength of the Russian peasant.

"You know, if you wanted to describe somebody as strong, muscular, a real man in Yiddish, a he-man, you called him a cossack," he recalled. "The Germans will never beat the Russians, not in the long run."

The entry of Russia in the war affected the synagogual life of the community. The synagogues had become desolate places. Lights were kept dim, and heating was kept low (or off) to save fuel, the children were evacuated to the countryside or seaside, the young men were in the forces, and the small handful of the old and the elderly who still came to synagogue sat huddled in their overcoats with troubled looks on their faces and muttering in anxious voices. Once Russia was in the war, however, they seemed rejuvenated. Their voices became louder and more confident, and everyone, certainly everyone who came from Russia, became a strategist.

"Do you know how big Russia is? You can travel a week and still be nowhere. . . . A tank isn't a horse, you know, you can't whip it along for a bit of extra effort if it runs out of petrol. . . . The Germans may be doing well now, but Stalin is giving them rope to hang themselves. . . . Wait till he throws the cossacks at them. . . . They'll never cross the Diniva . . . the Dnieper . . . the Don . . . the Beresina . . . the Volga. Tanks don't swim. . . . Once they get in really far, they won't be able to get their armies, they'll starve. . . . Trust old Stalin, he knows what he's doing . . . he's Georgian, they've always been known for their cunning, the Georgians."

Someone had heard that one of the Russian marshalls was Jewish.

"Timoshenko, I think."

"Not Timoshenko, Rokossovsky."

"Can't be Rokossovsky."

"Why not?"

"He's in the cavalry."

"So?"

"A Jew in the cavalry's possible—I had an uncle in the cavalry—but a cavalry marshall? Impossible."

"Since the revolution, everything's possible. And besides, Rokossovsky's a Jewish name."

"Voroshilov's a Jewish name. They're all Jewish names. They can't all be Jews."

Mrs Winston Churchill launched an aid to Russia fund, and Lotie promptly threw herself into the activities of the Glasgow branch, and, although she continued to complain of penury and that rising prices were eating away what little money she had, she donated five hundred pounds from her own account. Nahum organised special charity performances for the same cause and devoted one of his cinemas to Russian films. The quality of the films was not always of the highest, and apart from the first few nights when the cinema was packed with Jewish exiles, who would sigh over glimpses of the old country—attendance was sparse, but he felt it was his contribution to the war effort.

When, at the end of that year, America was also drawn into the war, the dominant opinion in the synagogue was that the war would end within months, if not weeks, an opinion which was revised as Japanese armies swept across Asia, and there was much shaking of heads when they over-ran not only the Philippines and the Dutch East Indies, but huge, pink-coloured chunks of the British Empire.

"They're giving them rope so that they can hang themselves," said a knowing voice.

"They're waiting till they come nearer India, so that they can throw the *schwartzes* at them. . . ."

"So even if the Japanese have got Burma, who needs Burma?"

"They're letting them get away with it, because they're preparing to invade Europe. That's the place that counts, Europe. What's happening out there is a side-show."

American troops soon began to appear in Glasgow, and Lotie threw open her home as a clubhouse for American servicemen, preferably of commissioned rank, though one could also encounter the occasional non-commissioned officer or even private.

Trude was a constant centre of attention. Nahum had offered her a job as a cashier in one of his cinemas, but she couldn't—or said she couldn't—count, and she found work as a nursing auxiliary in a local hospital. She would return home at night, white-faced with lank hair and on the point of collapse, but she had only to immerse herself in a bath for ten minutes and emerge a new woman, but she could rarely be induced to go out.

"Why doesn't she?" asked Nahum. "She should be enjoying herself while she can—especially after what she's been through."

"She's carrying a torch for Hector," explained Lotie.

"I don't think he's carrying a torch for her. She's got all these attractive young men coming to this house, why doesn't she go out with one of them?"

"Perhaps they've come to see me," said Lotie, which was indeed often the case, for, though nearly sixty, she continued to be a very attractive woman. Her face was beginning to acquire lines, but she knew how to hide them. Her eyes were lustrous, her figure was firm, her legs were shapely and free of protrusions. Her throat, which sometimes became red and raw, suggested her years, but otherwise she remained a pleasure to look at, and not a few of the men who came to court the younger woman remained to admire the older one.

One evening, Nahum came home and found a jeep parked outside his house, and, as he entered, he was greeted by a cloud of cigar smoke and the sound of a loud American voice.

Lotie was entertaining a lieutenant colonel to tea, a familiar figure in unfamiliar garb, with two rows of ribbon on his chest.

It was Kapulski who immediately rose and advanced upon him with an open hand.

"I knew you had a beautiful daughter and daughter-in-law, but you never told me you had such a beautiful and charming wife."

"I bet he's offered to put you into films," Nahum said to Lotie.

"He has."

"She's a natural. What Hollywood lacks is class, and class is what she's got."

He asked if he could take Lotie out to dinner.

"You had better ask her," said Nahum, "she's a big girl now." Nahum thought she would refuse, but she accepted with enthusiasm and rushed upstairs to see if there was anything left in her wardrobe worthy of the occasion. A few minutes later they were off, she looking a trifle out of place in Kapulski's battered jeep.

Nahum went into the kitchen to fry himself an egg and wondered what was happening to his womenfolk. Lotie was of an age when women in *der heim* became wrinkled old *babushkas*, wrapped up in shawls and self-pity, whereas Lotie seemed to be enjoying a second spring. He was proud of her appearance and took some pleasure in the fact that men still found her attractive. This was not the first time she had been taken out by an American officer, but her previous escorts had been remote relatives or friends of her family—decorous, sedate men—and even when she had returned in the early hours of the morning, he had felt satisfied that the association was innocent, but there was nothing staid or decorous about Kapulski, and he wondered if perhaps in this instance . . .

It seemed a ridiculous thought, but he could not dismiss it, yet what bothered him more than the possibility that his wife could be unfaithful was the thought that she could be unfaithful with a creature like Kapulski.

As he was eating, he heard the front door open, and Trude entered.

"You're late," said Nahum.

"This is my late night. Is Lotie in bed?"

"Lotie in bed? You don't know my wife. She's run off with an American soldier."

She looked at him aghast. "She *hasn't!*"

"You don't mean you believed me."

"I don't know when to believe you or not. I've never been able to get used to the English sense of humour."

Nahum found the fact that she could have believed him, even for a moment, disturbing.

"You shouldn't joke about such things," she continued. "American women don't seem to age. You're living for your children and grandchildren, and don't forget they're not *her* children and grandchildren. She's youthful enough to live for herself. American soldiers seem to go in for mature women—perhaps they miss their mothers."

"Not the soldier she went out with. I don't think he ever had a mother. He was found under a rock."

"Why don't you take her out sometime?"

"Take her out? Dear child, there's a war on."

"All the more reason."

He felt she had a point, and a few weeks later he took Lotie out, together with Trude and Benny. Benny was about to be posted overseas and was home on embarkation leave. It was not a particularly happy occasion. Benny was not sure where he was being posted, but he presumed it was somewhere in the tropics, for he had been pumped full of vaccines for every conceivable disorder—from yellow fever to the black death—and was beginning to feel their effects. He was sweating profusely, but he managed to raise a weak smile and said: "I think the vaccinations are part of the acclimatisation course. If you survive them, you can survive anything." When he stood up to go to the toilet, he swayed slightly as if he were about to faint, and they hurriedly summoned a taxi and took him home.

He spent the next day in bed. Trude looked after him, and when he got up the following morning to leave, both she and Gladys insisted that he delay his departure. Nahum pleaded with him to listen to them: "Trude is a nurse, you know, and Gladys is a doctor, they're not speaking from the top of their heads."

"I'm also something of a doctor," he reminded him, "and my prognosis is that I shall just about survive."

"Don't be an idiot," said Gladys, "your pulse is racing, go back to bed."

"That's because you're holding my hand. Now, if you'll excuse me." And a few minutes later, he was gone.

His departure filled Nahum with a sharp sense of foreboding. He had not experienced the anxieties in the second world war—except after Dunkirk, when there was the threat of invasion—that he had felt in the first. There wasn't the same incessant slaughter, and none of his children had been posted overseas, but with the departure of Benny, he felt as if he were suddenly back in the midst of World War I. He was aware that wherever Benny would be going, he wouldn't be facing the sort of dangers met by Hector in Flanders, but Hector was built for danger, whereas Benny—with his slight size, little ginger moustache and thick glasses—looked so small, so boyish, so vulnerable that the idea of him being a soldier at all seemed vaguely laughable, and from the day he left, Nahum braced himself for the worst. When he looked back on his life, his fortunes and misfortunes seemed to go in cycles—three or four good years, followed by three or four bad. He had now, in spite of the war, had three fairly good years and began to look apprehensively into the future. The more he had to be thankful for, the more vulnerable he felt, and, in moments of morbid contemplation, he would ask himself what form misfortune would take if it struck next, and whom would it strike. Benny? Hector? Jacob? (In an odd way, he had few worries about Jacob, as if he thought misfortune had no time for people like him.) Trude? Vicky? Sophie and her children? Or would Lotie perhaps leave him? He tried to dismiss such thoughts and recalled an old saying which his father often quoted: "If you prepare too well for the worst, you sometimes invite it."

Towards the end of the summer he had to be in London on business and wrote to Hector, who was stationed somewhere in the south, to join him for a meal in the Savoy, and Hector replied that he hoped to snatch an evening's leave to be there, failing which he would desert.

Nahum's train was delayed by repairs on the line, and when he reached the Savoy, he was afraid that Hector might have come and gone, but he was told that there had been no callers. He waited for a while but presumed that Hector couldn't make it, and it was about ten before he sat down to eat, with an evening paper propped up against the flower vase.

There had been an allied landing in force on the French coast at Dieppe earlier in the week. When he first heard the news, he had thought the "second front" had finally opened, but it soon became clear that it was a far more limited operation, and, as details began to emerge, it became evident that even that had not worked out as planned, and there was speculation in the papers on what, if anything, had gone wrong.

He was mildly depressed about it all, for the allies were suffering setbacks on every front—in Russia, in the Far East, in the Middle East—and they seemed incapable of staging an even limited operation without bungling it.

It never occurred to him that the news he was reading at that moment was to have a dramatic effect on him personally.

CHAPTER XXXV
EMERGENCY WARD

LOTIE WAS ALWAYS NERVOUS ABOUT HIS JOURNEYS TO LONDON; ever since the blitz, she had regarded it as a war zone, and he made it a rule to phone her last thing at night to assure her that everything was all right.

The lines were extremely busy that night, and it was nearly midnight before he could get through to Glasgow, and even then he could get no reply. He tried again half an hour later, and there was still no reply; instead of reassuring his wife, he was left feeling worried himself.

He had a busy round of meetings the next day and was not free to phone until the afternoon, but again there was no reply. He tried once more in the evening. This time Trude answered, and as soon as he heard her voice—she had said only, "Is that you, Nahum,"—he had the feeling that something unfortunate had happened.

"I have bad news," she said and paused for what seemed like an eternity. "Hector has been taken prisoner."

"Hector? I thought he was in London. I was to have had dinner with him last night."

"No, no. He was in the Dieppe landings and was taken prisoner-of-war."

"Is he all right? He wasn't injured or anything like that?"

"They only say he was taken prisoner," and she hesitated, as if there was worse to come, "and your son-in-law—"

"Son-in-law?"

"Major Edward Cameron."

"Was he also in the landings?"

"So it seems. He was severely injured and died of his wounds."

The name had come like a bolt from the blue. He had almost forced himself to forget about him. He had suspected that when Hector returned, Cameron was also somewhere about, but he hadn't dared to ask, as if afraid that the very mention of the name might pollute the air. He should have been overjoyed at the death of a man who had been the cause, directly or indirectly, of so many misfortunes, and yet, now that he was dead, he could feel only grief.

And again he could not fathom his own responses. Was he grief-stricken because he could not disentangle the news of Cameron from the news of Hector, or was it because he felt the pain which he thought Vicky must be feeling? He could not think properly alone in his hotel room. He wanted to know more details, to talk to Trude, to Lotie, to someone.

He looked at his watch. There was a train leaving for Glasgow in forty minutes. He grabbed his case, threw his few belongings into it and dashed into the street for a taxi. He managed to get fairly quickly out of the Strand and into the Aldwych, but halfway along Southampton Row the traffic came to a halt. He waited impatiently for three or four minutes, then he got out of the taxi and, with his case in hand, ran the half-mile or so to Euston and boarded the train as it was about to pull out of the station. He pushed his way along the entire length of the train, dragging his case, but there was not a seat to be had. The corridors were jammed with troops, and finally, after trying in vain to find a place in a toilet, he settled himself in a corner of the guard's van, sat down on his case, pulled a paper from his pocket and began reading. As he did so, the words started to dance before his eyes, perspiration formed on his brow and he gently keeled over.

He didn't know what happened next, or how long he had remained unconscious, but when he opened his eyes, he was in a hospital bed with Lotie sitting by his side, a bouquet in her hand.

"Where am I?" he asked.

"Tring," she said.

"Where?"

"Tring. A charming little place. I remember coming here as a child once. The Rothschilds have a place near here, or had."

"What am I doing here?"

"Resting. I don't know what you were doing with yourself in London, but you dropped from exhaustion."

Then he remembered. "Hector, Vicky—"

"Hector will be all right. I was a bit worried myself when I heard he was in German hands, but I spoke to a neighbour whose son was taken prisoner at Dunkirk. They're very correct in their treatment of prisoners-of-war, Jewish or otherwise. As for Vicky, I cabled her, suggesting she come back to Glasgow. I also cabled Edgar—who, as you know, lives in Vermont—to go up to see her, which he did, and he brought her back to stay with him. She's seven months pregnant."

"Vicky? Pregnant?"

"But she's all right, and everything will be all right, so will you, if you have a good rest."

"And Trude, how did she take the news? She seemed very calm on the phone."

"She's still very calm—in fact, she hardly said anything, though I could imagine how she felt, and I finally said to her: 'There's nothing wrong with tears. You can cry if you want, I'll cry with you,' and she said, 'No, I half expected it. He's alive. It could have been worse.'"

Nahum felt restive, if not quite rested, after about two days in bed, but Lotie made him stay in hospital for a week before allowing him to take the train back to Glasgow, and she did not let him resume work for a further week.

"You're not a wife, or even a nurse," he protested, "you're a jailer."

He tried to resume his normal routine but felt jittery and unsettled, possibly because the old adage, that misfortunes hunted in packs kept coming back to him, and he didn't really begin to relax or feel his normal self until a telegram arrived from America. He was half afraid to open it and asked Lotie to od it for him. Vicky had had an eight-pound boy, and both mother and son were well.

"Are you happy now?" Lotie asked. "Or were you expecting twins?"

Nahum couldn't wait to see them both and began to look into the possibility of travelling to America.

"You're mad," said Lotie, "you won't get on a boat, and if you do, you'll go down with it."

He had possibly not recovered from his earlier collapse, or perhaps the excitement of the news from Vicky, plus the frustration of his inability to see her, was too much for him, for a week later he was taken ill at work and brought home in a taxi. His temperature soared, his pulse was racing and he had turned deathly pale.

His doctor came, examined him at length and shrugged his shoulders.

"I can tell you what it isn't; as for what it is, God only knows. I could send for another chap. I shouldn't imagine he'll know, either, but he'll probably find a name for it." The other chap was sent for, but Nahum's pulse and temperature were almost back to normal by the time he came.

"I suspect," he said, "that you had touch of the flu and were walking around with it for longer than was good for you, but if it happens again, we'll have to take you into hospital for a close look."

It happened again a few weeks later, and he was rushed into hospital. He felt extremes of hot and cold and recurring dizziness.

"You know," he said to Lotie, "I think I'm dying."

"Now, Nahum darling, don't talk nonsense."

"What makes you think I'm talking nonsense?"

"Because you're not dying."

"Who should know if I'm dying or not, you or me? That's been my trouble all along, my word's never counted for anything in my household. I tell her I'm dying, and she tells me I'm talking nonsense."

"All right dear, have it your way, you're dying."

"It doesn't seem to worry you, but then, why should it? I'm leaving a fortune, you've got your own money, you'll be well looked after. You'll probably marry one of those Americans—Kapulski, or someone like that." Then he turned and looked around him. "Where's everybody?"

"What do you mean, everybody?"

"Does nobody want to visit me?"

"Nahum, dear, you only entered hospital this morning."

"Does Trude know I'm here?"

"She knows and will be coming later."

"Have you cabled Sophie, Vicky?"

"No."

"What are you waiting for, till I'm in my grave? Not that they would care if I were."

He wanted to redraft his will and asked young Krochmal, his solicitor, to come around to see him, but Krochmal was in the army, and an elderly clerk came instead. Nahum sent him home with a flea in his ear.

"If I pay Krochmal, I expect Krochmal. If he can't come, I can die comfortably without him."

By chance, Krochmal happened to be on leave the next day and came to see him, a neat little figure in a neat little uniform, with large glasses on his nose and three pips on each shoulder. Nahum looked at him disdainfully.

"You an officer, too? Everybody seems to be an officer. Don't they have privates in the British Army anymore? It's getting to be like the Polish Army."

"Is that what you wanted to see me about?"

"I want to make my will."

"You've made it."

"I want to remake it."

"You've remade it."

"I want to remake it again, do you mind? Are you listening?"

"I'm listening."

"I'm leaving my wife half my estate."

"If she survives you."

"What do you mean, *if* she survives me? Why shouldn't she survive me?

"Because wives sometimes don't."

"Have you seen my wife? She's good for another thirty years."

"You may be good for another forty."

"Another forty, eh? It's a good job you're a solicitor, Krochmal, not a doctor."

"You were saying, half your estate to your wife."

"Yes, half. Mind you, why half? She's got money of her own, you know."

"I didn't."

"I think she has. She must have. Do you know who her father was?"

"I do, but her father's in the ground, and so is his business."

"So you mean she mightn't have anything?"

"I don't know, you should know."

"The funny thing is, the one thing we don't talk about is money. All right, I'll leave her half—but supposing she marries? Of course she'll marry, attractive woman like her, she'll be snatched off. Why should I have to provide for some rich American—Kapulski, maybe—who's got lots of money of his own?"

Krochmal closed his notebook with a snap and rose to his feet. "I'll be back tomorrow when you're better."

"I could be dead tomorrow."

"So could we all."

He was having a doze the following afternoon, and when he opened his eyes he found Gladys by his side. He closed them again quickly, but when he reopened them she was still there.

"I'm sorry I haven't called before, but the children were both down with assorted disorders, so I had my hands full. Now, what's the matter?"

"You're asking me? You're the doctor."

"I've been looking at the records. They don't make sense. The symptoms are contradictory."

"Who says that symptoms have to agree with each other?"

"No, but your symptoms, taken together, suggest that you're dead, whereas you show passing indications of being alive. Can I have a look at you?"

"You are looking at me."

"I mean properly."

"What do you mean by properly?"

She said nothing but rolled up her sleeves and arranged the screen around his bed. When she tried to whip off his blankets, he struggled to hold them back, but she won. His pyjamas were undone, and he instinctively clasped his hands over his genitals, as if fearing rape. She made him remove his pyjamas and began handling his testicles, the effect of which was to give him an erection like a barge-pole, and he half feared—or half hoped—that she might mount him. He had never imagined that he could have thought of his daughter-in-law in such a context.

"How old are you?" she asked.

"Sixty-seven," he said with a slight swagger, hoping that she might comment approvingly on his salute (he thought she should have been flattered); instead she asked:

"How often do you go to the toilet?"

"What do you mean?"

"How often do you urinate?"

"I don't keep count. Who does? Do you?"

"Do you have to get up in the night?"

"Yes."

"How often?"

"Two or three times."

She slipped on a pair of rubber gloves and made him turn over on his stomach. He didn't know what she did next, but he had the feeling that she might be climbing up his anus. She then subjected him to further sundry humiliations before rolling down her sleeves.

"Well," he asked, trying to resume what dignity he could muster, "will I live?"

"Either that," she said, "or you won't."

She came back the next day with Lotie and told him that she had spoken to his doctors, and the general consensus was that he had returned to work too early and that he should eat less and walk more.

"And it took them a week to find that out?"

"They go through a patient process of elimination," said Lotie.

"And sometimes eliminate the patient in the process," said Gladys.

Although Lotie appeared to make light of his illness, she began to wonder if it had not been psychosomatic and asked Gladys if it might not be useful to consult a psychiatrist.

"Good heavens, no. This isn't America, where people are half expected to be off their chump. Leave well alone."

"But he's not all that well."

"Then leave ill alone."

When he left hospital, he and Lotie went up together to the high-lands. It was winter. The skies were clear, the air was sharp. The ground was firm underfoot, with a thick covering of leaves and pine needles, and they strolled together, arms about each other like lovers.

"If people could see us like this, they would laugh," he said.

"Let them."

They paused. There wasn't a sound to be heard except the noise of a distant tractor.

"You wouldn't think there was a war on, would you?" he said. "And that people were being killed." His voice broke as tears came into his eyes. "Poor Cameron."

Lotie wiped his eyes and blew his nose, and they sat down on a log pile.

"There's something about Cameron I don't understand," she said. "From what you told me about him, he must have been in his mid-fifties. Isn't that a bit old for a soldier?"

"I could show you generals in their eighties."

"Yes, but he was only a junior officer. I never thought they sent men of that age into action."

"He must have falsified his papers. There's a dreadful irony in that. He's been falsifying things all his life, and he may have falsified his way to an early death. But still, I'm upset. The man died a hero, and he was the father of my grandchild. And I can't help wondering what'll happen to Vicky. What that poor child's been through."

"She hasn't been through anything that she hasn't brought upon herself."

"It's true, but it's no consolation."

"Isn't it time you started thinking about yourself a little, and about us?"

"Us?"

"You and me. It's something you've never really done, and it's something you should do, before it's too late."

There was something ominous about the sound of "too late," and he asked her if Gladys had told her anything she hadn't told him. She looked at the ground for some time before answering.

"Yes, as a matter of fact. The doctors haven't gotten to the root of your trouble, but they suspect that what happened before will keep happening again, with increasing frequency and increasing intensity. The only remedy they can suggest is rest. She thinks you should retire."

"Retire? What are you talking about? My business is being run by schoolboys and old women as it is. If I were to retire now, the whole thing would fall to pieces. The least I can do is to hang on till the war's over."

"Who knows when it'll be over? I think you should sell out if you can."

"In the middle of the war? And what'll I do with myself if I do sell out?"

"You wouldn't have said that five or ten years ago, when you used to rush home early from work and couldn't stand the thought of being away from me. You've changed."

"I haven't. People don't change. They fade a bit, they become mellow, but they don't change."

"I'd have killed myself long ago if I had thought that. Do you remember what I was like when you first met me—silly, hare-brained, garrulous? I could never start thinking because I could never stop talking, and for many years afterwards when I thought back on some of the things I said and did—and I wasn't a child any more, but an adult woman—I shuddered. Perhaps with the sort of upbringing I had, it took me a long time to grow up, but I have grown up, and I have changed. So have you; you're more purposeful, determined, more self-assured—not always, perhaps. When Hector appears, I think you have the feeling you've got to jump to attention and salute, but otherwise you're much more of a man than you were, which is perhaps why you're less loving. I sometimes think that the only really affectionate men are effeminate. You seem to go away more often than you used to and to stay away longer. Have you grown tired of me? Don't you like being with me like this?"

He pulled her close to him and sat with his cheek against hers. "Of course I do."

"We won't have many more opportunities to do this if you don't retire."

"But Lotie, my love, I've still got dependents—Vicky, Trude."

"They'll both marry, and Vicky must be getting a pension—a generous one, probably. The Canadian Army is not the British Army. Besides, you can trust Edgar to look after her."

"But why should Edgar have to look after my daughter?"

"He doesn't have to, but you know Edgar."

"I don't know Edgar."

She sighed and said, half to herself: "Perhaps it's just as well that you don't."

CHAPTER XXXVI
THE YANKS HAVE COME

Dear Sophie,

Sorry for the delay in writing. It's taken me some time to collect my thoughts and, I suppose, myself together.

It's surprising what you can get through and get over if you have to, but, although I wouldn't have thought so, it helps to be pregnant.

An elderly army chaplain came to bring me the news, but when he saw my condition he felt he couldn't do it, but he didn't have to; his face told me everything, and he broke down and cried, which is more than I did, for by then I was convinced that whatever I had growing inside me was mine for keeps, and I think you will understand what I'm saying if I should tell you that it made Eddy's death seem impermanent.

Edgar (Lotie's brother) arrived that same day, scooped me up and took me back with him, and I was too dazed to protest. I am not quite sure what he does for a living, but whatever it is, he does very well, and he has a very large farm in Vermont, which is managed by his wife, who, I had been led to believe, was some sort of grand duchess. If one looks at her closely, one can still see about her face and figure relics of a fairly handsome appearance, but she reminds me mainly of a stately home which has come upon hard times, and she squelches around the place in Wellington boots with a clip-board under her arm and a pencil over her ear, and her talk is all of Fresians and calvings and milk yields. They have over four hundred head of cattle and two sons, one in the army and one in the navy, both serving somewhere in the Pacific.

Edgar is tall, white-haired and distinguished-looking, though I seem to remember him as being large and portly. He's been my fairy godfather, almost had an obstetrician in residence to look after me, and when it seemed that the birth might be a troublesome one, he arranged to have me taken to hospital, and the child—all eight pounds of him —was eventually delivered by Caesarian section. There were certain post-natal complications—of which more later—but they had nothing to do with the actual birth. I have called the boy Edward Charles (though, as an admirer of Bonnie Prince Charlie, I was tempted to call him Charles Edward), and he was circumcised in the hospital (as I believe most American boys are), though without any of the mumbo jumbo about the "Covenant of Abraham" (thank God). Father wrote to assure me that in Jewish life the identity of the father is immaterial, and that the child was "one hundred percent Jewish" and he hopes that he'll get "a good Jewish upbringing." I think that he's hoping he'll become a rabbi and atone for the sins of his father, to say nothing of the sins of his mother—which brings me to my post-natal problems, for I was hardly delivered of one child when my fairy godfather suggested that he was in a mood to get started on another. I think he looks upon it as his way of keeping up morale on the home front. He told me of all his conquests when he brought me breakfast in bed one morning, and they made Don Giovanni sound like a Trappist. Then, to climax the account, he threw off his dressing-gown, but I said no, not with my corn-flakes, and managed to fend him off with a fork. There have, however, been occasions when I was less well armed and less successful—besides, we all have our duties to the old. His wife's concern about his habits does not, I think, extend beyond curiosity. We were drinking coffee in the kitchen one morning when she asked me, in the sort of tone one might use to comment on the weather, if "the old goat" had tried to ravish me yet. The question was so unexpected that I blurted out a confession, and she said: "I'm not surprised, though one might have thought he'd wait till your uterus had snapped back. He tries them all, you know, young and old, black and white. Sometimes, in a fit of forgetfulness, he even finds his way into my bed, but, of course, I throw him out."

I think I would have been able to cope with Edgar, but in America every woman on her own—especially if she seems to be permanently on her own—is regarded as fair game, and I could hardly set foot out of doors without feeling a horny hand on my buttocks, which became a bore. Nor am I naturally cut out for the joys of rustic life. I began to yearn for Glasgow. When I told Edgar, he couldn't believe it and said: "London, yes; Paris, yes. But Glasgow? It's like yearning for Scranton. Hell, things can't be that bad here." Once he saw I was in earnest, however, he thought I was mad. Didn't I know there was a war on? The Atlantic crossing was extremely hazardous—the waters were teeming with U-boats—and he said I had no right to risk my life, and certainly not the life of the child. In any case, he didn't think I would be able to get on a boat, and if I did, he said he would get a court order to restrain me. Finally, as a sort of compromise, he got me a flat in New York.

Incidentally, while in New York I was visited by a sinister-looking figure with a short beard, a long nose and a Glaswegian accent, who didn't say who he was but claimed to be a friend of the family. He asked if I was being looked after, and I assured him that I was, and he questioned me at length about Hector, whom he had met in Egypt (I don't know when) and who, he said, was a hero. He wanted to know his address, but I couldn't help, and I was reluctant to give him Father's address (though, presumably, if he really is a friend of the family, he must have it). He's a man of about sixty-five or seventy and looks well-heeled materially, if decrepit personally, and I suspect that he's had more than his share of life's disappointments. I have the feeling that I've seen him somewhere before. I don't suppose you would know who he could be?

I have made quite a few friends, including a young major—a lawyer in civilian life—who wants to marry me, but I feel rather hesitant on the matter, first of all because I have only known him for about a month, second of all because he is about to be posted overseas—so that what there is of our relationship will be disrupted—and finally, because he is already married.

Life does have its complications, or perhaps I'm the sort of person who invites them.

Love,
Vicky

One Sunday afternoon, Nahum and Lotie received a visit from an American army major who introduced himself as Irving Krup and who brought regards from Edgar and Vicky.

Nahum questioned him closely about Vicky.

"She's beautiful," said Krup, which wasn't quite what he wanted to know.

"I mean, how is she managing all on her own?"

"Beautifully."

"And the baby?"

"Beautiful."

When he left, Nahum said to Lotie: "You know, for an officer, he's not very articulate."

"He's not only an officer, he's a lawyer who charges by the word, and I suppose he didn't want to give away too much without a fee."

He came to dinner the following week, and, as he had possibly heard too much about wartime shortages in Britain, he brought most of the meal with him, as well as a bottle of whisky; on this occasion, possibly because of the whisky, he was rather more voluble, and early in the course of the evening, he asked Nahum if he could call him by his first name, "because if things go as I hope they will go, there's every chance I may be your son-in-law."

Nahum gave Lotie a surprised look. She seemed rather less surprised, and he wondered if she knew something that he did not.

"Vicky didn't tell me anything about that in her letters," he said, "but then, she doesn't write all that often."

"Or say all that much," added Lotie.

"This is all very recent," said Krup. "I only asked her before I left. She didn't say yes, she didn't say no, she didn't say stay, she didn't say go, but hell, I can't be much of a lawyer if I can't persuade a woman to marry me."

He was tall, well-built, with dark hair growing grey at the temples, a sallow complexion and dark eyes. He reminded Nahum a little of Mittwoch, though he looked rather more polished and successful.

Lotie asked him what he thought of their visitor.

"Good-looking man, and he seems very fond of her."

"But you don't seem very fond of him. Don't you want to see Vicky married?"

"Of course I do."

"But you don't seem too happy about it."

"He's American."

"What's wrong with being American? You are prejudiced, you know. You're anti-American in the same way that some people are anti Jewish."

"I'm not prejudiced. I like Americans, or thought I did. They're open, friendly, direct, but I don't know—I suppose I'm disappointed in them. Remember the whole ta-ra-ra about the Yanks are coming, the Yanks are coming? I suppose we expected heros, giants, Sergeant Yorks, every man a Gary Cooper, and what did we get? A rabble— gum-chewing, flabby, badly turned out, undisciplined. I once saw a whole line of them ambling along Battlefield Road, with dirty boots, some in helmets, some in forage caps, some bare-headed, some with tunics buttoned, some unbuttoned, chattering among themselves, whistling at any girl they passed. It began to snow, and they reminded me a little of Napoleon's retreat from Moscow. In Russia, if a son was called up to the army it was a calamity, but people consoled themselves with the thought that it would make a man of him, and it did. They don't look like men, these Americans—at least, not fighting men."

"And the fact that they're fast with women has nothing to do with it?"

"The fact that they're fast with women has everything to do with it."

"Aren't all soldiers interested in women?"

"Aren't all men interested in women? But the Americans don't seem to be interested in anything else."

"No, my dear, all soldiers are after the same thing, but the Americans are better at getting it. It's jealousy, nothing more. Whenever you see an American out with a girl, you can already see them in bed together, but not all Americans are rapists, and Irving certainly isn't. But what I can't understand is this. You'd have been perfectly happy for Trude to marry an American, so why are you so hesitant about Vicky? Shall I tell you why? You think Americans are kosher enough for your niece, but not for your daughter."

"Trude is unlikely to have any children, that's why. Vicky has a son, and I'd like to see him brought up as a Jew. If she married someone here, I could help keep an eye on him—but in America? Of all the Americans who've been here, I haven't met one who's had a bit of religion in him. The Jews aren't Jews, the Christians aren't Christians. They're all pagans. What can happen to a boy brought up in such a country?"

Nahum was himself slightly surprised at his own lack of enthusiasm for Krup, but although he had been deeply concerned about Vicky, he had never for a moment believed that she would remain unattached for long. In that respect, he was rather more worried about Trude.

As the fourth year of war began, Nahum, like others, felt fairly confident that it would be the last, for the allies were advancing on every front, but Nahum could derive only limited comfort from their triumphs; it was becoming clear that—whatever the eventual outcome of events—the war, as far as European Jewry was concerned, was already lost.

He sat glued to the radio night after night, turning the dial this way and that while the air-waves crackled and whined, but the more horrific the details which emerged, the more difficult he found it to assimilate them, until they were brought home to him by a letter from Yankelson, who, in turn, had heard from a remote relative who had fled from Volkovysk in the face of the advancing Germans and had returned with the Russian army to find that the Jewish community had been wiped out. Of the five thousand Jews who had lived there before the war, only a few dozen remained. His Uncle Sender, whom his father had always spoken of as "the brains of the family" but who had never been able to make a living, had been "lucky," wrote Yankelson. There had been a heavy German air-raid on the town in June 1941 in which several hundred people had been killed, among them,

Sender, his wife—who had been ill in bed—and two of their grand-children. The Germans had entered the town a few days later, walled the Jews up in a ghetto and, in the following year, marched some two thousand of them to the nearby woods and mowed them down with machine guns. "You may remember the woods," wrote Yankelson, "your father had his *dacha* there." Many others had died of cold and starvation, and the rest had been deported to Treblinka or Auschwitz.

"There is one consolation to the story," Yankelson continued. "I'm not too sure what happened elsewhere, but in Volkovysk, they fought back. There was a Jewish underground movement in the town which established contact with the partisans. They killed some Germans and a few of their collaborators, and they helped some people escape. The movement wasn't large and it couldn't do much, but the fact that it existed at all gave some people the hope to survive. But the Volkovysk that you and I knew is finished, a *churban*. And, unfortunately, it's the same story everywhere. When we first heard the news, Sophie said to me: 'They're the usual wartime atrocity stories. We had the same sort of thing in the first war, don't believe a word of them,' and even I thought the Germans couldn't possibly be that bad, but I've spoken to people who have actually been to these places and seen it all with their own eyes, and it's far, far worse than anything you or I could have imagined."

Nahum recalled how they used to sit on low stools in synagogue on the fast of *Ab* and in subdued voices lament over the fall of Jeru-salem and the destruction of the Temple, and he sometimes wondered how he and his fellow worshippers could have been moved almost to tears by an event which, however melancholy, had taken place nearly two thousand years ago. The events surrounding the fast of *Ab* now seemed very trivial indeed.

He had been unprepared for the contents of Yankelson's letter and read it in the tram on the way to his office; when he alighted, he found himself unable to continue with his daily routine as if nothing had happened, and he walked around trailing his umbrella in a daze. He asked himself why he had not brought over his Uncle Sender and his family early in the century when he was still a ship owner. He could have done so without difficulty and could have managed to support them, if necessary, in their first years, at least. Had his uncle asked to be brought over he would have done so without hesitation, but why had he not urged him to come? Was it because he was anxious to get on, to make his first million, to have his fleet in the Atlantic? His uncle had, in fact, rarely entered his thoughts. He had been fond of him, for he was a kindly, amiable man, but in the last resort he was a *schleimazzle,* and everything he touched wilted, and he might have kept him out of his mind because he feared him as a burden. He had, after all, helped his mother, his sister, his cousin (and with what result!) and his aunt. He wasn't his uncle's keeper, as well. He had had no direct news of his sister, and he presumed she was dead, too.

Yankelson's letter somehow made him treasure Trude even more than before. She was to him the last relic of a lost world and an assurance that, whatever happens, life always goes on. Yet, at the same time, he had the unhappy feeling that no matter how great the calamities, she was moving away from him. She had lost much of her gaiety and freshness, and was becoming withdrawn and morose, and one evening, when he asked her in his hesitant, diffident way if anything was wrong, she turned upon him in a fury.

"No," she shouted, "nothing's wrong! Why should anything be wrong?"

It was the first time he had heard her voice raised, and it made her sound a different person. It upset him deeply, but he did not mention it to Lotie.

Some days later he and Lotie were having supper with Gladys, and he expressed the fear that his niece could be verging on a nervous breakdown.

"It shouldn't surprise me in the least," said Gladys. "I give her approximately another week."

"Why? Do you know anything about her that I don't?"

"I should imagine that I know everything about her that you don't. Didn't you know she works in the same hospital as me? Not that we have all that much to do with one another. She's virtually an orderly."

"What do you mean, an orderly? She's a nurse."

"A nursing auxiliary, which is a euphemism for an orderly, not that there's anything wrong with being an orderly. A hospital could function without surgeons, but not without orderlies. But that's all beside the point. The poor woman is having an unhappy love affair."

"Why? How? Who with? Why unhappy?"

At which point Lotie intervened: "One of the surgeons wants her to move in and live with him, but so far she's refused, out of consideration for your feelings, I suppose."

"My feelings? What about Hector?"

"It's more than a year since he was taken prisoner, and I suppose as time passes, she's begun to feel she has to settle for what life has to offer."

"But she writes to him nearly every night."

"For all I know, she could still be in love with him, only she's having an affair as a way of killing time, but she's obviously unhappy about it."

"Is the man Jewish?"

"He is, as a matter of fact," said Gladys, "but he's not single."

At which he doubled up and swayed back and forward, as he sometimes did when in distress. "Just like her mother," he said. "We're not free to live our own lives but doomed to play allotted parts. Just like her mother. Her mother couldn't form a healthy relationship—"

"I know very little about her mother," Lotie interjected, "but Trude happened to have spent over twenty years in marriage to a man she never cared for and probably detested, and now that she has met someone she possibly does care for—and who certainly cares for her—she feels unable to do anything about it out of consideration for her uncle. The woman's a saint, worse than a saint. She's crazy."

"The man *is* married, you know," said Gladys.

"I know he's married, but anyone who's been through what she's been through is entitled to snatch what happiness she can."

"Nobody's condemning her," said Nahum.

"As a matter of fact, I am," said Gladys. "I know it may be old-fashioned to say so, but I happen to believe in the sanctity of marriage."

"I also believe in it," said Nahum, "but we're living in confused times."

"It's the breakdown of old values which is confusing them."

"Let me finish, will you? I'm not condemning her. I also agree she's entitled to any happiness she can find, only she's anything but happy. She's miserable."

"She wouldn't be if she moved in with him," said Lotie.

"I wonder," said Gladys, "if you'd feel the same if your husband was the man involved."

At which Lotie gave Nahum an amused look which seemed to say "Him? He can hardly keep one woman satisfied, let alone two."

"If he's supposed to love Trude, why doesn't he divorce his wife and marry her?" asked Nahum.

"Because his wife, whom I happen to know, is unlikely to give him a divorce," said Gladys.

A few weeks later Nahum had to go into hospital for an operation. In spite of Gladys's dire warnings, there had been no recurrence of the illness which had laid him low some two years previously, but he suffered from considerable pressure on the bladder which made it impossible for him to have a decent night's sleep, and his doctors diagnosed an enlarged prostate. He had tried to delay the operation for as long as possible because Shyke, who had been operated on for a similar condition, had warned him: "Once they open you up, they let in the devil, and you're never the same again," but Lotie told him that if he delayed the operation further, she would have him chloroformed in his sleep and delivered to the operating theatre bound hand and foot, and he finally agreed to enter hospital.

By a grim stroke of irony, the surgeon who was to perform the operation turned out to be Trude's lover. He was a lean, grey-haired man with black eyebrows, a red nose and watery eyes.

"So you're the Casanova?" Nahum thought to himself. He must have been about seventy, and Nahum's last thought as he succumbed to the anaesthetic was, "If there's life in that old dog, then there could still be life in this one."

The operation was perfectly straightforward, but his convalescence took much longer than he or his doctors expected. He was two weeks in hospital and a further four weeks in bed, and when he eventually did get to his feet, he felt lifeless and shaky.

Old Mrs Mittwoch—or Madame Mittwoch, as the announcement had it—died about this time, and, against the advice of his doctors, he went to the funeral. It was a small affair, and most of the mourners looked as he felt, but her son Michael was there—a tall and robust figure—and the sight of him had an oddly restorative effect on Nahum, possibly because it suggested that there was still life on earth. He was an officer in the Parachute Regiment and had been flown over from France for the funeral.

"You married?" asked Nahum.

"No."

"Surprising, a good-looking young man like you."

"Not so young any longer, I'm afraid. How's Vicky?"

"Ah, don't ask. What she's been through. She's in America, you know."

"I know. I knew her husband."

"You knew Cameron?"

"I met him in the army."

"A hero."

"So I understand."

Nahum invited him to supper the following evening and hoped to introduce him to Trude. Trude had apologised for her outburst, and while he was convalescing she had spent long hours beside him, talking mostly about her childhood in Russia. When he had tried to direct her conversation to the here and now, she carefully steered him away from it, but he thought he had reestablished the warm relationship they had previously enjoyed. She, however, failed to turn up for supper and phoned from the hospital to apologise that some emergency had cropped up and that she would be late. Nahum prolonged the meal for as long as he could, and after the meal Lotie brought in coffee, and every time the young man showed signs of departure, Nahum introduced some new topic of conversation to keep him in place. But when midnight struck and there was still no sign of the girl, Nahum gave up, and the slight sense of well-being which had returned to his veins slowly ebbed out. The next day, Trude announced that she was taking another job at a hospital somewhere in the country and would be leaving Glasgow. Nahum felt too unhappy and too unwell to remonstrate, and went upstairs and took to his bed.

The war's end had been imminent for many months, and Nahum had dreamt of a grand victory celebration which would take the form of a family reunion, but when victory finally did come, his family was scattered throughout the globe, and he was ill with a recurrence of his previous undefined and undefinable complaint.

"It's a warning to retire," said Lotie. "You're seventy nearly, you're entitled to a rest. The boys will soon be home; Jacob can take over, or Hector—"

"What about this Irving fellow?"

"Which Irving fellow?"

"Vicky's young man, the one who wanted to marry her."

"There've been complications."

"What sort of complications? I suppose you want to tell me he's also married."

"How did you guess?"

He looked at her in bewilderment. "What's happening to the world? Are there no single men left any more?"

He sank under his blankets in despair, and when Gladys came to see him he said: "Leave me alone. The older you get, the more the heart-ache, the more the aggravation. I've got children and grandchildren. I've done my bit, now leave me alone and let me die. At my age I'm entitled to."

And for a time it looked as if he might die. Lotie wondered if she should cable Sophie and Vicky to come over, and if she should apply for compassionate leave for Jacob and Benny. Then came a cable to say that Hector was on his way home, which made Nahum sit up at once. The very name of Hector evoked what he thought of as his golden years—the holiday villa in Menton, hot afternoon and balmy nights, perfumed gardens and azure seas, Kagan and Wachsman, distant laughter and warm breezes, snatches of song floating on the evening air, Alex and Arabella. Whenever his thoughts turned to Arabella, as they did frequently, he wondered if she could have ever existed, and once Hector fell out of his life, he began to suspect that she had been conjured up by his imagination. Now that Hector was about to return, the memories of Arabella became more real, and he could almost hear her singing the Schubert songs she sang in Menton.

But when Hector finally materialised, Nahum sank back again. Hector was a ghost of his former self, a grey presence—grey hair, a grey bushy moustache, grey complexion—even his tired, world-weary blue eyes had assumed a shade of grey, and he came in a baggy, ill-fitting grey suit. He seemed commonplace, which was not a word Nahum would have previously associated with him.

"What are you doing in bed?" asked Hector.

"Dying," said Nahum.

"He makes it sound like an occupation," said Lotie. "It's general war-weariness, I should think, but now that you're here, he should be all right."

But he was far from all right and showed no signs of recovery until, in quick succession, there came a letter from Benny to say that he was engaged, followed by a cable from Vicky to say that she was on the way home.

CHAPTER XXXVII
BRIEFLY IN ZION

D EAR SOPH,

  I've been away for seven years, which you might think—and I thought—was not a long time, but I've returned to a different world. Britain may have won the war, but there is a general feeling of drabness and weariness which makes one wonder what it possibly could have been like to lose it. There is a shortage of everything and everything is still rationed, and the only things to brighten the spirit are the wild flowers flourishing on the bomb sites.

I was shocked by Father's appearance. You may remember he always used to be a rather smart-looking, smartly dressed man, though in a central European rather than an English way, but he's beginning to look a little drab, which is easy in post-war Britain—some might call it patriotic—though that may be due to the fact that Lotie, who is looking as smart as ever, probably pinches his clothing coupons. His little beard is a silvery white, and he looks like a once-prosperous Chekhovian family doctor who has come upon hard times. He and his cronies tend to address each other as *Gospodin* and break into Russian at the least excuse, but that may be in honour of Russia's part in the war. He also tends to revert to Yiddish with increasing frequency, even when speaking to non-Jews. His admirable grasp of English seems to be lapsing, and he is beginning to sound like his former partner, old Lomzer.

If I was shocked by Father's appearance, I was saddened by Hector's, and I almost broke down and cried. He says he was fairly decently treated in the POW camp—except after he and a number of others had made an abortive attempt to escape—but it must have been hell for a man of his spirit to have been incarcerated at all. I know that old soldiers only fade away, but he has begun to fade rather quickly and has lost—well, I suppose he's lost himself, for he's not Hector as you and I knew and loved him. I used to think I disliked Ara because she was hysterical, pretentious and spoilt, but I now see I was merely envious of her and felt she was bad for Hector. The process of deterioration which culminated in the POW camp really began with her. Poor, poor Hector. If I should tell you that he's agreed to join Father in the cinema trade, that should tell you everything.

The great news here is Pipsqueak's engagement to an Egyptian heiress from an old Jewish family. He has brought back photographs of his prospective wife, a dark-haired, pleasant-faced woman, who looks older than he and is certainly larger than he; of his prospective father-in-law, who looks like a Turkish wrestler; his prospective mother-in-law, who is about the size of the pyramids and the Sphinx thrown into one; and their actual home, which is a palace. They are to get married in six months, and Father plans to cart everyone over to Egypt—including you and me—for the occasion and has already booked a floor at Shepheard's Hotel.

You have not met—and it now seems that you will not be meeting —Trude, for she is living in sin with an elderly surgeon and wants to hide her shame from the family.

You have not met—but will no doubt be meeting—Jacob's wife, Gladys. She is very bright, highly regarded as one of the rising stars of her profession, very tart (without being in the least tarty) and very opinionated. I only knew her slightly before and disliked her slightly; now that I know her better, I dislike her a lot. Jacob is not yet de-mobilised. He seems to be taking his time in returning to the bosom of his family, but having regard to the sort of bosom he'd be returning to, I hardly blame him.

Lotie is still the queen she always was, but getting a trifle impatient with poor old Papa. These Americans are ageless. Who says money can't buy happiness? It can buy, and—from what I can see—it does buy youth, which is the next best thing. She and I get on very well, but I do resent the fact that she treats me as a contemporary. I know I look it, and I certainly feel it, but she doesn't have to rub it in.

You asked about Irving; I wish you hadn't. It was fun having him around while he was around, but once he left I hardly missed him. He phoned me about six weeks ago to say that his divorce was finally through, and I said how happy I was, both for his wife and for him, but told him I was going back to Daddy, and he said: "You can't do that," but I said I would, and I did. He threatened to come after me, and I was half hoping he would, but so far he hasn't, which is a pity. Mixed up, aren't I?

Yours,
Vicky

The prospect of Benny's wedding concentrated Nahum's mind wonderfully. He had up to then, possibly because of his illness, found it difficult to think ahead or, indeed, to put his thoughts into order at all. Now, suddenly, everything was clear. Hector was with him in the firm, and, after a desultory start, beginning to show enthusiasm, learning things quickly, and there was every chance that he would be in a position to take over within six months or, at most, a year. As far as the business itself was concerned, he had always wanted to have a cinema in London, in or near the West End, and he still hoped to acquire or build one. Once that was settled, he would feel his work was done and could hand over and retire from business life.

The next point he had to settle was where to retire. Lotie had suggested the south of France, and when he mentioned the matter of cost, she said that she still had "a dollar or two tucked away somewhere," but money was, in fact, a secondary—indeed, a tertiary—consideration. He already had Jacob and his family in Glasgow; Benny planned to settle there and he had every hope that Vicky would marry and do the same, and he wanted to be within easy reach of them. On the other hand, he still had not abandoned plans to settle in Palestine— "the call of ancestral voices," as Vicky termed it. Lotie was not too enthusiastic about the idea. "It has sunshine, which is more than can be said for Glasgow, but the way things are going, I don't know if Palestine will still be there by the time you retire." Hardly a day passed without reports of ambushes and attacks, deaths and explosions, and the country seemed to be on the brink of civil war.

"Things can't go on like that forever," said Nahum; "they'll settle down."

"If you ask me," said Lotie, "you and I will be settled in our graves long before things settle down in Palestine."

And they decided to leave the matter in abeyance until after the wedding. Shyke had said that he hoped to be at the wedding, and he suggested that when the celebrations were over, they should travel back together to Palestine and discuss the matter on the spot.

"Don't believe everything you read in the papers," he added; "things always look worse from a distance."

Nahum had hoped that the wedding would be an occasion for a grand family reunion, but the winter, which was one of the most severe and prolonged in living memory, had damaged several of his cinemas, some of them beyond repair. There were difficulties in obtaining the necessary material and permits for repair, and Hector had to stay behind to cope with the situation. Gladys didn't want to take the children out of school for the two or three weeks that would have been necessary and could not leave them behind, and Jacob could not leave

Gladys behind—or so Gladys averred—and Nahum began to wonder if Benny, too, might find some reason for not coming. Vicky, however, left her child with Gladys, and eventually four of them set out for Cairo. They travelled by train across France and then by boat from Marseilles.

On his first day at sea, Nahum was seized with apprehensions and half expected to be summoned home by cable as he had been the first time he and Lotie had sailed into the Mediterranean, but they reached Egypt without incident. In his hotel, however, two telegrams awaited him to say that none of his guests from Palestine would be able to make the journey.

Events in Palestine also cast a pall over the wedding itself. There were many guests, for Benny had married into a large clan, but everyone was apprehensive, not only about the future of Palestine, but what would happen in Egypt if a war were to break out between Arabs and Jews. Benny and his bride and their respective parents smiled until their jaws ached, but wherever one turned, there were anxious faces and anxious voices. There was a band and there were speeches, but it was all, as Vicky said, "like the last night on the *Titanic*."

The next morning at breakfast Lotie said: "I take it we're not going to Palestine?"

Nahum put a comforting hand on hers. "I understand how you feel, but as I've already gotten this far, I feel I've got to go on if it's the last thing I do."

"If you go on, it will be the last thing you do," she said.

"Why don't you and Vicky go sight-seeing, visit the pyramids, go down the Nile, while I go on to Palestine to see Sophie and have a quick word with Shyke? I shouldn't be away for more than a few days, and then we can all go back home together."

"I wonder what you would say if I really did leave you to go on, on your own?"

"I would say you were doing the sensible thing, and, in fact, I would much rather you did."

"If you act the bloody fool, why should we do the sensible thing?" asked Vicky.

"Don't say you're coming as well?"

"Do you think I'd come all this way without seeing Sophie?"

"What about the boy?"

"He's in good hands."

"But supposing something—heaven forbid—should happen to you?"

"He's still in good hands."

"Crazy."

Eventually the three of them set off. The train was stopped at the border and passengers and baggage were searched by tight-lipped Palestinian police. They were searched again at Beth Shemen, near Jerusalem. When they got to Jerusalem itself, the city was like a battle zone, with large areas cordoned off with barbed wire, armoured cars patrolling the streets and troops and police everywhere.

Jessie came to meet them at the station. She was silver-haired, and her skin was parched and a little lined, but her eyes were bright, and there was nothing in her manner or voice to suggest her age.

She rushed towards Nahum as he alighted, hesitated when she saw Lotie but still threw her arms around him in a warm embrace.

"Where's Shyke?" Nahum asked. "Why didn't you come to the wedding?"

"We're at war," she said; "the bloody Jews are rebelling against the British empire."

As she was driving across town, she gave them a summary of recent events, which made Lotie's hand tighten on Nahum's arm. "But all these are preliminaries," she added cheerfully. "Pasha is waiting for Armageddon."

"Pasha? Who is Pasha?"

"Shyke, of course."

"Why do you call him Pasha?"

"Wait till you see him, and you'll understand why."

Shyke had turned native. He had put on an immense amount of weight, was resting on a divan in an Arab *jellaba* and looked like an oriental potentate.

He lived in a spacious Moorish villa in Katamon, an area of the new city occupied mainly by Christian Arabs. The house was in semi-darkness with shutters drawn against the fierce sun, and a black servant brought coffee in a brass *hafinjan*.

Nahum looked around him, half wondering if he had not intruded onto a film set.

"What's happened to the boy from Volkovysk?" he asked.

"What should happen to everyone who settles here," said Shyke. "They should shake the blood-soaked dust of Europe from their feet and adapt themselves to their new environment, instead of trying to keep little bits of Russia, or Poland or, heaven help us, Germany alive. We've got Muslim Arabs here, and Christian Arabs, and unless the Jews here are prepared to become Jewish Arabs, they have no future in this part of the world. *You* are looking at a Jewish Arab."

"And it is not a particularly pretty sight," added Jessie.

"You mean if Jews assimilate, they'll live in peace?" said Nahum.

"But that sort of peace they could have had even in Europe. For two thousand years we've struggled against all odds to stay Jewish, and now you're saying that once we get back to our own land we should give up the ghost."

"We tried to assimilate in Europe and couldn't. Torquemada wouldn't let us, Hitler wouldn't let us. The first Jews Hitler went for were not the Hasidim, but the assimilated Germans who didn't even think of themselves as Jews. For a Jew to become a European it was to force himself into a mould for which he wasn't created, but to assimilate to the local setting here is to revert to his origins. All right, don't call him an Arab, call him a Palestinian, but he must stop being a European."

"And you think that'll bring peace?"

"No, nothing can bring peace. It's too late for that. The war's already started; in fact, it's been going off and on for the past thirty years, but it'll get worse, much worse. There'll be terrible slaughter."

"You speak about death like Englishmen speak about the weather," said Lotie.

"It's inevitable. No nation was born without it, it's labour pains, but after that, given a generation or two, things will gradually quiet down, and we'll be accepted, as long as we don't try and keep up our European pretensions. If we do, we'll be spat out like the Crusaders."

"Well," said Lotie to Nahum, "are you still thinking of retiring here, my dear?"

"That's an odd word, retirement," said Shyke. "It's not a word I'd ever heard of before I met the English—I think they invented it. In *der heim* you retired when you died—if then—but in England I met retired doctors, retired politicians, retired soldiers. To retire is to meet death halfway. Here, in this country, there is no such thing. I thought when you wrote to me about settling here, you wanted to start a new life."

"At seventy-two?" said Lotie.

"What's age got to do with it—specially if you've got children?" As he spoke, there was a dull crump. The house shook. Windows rattled, and flakes of plaster fell from the ceiling. Nahum and Lotie exchanged alarmed glances. Shyke jumped from his divan, pulled open the shutters and rushed out onto the balcony. A cloud of smoke and dust was rising from a building about half a mile away.

"It reminds me of the blitz," said Nahum, "except that we had air-raid shelters."

"We have one here," said Jessie, "only he uses it to grow mushrooms."

"What was I saying before I was so rudely interrupted?" asked Shyke.

"That this is an ideal place for a new life," said Lotie, "and—it would seem to me—a new death. I may be a simple-minded woman, but I have the feeling that people of our age in a place like this, at a time like this, would be a hindrance, both to themselves and the people around them."

Shyke put a hand on her knee: "I don't know how old you are, my dear. As my wife will tell you, I haven't been well—which is why we couldn't come to the wedding—but seeing you here, I'm already feeling better."

"What was the matter?" asked Nahum.

"He had a heart attack," said Jessie.

"A heart attack?"

"She's exaggerating."

"All right, he didn't have a heart attack. His heart merely stopped beating."

Shyke quickly changed what he obviously felt was an awkward subject. "Where is Hector, why isn't he with you, wasn't he at the wedding?"

"I'm afraid not. Somebody had to look after the shop."

"You mean he's with you in the business?"

"Why do you sound so surprised? It's not a tuppenny-ha'penny affair, you know. I own ten cinemas and am negotiating for an eleventh in London."

"I know, you're a very rich man."

"I'm not a *very* rich man."

"All right, a very comfortable man."

"I'm comfortable."

"It's just that I couldn't imagine Hector in the cinema business."

"He was in business before, you know, only I wouldn't like to say what sort of business."

"I know all about it, I set him up."

Nahum, who was taking a sip of coffee at the time, nearly choked. "*You* set him up?"

"Didn't he tell you?"

"My family never tells me anything. They think I'm too stupid to be trusted with serious things."

"I don't know if I should tell you, either, because the whole thing is supposed to be very secret, but I'm afraid if I don't tell you, nobody else will, and who knows for how long I'll be around? It all began in the 1920s, during the riots. You'll remember when I bumped into you in London during the first war, I was with Jabotinsky trying to raise a Jewish Legion, which we eventually did, but by the time it went into action, there was hardly any action to go into, for the war was more or less over, but the legion was not disbanded. In 1921, a Palestine Defence Force was formed with Jewish and Arab battalions, and an Australian by the name of Margolin—a good soldier and a good Jew—was made commander of the Jewish battalion, and the idea was that it should absorb what was left of the Jewish Legion. But before the force was established and Margolin's appointment took effect, Arab riots broke out, and the Jews, especially those in more isolated areas, were in danger. Margolin quickly brought together the few remaining units of the legion, plus a considerable number of ex-legionnaires, and managed to get hold of arms and stores without going through the whole business of filling in forms and getting permission. The British Army went into action fairly promptly, but it was thinly spread, and there were outbreaks in Jaffa, Rehovoth, Petach Tikva and elsewhere, and without Margolin's force there could have been massacres, I tell you, massacres. The military authorities, however, were not too happy about the way he took things over, and in particular they wanted to find out how he was able to get hold of the arms and stores. The legion, or what was left of it, was disbanded, and Margolin resigned his commission and returned to Australia, but questions continued to be asked, in particular how a train bound for Jerusalem managed to find its way to Haderah. Hector was never found in actual possession of a locomotive and rolling stock, but all the evidence pointed to him, and he followed Margolin's example and retired."

"But wait a moment, all that happened in the early twenties."

"All that began to happen in the early twenties, but Hector's part in it didn't come out till a few years later, when someone else was brought to court. Things don't move all that fast."

"And wasn't Hector in Egypt at the time?"

"He should have been, but it was the same command, so it wasn't too difficult to move around. And, of course, he had Cameron in Ramle."

"Cameron? Is that when their relationship began?"

"They were brothers, David and Jonathan. I can't make up my mind about Cameron—whether he did it for money, or for us—but I can tell you he did more for Zion than a congress of so-called Zionists. When I heard he'd been killed, I nearly dropped. I haven't been well since."

"If it wasn't for Eddy, Hector would have been court-martialled," said Vicky.

"Did Eddy tell you that?" asked Shyke.

"Hector told me that."

"I'm not sure. It would have been too embarrassing. Too many people were implicated. Some of them high up."

"But it was Eddy who implicated them. He spread the money around."

"I believe it. He had a mixture of Jewish *chutzpah* and Scottish cunning. Anyway, when things quieted down, I knew they wouldn't stay quiet for long, and that the troubles would continue and get worse. The Arabs had no difficulty in getting all the arms they needed, and I and others wanted to be sure that Jews, too, had a regular supply, but I thought it wasn't enough merely to procure guns, we had to be in a position to make them, and that's how the machine-tool business began. I didn't want to implicate the Zionist organisation, the Jewish Agency or any other official body in case our cover should be blown. I was head of a small bank at the time and organised the finances for the operation, and I got Cameron to run it. He, in turn, took on Hector, and between them they were perfect—energetic, enterprising, efficient, discreet. Mind you, you caused them a bit of embarrassment when you began poking your big nose into things."

"I wanted to see what they were up to," said Nahum.

"They weren't using your money—so it was none of your business."

"What went wrong?" asked Vicky.

"They got too ambitious. There were private armies all over the world, hungry for arms and with money to pay for them. It was always understood that they would be supplying others so that if they were caught, it shouldn't look like a Zionist operation, and also the profits from their other clients helped to pay for our part of the business—more or less. But they took on too many clients, which meant enlarging the organisation and taking too many people into their confidence, and eventually, of course, their cover was blown."

"How is it that your cover was never blown?" asked Vicky.

"I had a good middleman who organised things at the American end. He had contacts everywhere, including the FBI, and things got no further than him."

"Who was he?" asked Nahum.

"I don't know if I should tell you, but again, it would be a pity if you didn't know. The whole thing was almost a Volkovysk operation."

"So, *nu,* who was it?"

"Your cousin."

"Not Lazar!"

"Why not Lazar?"

"But how did you know about him? How did you get hold of him?"

"He got hold of me. When a boy from Volkovysk becomes a banker and makes a bit of money, other boys from Volkovysk get to hear of him. Maybe I wasn't a Wachsman, but I was something of a somebody in my own right, and he came to me once with a business proposal."

"Did you know what he did to me?"

"No, but I soon found out that he had a bit of a past."

"A *bit* of a past?"

"All right, more than a bit of a past, but for my purposes a past was useful."

"He did it for money, that much I can tell you."

"People who do things for money are reliable, you can reckon what they'll cost. Greed is fairly constant. It's the people who do things in the name of heaven that you've got to worry about. They've got a conscience, and when people start carting about their conscience, you've got the devil to play with. Lazar was quiet, circumspect, efficient and, unlike the others, he got away."

"He's the type that always does," said Nahum, "but start from the beginning. How was the whole thing organised?"

"That will have to wait for another day," said Jessie in a governessy voice, "it's long, long past his bedtime." And she propelled him to bed almost like a prisoner being taken to his cell. "Och, he's a terrible man," she said later. "He had no right to be up and dressed in the first place. He was at death's door three weeks ago, and I want to take him away for a bit of peace and quiet in Cyprus, but he won't hear of it. Mind you, I think it's the sound of gunfire that keeps him going. Did you see how his eyes lit up at the explosion?"

Nahum spent a restless night; the air was heavy and hot, and whenever he was about to sink into sleep he was startled into wakefulness by some distant explosion, the sound of gunfire or the whine of police sirens.

"Can you really see yourself retiring here?" asked Lotie.

He was up early next morning, partly because of his inability to sleep and partly because he had some business at the head office of the Zionist organisation, which he was anxious to settle for once and for all.

He had bought some land near Ashkelon earlier in the century—four acres of it—and still had a receipt to show for it, though it was beginning to fall apart at the folds. He had written to Zionist headquarters about it and either had received no reply, or when he received a reply had been told that the serial number did not correspond to any number in their files. Yankelson had also taken up the matter and had been given the same answer. The sum of money, though not large now, was at the time fairly substantial, and, whether large or small, he did not like to feel that he had been the victim of a fraud. But when he got to the building, he found it surrounded by sand-bags and barbed wire like a military outpost, and he felt it was too banal a matter to raise at such a time; on an impulse, he tore up the receipt and scattered the pieces to the winds.

When he got back, Shyke was entertaining Lotie and Vicky to breakfast on the terrace. For a sick man he seemed in fine fettle.

"Can you imagine having breakfast like this in Scotland in March? It's worth settling here just for the sunshine."

"There are other places in the world with sunshine, you know," said Lotie.

"But you can't call them your own," said Shyke, wagging a finger at her.

"You don't have to own a place to be happy there, you know. I've lived in Pennsylvania, in Vermont, in England, in Scotland, and I was happy in them all, and if I wasn't, it wasn't because of the place, but the people. To be honest, I'm nervous here. I don't like being in a place where people are killing each other."

"There was quite a bit of blood spilt before America became America, you know. We're in the process of being born. You're a cosmopolitan, my dear, and a pampered cosmopolitan at that, and you're at home anywhere, provided the comforts are there, but for simple Russian Jews like Nahum and myself, this is the only place. Everywhere else is quicksand. Here the ground is firm under our feet."

And as he spoke there came an explosion like a clap of thunder, and the house shook.

Lotie was by now quite rattled. There was a plane leaving for Rome the next morning, and she wanted to be on it.

"I'll drive you to the airport," said Nahum, "but I can't leave without seeing Sophie and the children."

They drove to Sophie that afternoon and reached her *moshav* just before nightfall.

She was not particularly pleased to see them.

"Really, what a time to come out, when the whole place is about to blow up."

"It's exactly what I keep telling him," said Lotie.

The twins were away. Sophie was not very forthcoming about their whereabouts, but it seemed they were both in the Haganah, the Jewish underground army. Sophie hadn't seen them for over a week and was plainly concerned about them. Yankelson, she said, was in Europe, and again she claimed not to know where he was or what he was doing.

"I wouldn't mind stopping here," said Vicky.

"We could do with an extra hand," said Sophie. "There's hardly an able-bodied man about the place."

"Don't encourage her," said Nahum, "she's crazy enough as it is."

Nahum would have liked to stay on for a few days. He hadn't seen the twins for seventeen years. There was the chance they would be home for the weekend, and he wanted to catch at least a glimpse of them, but Lotie was tense and unhappy and seemed to be verging on hysteria. They were in some danger, but they had been in greater danger in the blitz, and even when they had nearly suffered a direct hit, she had been calm and composed. He had, in fact, not known her to be like this since her mother died. He wondered what could have brought it on—the sudden change of climate, perhaps. He remembered her last breakdown, over forty years earlier, and the thought of it filled him with a dark dread.

He tried to cheer her up by suggesting they take a cruise on the way home.

"I don't want a cruise. I want to fly. I don't want to stay here a minute longer than possible."

They left by air the next day.

Nahum hoped that she would feel relaxed once they were air-borne, but he remained restless and unhappy, and they had been flying for about an hour when her head suddenly snapped back and she seemed to pass out. Vicky quickly called a stewardess and they gave her oxygen, which revived her, but she remained white and shaky, and the plane made an emergency stop at Athens. An ambulance waited by the tarmac as they landed, but when she reached hospital she was dead.

CHAPTER XXXVIII
MERRY CHRISTMAS

DEAR SOPH,

If all goes well I should be with you before this letter, but for the moment everything seems to be going ill, and I am writing this in what may be a vain attempt to keep my sanity.

The Greeks are the most bumbling and incompetent race out. Gladys, who arrived here this morning, said that it's as clear as daylight that poor Lotie died from a cerebral hemorrhage, but another passenger had died in the very same way earlier in the week, and the health authorities, fearing that they might have some sort of epidemic on their hands, are going over every organ in her body. It is also a good deal more difficult to get a dead person out of the country than a living one into it, and it doesn't look as if we'll be able to get to Palestine before Sunday at the earliest. I've been in touch with Shyke, and we've made provisional arrangements to have the funeral on the Mount of Olives on Monday afternoon. Shyke has all the details.

I've always thought of Lotie as an elegant and attractive woman, but it never occurred to me she was beautiful till I saw her laid out in the hospital morgue. She looked like a marble figure I once saw on a sarcophagus in Rome—white, flawless and with almost a glow to her face.

Father hasn't stopped talking from the moment we landed—in English, Yiddish, Russian—in an attempt, I suppose, to keep what's happened from sinking in. He hasn't shed a tear, and I suspect that he can't believe what's happened—I'm not sure that I can—but, as is usual in families, Father was the invalid and Lotie died. His decision to bury Lotie in Jerusalem surprised me, for as you may know, we left as soon as we did because she couldn't wait to get the holy soil off her feet, but apparently Father had reserved a plot next to Alex for himself, and another for Lotie soon after he married (could Lotie have known about it?). Her brother Edgar is here with his wife, and he is as surprised about the arrangements as I was, but, of course, he hasn't tried to interfere. He was in Rome when he received the telegram and is quite shattered. I gather Hector and the others have gone straight on to Palestine, and they should be with you by now.

Poor Lotie's death has settled one problem. Father will now retire to Palestine. He keeps talking about a property he's got near Ashkelon, but I think he'd be far better off in Jerusalem. I'm planning to settle there with him, and I shall look for a suitable property when I'm there next week, though, of course, one doesn't know what will be left of Jerusalem when the present troubles are over. In my present mood, I don't really care. Lotie was only my step-mother, but she was more like a sister, and of all the people and things I missed during the four years I was away, I missed her most of all—her vivacity, her intelligence, her warmth—and I must say that my estimation of Father rose at the thought that he could attract and keep such a woman; I want to settle in Palestine, not only because I think Father needs me (which, of course, he does), but because I couldn't contemplate returning to a Lotieless Glasgow.

I don't know what sort of person Father'll be when he wakes up to what's happened. He might take it all philosophically and tell himself that, after all, he's had a good life. He has suffered the tragedies of Alex and Ara. I have been a disappointment, and so, to a lesser extent, is Hector, but at least I've produced the compensation of a grandchild, and he has Hector to take over the business. On the more positive side, he has you, Yankelson and the twins, and he has had more joy out of Jacob and Benny than he could ever have hoped for. Even Gladys, who is more admirable than likable, can become vaguely human, and it is only since her arrival here that we have been able to make headway through the red-tape entanglements.

I'm not sure if Father is wise to retire. When he made his decision to hand over to Hector, he still had Lotie with him, but what will he do with himself by himself? He has often talked of returning to his studies—presumably the Talmud—but what capacity for study can one have at seventy-two? The best idea might be for him to buy or build a cinema in Jerusalem—except that he keeps talking about Goodkind-Raeburn, and I have the feeling that he thinks he's back in shipping.

We'll have a lot to talk about when I next see you.

Yours,
Vicky

It was a bleak day. The skies were grey and angry—"almost in mourning," said Vicky—and the winds howled across the exposed hillside and blew dust and grit into the eyes of the mourners.

Nahum remained oddly composed throughout the burial service, possibly because the family reunion he had hoped for at Benny's wedding had finally materialised at Lotie's funeral. Everybody was there—Sophie, Yankelson, flanked by their two sons, great, brawny giants; Jacob, Gladys and her father (her mother was looking after the children); Benny, his wife Yvonne and her father; Hector, Vicky and, rather unexpectedly, Trude; Edgar and his wife; Shyke and Jessie; and a tall, grey-haired figure whom Nahum could not at first place, until he introduced himself as Richard Kagan. Shyke had come over the protestations of both his doctor and his wife and was leaning heavily on a stick. After the service he said to Nahum: "You know, feeling the way I do, I might as well stop where I am."

They were beginning to descend the hill when Nahum suddenly remembered his grandfather and led the funeral party back along the lines of graves to his grandfather's tomb to read the inscription on the headstone.

"You know," he said, "looking at that name on that stone, I keep thinking it's me, and I don't know if I'm dead or alive."

Not to be outdone, Shyke remembered that he, too, had a grandfather *and* a great grandfather in the cemetery, and the mourners were led on a further pilgrimage, until Edgar protested: "If anybody else's got anyone in the ground, they can, as far as I'm concerned, stay there."

They all went back to Shyke's house where Jessie had prepared an elaborate tea, and Nahum was the main topic of conversation. Everybody seemed to be fighting over him. Gladys wanted him to come and live with them, so did Sophie and Jessie, while Trude offered to come and keep house for him wherever he planned to live, but that, said Vicky, was already settled, and during the week of mourning, in which Nahum remained indoors, Vicky and Jessie scoured Jerusalem for a likely property and found a small villa in a small garden not far from the centre of town. Because of the general tension in the country, and particularly in Jerusalem, prices were low; Vicky, who had a fairly developed commercial sense, thought she had found a bargain and paid the deposit out of her own pocket.

"If you don't want it," she told Nahum, "I'll buy it."

Nahum's immediate plans were to return to Glasgow, put his affairs in order and remain there until after the *bar mitzvah* of Jacob's son Aaron, who would be thirteen at the end of the year. Hector had also almost completed negotiations for the acquisition of a London cinema which they planned to refurbish and rename the *Charlotte*, after Lotie, and Nahum thought he might remain in the country for the official opening.

His experience of the unhappy flight to Athens had made him

nervous of air travel and, accompanied by Vicky, he returned by boat, travelling first on a cargo vessel to Gibraltar and then, in some luxury, in a P. & O. liner to Southampton. It was only when he opened the door of his house in Glasgow that the full force of his tragedy hit him—as if he were convinced that Lotie wasn't really dead and that she would be there to greet him when he crossed over the threshold—and he sat down on the stairs and wept. Vicky sat down beside him with his head on her shoulder and wept with him.

He went to the office the next day and resumed work as if nothing had happened, and when Vicky came to see him with some papers about the Jerusalem villa, he couldn't quite make out what she was talking about.

"What villa? Where?"

"Don't you remember, I—" But obviously he didn't. It seemed to her that the best he could do for the time being was to keep himself as busy as possible and leave the matter of retirement in abeyance, and she eventually acquired the villa in her own name.

Benny had bought a substantial house a few streets away from them, but it needed considerable repairs, and, while it was being prepared for occupation, he and Yvonne moved in with Nahum.

Their presence helped to cheer him immensely, as did Vicky's son Edward. She made a party for Edward when he was five to which she invited the whole family, and Nahum glowed with gladness, especially as Yvonne looked as if she were about to add to the number of his grandchildren. She had a daughter three weeks later, whom they called Lotie.

"Where there are children and grandchildren, there is no death," said Nahum, quoting the Talmud.

Vicky marvelled at his resilience. She had anticipated nothing ahead except decline, decay, senility and finally death, but he seemed to have taken a new lease on life.

"Look," he explained, "I'm seventy-two, nearly seventy-three, and for nearly fifty of these years I've lived on my own, so it's not too difficult to get used to my own company."

The next day he had to travel down to London on business with Hector. They had hoped to sign the contract for the London cinema, but at the last moment the vendors had introduced new conditions which they refused to accept. While the matter was being discussed by their lawyers, they found themselves with a day in hand, and, as an act of piety, Nahum decided to visit old Kagan. He had asked Richard about him in Jerusalem and been told: "The old man's pretty poorly, pretty poorly. He often talks about you. He'd welcome a visit."

Nahum was almost overwhelmed with nostalgia as he came into Liverpool Street station and took his seat in a first-class carriage. He recalled his meetings with Kagan to raise loans for his first vessel, and then the journey from Liverpool Street—possibly in that very carriage—to Matilda Kagan's wedding, where he first set eyes on Lotie, but when he reached the estate the glow in which he had travelled faded, for on every side there was dilapidation and decay. The driveway was full of cracks and potholes with grass growing everywhere. The neatly cropped parklands had been plowed up. The trees were smothered in ivy. The house, which Nahum remembered as a gleaming palace, was crumbling, with numerous moth-eaten cats lurking in the shadows and the musty smell of a neglected museum. A decrepit servant with a slow walk and bandy legs like a crab led them to old Kagan, who was sitting in an armchair in front of a blazing fire with a blanket around his legs, and who seemed even more dilapidated than the house. Most of his magnificent beard had fallen away, and he was left with a few straggling white hairs; the chin underneath was raw and covered in sores. His eyes were red and swollen, and he looked less the regal patriarch than one of the decrepit *schnorrers* Hector used to see haunting the synagogues when he was a boy.

"Raeburn, yes, remembered the name as soon as you called," croaked the old man. "Shipping, correct?"

"I used to be," said Nahum.

"Retired, I suppose. Handed over to your children. Big mistake. My son's in charge of the bank now, you know. Good war—my son, I mean. Not much of a banker, though." Then he pointed to Hector. "Who's this young man?"

"My son."

"Son? Ah, yes, married an Althouse. Memory's still there, you see."

"No, I married an Althouse."

"Ah, yes, of course, you married my daughter-in-law. Makes us relatives of a sort. Dreadful weather. Can't keep warm. Had lunch?"

"We had a good breakfast," said Nahum, "we're not hungry."

"I am. Let's see if we can rustle up something." And he pressed a bell which remained unanswered. "Wife's dead, you know."

"I'm sorry to hear it."

"What's that?"

"I'm sorry to hear it."

"Hard of hearing? Aren't we all. Yes. Nice of you to come. Don't have much company these days. Wife's dead, you know."

"I'm sorry to hear it."

"What's that?"

"I'm sorry to hear it."

"Nobody lives forever, you know, though she had a jolly good try. She was a good bit older than me. She was in that very chair you're sitting in now. Popped off suddenly, just like that. Decent type, the wife. Did you know her?"

"I met her once or twice."

"Good type, nice family, rather plain. Children took after me, thank God, but he's not much use in the bank—the boy, I mean. The girl married an American, you know."

"I know. He's my brother-in-law."

"Is he? That makes us relatives of a sort. Come to think of it, I'm related to almost everybody. Large family, my wife's. Dead, of course, most of 'em. Very old family, you see. Had lunch?"

Nahum and Hector exchanged glances and rose.

"You're not going yet, surely, you've only just come."

"We're in a bit of a hurry," said Nahum.

"That's the trouble, everybody is, or at least they seem to be every time they come here. Funny that. People seemed to have all the time in the world when I was younger. Smoke?"

"Yes."

"Cigars?"

"No."

"Pity, I could do with a good cigar."

As they hurtled back towards the station, Nahum said to Hector: "When I was in my forties, I had an awful premonition that I would die young; now that I'm in my seventies, I have a terrible premonition that I may live to a ripe old age. We have all sorts of prayers asking for long life. Who wants it? From now on I'm going to say a daily prayer to be saved from old age."

"Be careful," said Hector, "you never know with God, he could be listening."

"Your mother used to say that."

"I know, that's why I never pray."

They had dinner in their hotel with Michael Mittwoch that evening, and he asked them whether they had exchanged contracts.

"Nearly," said Hector, "but they keep. introducing new conditions. I wonder who the hell they think they're dealing with."

"I wouldn't accept the cinema as a gift," said Mittwoch.

"Have you seen their receipts?" asked Nahum.

"Oh, they're riding high now, but I can tell you the whole industry is doomed. There're all sorts of new developments in the wings. Twenty years from now, people will have private cinemas in their own homes."

"What happens in twenty years' time doesn't worry me," said Nahum.

"But you'll begin to feel the effects in ten years' time, perhaps even five. I'm telling you what I've been trying to tell my own people. As a matter of fact, I'm leaving the cinema business."

"Leaving the cinema business? To do what?"

"I'm nudging forty and feel bogged down. I might go to Palestine. I've had an interesting offer from an old army chum who may become chief of staff once the underground comes above ground."

"Put in a word for me," said Hector; "if they can use middle-aged soldiers, then perhaps they can use old crocks as well."

"And who's going to look after the shop?" asked Nahum.

Nahum had eaten sparingly but possibly had drunk too much, and that night he was taken ill, and they had to call a doctor. He was a good deal better by the morning, but Hector cancelled all their meetings and hurried him back up to Glasgow. When they were home, Hector urged Nahum to go straight to bed.

"All right," he said, "I'll go, if you promise not to call Gladys."

"What's wrong with Gladys? She's a good doctor."

"She may be, but she puts the fear of death into me."

Three weeks later came his grandson's *bar mitzvah*, and by then he felt fully recovered and donned his top hat, frock coat and striped trousers, an outfit he hadn't worn since he was a warden of the synagogue some ten years previously; he didn't realise until he put it on how much weight he had lost. Vicky suggested that he might be better off in a lounge suit, but Nahum thought it would have been unworthy of the occasion, and he set out in full regalia. His grandson was in fine voice and rendered his portion of the Torah beautifully.

The synagogue was nearly full, and Nahum was flanked by relatives, friends, well-wishers, acquaintances he had made at various stages of his life—as immigrant, ticket agent, carter, ship owner and in the cinema trade—his daughter-in-law's family and their friends—schoolteachers in crumpled suits and shapeless hats, doctors in bowlers and hand-tailored worsteds, smelling of ether and brilliantine. In the ladies' gallery sat an impressive array of handsome women—Vicky, her hair cut short, in a black suit and a tiny black hat with a short piece of black netting over her eyes; Trude, less elegant but still attractive, in a large straw hat with a broad band under her chin, which made her look as if she had strayed from a garden party; Benny's wife Yvonne, with her large, dark eyes and sallow complexion, looking extremely exotic in a fur hat and velvet costume; the grandmother in scarlet, like a setting sun which had been stopped in its course. Even Gladys, without her glasses and her eyes screwed up to absorb the scene, looked vaguely handsome.

Nahum sighed with gladness and said to himself: "If I should die now, I would die a happy man."

At the reception which followed, an aged rabbi came up to Nahum and asked him how long he had been widowed.

"Eight months, nearly."

"A long time to be alone. You're a fine-looking man still, prosperous. You should think about taking another wife. Do you remember Mr Black? He had three daughters, beauties all of them, especially the youngest. Her first husband was a Dacosta, left her very comfortable. The second, a Kunzler, left her even more comfortable. She's not a young woman, but she's not so old, either, or, at least, she doesn't look so old, and I was thinking—"

"It's a nice thought, Rabbi, but not for the moment, I've got too many things happening."

"Shall I tell her you're thinking about it?"

"You can tell her I'm thinking of thinking about it, but I've had two wives and she's had two husbands, and I think it's maybe enough— at least, for the time being. Maybe when I'm older."

There were many doctors at the reception, and one of them asked Nahum what he'd done to his lip.

"A silly thing. I like a hard toothbrush, and while I was brushing my teeth last night, the thing slipped and I scratched my lip."

"You should have it looked at. It's beginning to swell."

There was a dance in the evening, and while he was wrestling with Gladys in what he thought was a tango, she also asked him what he had done to his lip, and he told her.

"I don't like the look of it. As soon as this is over, I'm going to take you into hospital."

"Just for a scratch? You're being funny," but just in case she was not, he fled before the last dance had been danced and was to regret it. His lip kept him awake half the night, and by the morning it had turned purple. When Gladys saw it, she drove him straight to hospital. He was given a local anaesthetic, and when it was lanced and dressed he felt somewhat shaky, but he thought he would be able to go home.

"Not on your life," said Gladys, "you're stopping right here."

Later in the day, Vicky came to see him and brought his pyjamas, dressing gown, slippers, toilet bag and reading material.

"Good God," he said, "how long do you think I'm going to be here?"

"A day or two yet, according to Gladys."

"Just for a bleeding lip?"

"Don't ask me, I'm not the doctor."

He was seen by a succession of doctors over the next few days, and at the end of the week he was still in hospital, and when Gladys came to see him he grabbed her by the arm.

"I want to know what's happening. Why are you keeping me a prisoner here? I'm all right. I'll get my lawyer."

"We're making tests," she said.

"That's what they told me earlier in the week. How long does a test take? What are you testing?"

"To be honest, we're somewhat in the dark ourselves."

The next morning he was brushing his teeth—carefully now, and with a soft brush—when he felt the taste of blood in his mouth and saw that the toothpaste foam had turned red. He stopped, rinsed out his mouth and examined his teeth carefully in the mirror; he noticed that his gums were a blackish red. They were causing him some apprehension but no discomfort, and he was half afraid of mentioning them to the nurses or doctors, but that night, to be on the safe side, he did not brush his teeth. The next morning when he opened his eyes, he found two doctors standing over him, both looking closely into his mouth. He felt as if he had a gum-shield under his lip and could barely shut his mouth.

Gladys arrived, a trifle breathless, about half an hour later, and for the first time in his life he was glad to see her.

"We are in a sad state, aren't we?" she said.

He was given some drugs which made the swellings subside, but they left him drowsy and nauseous, and he noticed that whenever he stroked his beard, whole tufts of hair came away in his hand. His pillow was covered with hair. When Benny came to see him, he was almost in tears.

"Do you know what's happening to me? I don't, and nobody tells me anything."

"I honestly don't think they know, but you've got the best people in the profession looking after you."

The swellings on his gums returned, and Gladys told him that he would need "another little operation."

"I don't like these little operations," he mumbled; "can't they give me one big one and get it over and done with?"

"Well, this one isn't going to be so little, unfortunately. I'm afraid you're going to lose all your pretty teeth."

"My teeth? There's nothing wrong with my teeth."

"I'm afraid there is, they're giving you blood poisoning."

At which he felt a stab of despair. He had always taken great care of his teeth and had been inordinately proud of the fact that even at his age they were all his own.

"Look," he said, "why don't they put me to sleep and finish with me? Why all this messing about? I've had a good life, my children and grandchildren are all well-looked-after, what's the point of it?"

"Because you're basically in good shape, and if we can get over this bit of bother, you're good for another ten years."

He felt too weary to protest further, and about an hour later he was wheeled into the operating theatre.

He didn't know how long he had been under the anaesthetic, but when he opened his eyes he was dimly aware of vague figures by his bed and of hushed voices, and he closed them again. His mouth felt like a mangled piece of raw meat, and he settled back on his pillow and fell asleep.

When he opened his eyes again, the ward was in darkness, except for a dim light over the sister's desk. He wanted to go to the toilet, but as he lowered himself from his bed, his legs gave way. He snatched at the screen to steady himself, but it tore under his weight, and he fell to the ground. The noise brought the sister to his side and she helped him back into bed and brought him a bed-pan. "A bed-pan," Lomzer had once told him, "is the beginning of the end."

The next day, however, he felt able to get out of bed and go to the bathroom, but when he saw himself in the mirror, he thought that the wrong person had looked into it by mistake and staggered out to another bathroom to have a look in another mirror, but the same reflection greeted him, and he failed to recognise it, for he was looking into the shrivelled face of an old man, with sunken cheeks, contorted mouth and a few straggling white hairs on the point of his chin. He was convinced this couldn't be him, and when it finally dawned on him that it couldn't be anyone else, he arranged the screen around his bed, told the nurse that he didn't want to see anyone and got into bed to die.

When food was brought, he refused to touch it.

"Give it to the living," he said. For a while he hovered between fitful wakefulness and sleep and lost all sense of time. Then, as he was about to turn over, he felt held back by something, and, looking around, he found that a feed-drip was connected to his arm.

"And how are we this morning?" a voice asked him brightly.

It was Gladys. "Actually, you're making good progress," she said. "With any luck, you should be out of here in a week or two."

"Feet first," he muttered hoarsely.

"But you are much better," she said. "Forty-eight hours ago I thought you were over and done with, but you've pulled around smartly. Now, would you like to have some visitors?"

"No," he said.

"Not even Sophie?"

"Sophie? What's she doing here?"

Before she could answer, Sophie materialised and enveloped him in a suffocating embrace and drenched him with tears.

"What are you doing here? Did they send for you? So that's it, I'm dying. No, I'm not. I'm dead. Look me straight in the face, Sophie, and tell me if the toothless old *cacker* you're looking at is Nahum Raeburn. I knew him well, he was a good-looking man, but he lived a good life and is dead. What you see here is some old *cacker* who's wearing his pyjamas and maybe even has the same name."

"Don't talk like that, Father. Gladys thinks you've got a good chance of recovery."

"Who? Me or Nahum, because Nahum died on the operating table yesterday, or was it last week? I don't even know what this month is. Those decorations out there, is it Christmas already?"

"Yankelson and the boys send their love, they—" She couldn't contain her tears and fled from his side.

Nahum dozed for a while, and when he opened his eyes he saw a tall figure in a long white beard standing over him and thought that he was already in the next world and this was the Prophet Elijah come to greet him, but when he tried to sit up, he noticed the apparition was wearing a red pom-pom hat and a long red coat.

"And a Merry Christmas," said the figure. "Now, let's see what we have for you here," and he began rummaging in a bag and pulled out a paper hat which he put on Nahum's head.

"There, and the right size, too. I think you unfortunately missed our carol service, so do you know what Santa Claus has done, he has brought the choir right here. Isn't that nice?"

And before Nahum could say anything, they began:

God rest ye merry gentlemen,
Let nothing you dismay . . .

He must have dropped off for a minute—or perhaps he had dreamed the whole episode—for when he opened his eyes, they were gone.

Nahum had asked for a rabbi earlier in the day, and towards evening a small, wizened, bearded figure with large glasses arrived.

"Not looking so well, Mr Raeburn?" he said.

"Raeburn is dead," said Nahum.

"Heaven forbid, it's a sin to talk like that. Where there's life, there's hope."

"I'm still alive, in a manner of speaking, but I'm not Raeburn."

"You're not Raeburn?"

"Do I look like Raeburn?"

The rabbi rose. "Oh, I'm sorry, I must have come to the wrong ward. I was told Mr Raeburn wanted to see me. You look a bit like him, you know."

"Mr Raeburn is past seeing anyone."

"You mean I'm too late, *boruch dayan emes*—what a shame. That's what usually happens, unfortunately. By the time anyone wants to see a rabbi, they're already with God. So Nahum Raeburn is dead. Not many people like him in Glasgow, not anywhere. A good man, a pious man, a generous man, a *tzadik bedoiroi*, a saint in his generation. You know, usually when a man's made a bit of money and come up in the world, he thinks he can do without God; with Raeburn, it was the other way about. In his youth he was a bit of a *sheigets*, but when he made his money he remembered that 'the world in all its fullness is the Lord's.' He was a pillar of his congregation, helped the needy, fed the poor, and if a man was in difficulties and needed help, the first person you thought of was Nahum Raeburn. As a matter of fact, he wasn't all that rich, and, believe me, he went through difficult times himself. One year he was in a palace in Mansion House Road, the next he was in the Gorbals, but God helped him and he rose again, but whether risen or fallen, he was the same good man. Dead? What a tragedy. Why did nobody tell me?" He took off his glasses to wipe away a tear, and, as he did so, Nahum also began to cry.

"You knew him?"

"Very well."

"A saint." He blew his nose and pulled himself together. "But still, he's with God, at his right hand, I can tell you, but my work is with the living. You been here long?"

"Who knows? Weeks, months, who knows?"

"What's your trouble?"

"God knows."

"We're all in God's hands—the healthy, the sick, the living, the dead."

"I want to say *vidui*."

"*Vidui?* Heaven forbid. You know what *vidui* is?"

"Yes, the death-bed confession."

"You don't look that bad."

"I don't feel that good."

"They do wonders with medicine these days, with all these clever Jewish doctors, miracles."

"But even with all the Jewish doctors and all their miracles, you don't live forever."

"You'll live till a hundred and twenty."

"Such favours I can do without. With respect, Rabbi, who's the patient, you or me?"

"It's a sin to give up hope."

"I'm facing reality."

"That's exactly what giving up hope is."

"Rabbi, I'll feel better if I say *vidui*."

The rabbi sighed. "How do you want to say it, in Hebrew or in English?"

"Does it make any difference?"

"No, God speaks both."

"I think I prefer it in Hebrew."

"All right, now, say it after me. *Modeh*."

"*Modeh*."

"*Ani*."

"*Ani*."

The rabbi paused for a moment.

"What's the matter?"

"I just noticed you ain't got your teeth on."

"Do you have to have teeth to say *vidui*?"

"You don't have to, but it's more respectful to wear them, if you have them."

"I haven't got any."

"That's another matter. *Lefonecho*."

"*Lefonecho* . . ."

EPILOGUE

Hector died at the end of 1968, twenty-one years to the day after his step-father. The cinema chain he had inherited had by then atrophied to one, a drab building in a drab street which Nahum had renamed the *Volga* during the war, and which managed to survive on nostalgia, showing ragged prints of forgotten films from the thirties.

He had not seen the final draft of my book, but I had shown him some of the work in progress, and he read it with a disapproving face. "But.it isn't me," he protested, "it's not me at all."

"O wad some Power the giftie gie us, to see ourselves as others see us," I said.

"What do you mean by that?"

"You think it isn't you, or rather the you you've been trying to play, but you're a sham, a fraud."

"Oh, no doubt, but you wouldn't think so from what you've got here."

"Forgive me, Uncle Hector, but you're a perfectly good man masquerading as a rogue. I know there are Englishmen who regard virtue as a private vice, but you've carried it to unlikely extremes. The whole wicked-uncle saga is spurious."

He shook his head slowly, put his hand on my shoulder and said: "You've done your homework badly, my boy." It was the last time I spoke to him.

All the surviving members of the family assembled for the funeral, even my mother, whom I had convinced that the Hector she thought she knew was not the Hector I had discovered. I think she felt a trifle let down by my discovery; so did I.

Sophie flew in from Israel with Vicky, who had settled there shortly after Nahum's death and was now Mrs. Mittwoch (yes, Nahum's attempt at matchmaking finally succeeded, if only posthumously) and a grandmother, and Trude flew in from America.

Trude had, for a time, faded out of the family, as if anxious not to embarrass us by her domestic circumstances. The man she had been living with did, in fact, eventually marry her, but he died shortly afterwards—another instance, I suppose, of what she called "the black touch," though he was by then of an age when he was fully entitled to die. A year or two later she went back to Russia in search of her parents. Astonishingly, she did find her mother, alive but senile, in a mental hospital in the Ukraine. She could find no trace of her father but does not appear to have exerted herself unduly in the effort.

While in Russia she met an American, a widower with three children, who was engaged in a similar search. He went back to the United States, whence he wrote her long (he devoted his weekends to them), affectionate and happily detailed letters about life in Boston, where he was the head of a large real-estate company. After four months of this, Trude succumbed. Sophie organised the wedding, which was held in her *moshav*, and Vicky wrote to say that "Trude and her husband look so much alike that their union seems almost incestuous," but their marriage is a very happy one, far more so than Vicky's, who separated from Mittwoch and went on to live with a South African tennis player half her age.

Hector's funeral had to be delayed to give the various relatives time to assemble, and they formed a sizable crowd, but during the course of the funeral service I noticed a plump ruddy-faced figure with thick glasses, thick lips and a tiny nose, who didn't seem to belong there and stood, self-consciously, a little apart from the rest. After the service, I was moved by curiosity to ask him if he was a friend of Hector's.

"No," he said firmly, "not a friend, a relative." He had an American accent. "My father and his were cousins."

"Who was your father?"

"A bastard. I wouldn't mention his name on consecrated ground."

I arranged to see him that evening at his hotel, a musty little hole near the centre of town reeking of stale men and stale beer.

"My father—may he roast in hell," he began—"was Lazar."

"Lazar! The—"

"The lawyer, the shyster, the robber, the crook. If there's a God in heaven—and Christ, there had better be after all I've been through—he must be sizzling away in the other place, except that he's probably done a deal with the devil. He was a millionaire, my father, a millionaire, but left me and my mother, a sick woman—not that I'm all that well myself—almost penniless."

"Can a man disinherit his family just like that?"

"Not normally, he can't, not in New York, but if you knew my father, you'd know he could find loopholes in a brick wall. He was the sharpest shyster-lawyer in the state, which is saying something. In any case, he passed the money over while he was still alive, and the whole legacy story was a smoke-screen. I had heard about Hector coming into a fortune, and I wondered who the fairy godmother could have been. Within ten seconds I knew—I *knew*—it was the old man. Hector stayed with us during the war, just before he went back to England, and Father's eyes would light up at the sight of him. 'Why couldn't you be like him?' he kept saying to me; 'why can't you be a soldier?' A soldier? I couldn't even stand up straight. I had back trouble and asthma, and still have. Anyway, the old bastard dropped dead about a year ago, and not before time, and I was rummaging through his papers when I found out about the so-called legacy. I thought, this can't be fair, I'm going to challenge it in the courts, and went to see my lawyer, and he said, it's too late, the money's been transferred, you'd better try the Scottish courts. That's why I'm here, but the moment I set foot in Scotland, he drops dead. I'm a born loser if ever there was one." He was nearly in tears. "Two million, he left him. He didn't leave us two hundred thousand, and it's all gone on hospital bills. What do you think Hector did with the money? He couldn't have spent two million, not in two years."

The sum was, in fact, one and a quarter million, of which he had spent about a fifth. He left the bulk of his fortune to his sister, half-sister and half-brothers, though he referred to them all as "brothers" and "sisters" in his will. "He liked to think that Nahum was his natural father," said Sophie, "and it's quite possible that he was." He also left a substantial sum to an old school friend, Cyrus (about whose existence I had almost forgotten and who, as far as I knew, he hadn't seen in years), and a generous bequest to me. In turn, this book is my bequest to the man who, whether or not he was Hector's natural father, was in one way or another, the father of us all.